'PEDE

By

James H Longmore

A HellBound Books Publishing LLC Book
Austin TX

James H Longmore

**A HellBound Books LLC
Publication**
Copyright © 2021 by HellBound Books Publishing LLC
All Rights Reserved

Cover and art design by Kevin Enhart for
HellBound Books Publishing LLC

Edition 2

**No part of this book may be reproduced, stored in a retrieval system, or transmitted by any means, electronic, mechanical, photocopying, recording or otherwise without written permission from the author
This book is a work of fiction. Names, characters, places and incidents are entirely fictitious or are used fictitiously and any resemblance to actual persons, living or dead, events or locales is purely coincidental.**

www.hellboundbookspublishing.com

Printed in the United States of America

2

BY JAMES H LONGMORE

HORROR
Blood & Kisses
'Pede
Tenebrion
Flanagan

BIZARRO
The Erotic Odyssey of Colton Forshay
Buds
And Then You Die
Feeder
I Am Joe's Unwanted Penis

'PEDE

PROLOGUE

MOUNTAINVIEW HOTEL AND NATURAL SPA, DESERT HOT SPRINGS, COACHELLA VALLEY, CA.

FIVE YEARS AGO

Jahanzeb Ebrahimi was making a dirty bomb: a modest device that combined a small amount of radioactive material with more conventional explosives which, upon detonation, would spread a radioactive cloud across two to three square miles of prime California real estate and render the entire area uninhabitable for a decade or two.

Sweat dripped from the terrorist's face and into the bathtub he'd filled with the fifty pounds of ice he'd had the Idiot Boy haul up from the hotel's ice machine two floors down. He wiped away the sweat with the back of a trembling hand and absently dried it on his full, white-streaked beard, and the unkempt, wiry hair snagged at his skin like tiny, grasping fingers. Ignoring the pain that screamed from his knees at having been knelt down for so long, Jahanzeb added another drop of thick, clear liquid from the glass pipette into the Pyrex beaker that nestled among the ice; adding to the 1-2-3 trinitroxypropane he was making for the Great Cause.

Along with the crates and boxes filled with bomb paraphernalia, Jahanzeb liked to keep a small revolver – for emergencies only – nearby. His sat innocuously on the countertop among the complimentary shower gels and revitalizing shampoos. The gun's dull, gray metal perfectly matched the pewter bathroom fittings, almost as if it had been purposefully accessorized.

Desert Hot Springs was a small, tourist-trap town one hundred miles as the crow flies west from Los Angeles. It had a population of less than thirty thousand residing souls – fewer than some football games – its one claim to fame being the overabundance of boutique spas, hotels, and swingers' sex clubs. They had been built in the desert over and around the geothermal spas that bubbled up from the San Andreas Fault like gangrenous fluids from a putrefying wound. It was, Jahanzeb's superiors had explained, a *soft target. He'd* recommended Wall Street, Broadway, or even Rodeo Drive – but no. Coachella Valley was the very *last* place the Americans would expect an attack, apparently.

He snorted his derision and added another two drops to his hellish concoction.

In an instant, an opaque film formed between the two liquids in the beaker, and it let out the tiniest wisp of brownish smoke. Jahanzeb couldn't help but smile; the smoke looked exactly how he'd always imagined farts would appear should you be able to see them.

The smile belied an inner panic, though. The smoke was nitrogen dioxide gas, and experience had taught that the noxious brown whiff indicated that the mix was too warm. And *that* meant dangerously close to the exothermic reaction, which would set off the whole shebang in a flash of blinding light and the searing heat of rapidly expanding gas.

The bomb-maker froze, held his breath, fearful that the heat from his mouth might add an unwanted catalyst to the unstable mix.

He wasn't ready for his martyrdom just yet.

The brown smoke dissipated harmlessly into the cool air.

Jahanzeb allowed himself the luxury of a long, noisy exhale and squeezed the rubber pipette bulb again.

Atop the toilet cistern, next to his left shoulder, there was a *Dora the Explorer* Thermos flask. The flask contained the nitro-glycerin Jahanzeb had made thus far – barely enough to blow the skin off a rice pudding, as his Grandfather would have put it, and a sorry amount for four days' work. But, this wasn't a race, Jahanzeb reminded himself, he knew better than to rush the process: Too many hands, faces, and lives had been lost by those not mindful of the patience that was needed to create the explosive.

The *Dora* flask was perched on top of a silver metal box that spanned the length of the cistern. The box was stenciled with the universally familiar yellow trefoil that was the international symbol for radioactivity; the symbol had faded with age to a pale bile color, as had the indiscernible Eastern-European wording beneath it. The box and its deadly contents had been shipped direct from one of the lesser ex-Soviet bloc countries since low-grade radioactive material was ridiculously simple to obtain from the former communist states. They simply salvaged it from source capsules of defunct radiotherapy machines that Jahanzeb had heard were just dumped into landfills along with the other vestiges of failed communism. The terrorist was awaiting another two shipments to complete his bomb since there was not quite enough in the silver box for the results he was hoping to achieve. Jahanzeb had been given firm assurances that the shipments would be with him within the week.

The hotel suite door opened with a crash, and Jahanzeb snapped his head around with a start, his heart racing with the sudden rush of adrenaline. In doing so, he almost dropped the pipette into the acid mix, and he cursed silently to himself.

"Uncle!" Rakeem – the Idiot Boy – stomped into the room with a big, stupid grin across his face and a brown bag of groceries clutched to his chest to obscure his black Darth Vader T-shirt. "I'm back!" the product of Jahanzeb's martyred brother's loins declared as he kicked the door shut with a sandaled foot and made his way over to the bathroom, his white, cotton pants flapping about his skinny legs as he walked.

At least he'd *remembered* the groceries this time, thought Jahanzeb. He cast his mind back a few days, to when the Idiot Boy had been gone almost an hour only to return having completely forgotten what he'd been sent out for.

"Allahu Akbar," Jahanzeb declared with sarcasm that was lost on the boy, "you were gone so long I thought you'd already sought your glorious death!"

"I'm sorry Uncle, I was …"

"I know what you were doing, boy," Jahanzeb barked. "You were dallying with those filthy harlots around the swimming pool. Don't think that I don't know what you get up to when you're out of my sight, Rakeem. Your shame is visible, you disgusting boy!"

Rakeem looked shamefaced and glanced down at the diminishing erection that tented his white cotton trousers. He was nineteen, in the prime of his life, and the hotel was filled to bursting with tanned, nubile females who wore incredibly small amounts of clothing and skimpy strips of swimwear that left absolutely nothing to the imagination; what else was Rakeem to do but become distracted?

"I have the bananas you asked for, Uncle," Rakeem said and held out the grocery bag, "on the stalk, just like you said."

"Well, at least you got that much right, boy," Jahanzeb growled. He laid his pipette in the bathtub and stood up; his knees cracked like dual shots from a starting pistol. He shuffled toward Rakeem, the feeling in his legs taking its own sweet time in returning. As much as the Idiot Boy irritated him, Jahanzeb couldn't bear to see that kicked-puppy face when the boy thought he had earned displeasure. He forced a smile at the Idiot Boy.

Rakeem smiled back at his uncle and rummaged around in the brown paper bag.

The centipede sensed the warmth of the hand as it moved close to her. She wrapped her long body around the banana stalk, gripped its roughness with her myriad feet.

She was fully awake now, awakened from the near-comatose state that the cold storage of her overseas trip had induced, warmed now by the dry heat of the California sun. The creature tapped at the human skin with her antennae to sense its salty secretions, alert to the danger it presented and poised ready to strike; the centipede's upper body coiled into an S, she flexed her fangs and minuscule droplets of venom oozed from their razor-sharp tips.

And then the hand was gone.

"Uncle?" Rakeem plucked a shiny red apple out of the bag and took a wide bite.

"Yes, Rakeem?" Jahanzeb sighed, rolled his eyes upward. Here it comes, another one of the Idiot Boy's dumb questions. What was it to be this time? *What does vampire shit smell like? Why are there so many Gods?* Or perhaps something a little more philosophical as in last nights' *why don't the girls like me?*

"When we become martyrs, why does our reward have to be virgins?" the Boy asked through a mouthful of chewed apple pulp.

"Because that is the way it is," Jahanzeb snorted, "you really ought to know better than to question Allah's will."

"But, if they're *all* virgins, they will have no experience in the carnal pleasures."

"Of course they will not," Jahanzeb retorted with impatience. "They're virgins, so how could they possibly be experienced?!"

"But, if they have no experience…"

"You will have eternity to mold them, to teach them the skills that will give you all of the pleasures you desire from them."

"But, Uncle," Rakeem struggled to express his thoughts, as he always did. "I am a virgin, also. I have no experience to teach."

A leaden silence filled the room.

Jahanzeb, for once, had nothing to say to the Idiot Boy. This was the problem, he thought, of recruiting boys to do suicide missions. They simply were unable to blindly accept Allah's will and thought far more than was good for them.

"Oh, for Allah's sake, Boy!" Jahanzeb hid his own misgivings behind brusqueness. "You ask too many questions!" He beckoned the boy toward him and barked, "Now give me the fruit and go find something useful to do." He snatched the bag from Rakeem and thrust his hand in to retrieve a banana.

Jahanzeb screamed out in agony as white-hot pain flared through his hand. He dropped the grocery bag as if it were burning, and fruit and tinned tuna spilled out across the bathroom floor, the apples rolling lazily toward a startled Rakeem. Jahanzeb lifted his hand up to see what his panicked brain was telling him was a snake clinging to his arm, its fangs buried deep into his flesh.

Shocked, Rakeem jumped at the sound of his uncle's cry, having never heard the man raise his voice in anything other than annoyance. The boy stared open-mouthed at the chestnut-red snake thing that had dug fat, black fangs into his uncle's hand and wrapped the entire length of its body around his arm – coiling up almost as far as his Uncle's elbow. As Rakeem watched, Jahanzeb flailed his arm around and continued to scream as the creature clung to him with scores of pointed legs.

"Get it off me! *Get it off me!*" The pain in Jahanzeb's hand was unbearable, and he saw nasty red welts appear on his skin in reaction to the poisons that were already spreading through his veins. It felt to him as if his blood was a boiling, bubbling mass beneath his skin, and his nerves were screaming out their protests. He felt the agony spread up along his arm like creeping acid to leave a strange, tingling numbness in its wake. His racing mind, flooded with adrenaline, registered that it wasn't a snake that had coiled tightly around his arm, but a centipede of horrific proportions – a thing of schlock creature movies and nightmares. The creature spanned easily over twelve inches long and was three inches wide with a hard, segmented body that glistened as if it had been lacquered. Each of the creature's segments sported a pair of keen, tapered legs – some easily an inch long – which dug into Jahanzeb's skin for purchase while the animal's formidable fangs buried deep and pumped venom into the soft palm of his hand.

"Do something, Rakeem!" Jahanzeb bashed his arm against the wall, in an attempt to dislodge the centipede, but it dug its feet further into his flesh and created yet more suffering.

And then Rakeem was holding the gun. "Hold still, Uncle! I will kill it!" he shouted above his uncle's screams and aimed the gun.

"No!" panic strangled Jahanzeb's voice. "Don't be stupid, boy!"

The gun's report echoed around the tiled bathroom, and

shattered pieces of Jahanzeb's fingers spattered from his hand. He stopped his screaming and stared in disbelief at the thick flow of blood that poured from the ragged, fleshy stubs of his fingers from which bone shards poked out like miniature stalagmites.

"You shot me!" he screamed and waved his wounded arm at the Idiot Boy. Blood splashed around the bathroom, into the ice bath and flowed down Jahanzeb's arm to soak the centipede that Rakeem's bullet had completely missed.

"Rakeem!" the terror and pain in Jahanzeb's voice made it sound shrill, almost feminine, "you Idiot B —"

Rakeem's second shot fared little better than his first. The bullet zinged harmlessly by Jahanzeb's face, and in the fraction of a second, it took the bullet to hit its final target. Rakeem imagined his Uncle had actually turned his head to *watch* the lead go by.

By sheer fluke, the bullet hit the flask on the toilet cistern, directly between Dora's big brown eyes.

The blast from the nitro-glycerin ripped apart the hotel bathroom; disintegrating crates, bomb-making equipment, the silver radiation-proofed box and its deadly contents, and the two would-be terrorists.

Rakeem and Jahanzeb were in an instant dismembered by the searing breath of expanding gasses that turned their blood and internal organs into a fine liquid which spray-painted the room a wet, scarlet red. Their bones shattered into myriad fragments, forced out through their flesh like tiny white splinters, and those body parts that escaped atomization were scattered to all four corners of the fifth-floor suite.

Jahanzeb's arm was ripped deftly from his shoulder and hurled like bloodied, wind-tossed flotsam out into the bedroom with its resilient passenger still clinging to it. The severed limb flopped on to the blood-spattered bed sheets, and the centipede seized its opportunity to crawl away toward the cool, dark space beneath the bed. As the creature crawled away, the radioactive dust from the devastated room settled on and around it like fine, toxic snow.

CHAPTER ONE

MOUNTAINVIEW HOTEL AND NATURAL SPA, DESERT HOT SPRINGS, COACHELLA VALLEY, CA.

PRESENT DAY

"Come on, baby girl, there's nothing to be scared of!" Stevie Johnson cajoled. He thought that his new girl looked mighty fine in her tight pink T and Daisy Dukes, the latter accentuating the deep 'V' of her crotch just so. It was girls like Virginia Mendoza that drove him – and all the other older boys – batshit crazy, and they sure knew just how best to play what God gave 'em. "Jimmy found this way in not long after they boarded the place up," Stevie told her. "He used to bring girls here all the time."

"Jimmy's your brother who…" Virginia toyed absently with her ass-length, black hair that shone iridescent in the clear desert sun.

"…who died?" Stevie finished the sentence. He set his face to *sad* to best attract the girl's sympathy. He was by now a grandmaster at rolling out the *Dead Brother* card to grab himself a piece of impressionable High-School ass. It was a ploy that hadn't failed him yet.

"I'm sorry. I didn't mean to upset you," Virginia apologized as her cheeks reddened.

"It's okay, baby. It's hard, but I guess it's something you just have to learn to live with," Stevie's faux-bravery put the perfect quiver in his voice. "Although, sometimes, it can be difficult when I think about all the good times we had together."

Stevie bowed his head and allowed the girl to get closer. She put a comforting arm around his shoulder and rested her head against his. Stevie's skin tingled where their bodies touched, and blood rushed to his dick at the feel of the hard lump of Virginia's pert breast digging into his bicep. "It was a year ago, leukemia…"

"That's blood cancer, right? I am so sorry." Virginia was suddenly conscious that she was wearing a *Breast Cancer Awareness* T-shirt, one with a little pink bow silk-screened onto it – she'd lost an Aunt to the disease a handful of years ago and tried to support the cause wherever she could. Having said that, she'd chosen the shirt from her closet that morning because she knew it looked hot when she wore it knotted at the front to reveal her tan, toned belly and the diamanté navel ring that dangled down to the top of her pubic bone.

"It's okay, babe," Stevie reassured and smiled his sweetest smile. "What hurts my heart most is that they tested me as a bone marrow donor, and I wasn't a match." A well-rehearsed tear escaped the corner of Stevie's eye. "And what's *even* worse is that's how come Dad found out that Mom had cheated on him, and I wasn't his kid," he sniffled, "and then he split." Stevie glanced across at Virginia and saw with some satisfaction that she was practically in tears herself.

"Oh, you poor, poor thing," she consoled as she held him tight, and Stevie inhaled the sweet, sweet smell of her skin. "It must have been terrible to lose your brother *and* your Daddy at the same time."

And there it was, *ka-ching*!

The deal was sealed! It really was easy as that; the dumb broads fell for it every time. Stevie reveled in yet another soon to be conquest, smug in the knowledge that he'd be balls-deep in the soppy bitch just as soon as he could get her inside the hotel.

"Yeah, it was. Really hard," Stevie fought hard to keep the glee from creeping into his voice. "That's why I am so happy that *we* found each other, Virginia. I knew from the moment we first met that we had a connection." The tried and trusted lines spilled from Stevie's mouth like sewage from an overflow as he reeled in yet another naive catch.

How did the saying go? The best lies were those closest to the truth? Yes, it was certainly no lie that Stevie's older brother had actually died of Leukemia a few years' back. And it was also true that Dad had split shortly after Jimmy had passed on. Where the truth and Stephen Johnson parted company was that Stevie *had* been a tissue match, but the marrow transplant had failed after so many hours of agonizing extraction and endless, agonizing months of praying for it to take. In the end, Jimmy's immune system had simply rejected his younger brother's marrow, and he had died.

It really had been as simple as that.

Stevie's father had taken the death of his eldest – and although he would never admit it, favorite – son terribly and had plunged into a deep, dark depression that had consumed him both mentally and physically. He'd eventually sought solace in the bottom of a Jack Daniel's bottle and some guy from the office at the computer software company he'd worked at for thirteen years.

It was probably that which had irked Stevie most of all. His brother's death, he had handled with help from bereavement counselors and Ritalin, but there was nothing that could diminish the curveball of a tragic death in the family that outed your Dad as a fag!

Stevie lead Virginia by the hand around to the rear of the hotel. He felt her tense a little and slow her step in hesitation. He gave her a gentle but persuasive tug.

"Are you sure it's safe to be here, Stevie? It doesn't look safe to me," Virginia said as she strained her neck to glance up at the abandoned building that loomed over them, and its boarded-up, lifeless windows that seemed to stare right back at her with malevolent curiosity.

"Will you quit worrying and trust me?" Stevie barked, possibly with more curtness than he'd intended. "I've been here loads – err, a *few* times before," Stevie corrected himself and was positive he'd gotten away with the *faux-pas.*

Of course, he'd had dozens of girls in the hotel before Virginia, so many in fact that he'd have lost count had he not had the foresight to have kept a record in his cell phone. Each and every one of Stevie's conquests was logged and filed away with an accompanying photograph in his phone's *notes* app, lest he forgot what an absolute stud he had become.

But Virginia, well, Virginia was something special, and Stevie had not been afraid to embrace his sensitive side and tell her as much. What he omitted to tell her, of course, was that she was only special insomuch that he hadn't put his thing inside of her.

Yet.

"Just wait until you see the inside," Stevie enthused, "you're going to love it!"

"But it's broad daylight." Virginia cast a furtive glance across the desolated parking lot. "What if that creepy old caretaker guy comes around?" her voice wavered. She'd heard the stories from friends at school about the old caretaker – *or was it the* ghost *of the old caretaker?* – who hung around the old hotel. Although no one she knew had actually seen the man, the thought of him scared her very much.

"We could always let him watch?" Stevie smirked, quite possibly only half-joking. "You never know, we might be able to teach the old pervert a thing or two!" Stevie laughed. Virginia laughed along with her beau with a soupcon of nervousness.

"You know I'm trusting you with this, right?" Virginia's resolve was eroding as quickly as a sand castle on the beach as Stevie deftly sideswiped her objections with well-practiced ease. "You *are* sure that this is a good idea, though?" she eyed her boyfriend with a serious look in her eyes. "Us – *this* – I mean?"

"Of course, I do, baby," now Stevie was struggling to hide his impatience; he'd be damned if he'd taken a day off work to spring the skittish virgin out of high school just to have her go all frigid on him now. He'd worked hard to plan the day's excursion, even paid out for beer and a new shirt, so this thing was damned well going to happen, come hell or high water. "Everything's gonna be okay, baby. I promise," he said through clenched teeth and a forced smile, "and remember, Virginia, once we get inside, you don't have to do anything you don't want to."

"Yeah?"

"Yeah," Stevie whispered and hit Virginia with his best *I'm an honorable young man, trust me* smile, all the while thinking *like fuck, you don't have to, bitch*. No way was the notorious pussy-hound Stevie Johnson going home without another notch on the bed post, no matter what it took.

"Okay, here we are," Stevie pointed to the trash chute that puckered from the hotel's wall like a giant, sheet steel anus. "There's our gateway to paradise, baby," he leered. "I'll give you a leg up."

"Seriously?" Virginia balked. "You're expecting me to climb up there?"

"It's the only way in, Sweetheart. This place is boarded

up tighter than that sweet pussy of yours."

Virginia giggled, her face flushing coy pink. "Okay, lover boy – if you're gonna sweet talk me like that, how can I possibly say no?"

You fucking can't, Bitch.

Virginia smiled at Stevie and kicked off her sneakers. She slipped her dusty foot into Stevie's cupped hands and pushed against his strong grip. As he lifted his girl up to the chute, Stevie took great delight in the silky softness of her foot, the faint, musty scent of its sole, and he gazed with wanton lust at the denim-clad derriere that passed just a hair's-breadth by his eager face. Stevie inhaled deeply through his nose, trying to catch her aroma.

Once Virginia was safely ensconced within the trash chute, Stevie followed suit. He knew the technique by heart, taught to him by his dear, departed brother. He jumped with a bend at the knees and grabbed a hold of the smooth rim of the chute. He then hauled himself up by the sheer strength in his bulging arms until he could heave his torso into the chute's cool interior. Once in, Stevie followed Virginia as they crawled into the bowels of the Mountainview, all the while keeping a watchful eye on her incredibly perfect rear end.

"Wow!" Virginia gasped, "this *really* is awesome!" Her face lit up with the broadest of smiles, her eyes sparkling with delight at the sight that greeted her.

She'd been disheartened after ten minutes of crawling on her hands and knees to discover that the business end of the chute was housed in a gray, grimy room that stank of pee. It was hardly the romantic love nest that Stevie had promised, and most definitely not the perfect venue she'd fantasized about for the giving up of her virginity. She'd been relieved when Stevie had taken her out of the trash room and guided her along a utilitarian, concrete passageway, down two flights of stairs and into the hotel's underground spa.

Stevie had then made his famous *Big Reveal*; waiting until the last possible moment to hit the switch on the spa's subdued lighting, he knew from experience that it was guaranteed to take a girl's breath away.

To date, it had never, ever failed him. The Mountainview's natural underground spa won them over every single time. Stevie studied Virginia's glowing face and knew her expression meant she was now his for the taking, and he felt incredibly pleased with himself.

The spa comprised a large pool of thirty feet by fifty feet at the very least, filled to overflowing with fresh, warm spring water that bubbled up from deep within a fissure in the Earth's crust. The water was clear as crystal and infused with billions of microscopic gas bubbles that gave it a faint sulfurus scent – as if Mother Earth herself was passing gas. The spring provided the spa with an endless renewal of fresh, mineral-infused water that had continued to flow long after the hotel closed. The pool's overflow siphoned off into the desert behind the hotel and was constantly replaced by fresh spring water that kept the pool clean and clear.

Surrounding the pool was a broad walkway of gray, natural slate tiles embedded with fossilized corpses of long-extinct sea creatures. Sitting neatly on the slate was a uniform row of dark wood beach recliners. On some of the recliners, there were dusty but neatly folded purple towels that sported the hotel's distinctive logo of three snow-topped mountain peaks.

At the far end of the spa room were three poolside cabanas. Each one enclosed a four-poster bed draped with diaphanous material and laid with crisp, white sheets. As with everything in the spa, the cabanas were covered with the thick film of dust that bore testimony to their abandonment. There was also the evidence of nefarious use in the form of stained sheets and used condoms, and yet the beds still managed to cling to their erotic allure like an aged screen siren long past her day.

Behind the cabanas sat a small wet bar – long since emptied of its contents – and the door to the steam room that had lain dormant for five years. Adjacent to that was the door to the changing rooms, which hung open like a gaping mouth.

"Didn't I tell you this would be amazing?" Stevie gave his awestruck gal a Cheshire cat grin. "Just like you," he added and reached in for the kiss that would seal the deal.

Virginia pulled away. "Oh, no, you don't!" she laughed at the disappointment in Stevie's face. "Did you really think I was that easy?" she wagged a finger and moved away from him. "I know all about you and your reputation, Stevie Johnson. You thought you'd get me to just drop my panties with this place and your cheesy lines?" She laughed at him again; her eyes twinkled with the pool's reflection.

The muscles on either side of Stevie's face bulged as he ground his teeth together and a sharp pain shot up into his head from the cavity he'd been putting off getting plugged. The prick-teasing bitch had been leading him on? He couldn't believe it, *nobody* played Stevie Johnson, especially not some slip of a girl, no matter how fucking hot she was. Stevie stepped toward Virginia, a smile fixed on his face to mask his anger. They could do this the easy way, or the hard way, as far as he saw things – but *either* way, they were not leaving until he'd gotten his dues from Virginia.

"I'm sorry, Stevie," Virginia said as she offered up a sincere smile, "but you can't expect to bring me to a place like this…"

Stevie moved toward her with purpose, fists clenched tight by his sides, but Virginia backed further away.

"…and not go skinny-dipping!" she giggled, and sloughed off her shorts and panties in one fluid movement. She pulled her T off over her head, unhooked her bra, and her bountiful breasts bounced free. "Care to join me, lover boy?" Virginia took a running dive at the inviting pool and hit the warm water with an almighty splash.

It was the quickest Stevie had ever undressed in his life, and by Christ, he *could* be quick when he needed to be. He threw off his jeans and white wifebeater like they were on fire, and within seconds he and his conquest-to-be were splashing around in the water.

"Hey, look! I'm floating!" Virginia laughed as she lay on her back. The mineral-laden water supported her body as she arched her back and threw back her head, her hair spreading in the water as a feathery black halo. Stevie studied the girl, his erection building as he marveled at the view of the girl's firm, round breasts that pointed at the domed ceiling with delicious, jutting nipples. Those and the black tangle of pubic hair that she thrust clear of the water. As much as he wasn't a big fan of a full bush – much preferring the Brazilian look – Stevie was beguiled by the silky curls and the pink hint of fleshy labia that poked through them.

"It's all the minerals and crap in the water," Stevie offered as he sidled up to Virginia, "you know, from underground." He stroked her glistening, flat stomach and delighted in how her skin trembled at his touch.

"Hey, listen to you, Mr. Geologist," Virginia snorted, "anyone would think you were actually learning something at college."

Stevie ignored her jibe and slid his hand downwards along her belly, his fingers reaching for the dark triangle that nestled between her legs.

Virginia stopped his errant digits with a playful slap and stood up in the water to face him, her tits bobbing in the water like seaside buoys. "Not here, not like this," she said, "I want our first time to be perfect." With that, Virginia waded to the side of the pool and climbed out.

Stevie sighed, barely able to control his exasperation. He was still damned annoyed at her earlier joke and doubted he could take much more teasing from the bitch before he just took what was rightfully his. He watched Virginia's wet, perfect ass glisten as she climbed the pool steps and hoped to God that she wasn't going to wuss out on him; he'd hate to have to *persuade* her like the last one he'd brought down here. That particular episode had shredded his nerves somewhat since she'd been a screamer, *and* she'd threatened to tell the cops, the school, and pretty much everyone she knew. But, lucky for him, her own shame had prevented her from doing so, and the legend that was Stevie Johnson had lived to love another day. Stevie had made a mental note at the time – *definitely* no more virgins, although as quickly as he'd made the note, it was forgotten.

Stevie climbed out of the pool and followed Virginia's naked form to the cabanas. "Which one should we use?" she asked with a playfulness in her tone that gave Stevie a good feeling that she *wasn't* going to back out on him, virginity or no. He fancied he sensed her inner lust like a predatory animal sensed fear: it was most definitely the carnal wantonness experience had taught him would soon have her begging him to fuck her 'till she wept.

Virginia turned around to face him and walked backward toward the cabana bed to better give her man a good look at her lean, olive-skinned body. "Although, I am beginning to have second thoughts about letting you fuck me now. Perhaps, I should be saving myself for my future husband?" she teased.

"And why would you want to do a dumb thing like that?" Stevie tried to keep his voice level, still unsure if she was one-hundred percent joking or not, "when you can have a piece of this." He pointed to his impressive erection, which in turn pointed eagerly at Virginia like a gun dog at a downed bird.

Virginia reached the bed and stopped, with the back of her legs touching the soft, cotton sheets. She spread out her arms, palms up, and she looked like a wanton, naked angel.

"They called me Virginia for a good reason, you know," she purred.

"I know, babe," Stevie said with a lascivious laugh, "but after today, they're gonna have to change your name to Cock-Hungry Bitch."

"Stevie Johnson!" Virginia feigned horror, "with talk like that, you're likely gonna get your brains fucked out." She squeezed her dripping, wet breasts together, pulling her hands toward their tips; she tweaked the angry nipples with an extra hard tug. Then, maintaining lustful eye contact, Virginia snaked one hand down to her pouting vulva.

The cabana bed was tipped roughly onto its side as something immense lunged forward with lightning speed. In a reddish blur, the thing reared up and grabbed Virginia with long, monstrous legs and lifted her clean off of her bare feet. Virginia had no time to form a scream before long, sharp, black fangs dug into either side of her abdomen, sliding with ease into her lithe body amidst a thick gout of blood; they punctured Virginia's diaphragm and silenced her voice.

Paralyzed with terror, Stevie gawked in shock at the scene that unfolded before him, his mind simply refusing to believe what his eyes showed it; the colossal creature that had lunged out of the darkness and grabbed his gal looked like some kind of bizarre, oversized snake. It had a head the color of dried-blood that was broad as his car's hood, its body a touch wider than that. The grotesque, serpentine body was carried along on countless legs and snaked back so far into the shadows that Stevie could only see but half of the monster. And it was the pointed, yellow legs that finally registered some form of recognition in Stevie's panicking brain and he knew in that instant what the gigantic thing was – but still he refused to comprehend.

The creature held Virginia aloft with its huge legs that appeared to be giant spikes as its huge jaws penetrated her smooth, tanned skin. She struggled valiantly, smashed her fists into the wicked, black jaws and kicked her legs against thin air; all the while her mouth gaping in a long, breathless scream. Then, the girl's smooth, toned belly distended, and her navel popped outward as if violently pushed from inside, as the giant centipede pumped its lethal venom into her body.

Stevie found his feet and staggered back from the horror. As he did so, Virginia's eyes met his, imploring him not to do what he was about to do. What he *had* to do.

"*Don't leave me*," she mouthed, "*please*."

The centipede sensed the vibration of Stevie's movement and turned its gargantuan head to face him. Its array of black, dull eyes – each one a dinner plate across – stared unblinking toward Stevie, and although it could only make out his dark shape in the dimly lit poolroom, that was enough for the creature to register fresh prey.

Stevie froze.

His mind raced. He knew he should run whilst the monster was occupied with the girl – what the fuck *was* her name again? – she was his ticket away from this nightmare. Yet his body was once again refusing to move. It was as if he knew by instinct that if he moved, the hellish creature would follow.

Virginia's struggles grew weaker as the venom bloating her body worked quickly to poison her heart and destroy her nervous system. Her body flopped around like a deflating toy in the centipede's mouth, feet slapping against its burnished shell with a hollow *pitter-patter-pat*. Virginia was still beating her hands on the cold, hard fangs that were ensconced in her body when her belly split open. The built-up pressure of the monster's poison, along with the digesting action of the enzymes that it contained, had weakened the girl's abdominal muscles and her body ripped itself apart.

Virginia's digestive tract slopped out onto the cool, tiled floor and laid pulsing and steaming before her shocked eyes.

Washes of blood gushed from her eviscerated body and poured into the spa pool to turn its warm water a disgusting, fleshy pink. As her life ebbed, Virginia felt the centipede's rigid mouth parts caress the soft flesh between her shoulder blades like a lover's kiss and mercifully, her dying senses didn't register that it had, in fact, begun to feed.

Finally, Stevie summoned the wherewithal to turn and run, and as he high-tailed it away from the impossible creature and the gore-soaked ruin of Virginia Mendoza, his rapidly diminishing erection flapped noisily against his thighs.

As he ran – the fastest he'd run since quitting college football – Stevie dared not glance back, because he knew that to do so would be to court bad karma and the beast would be upon him. He was in no doubt that it could easily outrun him – what wouldn't with that many legs? – he could only hope and pray that the monster with a thousand legs would stay put to finish its meal and leave him the hell alone.

Stevie raced out of the poolroom and flew up the two flights of stairs beyond the door, taking the steps three, four at a time. He burst through the door at the top of the stairs and into the hallway leading to the trash room. He allowed himself one twinge of relief at having the solidness of a door between himself and the monster centipede, although he knew a thing that size would most likely make short work of the lightweight door. The hallway lights were on a timer and had switched themselves off ten minutes after he and Virginia had ventured down into the bowels of the hotel, but Stevie ran headlong into the darkness anyway; knowing what may well be hot on his tail by now, the dark held no further terrors.

Stevie ran blindly toward the trash room, forcing his breath in shallow, painful gasps that tore at his lungs. As he ran, he batted away the things in the blackness that brushed against his face like the fake spider webs in a ghost train.

Whatever the things were – and Stevie's horrified mind was already making an educated guess – they seemed to be coming down from the ceiling to grab at him. They snagged in his hair, pulling at it as myriad tiny shards prickled his skin, scratched and pinched him. Stevie held his head down and ran like the Devil himself was after him.

When, at last, Stevie plopped out of the trash chute like a fat, bloodied turd, he crashed into the dirt with a *thump* that knocked the wind out of him and rattled his teeth. A plume of pale dust clouded up around him to herald his escape from the horrors he'd witnessed deep within the bowels of the Mountainview.

Stevie's head was a seething mass of chestnut colored centipedes that clung on to his scalp with sharp, pointed legs. He felt their scratching, prickling movements as they crawled around in his hair to bite at his skin and explore his ears, his nose, his mouth.

Stevie screamed and pulled at the creatures, no longer caring that their hard, fat bodies and pointy legs repulsed him. Each one of them he yanked from his hair was almost as long as his arm and a perfect miniature of the monster that had killed Virginia. Stevie yowled as he tugged, and the centipedes tore away with raw clumps of bloodied scalp clutched between their legs, and they bit at his hands with vicious fangs until his flesh ran slick with blood and poison.

Struggling to his feet with a curtain of blood pouring down his face and into his eyes, Stevie ran for the road. His Corolla was around somewhere, he was sure of that, and he knew he had to get to it and fast. Perhaps, he could get away, find help, and come back for the girl: although, he knew this to be a dumb thought because Virginia was already dead. He'd seen her guts spread out beneath her dying body like some sick buffet, so any thoughts of rescuing her served only to assuage Stevie's selfish conscience.

Stevie tore the last of the centipedes from his hair,

wobbled to his feet – unsteady because of the venom that worked its way through his blood stream – and zigzagged to where he thought his car might be. What Stevie didn't see was the Airport Shuttle bus thundering toward him as he blundered out onto the blacktop.

It was fortuitous that the shuttle bus driver saw *him* otherwise Stevie would have become just another mangled lump of roadkill on the hot California road; something else for the fat, waddling buzzards to pick at. It took the driver a double take to register what he was seeing, but instinct took over, and he slammed his foot on the brakes.

It wasn't every day that a naked, blood drenched boy ran in front of the Happy Shuttle Coachella Valley Airport Bus.

The small group of passengers stood around the boy's body, holding handkerchiefs, hats, hands, *anything* up to their noses to stifle the dreadful blood and piss-stink wafting from him. They gawked and fought the urge to point at his shriveled genitals, the countless abrasions over his upper body, and the congealing mask of blood that covered his face. Behind them, the bus driver was busy calling 911, doing his damndest not to throw up while explaining to the operator what was going on, and where he was.

"Is he still alive?" a fat woman asked.

"Yeah, he's still breathing," a guy in a too-wide Stetson replied, blinking hard against the harsh California sun, "and you can see his jugular moving." He pointed at Stevie's throat, and at the faint throbbing exaggerated by the slick blood coating it.

"What the heck happened to him?" Fat Woman said with some difficulty as her breathing was coming in short spasms from the sheer exertion of getting off the bus and standing upright.

Stetson eyed the fat woman with disdain. He'd hoped to Dear God when she'd clambered onto the bus at the airport that she wasn't going to the same swinger's resort as himself and his good lady wife. And if she was, how he'd pity whichever poor sap destined to pull *her* keys out of the goldfish bowl.

"Damned if I know," Stetson offered. His eyes followed the fractured blood trail that ran from the boy and back to the abandoned hotel, disappearing behind it. "Looks like he came from that away though," he said, and from the corner of his eye, he saw something move. It darted into one of the scrawny, desiccated bushes that specked the roadside. Probably a snake, he told himself, cringing; he hated snakes.

Stevie's body began to convulse. His head snapped back, eyes bulged open, and he twitched and shuddered. A watery spout of blood coughed up from his gaping mouth, and in unison, his bladder and bowels let go with a strident gurgle and a splash. The bus people gasped and took a step back as one, a look of utter disgust on every face as the unfortunate boy jigged as if a million volts were passing through his body and he peed and crapped on the road in front of them.

"Areany of you a doctor?" the bus driver shouted over; cell phone still stuck to his ear.

They all shook their heads.

"A nurse, paramedic? Has anyone got a fucking First Aid certificate?!" he shouted at them all, angry and frustrated.

"I'm a lawyer," Stetson offered.

"Then why not give him your goddamned card so he can sue some fucker once he's finished puking blood?!" the bus driver fumed.

As if on cue, Stevie coughed up another fountain of blood that sprayed on everyone's feet and elicited groans of revulsion. Then, as quickly as the seizure had begun, Stevie quit moving and lay quite still.

"What the fuck is *that*?" Fat Woman pointed a chubby

finger at the bloodied head that appeared in Stevie's twitching mouth. It was wide and fat, a thumbs-length across, and sported sturdy, segmented antennae that twitched around to taste the air.

"Oh my dear God!" shrieked a young, pale skinned woman. She clamped her hand to her mouth, turned away, and puked through her fingers.

The centipede crawled out of Stevie's mouth, its passage eased by the slickness of the blood and fluids that oozed up from the boy's stomach. The creature hauled its body out of Stevie's esophagus and onto the hot road where it stretched the full length of one of the fading white stripes that ran along the centerline.

"Jesus H –!" Stetson lunged forward and stamped on the animal's head. It *smooshed* on the tarmac with a satisfying crunch; clear fluid and chunks of shattered exoskeleton splattered across the road as the centipede thrashed and twisted in its death throes. Before Stetson could lift his Croc away and contemplate looking for something with which to wipe off the mess, the centipede had whipped its tail end around and slashed at his bare calf with its rear legs.

"*Sonofabitch*!" Stetson yelped and hopped away from the creature that still squirmed on the road, stuck there by the gore from its own mangled head. Blood oozed from the twin cuts on the man's leg and soaked into his brown sock.

Stevie Johnson's body twitched again, and his eyelids flickered, and as he faded into a most welcome and merciful unconsciousness, he heard sirens in the distance.

CHAPTER TWO

1

UNIVERSITY OF CALIFORNIA, SAN DIEGO,
DEPARTMENT OF BIOLOGICAL SCIENCES.

Professor Jane Lucas nuzzled at the student's clitoris with her nose and relished the sensation of lustful power as the girl squirmed her response. Venturing downward a little more, Jane replaced her nose with her lapping tongue and applied just the right amount of moist pressure on the girl's swollen organ, and this time, her student moaned out loud.

Pinned beneath her Professor, Melanie Hernandez tried to suppress her groan and focused on slurping between Jane's legs as she struggled to breathe against the hot, slick flesh that pressed into her face.

Jane stretched Mel's slippery labia wide apart with her fingers and inhaled the heady scent that entranced her. She wriggled her tongue deep into Mel's vagina and relished the slightest taste of copper that permeated the faint piscine perfume. Jane recalled that Mel had informed her she'd just started her period, or had just finished – Jane was damned if she could remember which – and knowing that always made their trysts all the more salacious for the taboo. Jane did, however, resolve to chastise her lover to shave her nether regions a little more often, as she could already feel her face beginning to chafe with stubble rash.

As seemed to be the norm in their illicit relationship, Professor Lucas was entertaining the student in her faculty office, away from the prying eyes of Mel's shared house and her own faculty apartment. Lost deep within their own pleasures, immersed in their intimate *soixante-neuf,* naked and sweating on the cold, hard floor, it was always a delight to shut out the world for an hour or so. Of course, such liaisons between students and staff were the ultimate no-no, but the risk of being caught brought much-needed frission for Jane to counteract her lover's lack of experience. Having said that, Professor Lucas wasn't quite *that* reckless, and she'd secured her office door with an old plastic chair propped under the handle.

Jane's office was, at best, utilitarian: its whitewashed walls and ancient furniture came across as drab, unremarkable, and devoid of personality. A gray, melamine desk with dented metal legs sat at one end of the room – its companion chair was currently the makeshift door blockade. The desk was laden with mountains of haphazardly discarded files, academic books, and carefully bound student papers that looked as if they would topple over at the slightest provocation to spill onto the beige-tiled floor.

A solitary, wooden bookcase stood against the windowless wall, the only other concession to academia in Jane's sparse office. As with the desk, the bookcase was crammed with fat books, journals, and published papers that bore testimony to Professor Jane Lucas's specialization in the phylum *arthropoda;* the literal translation of the Latin-derived word being '*jointed legs*'.

The phylum comprised over eighty percent of the

animal life on the planet, which were more commonly known as insects and spiders to most people; they were 'bugs' to others, although only a relatively small number of said creatures were classed as true bugs – the order *Hemiptera*, to be precise – and the more general *creepy-crawlies* to the majority. Jane had never cared much for that particular epithet as, since childhood, she had always found the arthropods an endless fascination and to be neither creepy nor crawly – she loved 'em all.

All, that is, except one.

The myriad arthropod eyes – some compound, some single, others in pairs, in fours, sixes, eights, and more – stared out from the vibrant book covers. one might imagine that some were casting judgment over the Professor and her latest conquest, whilst others played voyeur as both women worked diligently toward their mutual satisfaction on the cold floor.

With an expert's ease, Jane slid her tongue in and out of Mel's succulent vagina to tongue-fuck the girl to orgasm and savor its warm taste and slippery texture. With an index finger, Jane maintained the stimulation of Mel's swollen clitoris, pushing the girl closer to the edge with every swirl and flick whilst Mel reciprocated with a busy mouth on her Professor's sex.

Jane kept herself under no illusions whatsoever about the Hernandez girl. She knew full well that Mel was only screwing her to bring her grades out of the doldrums, and Jane had good reason to believe that the girl was nowhere near as bisexual as she'd made herself out to be. There always seemed to be an inherent hesitance about the girl, as if she were going through the motions with Jane and her heart was not one-hundred percent into their fucking. Having said that, Mel always seemed to put in a sterling performance and left Jane more than satisfied – good sex was good sex; Jane had never been too fussy about from where – or whom – she got it .

Jane figured she couldn't be too hypocritical about Mel's potential motive for their relationship – if screwing in Jane's tiny office could ever be called a relationship, that is. Jane herself certainly hadn't been above using her pussy to get what she wanted, when the need arose: she hadn't got to be Professor of Zoology, at one of the West Coast's most prestigious universities before the age of thirty-seven, because of her outstanding contribution to the planet's understanding of myriapods. In that way, at least, Jane had to admire her eager student and her beautifully proportioned, hard body as the girl was most certainly reminiscent of a young Jane Lucas.

A knock on the door.

"Professor Lucas?" a nervous voice enquired, "are you in there?" It was Dorothy Manning, the faculty secretary, PA, and general busybody – Dotty to her friends. The doorknob twisted, and thankfully, the plastic chair held its place. "There's someone here to see you, Professor Lucas," Dotty insisted.

Jane snorted her impatience, which sent shivers of unintentional ecstasy through Mel's body. The girl let out a soft whimper and pressed her thighs tight against Jane's ears, which dampened Dotty's voice somewhat. Close to achieving her climax, Jane was reluctant to break away from Mel's industrious tongue and fingers. "Dotty, I'm busy!" she replied, her voice was muffled but civil, as Jane could manage, given the circumstances.

Jane's sexual indiscretions with students and staff were no secret to Dotty. The old woman had covered for the Professor more times than Jane could care to count, so in that respect, at least, Dotty was a saint. But knocking on the door when she knew Jane was *busy*, that was most unforgivable. What was a girl supposed to do for privacy: hang a fucking sock on the doorknob?

"I'm sorry, Professor Lucas, but he says it's quite urgent," Dotty continued, "he's a police officer."

Jane stopped dead, her tongue resting still and lifeless against Mel's labia as a cold shiver coursed up and along her spine – the police always made Jane nervous. Placating herself that it was probably nothing too serious, Jane went back to work on her lover with increased vigor. She absently wondered if Dotty could hear the slurping noises through the door, or the wet fart sounds that squeaked out as air trapped between her and Mel's sweating bodies made its escape.

Mel lifted her head, pushing Jane's bottom upward. "The police?" there was panic in her voice.

"Take him down to the laboratory, Dotty," Jane instructed, "I'll be done in a few minutes."

"Perhaps, we should finish up now?" Mel suggested and then gasped as Jane nibbled gently at her clit.

"You'll be finished when I am." Jane thrust her crotch into Mel's face and forced the girl's head back down to the floor with a hollow *thud*.

Mel renewed her enthusiastic lapping at Jane's vagina, though more now to get things over and done than with inflamed passion. Jane moaned, grateful that her voice was muffled by Mel's firm thighs as she could sense that Dotty was still lurking around on the other side of the door. Jane felt the intense orgasm as it welled up from deep inside her body - this was going to be a good one.

"Okay, Professor Lucas," Dotty said, "but please don't be too long: he's driven all the way from Coachella Valley to see you."

"Okay, Dotty," Jane growled in a breathless pant, "I'm coming."

2

True to her word, Professor Jane Lucas strode into the Zoology Laboratory a few minutes later. Seven minutes, to be precise, just long enough for her breathing to return to normal, after an orgasm so intense she'd bitten the back of her hand to quell the inevitable scream, and to pull on her clothes – faded jeans, yellow tank top, white laboratory coat, and strappy pumps. There'd been no time for the niceties of brushing her hair or washing up, so she'd tied up her mess of long, red hair into a rough ponytail and decided that she could live with the musky scent of Melanie Hernandez on her face for as long as it would take to find out what had brought a cop a'calling.

"Hi, I'm Professor Lucas. Call me Jane, please," she greeted the cop with a hand outstretched, and her warmest, most disarming smile. "And you are – ?"

"Lieutenant Newman, call me Don." He smiled back and shook Jane's hand. "Thank you so much for taking the time to see me. Really appreciate it."

Jane studied the cop. He was tall and thin, almost wiry-looking. His hair was almost totally gray – prematurely, she would have guessed – she put him at late forties/early fifties – and his face was rugged, etched with crevices and wrinkles: character lines as her Gran'pappy used to call them. Newman's eyes were a heavenly, twinkling blue which sparkled with life of its own, as if they were simply refusing to age, along with the rest of his body.

They were also giving nothing away.

Jane began to feel a little nervous: why was he here? What did he want? Had another student's pissed-off family found out that the esteemed Professor Lucas had slept with him/her and had reported her for dereliction of her duty of care? No, it couldn't possibly be that – the cop wouldn't be talking to her here in the Lab and certainly not within earshot of the three students in the background who were busy pretending not to have noticed that there was a cop in their midst.

"It's no problem at all, Lieutenant Newman, how can I help you?" Jane said.

The cop studied the Professor who looked much too young to be a Professor of anything. She stood – in heels, he noted – a good eight or nine inches below his height, which he figured would put her at five feet and change. Her dazzling, hazel eyes twinkled with bright intelligence, and the pale, flawless skin of her round, handsome face had a glow that married just perfect with the tousled flame of hair that she'd obviously tried to contain in a hurry. At this, Newman's mind wandered a little, part cop curiosity, part flight of fancy.

"I was hoping you could offer your expert opinion on this." Newman brought his mind back to bear and held up a Wal-Mart carrier bag – double bagged – with its contents close to bursting out. "And please, call me Don." He plopped the bag on the closest workbench, lifted a flap, and invited Jane to take a peek: his trained eyes noting the Professor recoiled from the bag, just a little.

"Dead?" Jane asked.

"As a doornail. Some tourist stepped on its head good and proper," Newman told her. "The paramedics brought it in."

"Paramedics?" Jane questioned with a playful smile on her lips, "They have 911 for 'pedes now?"

"Not quite," Newman smiled. "It's standard procedure with animal bites. It helps the hospital to identify what did the biting so they can get the right anti-venom into the patient," he explained.

"This bit somebody?"

"Yeah, I'll fill you in once you've given me the run down," Newman teased. He let go of the bag and took a half-step back: a gesture that said: *you're the goddammed expert, it's all yours now*.

Jane pulled a pair of blue heavy-duty rubber gloves from her lab coat pocket. She snapped them on and gingerly pulled open the mouth of the Wal-Mart bag. With a firm grip on a bottom corner, Jane tipped the bag up and poured the deceased centipede out onto the dissecting table. It slithered from the bag in one fluid motion, and as it clattered onto the steel topped table, a viscous fluid dribbled from its crushed head, and Jane caught the strong, acrid stink of urea.

"It's some kind of millipede," Newman ventured, not sure if he was trying to impress her, or why.

"It's a 'pede. Sorry, I mean a *centipede,*" Jane corrected.

"Oh yeah, a hundred legs. I guess I should have counted 'em," the cop grinned.

"They don't actually have a hundred legs, Lieutenant; none of them do. It's a common misnomer amongst people —"

" – like me?" Newman interrupted.

"What I was *going* to say that people don't know Arthropods like we Zoologists do." Jane laughed to diffuse the tension that she felt was stirring between herself and the cop: the man was a tad too serious for her liking. She fished a pair of extra long tweezers out of a drawer beneath the benchtop and used them to layout the animal. She marveled at the size of the thing, it was far bigger than any specimen she'd seen before, and she'd certainly seen plenty.

"Forty-six," she said, "legs, I mean. There are twenty-three pairs of legs, one per segment; I guess that makes our big boy here a *Scolopendra gigantea.*"

"A what now?" The merest hint of a smile danced on Newman's lips. "I thought you said it was a centipede, Ma'am. Now you're trying to confuse a poor Hicksville cop with ya'll's fancy talk."

"I'm sorry, Lieutenant, I don't usually get to talk about these things with anyone outside of the University, I didn't mean…" Jane stopped herself there. "You're joking, right?"

"I'm sorry, Professor Lucas, couldn't resist," the cop said and laughed along with Jane, the tension duly dissipated.

"Hey, guys!" Jane called to the students who were still trying their best to be invisible whilst rubbernecking at the same time. "Come take a look at this beauty."

The students drifted over, and Jane introduced them.

"Lieutenant Newman, meet some of my best students, and by best, I mean those who stay awake during my lectures." She laughed, although there was a painful grain of truth in her comment. "This is Martha-Ray Penderson: her specialty is *'Parasitic Diptera'*.This is Darlene Buchanan, specialty *'Ephemeroptera'*. And the big guy here is Fred Westendick: specialty – his football scholarship." They all, in turn, dutifully shook hands with the cop.

"I'm sorry, Professor, but the only one of those I got was *football*," Newman laughed. "Quarterback?" he asked Fred.

"Yes, Sir."

The lab door swung open, and heads turned. Melanie Hernandez sauntered in, smoothing her pristine white lab coat over her round hips as she walked.

"Ahh, Miss Hernandez, pleased that you decided to join us," Jane announced. "This is Lieutenant Newman, and he's brought us a prize. Lieutenant Newman, this is Melanie Hernandez, my star student. Her specialty is the same as mine, the *Myriapods*."

"Call me Don." Newman extended his slender hand to Mel. She shook it with reluctance, wary of the tall detective.

Jane looked the Hispanic girl up and down, soaking up her doe-eyed Hispanic features and voluptuous figure. Relishing the fresh memory of that delicious body, she was a little hurt to note that Mel had taken the time to rinse her face on the way down to the lab.

"Okay folks, it's quiz time," Jane declared. "Our dead guy here is a – what?" she threw the question out to her students. They all stood stock-still and stared at the thing on the table as if it were about to give them the answer.

The centipede stretched two-thirds the length of the yard-long dissecting table, its segmented body glinting like cheap plastic jewelry beneath the laboratory's fluorescent light. The creature was a deep maroon color, a color that always reminded Jane of dried blood. Not including the head, she had counted twenty-three leg-bearing segments. Each one of those housed a pair of bright yellow legs, one on either side. The legs, typical of the species, were long – some over two inches and each pair of limbs tapered to a sharp point and was progressively longer than those immediately in front of it – evolution's key in preventing the centipede from tripping itself up.

"*Scolopendra gigantea,*" *Mel* answered, "also known as the Peruvian Giant Yellow-Leg centipede or Amazonian Giant Centipede. It comes from the family *Scolopendridae*, subphylum *Myriapodia;* members of the largest animal phylum – the arthropods."

"Well done, Melanie." Jane smiled at Newman. "You can see why Miss Hernandez is my star student."

The other students cast sly glances between themselves. Most of them knew precisely *why* Miss Hernandez was Professor Lucas's star student, and it had absolutely squat to do with her knowledge of the *myriapodia*, as impressive as that may be.

"And you can see here," Jane snorted as she prodded at the rear end of the 'pede with the tweezers, "these fake antennae are actually adapted legs. You see how they are colored red like the real antennae? The 'pede holds them upward when it walks, as a decoy." She invited Newman to take a closer look. "They make the back-end look much like the front end. This animal exhibits a bizarre type of Batesian mimicry in that its backside mimics its own head."

"It's to confuse predators," Mel chipped in. "Much like the fake eyes on Owl Butterflies. The predator attacks what it thinks is the head to disable its prey –"

"– and gets a nasty surprise as our guy here whips his *real* head around and predator very quickly becomes prey," Jane concluded. "Having said that, these fake antennae do carry a little venom. Not as much as the front end, but more than enough to spoil your afternoon."

As the familiar words from countless lectures tumbled from her mouth, Jane felt a long-forgotten twinge of exhilaration stab at her gut. The cop's 'pede certainly looked to all intents and purposes to be *gigantea*, but it was far larger than any recorded specimen she was aware of. It was always possible that an animal of this size could be a one-off mutation, but there was always the – more exciting – chance that it could be an entirely new sub-species! Zoologist Jane allowed herself the buzz of excitement at this: a discovery like this could secure her tenure at the University, and elevate her to the top echelons of the international zoological fraternity. Think worldwide lecture tours, book deals, even TV,and she'd no longer have to be the gal who'd screwed her way to Professordom!

"It's big," Martha-Ray understated, as was her norm, "where did you find it?"

"On a freeway a couple of miles outside Desert Hot Springs," Newman replied. "We think it came out of an old hotel that's been boarded up a while."

"Well, thank you for bringing it in for us, Lieutenant; it really is a fascinating specimen." Jane was keen to hurry the cop along now; there was something in his eyes that was beginning to make her nervous. "Is there anything else you'd like to know?"

"Actually, I didn't bring this beastie along for show 'n' tell," Newman said. "It's part of a murder investigation."

"Seriously?" Darlene gasped.

"I don't ever joke about murder, Miss," Newman said solemnly and then followed up with a sly wink at Jane.

Did the cop just *flirt* with her? Jeez, you show a guy a little civility, and you get hit on. An inward smile; *you still got it, old girl.* Of course, it could always have been the scent of another woman's sex on Jane that was attracting him, like *formicidae* to jelly. Another inward chuckle; even her private, most lewd thoughts were zoological!

"I was told that you were the authority on centipedes and such," Newman continued.

"I'd hardly say I was an authority, Lieutenant. I've written a few papers and a book or two on this particular 'pede, and that's about far as it goes," Jane replied with a false modesty that didn't become her. Dammit, why did she always do this? She was *the* goddamned authority on the *Scolopendridae*!

"Well, that's much authority as I need, Ma'am."

Jane prodded the dead centipede once more with her tweezers and tried to repress her revulsion. Twenty years of studying 'pedes, fifteen published papers, sole author of *the* reference book, and she still couldn't stand the sight of the God-awful things. Hell, she could barely force herself to say the damned word in full, which is why she always insisted on calling them by the abbreviated name she'd coined.

In short, centipedes of this particular variety made Jane's skin crawl and creeped her the fuck out.

"You can see by the maroon coloring and the yellow tinted legs that this is *gigantea*. Although I have to say, it does appear to be an unusually large specimen, and that would make me question its integrity as one of the species."

"Didn't you say that these things were *supposed* to be giant?" Newman queried.

"Yes, I did." Jane narrowly avoided a patronizing smile. "*Gigantea* typically achieves a size of around twelve inches. As you can see, this one is more than double that." Jane indicated the brass ruler embedded into the top edge of the bench.

"Okay, so, are these things poisonous?" Newman asked. Time to cut to the chase.

"Not in the least, Lieutenant. In fact, I'm told they have quite a pleasant, nutty flavor," Jane told him with a smile.

"People eat those things?" Newman wrinkled his nose.

"You eat shrimp?" Jane retorted.

"Yeah, but – "

"Well, then," she grinned at the cop.

"So, you're saying that this thing *isn't* poisonous?" Newman queried. "It sure as shit looks like it ought to be, pardon my French."

"I'm sorry, Lieutenant, just a little zoological humor," Jane laughed. "Would you care to explain, Martha-Ray?"

The black, pudgy girl with wide spectacles and cornrows spoke up, "When something is poisonous, it means it causes harm when ingested, like a toadstool. For something to be classed as *venomous*, it has to cause harm through a bite, a sting, or some other means of getting toxins *into* its victim." Pleased with herself, Martha-Ray beamed at Jane for reassurance.

And got nothing.

"Okay, okay, I get it." Newman laughed a weary laugh. Time was running on, and he had half a girl's corpse and a suspect who wasn't likely to talk anytime soon – if ever – back home.

"I'm sorry, Lieutenant, no offense meant," Jane apologized.

"None taken, Ma'am. So, is this thing *venomous* enough to kill someone?" Newman asked, "or to make someone do this?" He pulled out a photograph from an inside pocket and showed it to Jane, at the same time taking great care not to let the students see.

Jane shuddered. The picture was of the shredded remains of a girl's torso. The head was chewed down to the jawline, both arms were missing, and a single, bloodied breast jutted out defiantly atop a hollowed-out rib cage. The girl's stomach was slopped out onto an autopsy table, and there were four or five feet of intestines snaking from it.

Below that, there was just a pool of congealing blood.

"Oh, sweet Jesus," Jane gasped and turned a translucent greenish-gray. Her students all craned their necks to see, but Newman was too quick for them, spiriting the photograph back into his pocket like a sidewalk magician.

"I'm guessing that this thing wouldn't be big enough to do that amount of damage to a person?" Newman ventured. "So I guess my real question is – could a bite from one of these things make a guy do this to his girlfriend?"

"There was another victim?"

"Yeah, a boy of nineteen. He's messed up pretty bad, but not as badly as his girlfriend, though." Newman paused. "He's still in a coma, bitten to hell and back by something, and this guy here is my prime suspect." He nodded to the 'pede on the dissecting table.

"Well, Lieutenant," Jane said, slipping into *lecture mode* through habit, "you are correct in your assumption insomuch that this critter couldn't have done *that* to a human body. Whilst its bite is a nasty one…" A visible tremble as she extended the centipedes' remaining, inch-long fang, as she suppressed the urge to cringe. "…I'm told it is intensely painful, but no more dangerous than a hornet sting. Unless you are allergic to the venom, of course, in which case it's anaphylactic shock, followed by respiratory failure, and then death if adrenaline is not administered quickly." She smiled at the look of distaste on the cop's face. "But don't forget, Lieutenant that one can also get the same effects with a bee sting, contact with rat's pee, or eating peanuts."

Jane poked around some more inside the creature's crushed head.

"The fangs – and there are normally two by the way – are not really fangs at all," Jane explained, "they are actually modified from the first pair of legs. They are what we in the business call maxillipeds, or more often in this case, *forcipules*. They tend to be used solely for venom injection and are quite unique to the 'pedes."

"It's something they have in common with the crustaceans; modified legs for mouthparts," Mel chimed in and looked particularly pleased with herself.

"Miss Hernandez is correct. We think that it goes some way toward proving a common ancestor between the *Myriapodia* and the crustaceans," Jane lectured. And then, "I'm sorry, Lieutenant, you didn't come all this way for a lecture on evolution." An awkward look shot between Professor and cop. "You're not one of those weird Creationist who thinks God did it all in six days, and the Earth is only four thousand years old, are you?"

"No, Ma'am, I'm all up for your Darwin fella," Newman laughed, "some of the reprobates I have to deal with on Saturday nights could also go a long way towards proving that we descended from the apes – some more recently than others." Newman allowed himself a hearty laugh, relaxing a little, and the students laughed along politely.

"A dose of venom from this 'pede would cause searing pain, numbness, disorientation, and delirium," Jane said, "quite possibly necrosis at the site of the bite, maybe even heart palpitations. But it won't kill a healthy, unallergic adult. In fact, the only recorded instance of human death by *gigantea* was a child in Peru who got bitten in the scalp." She forced herself to peer even closer at the centipede's unsightly head. "Research shows that it would take the venom from approximately five hundred *gigantea* to kill a healthy human." She stepped back a little, the ammonia smell the specimen was giving off was starting to make her stomach feel queasy. "Although, this venom gland *is* unusually large, even for such an oversized specimen; you could probably take that number down to a couple of hundred."

"You're telling me that this thing *could* have killed the girl?" Newman asked.

"I doubt that very much, Lieutenant. Taking into account the damage her body has sustained. There's no way one 'pede could have done that. And I really don't think any number of them could have, either," Jane explained. "Perhaps some of the neurological effects of the venom could have been exaggerated, given the size of the creature and the disproportionately large venom gland."

"You think the boy could have been bitten and then gone crazy enough to butcher his girlfriend? Jesus H Christ." Newman looked nauseous.

"I guess anything's possible, Lieutenant." Jane felt sorry for the cop. She figured that things like this rarely happened out in Desert Hot Springs. She added, "Although there's not been all that much work done on the neurological effects of *gigantea* venom."

"There's your next doctorate right there, Professor Lucas," Darlene piped up with a wry smile, "a great opportunity for you to work with the centipedes again. We could all help."

"Thank you, Darlene. One for the back burner, I think," Jane said and smiled sweetly at Darlene's sarcasm. She was not at all sure how her students could possibly know about her hatred of 'pedes, she thought she kept it well hidden. But they knew, of that, she was positive – had she been *that* obvious?

"I guess that answers my question, Professor." Newman rubbed his temples, trying to fend off the headache that was forming behind his eyes like storm clouds on a fall evening. "Kind of," he said, the case was beginning to show all the hallmarks of a complete and utter nightmare. Newman was the kind of cop who preferred his crime simple and straightforward: not the variety that insisted on throwing curve ball after curve ball at him. He'd initially had this one figured as an open-and-shut: freaky boyfriend lures impressionable girl into the abandoned hotel, and then goes all crazy and butchers her up for his own gratification – end of story. But now – now there was a possible defense: *the fucking centipede made me do it.*

"I'm sorry I couldn't give you more, Lieutenant." Jane felt genuinely sorry that she'd appeared to have just made the cop's day a shit-load worse. "But, as I said, this is not a typical specimen. You say it came out of an abandoned hotel?"

"Yeah, the Mountainview," Newman told her. He decided against explaining how he'd followed the blood trail from the middle of the freeway where they'd found Stevie Johnson barely alive and looking like he'd stuck his head through a windshield. He wasn't in the mood for long stories: he just wanted to hit the road and get back to familiar territory. "It's one of those fancy ones with a natural hot pool in the basement. They had a gas explosion about five years ago, and it's been closed up ever since," Newman added.

"It may be worth us having a look around to see if there are any more specimens inside," Jane offered. "It may help your case."

"I doubt that, Professor. It doesn't matter if there's just this one or a hundred of 'em. The girl's still dead, and Coma Boyfriend's gonna be better off if he never wakes up." Newman was getting antsy: the laboratory was making him feel out-of-place. Colleges always had that effect on him, even back when he was a student. Newman had never been much of an advocate for learning for its own sake.

"I'd love to have the opportunity to see what there is to find," Jane said, trying her best not to sound too much like a ten-year-old girl who just got invited to the cool kid's sleepover. "I think we're all free this weekend, aren't we people?"

Her students' nods were lackluster at best.

"I'm not sure how easy that would be: the place's boarded up pretty tight," Newman told her. "But if you are planning to come over to Coachella, I'd wait a week or so, we're expecting a wind storm this weekend, and the last one we had, the winds reached eighty miles per hour."

"I grew up in Florida, Lieutenant. It'd take more than a desert fart to scare me off!" Jane's laugh was a young girl's laugh.

That old, long-forgotten excitement had crept over Jane. It was the feeling that had pulled her toward science in the first place, which in turn fuelled her inextinguishable love of crawling, slithering things. At the very least, this could be a golden excuse to get out beyond the confines of the lab, away from the books and papers, back into grubbing around in the dirt and those dark, damp corners that she'd been drawn to since she was a kid. That and the thrill of discovering creatures that most people never even knew existed. Seeing the oversized 'pede stretched out before her – as revolted as she was by the sight of its disgusting body – had given her the itch again, and this was an itch that not even the most depraved sex could scratch. And wouldn't it be so wonderfully ironic to have the one creature on God's Own Earth that she truly despised named after her? *Scolopendra gigantea lucasii.* Yeah, that had a nice ring to it.

"I thought you might say something like that," Newman smiled. "You're all the same, you academic types: never take no for an answer." Newman handed Jane a tattered, white business card. "Give this guy a call. He's the caretaker up at the Mountainview. I'm not promising he's gonna help you because he's a strange old bastard. But, you never know."

Jane read the card. There were three words on it, printed in plain Arial: *Lenard Levandowski – Caretaker.* Scrawled on the back of the card in green Crayola was a phone number.

"Give the old boy a try," Newman suggested. "And in the meantime, I'd appreciate it if you could write me up a few notes on this millipede thing for my report."

"No problem, Lieutenant, happy to help." Jane held up the card. "And thank *you*."

"Don't mention it. Be sure to let me know how you get on," the cop replied. "Time to hit the road, it's been a pleasure," Newman said and stepped away from the table, walked toward the door.

Jane hoped he'd not heard her sigh of relief behind his back.

"Oh yeah, one last thing…" Newman turned around, and Jane swallowed hard. Was this the part where the cop turned all Columbo on her? Where he'd explain in that inimitable, bumbling manner that the whole 'pede thing had just been a ruse to lull her into a false sense of security? And now would she care to answer questions as to how come her face smelled of student pussy?

"Yes, Lieutenant?" Jane forced a smile.

"One of the bystanders we spoke to reported that he saw this thing crawl out of the boy's mouth. Probably BS, but that's bystanders for you. I have to ask, though – is that possible?"

"If the boy were dead, I guess the 'pede could have sought refuge inside his body," Jane slipped into *Professor* mode again, relieved that this was all the cop wanted her to answer to. "They don't have a waxy coat on their bodies like most other arthropods, so they have a tendency to dehydrate. I like to think of it as nature's way of keeping them under rocks –"

– where people like me don't have to face them –

"– but since you say the boy was alive, I doubt it very much. It probably just crawled out of his shirt."

"That's pretty much what I thought," Newman said and decided not to bother mentioning that they'd found the boy buck-naked, "hencemy previous comments regarding bystanders."

And with that, the cop was gone.

CHAPTER THREE

1

Jackson Booth was a self-proclaimed *badass*. It was an image he'd had spent most of his years cultivating, and one that kept his people precisely where he wanted them.

He stood naked in the bathroom and stared at his reflection in the mirror, admiring the contours of his body that were emphasized by thick tribal tattoos that had been etched into the ebony skin that stretched taut over his well-honed muscles. At the ripe old age of twenty-six, Jackson figured he'd finally reached his prime, and he was already long past the half-way mark of his *gangsta* lifespan.

"You gonna be long in there, baby?" the soft voice of his girlfriend – no, his *bitch* – called through the door. "I really need to pee!"

Jackson smiled and reached out a hand to touch his fingertips to the cold metal of the gun that peeped out from the stack of pink fluffy towels on the counter top. He caressed it as he'd caressed his woman not five minutes before, enjoying the chill of the muzzle against his warm skin.

"Can't a man take a pee in peace?!" he shouted, "you know how I can't go 'till my boner goes down!"

"S'okay, I can wait!"

Something was bothering Jackson.

There was something going on with his girl, and he reckoned that he'd finally got her figured out.

She was seeing – and by seeing meant *fucking* – somebody else. He was sure of it, he *knew* even though he had no concrete evidence, but he could feel her infidelity in the pit of his belly every time they were together.

There was a small part of Jackson that couldn't help but think that he should feel a little hypocritical since he was now besotted by an older chick he'd been seeing (read: *fucking*) for a couple of months now. What had started off as a casual bar pick up and one-night-stand had left him addicted to the mind-blowing sex that her maturity offered. Ah, the exotic beauty of experience.

The girl pestering him on the other side of the bathroom door was the first properly educated girl he'd been with, a post grad student at the University. She had been a little too inexperienced sexually for his tastes at first, but Jackson had quickly brought her up to speed. She was a classy gal for sure: cute, sexy, smart, *and* she had this fantastic apartment – paid in full by Daddy.

More importantly, she had been Jackson's 'in' with the lucrative University crowd. Through her, he'd soon gotten his hooks into college funds, trust funds, seemingly infinite student loans, and rich parent's credit cards: the student body's appetite for the Class B drugs that Jackson pedaled had proved insatiable. He had rapidly spread his insidious business throughout the University, selling all the varieties of weed and MDMA that the students – a fair number of the staff – could ask for.

In building his mini empire, Jackson had pushed out the weaker dealers through fair means or foul until he had the place pretty much sewn up. A man of few moral codes, Jackson did take great pride in the fact that he'd never, ever dealt in anything Class A. Truth be told, that was more to do with his inherent fear of the serious gangs who did deal in that particular range of merchandise than any kind of misplaced altruism: there was no way he intended ending his days face down in a ditch with his brains in the dirt.

In the year or so he'd been banging his student chick, Jackson had amassed a small fortune. He'd squirreled away as much of his ill-gotten gains as he could, being careful to squander just enough on the required trappings to maintain his status as Number One dealer on the north side of San Diego. He had the ubiquitous, pimped-out black Challenger, the sharpest clothes, and *always* splashed out for VIP seats and the most expensive champagne at the clubs he frequented.

And of course, he never, ever took his own drugs.

As for the girl, he had been surprised to find that he had grown to like her for more than her bangin' body, even though he wouldn't freely admit it, and was constantly unfaithful. Jackson had actually grown quite fond of her nerdy ass.

"Okay, let's do this." He instructed the reflection that mouthed the words straight back to him. He pushed the gun back under the towel pile, safe in the knowledge that she'd never find it there. Those towels were her *'for nice'* towels and not for everyday use. And most certainly not for the likes of him.

"Okay, baby, it's all yours," Jackson said as he finished up peeing and flushed the toilet. He opened the bathroom door and strutted past his nude girlfriend, proud and confident. A tiny smile curled up the corners of his mouth as he caught her totally checking him out.

"Thank you so much! I'm bursting," Melanie Hernandez thanked her boyfriend as she rushed into the bathroom and slammed the door shut behind her.

"Why don't you take a nice, hot bath while you're in there?" Jackson shouted after her. Mel didn't reply, but Jackson could already hear the waterfall sound of the bathwater as it ran into the deep tub.

Seizing his chance, Jackson grabbed Mel's purse from its usual perch on the breakfast bar stool. Keeping one ear on the bathroom sounds, Jackson began to rummage.

"Holy shit, girl, you've got everything in here," he exclaimed to himself as he moved aside the jumble of items within; keys, loose change, tampons, candy wrappers, empty perfume bottles, *Tic-tacs;* a whole world of debris. And then he found exactly what he was searching for.

Mel's notebook.

It was a tattered, pocket-sized book with pink floral patterns and *'MEL'S NOTEBOOK'* written in neat handwriting on the cover in White-Out.

"Gotcha!" he said, a little too loudly.

"What's that, baby?" Mel shouted from the bathroom, her voice almost inaudible against the splashing of hot water.

"I said, I'll be in to scrub your back later!"

"I'd be much happier if you scrubbed my front!" she replied with a dirty laugh that once more stirred the blood in his loins.

Jackson flicked through the well-worn pages of the notebook, knowing that he was sure to find what he was looking for somewhere in there; Mel was so scatterbrained that she *had* to write everything down otherwise, it would simply fly straight out of her pretty little head. There were some days that Jackson figured he wouldn't be in the least surprised to find his woman had left herself a Post-It by the lavatory that read *'wipe ass'*.

As Jackson flicked through the book, eyes scanning the innocuous memoranda for her university work, complete with the indecipherable, foreign-looking names of bugs nobody gave a crap about, and reminders for 'flu shots and hair appointments, he began to feel a rage bubbling up inside.

Mel had told him, "She's making us all go on this lame field trip," and there had been guilt etched all over her beautiful face. "You don't mind do you, Jackson, baby?" Her long, sensuous toes had been stroking his dick at the same time as her eyes were lying to him.

He'd told her no; he didn't mind her going on some dumb bug-hunt with her dumb Professor. After all, it was not like Coachella Valley was the Amazon rainforests now, was it?

And she'd gushed, "Thank you, baby, I didn't want you to be mad at me." And then in her baby voice, "You know that your ickle Melanie doesn't really want to go, don't you?"

He'd reassured her that yes, he knew that, and no, he wouldn't get mad at her for being away all weekend. What he was mad at, though, was her for feeding him this bullshit story and expecting him to swallow it like some lovelorn cuckold. She was going away alright, that much he believed, but he just knew in his gut that she was planning something.

The rage was an old, familiar one – kind of like an old friend who popped up unexpectedly every once in a while. It had gotten Jackson thrown out of three schools, two foster homes, and into the detention center. Throughout his far from illustrious career, he'd lost count of the number of people who had said that if Jackson could apply his brain as well as he used his fists, he could have made something more of himself than the thug he'd become. Well, now he had done just that, and by using both! Two-hundred-grandin the bank, a thriving business, and his pick of the hot chicks wasn't bad at all for someone of Jackson's age and background.

What angered Jackson the most was that, despite all the minutiae contained within Melanie's stupid little book, he couldn't shake the feeling that she wasn't writing *everything* down. And that meant she was keeping something from him, which in turn made him even more determined to find out who she was fucking and make sure the sonofabitch never fucked with another dude's lady again.

There it was. On the penultimate page, scribbled in Mel's unmistakable, girlish handwriting -

Saturday, Mountainview Hotel & Spa, Coachella V. Meet J.

"Gotcha!" Jackson growled.

2

Jane toyed with the grubby business card the cop had given her. She turned it over in her fingers whilst she sat in her drab office, waiting for her call to pick up.

She pinned the phone to her ear with her right shoulder and idly flicked through the aging heap of student essays that dominated her desk in a tall precarious pile. The papers were gradually inching their way toward the edge of the desk and, ultimately, the trash can. Jane reminded herself that she really should either read and grade the essays, or bin them, but throwing stuff away had never been Jane Lucas's strong point. She knew in her heart of hearts that the papers would still be on her desk when the students who had labored so intently over them had graduated and made their way out into the big, bad world.

Jane sighed and tuned her mind out to the monotonous ring tone; its electronic purring was beginning to drive her crazy. She checked her watch and lamented that she was still in her office at a quarter after nine on a Wednesday evening when everyone else in the faculty had gone home to their non-academic lives.

She'd had spent the remainder of the day following the

cop's visit engrossed in the 'pede specimen he'd brought along with all the eagerness of a cat who offers its owner a mangled bird to curry favor. She had dissected the creature with precise care, blunting three pairs of surgical scissors in the process of cutting through the tough carapace to expose the 'pede's alien innards. Jane had become so absorbed in her scrutiny of each of the animal's systems – nervous, digestive, respiratory, and reproductive – of taking copious notes and making detailed sketches, that time had quite gotten away from her.

It had been exhilarating, a welcome distraction from the more mundane rats, frogs, and cockroaches she and her students dissected during her anatomy classes. Sure, she'd taken apart plenty of 'pedes during her research into the creatures – could most likely dissect one blindfolded – but there was something wonderfully *different* about the cop's specimen, size notwithstanding. Whether it was the frustratingly tough, chitinous exoskeleton, the disproportionately oversized venom glands, or the unruly jumble of the myriapod's insides, Jane couldn't be entirely sure. All she had been aware of as she'd taken the thing apart and peered into the mystery of its interior was the heart-pounding thrill of the new that had been absent from her career for far longer than she cared to remember. It was the rare times such as this that Jane was actually pleased she'd not given up and quit zoology after she'd graduated.

She had originally majored in the subject because of her life-long love of animals; it really had been simple as that. Life in all of its miraculous forms had been an endless fascination for Jane from her earliest memories onward. The anatomy, physiology, chemistry, behavior – everything about the creatures she shared the planet with had caught and held Jane's attention. And as the years advanced and Jane soaked up every shred of information about the animal kingdom, it transpired that the more creepy, slimy, or dangerous the subject, the deeper the attraction.

However, Jane's four-year zoology course had entailed far more dissection than she had the stomach for, and she soon grew tired of killing in the name of science, sickened at the constant presence of death. And her defining moment had come one winter afternoon in her final year.

There had been a lab class in which the objective had been to trace the path of radioactive iodine inside a pigeon. Of course, the stuff was going to end up in the poor bird's thyroid gland; anyone with high-school biology 101 would have known that. But, science being science, the students just had to see it for themselves. Jane had dutifully injected her allocated bird with the iodine solution and then waited the required sixty minutes for it to circulate.

When it was time for her pigeon to die, Jane's professor had dealt with that particular unpleasantry, and not without some aplomb. Without a second thought or undue hesitation, he'd plucked the flapping bird from its cage, held it over the laboratory sink, and hacked off its head with a pair of kitchen scissors.

To this day, it still made Jane feel nauseous to remember just how sick to her stomach she had felt as she watched the pigeon's severed head twitching and jerking in the sink. The head had landed upright, stuck in place by the raw, bloodied stump of its neck, the crimson splash of the bird's blood painting a vivid contrast against the white porcelain as it trickled ever so slowly toward the plug. But the thing that had haunted Jane's dreams for months afterward was how that bird's beak opened and closed as if it were trying to speak, and how its eyes blinked furiously at her as it died.

It also hadn't helped that her professor, with his white stubble beard, round wire spectacles, and shiny bald head was the spitting image of Josef Mengele.

That was the point in time when Jane had vowed to complete her degree – she was at least that mercenary – give up on science completely and go into marketing, accounting, anything that didn't involve the merciless slaughter of living things.

However, the opportunity to research the *Scolopendridae* for her post-grad had come along, and Jane had seized it with both hands. Despite the utter distaste she felt for the killing that her science demanded, her dislike for centipedes outweighed it. Jane knew that she could quite happily kill and cut up those ugly fuckers twenty-four-seven.

When Jane had finally broken from her reverie, and from dismembering the cop's 'pede specimen, the faculty had been empty a longtime,, and the cleaning staff was buffing the hallways into slippery death traps.

Usually, Jane was the first one out of the door once classes ended; keen to get out of the stifling academic atmosphere, even if it meant going home to her empty apartment or trawling the early evening bar scene for a temporary bedfellow. But tonight, Jane hadn't minded staying late at all, had rather enjoyed it, in fact. It had been the first time in far too many years that her inner scientist had been coaxed out. Of course, the irony was not lost on Jane that it had been a damned 'pede that had done the coaxing.

Jane already knew that she wouldn't – couldn't – rest until she'd found a living specimen, as much as that thought made her skin crawl. Then, she would be able to study what the corpse hadn't been able to offer up more than a few hints about - its behavior. With a live animal (or, dare she hope, two?) she would be able to study how they hunted, their social behavior, and how they fucked. She also thought it would be interesting to see if these creatures were capable of growing even bigger than the cop's: an experiment she would conduct from the safety of a securely locked terrarium in the faculty's animal unit. She'd be damned if she was going to run the risk of having a *gigantea* scuttling loose around her office.

"Hello?" Jane almost dropped the phone as an old man's voice crept into her ear, "who is this?"

"Oh, hello," Jane sputtered for a split second, she'd forgotten just who it was she was calling. "Is this– Mr. Levandowski?" She had to read the surname from the card and hope she'd nailed the pronunciation.

"Might be," guarded. "Who wants to know?"

"My name is Professor Jane Lucas from the University of California: I was given your card by Lieutenant Newman."

"The lanky cop? Yeah, I remember him."

An awkward moment of silence passed between them. Jane could hear a TV playing in the background, and it was clear to her that Mr. Levandowski was watching porn. Jane pushed that particular mental imagery to the back of her mind, figuring that the onus was on her to keep the conversation going despite the old man's obvious distraction. "He told me that you were the person to speak to about the hotel," she ventured.

"The Mountainview?" The old man now sounded more obstructive than hostile.

"Lieutenant Newman brought me an interesting specimen today. He said it came from the hotel."

"That fucking millipede thing?" there was repugnance in the old man's voice.

Best not muddy the waters by correcting him, Jane thought and physically bit her tongue – so hard that she tasted the coppery tang of her own blood. "Yeah, that's the one."

"What about it?"

"Well, I would really appreciate it if you could allow me to take a look around," Jane said. "I'd like to see if I can find any more of them inside the hotel," she explained, "this weekend, if possible." She'd done the calculations: it was one-hundred-thirty miles to Desert Hot Springs from where she was sitting right now – she could be there in less than three hours if traffic wasn't a bitch and she hit the gas on the interstate.

"Can't do that, Missy," Levandowski barked, "no one's allowed in, them's my orders. Not even the damned cops are allowed back in to the place."

"The University would be happy to pay you for your time, Mr. Levandowski," Jane offered. Actually, no, they wouldn't, but she'd pay the obstinate old fart out of her pocket if she had to.

"I have no need for your money. I'm very well taken care of in that respect, thank you very much."

"I understand that you have a job to do, Mr. Levandowski," Jane struggled to keep the desperation out of her voice; she'd already planned on taking the trip, told her students to keep the weekend free – she was going to get in to that hotel, obstinate old man or not. "I promise you that no one would ever find out about you letting us in. You'll never even know we've been there," Jane promised.

"It's not that, Missy," The old man snorted down the phone. "I don't need your assurances any more, than I need your fucking money. I do believe that you wouldn't be no bother, but if my bosses ever found out –"

"I can make sure they wouldn't."

"Nah, keep your money. Spend it on chasing some other damned bug." Jane sensed that she was losing the fight against Levandowski's background smut and that the old man was rapidly losing interest in their conversation.

"There must be something I can do for you, Mr. Levandowski? *Anything* at all?" Jane lowered the tone in her voice so that it oozed suggestion. Plan B was always a good back-up: if all else fails, go for a hint of the sexual – the lowest common denominator.

The following pause was a pregnant one, to say the least. Jane pressed her ear into the receiver and listened to the irregular snorts of breath from the other side, along with the shrieks, squeals, and grunts from Levandowski's pornography.

"Anything?" it was the old man who broke the silence.

"Yes, Mr. Levandowski," again, Jane's voice loaded with suggestion; a little flirting could go a remarkably long way. She'd make the old boy feel special and that he may just have a chance, even though he sounded twice her age, and she pictured him as a shriveled, gray-haired old pervert that she'd cross the sidewalk to avoid. "As I said, I would *love* to take a look around your hotel," Jane purred.

"Well, Missy, why don't ya git yourself down here on Friday night?" Levandowski grunted, "I'm not promising anything, but we can at least meet up and see if maybe we can come to some arrangement," now it was Levandowski's turn for the suggestive undertones, and he did sound quite hopeful. Forgoing the niceties of a goodbye, Lenard Levandowski then hung up the phone on Jane.

Jane rested the receiver back onto its cradle and relished awhile the butterflies that fluttered around in her stomach. She was about to embark on her first research field trip in a long, long time, and there was the chance of discovering something truly remarkable – the excitement she felt was most invigorating.

Jane made the executive decision that she would finish up writing Newman's report when she got the analysis results on the clear liquid she'd milked out of the 'pede's remaining venom gland. She'd sent it straight off to her good friend Geoff Simpson in the Department of Toxicology. He owed her a big favor and had promised he'd expedite it; the report would be on her desk when she got back on Monday.

She picked up the copy of the book she'd rescued from the chaotic bookcase. It was a first edition (there had been four to date); *Scolopendra gigantea; Anatomy, Physiology, and Behavior – by Prof. J. Lucas Ph.D.* She had deliberately pushed it beneath a sheaf of loose papers on her desk because the dust jacket illustration made her feel queasy, even though she had chosen it herself. It showed a full color, extreme close-up of a pede's giant head, glinting black fangs gaping open as if ready to strike, the vicious jaws that gnashed beneath them, and the dull, flat eyes that Jane always imagined belonged in the netherworlds of hell.

It was funny, Jane mused, as she flicked through her book, whilst the creatures repulsed her, they also somehow managed to entrance her at the same time, as if fear was feeding her fascination. It was much like, she guessed, the fascination that people held with rollercoasters, horror movies, and other people's car wrecks. Deep down, you know that they can't hurt you, but there is always the frisson of danger at the back of your mind. What if the rollercoaster tracks broke and sent you hurtling to the ground? What if the slithering, toothy things that lurked in the horror movies turned out to be real after all and grabbed at your ankle in the middle of the night? What if you wound up watching the drama of the next car wreck you saw from the *inside* of a smashed car, your life ebbing as other people drove slowly by to gawk at *you*?

And what if the 'pede she had just dissected *could* kill you? Or even worse, what if its bite could make you brutally butcher someone else? The image of the ruined girl's corpse in the photograph the cop had shown her flashed into Jane's mind and caused a wave of nausea that threatened her lunch.

The root of Jane's decision to specialize in *myriapods* had been more than a nose-thumbing at an animal that scared her; it had been about facing her lifelong, personal demons, and it was that which made Jane feel more alive now than she had felt in as long as she could remember.

Taking great care not to touch the front of it, Jane tucked the book into her bag.

3

The centipede uncurled her immense bulk from around the clutch of soft, yellow eggs. She stretched her huge, segmented body out of the room in which she'd nested and down along the hallway, her full length almost equal that of the dark corridor. She twitched her antennae, and they pointed this way and that to taste the air.

As the creature crawled, her legs moved in ordered waves that propelled her giant body along. All the while, her rudimentary eyes remained alert for signs of movement.

She was hungry. Her last feeding had barely sated her appetite, and half of that particular meal had been taken away by the hordes of noisy but sweet-smelling creatures who had invaded her territory. She'd followed the scent of the other pink creature, but it had escaped through a hole far too narrow for her enormous body to follow. She snatched at a centipede a fraction of her size that was unlucky enough to scurry by, grasping it tightly with her fore legs; she lifted it to her mouth. The smaller creature wriggled in her grasp and bit in vain at her legs as her mouth loomed closer to chew at its flesh. The smaller creatures' forcipules were too weak to penetrate her exoskeleton, and even if they had managed to penetrate the armor, she was immune to the venom of her own kind.

They had sealed up her one and only egress from her warm, damp home; the weird reek of ozone and damp cement from their work still hung heavy in the air. Prior to this infraction, the centipede had enjoyed the freedom to come and go as she pleased, and each night she had ventured from the sanctuary of the hotel to hunt in the desert. Birds, snakes, skunks, raccoons, feral, domestic cats, and stray dogs had all fallen prey to the centipede, along with the occasional human who happened to stray too close to the Mountainview at the wrong time of night.

But now she was trapped, and she had the energy and nutrients that making her eggs had drained from her to replace. The smaller ones of her kind with whom she shared her domain were still able to find ways to leave, although they always returned with the arrival of dawn. They were small enough to squeeze themselves through the narrowest of cracks to escape into the desert to feed while she remained behind, a prisoner of her own bulk.

The gargantuan centipede finished crunching through her inadequate meal and continued on, the relentless instinct to feed driving her to hunt.

CHAPTER FOUR

1

Professor Jane Lucas Ph.D. hunched her backpack on her shoulders and braced herself against the hot desert wind that buffeted into her. The abrasive, windblown sand whipped against her bare arms and drove stinging grains behind her Ray-Bans and into her eyes. Jane poked a finger behind one dark lens and wiped the grit out of her watering left eye and made her way toward the old man who stood in front of the Mountainview Hotel. Jane felt more than a little discomfort as she walked: she would have worn a skirt instead of tight Levis had she known just how sore she was going to be this morning.

So this was it. She looked around at Desert Hot Springs in all its glory. She was seeing the outskirts of said town that was home to 26,000 souls and just eleven miles north of the larger and more renowned Palm Springs. This side of town was chiefly reserved for tourists and was adorned with hotels, motels, and stores that specialized in the usual touristy crap. A leisurely trip across the Coachella Valley – still called Desert Empire, although no one seemed to know exactly why – would take you to the Joshua Tree National Park, and Jane thought that she might just treat herself to a trip there to see the old trees in person on the way back home from this adventure.

Jane gazed around as she walked from her Hyundai, soaking up the breathtaking view of the craggy, snow-cappedmountain range, which thrust up like a giant's crooked teeth from the horizon up in stark contrast with the beige expanse of the cactus-speckled desert. Despite their distance from her, the mountains appeared so imposing, so close, that Jane imagined she could reach out her hand and touch them. This picturesque scene was marred somewhat by the sad neglect of the boarded-up hotel that cast its shadow over Jane and the road, which reminded her of a tall, miserable tombstone. There was also the sun-faded bloodstain in the middle of the road: a brutal Rorschach image spread out across the tarmac. Something flapped against Jane's leg, and she jumped, heart in her mouth. She turned with a start and saw a flailing yellow ribbon of police tape that was being whipped about by the wind. The tape grabbed at her jeans as it thrashed around as if desperate to be free of the thorny bush that held on to it.

"Told ya, there's a storm comin'," Lenard Levandowski called over to Jane. "They've been forecasting it all god-damned week." He was an odd-lookingman, had probably been quite the lady-killer in his day. He was short, slightly overweight with crooked teeth and a full head of greased-back, thin, graying hair. "Of course, I never believe 'em 'till it's whippin' at ma long johns," he laughed.

Jane stopped in front of Levandowski. "Yeah, you said," she said and took a step to the side, much preferring her view of the mountains that bordered the valley and the still majestic hotel that rose up from the sand before her.

The *Mountainview Hotel and Natural Spa* loomed like some great tragedy from the desert. Its parking lot had been all but claimed by the drifting sand, and the once immaculately manicured flower beds and lawns had long since been desiccated by the heat of the relentless sun. Close to the road was the neon sign that bore the glass tube outline of the hotel's name, perched at the top of a thirty-foot metal pole, having remained dormant for the five years since the hotel closed down.

The whitewashed, sandstone hotel was once the biggest and most exclusive of all the spa hotels in Desert Hot Springs. It had always been busy and bustling, full of life, and in its heyday, it had rarely known an unoccupied room: there was always a party going down somewhere in the Mountainview. It had garnered the reputation as *the* go-to hotel in the valley, *the* best place in town for whatever hedonistic pleasures one might desire.. But that was in the halcyon days before it was hurriedly boarded up and left to rot.

Each and every window had been sealed with a sheet of thick steel that wept bright rust down the walls like tears of blood. The balconies outside of each room, designed to catch the very best of the afternoon light for sun-seeking guests, were now home to storks and grackles that squirted their white-and-black shit dots onto the rust covered walls, adding their own illustration to the pitiful sight.

But Jane could see through the decay and neglect, and she could imagine the Mountainview as it must have been in all its decadent glory: a beautiful, thrilling place brimming with excitement and forbidden pleasures. Perhaps, she thought, the ghosts of said pleasures still cavorted along the abandoned hallways and empty rooms?

"Need to be careful, you city folk. Comin' out here in storm season," Lenard's voice was hoarse and rasped as if he'd inhaled too much of the swirling desert. He grunted and bent down to straighten his knee-length brown socks. He rolled the errant tops back up his legs and pulled the feet up tight in his sandals. He stood back up and squinted down at Jane with an amused glint in his rheumy eyes.

"I'll be fine, thank you," Jane asserted. "My students will be along any minute, they just texted." She composed herself, "And what was it you said again about not leaving me with the keys?"

"Like I said, Missy, I'm risking ma job just letting you into the hotel in the first place. I can't just leave ya all alone with the keys."

Jane lowered her shades and gave him a hard stare over the top of them. She figured she had every right to be annoyed with Levandowski for not telling her this last night – he could have let her know about the damned keys before he'd stuck his dick so far down her throat that she'd damned near passed out.

"And I can't leave it unlocked neither," the old man added, "on account of the fact *they'd* be awful pissed at me if they found out I'd left the Mountainview unlocked; definitely cost me the job, that one."

"They?" Jane fought to hide her gradually rising contempt toward the sweating, chubby-faced man, "who are *they*?"

"The *Gummint*, that's who," Lenard snapped. "Them's that pays my wage – and pays it well – to keep an eye on the place and keep horny kids, vagrants, and the likes of you out." Lenard laughed and eyed Jane up and down, which made her feel even more uncomfortable in his presence.

"The likes of me?" Jane was curious. Did anyone else among the scientific community know about the giant 'pedes? Surely she would have heard something if that were the case: biologists were notoriously incestuous with their information.

Lenard ignored Jane, possibly choosing not to hear her on that particular occasion.

A blast of loud music and a cloud of fine dust heralded the arrival of Jane's students, and she'd never been more pleased to see their disinterested little faces. "Ah, here they are now," the relief in Jane's voice was painfully obvious.

Fred, Darlene, Mel, and Martha-Ray clambered out of Fred's battered green Wrangler Jeep. They were dressed more appropriately for a beach party than a serious, zoological field trip; baggy shorts, beach tops that flashed fashionably inadequate swimwear beneath, and – much to Jane's chagrin – flip-flops.

However, Jane was so relieved to see them that she wouldn't have cared less if they'd shown up naked. She did, however, realize that she'd have to have a quiet word about field-trip dress codes once Lenard had crawled back under his greasy little stone.

"Hey there, Professor Lucas!" Martha-Ray called out and waved both hands above her head like a lunatic. Jane returned the wave, and the students bounded over. Jane sighed and rubbed her aching head: all of them were far too lively for a Saturday morning.

"Hi, Prof'!" Mel shouted. "Nice day for catching stuff!" She hefted the equipment bag over her shoulder, grabbed a second bag with her free hand, and groaned against the weight.

"Hey, Mel," Fred smiled, "don't struggle with all of that."

"Thanks, Fred, that's very kind of you –" Mel returned the smile and eased the bag's strap off her shoulder.

"– nah, you should take two trips!" Fred laughed out loud and jogged on ahead.

"Prick!" Mel shouted at his back.

"Okay, Mr. Levandowski, now that we're all here, allow me to make the introductions," Jane said as pleasantly as she could.

"No need." Lenard gave a dismissive wave of his hand. "I don't need to know any of you lot, and you –" a lascivious wink at Jane "– you, I already know." Lenard was oblivious to the quizzical looks that passed between the students, either that, or he just enjoyed stirring things up and didn't give all that much of a shit. He turned his back on Jane and her students and walked toward the Mountainview. "Better get a move on: I want to get you into the hotel before anybody sees us loitering and calls the authorities."

Lenard stuck the large, metal key into the lock and made a big show of jiggling it around. "Damn thing sticks," he said. "There's a knack to getting it right. I guess I should lube it up some. What do ya say, Missy? Got to be a way to get 'er lubed up right." Another wink at Jane which she duly ignored.

Eventually, the lock gave in and allowed the heavy key to twist with a resounding *clunk*. Lenard pulled the sheet-steel door open, wincing as the sound of screeching metal dug into his ears. He then unlocked the hotel door within with a more modest sized key and swung it open.

Stepping inside, Lenard flicked a light switch and beckoned Jane and the zoology students inside. Behind them, the huge steel door swung shut with a loud *CLANG!*

"There's electricity!?" exclaimed Darlene with all the excitement of someone who'd just discovered the wheel. She then sighed and wished she'd packed her curling iron after all.

"Yep, we're not in the Dark Ages here, ya know," Lenard laughed at her. "Some folk 'round these parts have even got them outside lavatorials!" He laughed his rasping laugh.

"No. I meant here, this place. It's all abandoned, and the power's still on," Darlene explained. Her face had flushed a deep pink with the embarrassment at finding herself the foil to the old man's lame joke.

"I know what ya meant, Darlin'. I was just messing with ya," Lenard chuckled. Then, to Jane, "Your Professor here knows how's I like to mess around a little!" Again with the laugh.

"Does *everything* still work?" Fred asked.

"Pretty much," Lenard answered him. "The electrics are still on, as well as the gas, running water, the whole she-bang. Even the ice machine on the third floor is still working." The old man grunted. "Got clogged up a couple of years ago and shat ice all over the carpets, but I fixed her up good, and she's as right as rain now."

Jane and her students followed Lenard as he traipsed across the beige, polished marble floor, weaving between dusty sofas with rattan frames and tall, glass-topped drinks tables. Their footsteps were muffled by the huge, exquisite antique Persian rug that sat in the dead center of the sand-white painted room. The lobby's dusty walls were adorned with an eclectic array of large, artistic desert-themed photographs: a majestic cactus straight out of a western movie, its branches pointing upward like a bad guy *reachin' for the sky*; a close up of a gold-rimmed lizard's eye, the snow-capped mountains, endless acres of golden sand punctuated by sparse, sun bleached vegetation – lots and lots of sand. In the far corner, there also stood a massive grandfather clock – its face the size of a truck wheel – that had stalled at a quarter after six a long, long time ago.

Lenard ushered his eager guests toward the double doors that led out of the lobby. They brushed past the once highly polished, mahogany reception desk behind which stood the matching its key cubbies. Jane noted with a wry, nostalgic smile that the hotel had an old-fashioned key system, even though the hotel was relatively modern; someone in the corporate marketing department no doubt thought it terribly cute at the time.

"The air conditioning probably still works, but there's been no point putting it on, what with the place bein' shut up and all," Lenard continued his droll, Tour-Guide speech. "And I'd stay out of the elevator if I were you. Still works, but it's not seen any maintenance in five years – not my remit – and you know how temperamental those things can be at the best of times." He laughed his rusty laugh, which then broke off into a disconcerting, hacking cough.

The hotel had that warm, damp feeling that an uninhabited building adopts over time, without the hustle and bustle of people to stir the air, compounded by the fact that the place had been sealed up tight against the outside elements. The resulting stillness had enabled a thick layer of dust to build up and cast a powdery veil over everything, whilst the air itself hung thick, cloying, and moist, and carried a faint odor of ammonia that reminded Jane of stale cat pee.

"This way's the pool room. I figured you'd want to know where that is, what with ya coming all prepared an' all." Lenard stared directly at Mel's jutting breasts that strained against the bikini top she wore beneath her flimsy, white cotton beach shirt.

Jane corrected him, "I can assure you that we are here for scientific purposes only, Mr. Levandowski." She put on her very best schoolmarm tone, "Isn't that right, people?"

Mel, Fred, Darlene, and Martha-Ray mumbled their agreement. Only Martha-Ray — ever the nerd of the group — sounded like she actually meant it.

They followed Lenard down the two flights of whitewashed stairs to the poolroom. The stairs were molded from rough, chunky concrete that was most likely supposed to have given a primitive feel to guests descending to the natural spa, but which Jane thought gave the place a more institutional air. The stairwell walls were painted as white as the stairs and were in dire need of a touch-up. The paint was cracked and peeling through the years of neglect and was decorated with patches of powdery black mold that crept out across the spreading decay like a corpse's veins. The mold gave a dank, musty aroma to the stagnant air, which became warmer and ever more humid with the descent to the basement and it brought everyone out in a light sheen of sweat.

"Well, here ya are," Lenard announced as he pushed open the pool room door and flicked on the light, "your one-hundred percent natural geothermal spring. Fresh from the bowels of Mother Earth herself!"

"Wow! It's beautiful," gasped Darlene. "Is it clean?"

"As clean as a fresh-wiped ass, my darling," Lenard grinned. "It bubbles up from deep below, and the overflow is channeled out into the desert somewhere out back like its one big, natural filter system. I think the whole pool is replenished once every two days or so if ya believe what ya read in the brochures."

The room was pleasantly warm and humid with a slight sulfur smell that emanated from the pool, along with the faintest tinge of a coppery scent. Small blotches of the black mold had taken root at the lower half of the walls, and there was a thin layer of the ubiquitous fine dust clinging to every surface.

Jane studied her surroundings: the dark painted walls, the gray slate floors, the no-doubt extremely comfortable recliners, the poolside cabanas. She sighed, knowing in her heart of hearts just how difficult it was going to be to keep her students on task with all of this as a distraction.

"Over there's where the girl got all messed up," Lenard continued, once more relishing his role of macabre tour guide a tad too much. "Cops reckoned the boyfriend did it while he was high on drugs. Ate some of her innards too, most likely while she was still breathin'," Lenard told them with a grin, pleased with his embellishment. He leaned nonchalantly against the damp wall, soaking up the power his tale telling held over the young, impressionable, and oh, so lithe girls.

"Oh, sweet Jesus," Martha-Ray groaned. Her eyes fell upon the up-ended four-poster at the opposite end of the room and the faded bloodstain that spread across the floor beside it. "Is that where –?"

"– they found her?" Lenard pre-empted. "Yep. Well,

some of her, anyways." He chuckled at Martha-Ray's wrinkled nose. "Did my best to clean it up, but you know just how stubborn blood stains on real slate can be."

"Err, no, actually, I don't," Martha-Ray told him as she fought the bile that crept, burning along her throat.

"So, this is a crime scene?" Fred chimed in.

"Not anymore, the cops are all done."

"They've finished the investigation already?" Jane asked.

"Don't know anything about that, lady. What I *said* was the cops were done. Not coming in here again. Ever," Lenard added a sinister tone to his voice for extra effect, and as he spoke, Lenard was unaware of the dark red centipede – thin, a man's-forearm long – that crawled from the wall and down inside the collar of his jacket. "So you see just how privileged you are to be in here," Lenard addressed Mel directly to have an excuse to glare at her body. "And it's all thanks to your professor here," he grinned.

Mel ignored the old man – there was something about him that disgusted her. She was used to men leering at her body, since she did little to hide what the good lord had given her, but there was something about Levandowski and his lasciviousness that made her feel uneasy; she wouldn't be at all surprised if he spent his sad old man days trawling the darkest, *TOR*-protected corners of the internet and had a hard drive filled with kiddy porn. Mel sauntered around the pool, marveled at how clear the water was, and enjoyed the sinus-cleansing aroma of its minerals. "I've never been anywhere like this before. It's awesome," she breathed.

"Remember what we're here for, Miss Hernandez," Jane told her. "This is supposed to be a zoological expedition. I know it's not quite the Galapagos archipelago, but we're not here to enjoy the facilities." Jane risked a knowing smile at Mel, the fond memory of the girl's sweet taste still with her. "But I'm sure we can find time for some down-time once we get what we came here for," she said.

Mel and the others grinned. This might not have been a complete waste of a weekend, after all.

"Well, I'm gonna leave you good people to it; get myself home before this storm whips up good'n proper," Lenard said as he made his way back toward the door. "You got the run of the place for as long as ya need it, just call me when you're done." He awarded himself one last, lingering letch at the three girls in order to commit to memory their smooth, flawless skin, young, heady scent, and perky untouched-by-gravity breasts. "Oh yeah, almost forgot. Stay off the fifth floor. It's where the gas blew up, and it's none too pretty up there: the floor and ceiling are unstable. More'n likely either you'll fall through it, or it'll fall in on you. And I'd hate to have to explain that to ma employers!" He laughed at this as if it were some infinitely funny joke that only he had the punchline to.

"Fifth floor. Got it," Jane repeated back to him, "you hear that, people?"

"Okay folks, enjoy your bug-hunt!" Lenard smiled at the pretty girls as they nodded back at him.

And with that, the old man was gone.

2

Jackson Booth screwed up his eyes against the driving wind. He flicked his spent Camel onto the desert floor in the cool manner he'd copied from countless movies and chased the butt with a thick gob of mucus he'd hawked from the back of his throat.

"We're going in," he informed his boys. He nodded toward the heavy steel door of the Mountainview. His boys: Lee, Mikey, and Johnny Psycho followed his instruction without question, all the while gawking up at the grand facade of the building like they'd never seen a hotel before. "Keep it quiet; make sure they don't see you," Jackson growled. The gang members – if you could call three such rag-tag misfits a gang – nodded in silence and made their way toward the hotel entrance, struggling against the wind that buffeted warm, stinging sand at them.

Jackson cast a cursory glance behind to make sure that there was no one around to see them enter the hotel. The road was empty as far as the wind-blown sand would allow him to see. Upon arrival, Jackson had noted that the hotel parking lot had contained only three vehicles; a vaguely familiar Hyundai, a beat up old Jeep, and a White Lexus SUV. Jackson had parked his Challenger to the rear of the hotel to keep it away from inquisitive eyes.

The place puzzled him, and Jackson was forced to admit that this did seem to be an unlikely venue for an illicit tryst. The place was just some abandoned craphole and not the luxurious love nest he had envisaged he'd find Mel in, but this *was* most definitely the address that he had found in her note book. He'd driven by three times earlier that morning to make sure that he'd found the right hotel and that Mel was not holed up with her fuck-buddy in one of the more salubrious – and open for business – hotels farther down the valley. But no, it was the right one, alright. Perhaps Mel craved the excitement of somewhere dirty and forbidden? A spoiled little rich girl like her was bound to like it rough and ready on occasion – how else could he explain her relationship with himself? And, if she really was just the clichéd rich bitch that wanted to play rough, then Jackson could give her rough any day of the motherfucking week.

Jackson peered into the dim lobby, affording his eyes time to adjust. He could hear the faint voices as the hotel's occupants made their way down the stairs beyond the door at the far end of the expansive room.

Just how many people was his girl here with? Four, five, more? Jackson could, for sure, make out two guy voices and at least two other female voices in addition to Mel's. Were they all here for some kind of kinky sex party? He'd read about the valley and its hedonistic reputation when he'd Googled *'Coachella Valley/Desert Hot Springs'* for directions to plug into his GPS. He'd read with growing interest about the nudist *'clothing optional'* – although the pictures he'd seen certainly didn't denote *'optional'* at all – and swingers' hotels famous for their anything-goes orgies and sex parties. Jackson snorted his distaste, although he was somewhat confused as to whether he was more annoyed that Mel was cheating on him and was here with someone else or that she'd not invited him along for the fun and games.

"In," Jackson barked. He pulled the resisting steel door open just wide enough for him and his boys to slip through. He grimaced as the door let out a loud, complaining creak on its rusted hinges and hoped that the people they were following hadn't heard.

They crept carefully across the lobby, tiptoed around the heavy-looking canvas bag in the middle of the rug floor, their Nikes puffing up eddies of fine dust. Jackson heard the sound of heavy, deliberate footsteps from the pool room stairway.

"Shit!" Johnny spat, "there's somebody coming!" The thug's hand went instinctively to the oversized knife that he always seemed to be carrying these days.

They all froze, ears straining at the sound of wheezing and approaching footsteps, Mikey, Lee, and Johnny looking to Jackson – their esteemed leader – for direction.

"This way!" Jackson commanded. He ran toward a doorway sporting a fading *'To The Bedrooms'* sign on the opposite side of the lobby from where the footsteps emanated, his motley gang following hot on his heels.

Jackson eased the door closed behind them, mindful of the noise it would make should it slam shut. From there, he watched as the old caretaker dude shuffled across the lobby and headed outside through the steel door. Heard the wind whistling in from the desert, the steel door clanging shut, and the metallic rattle of keys. Jackson allowed himself a sigh of relief, only just realizing that he had been holding his breath the entire time it had taken the old bastard to cross the lobby.

"He's gone," Lee stated the obvious.

"No shit, Sherlock," Mikey chastised. "I think he locked us in."

"Does that mean we're trapped in here?" Johnny asked with a tinge of panic in his voice, he never had been the brightest button on the shirt.

"No, we are not trapped," Jackson explained, his exasperation at his gang's outward lack of intelligence are all too transparent. "He's gonna have to come back for Mel and whoever the fuck else he's just let in, unless he's given 'em a spare key. Either way, we can get out."

"Fuckwit," Mikey muttered at Johnny Psycho, as always enjoying playing the big man.

Jackson slapped Mikey around the back of the head.

"Ow, that hurt!" Mikey yelped.

"It was supposed to," Jackson told him. "Show some respect, man."

Mikey sulked, and Johnny and Lee smirked at him as they all made their way upstairs.

3

Jane studied the pool room using her expert eye to gauge where the possible 'pede hidey-holes would be. She'd made an educated (very *well*-educated, thank you very much) guess that if there were to be more of the animals at the Mountainview – and she had every reason to believe that there would be – this room would give an ideal habitat. It was warm, damp, dark, and secluded – perfect 'pede territory. Although, having said that, the rest of the hotel also appeared to be warm and damp: so pretty much anywhere in the abandoned building could be a likely home for the creatures.

She'd sent her students back up to the lobby to gather the equipment she'd instructed Mel to bring along from the University. There was everything a zoological expedition could need to track down and capture what could well turn out to be the discovery of a lifetime. Jane could hear the youngsters larking about upstairs, and again she fretted about keeping their attention.

She smiled to herself. Sure, this was all big-fish-small-pond stuff, insomuch no one outside of the zoological community was likely to ever know about – or care about for that matter – a new sub-species (or *species*, dare she hope?) of 'pede, no matter how big. There were new species of animals discovered almost every day (most of which were tiny, insignificant rainforest bugs) and unless they were cute, or ugly, or deadly, nobody really gave a damn. But still, it mattered to Jane and her career; and that, right now, was the main thing.

She paced a circuit around the warm pool that looked oh, so inviting. She took great care to skirt around the badly scrubbed bloodstain: whoever had tried cleaning up the girl's blood had succeeded only in spreading it into a wider pattern, and it looked most unpleasant. Jane's eyes darted this way and that, alert for movement or any other sign that would give away a hiding 'pede: track marks, half-eaten prey, feces – all your basic Discovery Channel stuff.

It felt good to be away from the confines of the University, if only for a weekend. This was a pleasant hark back to better times, the good old days before the vicious budget cuts; there had been field-trips to many a far-flung, exotic place – South America, Australia, Antarctica, England, the latter of which had reported sightings of *Scolopendra gigantea* in the London Docklands. Sadly, Jane had turned up squat on that trip, but had nonetheless, enjoyed a fantastic all expenses paid week sight-seeing in the bustling, tourist-friendly city, all courtesy of the

University of California.

The professor smiled and reminded herself of the more personal fun she had afforded herself on her excursions and decided that she should cut her four students a little slack. After all, this was their first field trip with her, and it had been three long years since Jane's last bug-hunt.

Prompted by the familiar turn of phrase, Jane's mind switched tracks. Lenard Levandowski had referred to this expedition as just that – *'enjoy your bug-hunt'* had been his precise words. Against her will, Jane's mind jumped to the old man and her dealings with him and his reprehensible friend the previous night.

She'd driven to Desert Hot Springs, and the usual Friday Night rush traffic leaving San Diego had been horrific. But, three weary, ass-numbing hours after leaving, Jane had arrived in town and checked into the hotel she had gotten Dotty to book for her. The hotel had turned out to be a cheap one – more budget cuts – but she didn't mind too much since she'd not been planning to stay long.

Jane had arranged to meet up with Lenard Levandowski at his apartment across town: in retrospect, a potentially stupid decision. Although she had gone to all the trouble of checking out his address and found it to be a condo in the more respectable part of Desert Hot Springs, she figured she'd be quite safe. Besides which, she was a grown woman and could take care of herself, right?

She had been expecting to be expected to give the old pervert a blowjob at the most for his granting her entry to the elusive Mountainview, a small price to pay to get what she wanted. Hell, she'd done a lot worse for a lot less in her past.

But no. It was obvious from the jump off that the old man had been making plans since their phone conversation earlier on in the week.

She'd put on a thin, floral summer dress that had a cleavage-revealing halter-top, paired with four-inch strappy pumps. She'd arrived at Levandowski's apartment around eleven, and the caretaker had ushered her in with little ceremony.

Jane recalled how taken aback she'd been at the eclectic mix of old man stuff and bachelor-about-town trappings Lenard had in his apartment. There was an ancient, battered, and chipped writing desk, a fifty-five inch, 3D plasma TV anchored to the wall, a Bose *hi-fi system on a rickety pine coffee table next to an ostentatious cream-leather sofa which in turn nestled up to a tattered, pale blue velour armchair that had stains that made her cringe even now just thinking about it.*

Oh yes, and then Lenard had introduced Jane to his best friend.

"Larry-Wayne Williaford," Lenard had announced with good cheer.

"Call me Larry," Lenard's strange looking friend had offered with a handshake. "All my good friends do." Jane had taken his leathery hand and shook it in the most professional manner she could muster.

Larry-Wayne was in his early sixties, a tall, wiry man who sported an impressive Victorian strongman mustache. His mousey-brown hair was thin and graying, and his eyes sparkled with something one could very easily imagine to have been malignant. He wore an ill-fitting, beige suit that hung loosely from his thin frame, the pants of which stopped mid-calf to reveal knee-high, red striped socks – those he'd kept on all *night - that made his bony legs look like bowed candy canes. He carried himself with a polite, at times haughty, demeanor and was nothing less than a complete gentleman throughout the debauched proceedings that followed.*

The night had quickly progressed from token politeness to what Lenard had really been expecting for breaking his employer's golden rule of 'no-one-in-the-Mountainview – ever'.

The old man had, indeed, gone to a whole load of trouble for Jane's visit: dimmed lights, make-out music, scented candles, fresh bed-linens, and Jane had an inkling that both men had even washed their pits especially for the occasion. The creepy friend – Larry-Wayne – had even sprung for Thai food takeout and a bottle of fizzy wine – screw cap of course. Nothing like screw-top wine to make a girl feel special!

Jane had it figured that Lenard was quite determined to get his money's worth. She'd clearly ensnared him with her suggestive tone, and he'd picked up on something in her voice that had more than piqued his interest. Indeed, her own heart had beat just a little faster when she'd recognized the want in his voice during their brief telephone conversation. Despite the surly tone and distance in years between them, like it or not, she and Lenard were kindred spirits.

What had followed between the three was the stuff of the wildest porn movies. As old as the two men were, and as sexually worldly-wise as Jane imagined herself to be, she was astounded by what was asked of her: the myriad positions, the dirty talk, the rough fucking, the role play, the kinky bondage/punishment stuff. They had used and abused her body, and she theirs, and it was like the guys had a lifetime's worth of pent-up dark fantasies that they simply had *to get through in the one night.*

Which explained why Jane ached so much today and how come she now knew first-hand that, despite the (faked) ecstasy of seasoned porn actresses, double penetration damned well hurt!

Of course, Jane had thrown herself whole-heartedly into the night's debauched activities, had taken great delight in each and every disgusting, perverted act they'd asked of her – and had even requested some of her own. So much so that she had left both Lenard and his good friend Larry-Wayne in the small hours of this morning exhausted and spent and barely able to utter a word between them.

And, as the night's activities progressed, Jane had realized that the tryst had become less and less about how badly she wanted in the Mountainview, and the lure of research grants and new species and recognition. It had become, pure and simple, all about enjoying every dirty, filthy –

4

- depraved minute of it. Every lewd, debauched act – and the Bug Lady had absolutely *loved* everything Lenard and Larry-Wayne had thrown at her!

Lenard smiled to himself as he drove his pristine Lexus away from the hotel and made his way back into town, straining to see through the thick dust cloud that swirled across the road.

He and Larry-Wayne had started her off slow, but Oh Lordy, the young University woman had gotten into the whole sordid scene with aplomb insatiable to the point of being greedy. It had seemed to Lenard that no sooner had he let her into his apartment and introduced her to his good friend that she'd stripped buck naked and was chomping down on his dick. Her oral technique was especially mind-blowing, and Lenard had to pull her away hard by the hair to prevent her finishing the night for him before he'd even gotten started. And, once they'd gotten her into the bedroom and onto the Queen-sized bed, boy, she had really pulled out all the stops.

As far as the professor chick was concerned, everything he and Larry-Wayne's twisted minds could ever have imagined was game-on. She took them both in her mouth – at the same time – on her surprisingly-pert-for-her-age titties, in her pussy, between her toes, inside her ass. She'd let them tie her up, pour baby oil all over her firm body, and use impossibly oversized sex toys on her.

She'd also turned the tables on them, wielding the huge

flesh-colored strap-on that Lenard kept for very special occasions with such expertise that there was no doubt at all in his mind that she was into chicks in a big way. She'd fucked his ass long and hard, tugging on his dick as she thrust into him, all the while slurping away on Larry's cock with that hot little mouth of hers. And then she'd swapped the two men over and started all over again.

It had all been so intense for Lenard, that at several points during the night's proceedings, he had found himself wishing that he'd not invited Larry over and had bought in a whore instead. 'He'd have loved to have seen Bug Lady skewered on one end of the double-dong dildo, and a young hooker on the other instead of Larry's sagging, hairy ass.

Maybe next time.

Lenard grinned as he felt his aching dick twitch at the recollection.

As a finale, he and Larry-Wayne had double-teamed Bug Lady 'till her eyes watered, and she'd screamed the house down. Lenard had discovered for the first time in his fifty-four years that there was nothing in the world quite like feeling another dick through that thin piece of flesh that separates a woman's ass from her pussy. Nothing gay, thank you very much, just two good friends enjoying an incredibly horny experience. And next time, he would make sure it was himself who got the woman's pussy hole!

Lenard Levandowski's preference was for younger women, especially when he paid for his company, as was his usual practice. But, this one was for *gratis*, and as the saying goes, beggars can't be choosers. He'd taken a calculated risk on Bug Lady: she could easily have been some pig-ugly, two-hundred-fifty-pound heifer for all he knew since he'd only spoken to her on the 'phone. But there had been something in her voice that had given him that old familiar tingle in his gut. Something that told him that she would be to his taste physically and that he was dealing with a like-minded soul when it came to the more deprived levels of the carnal pleasures.

He fidgeted in his seat to ease the prickling sensation that coursed down his back – it sure felt like Bug Lady had done a number along his spine with those nails of hers. He reminisced with a dirty smile, felt once more her blood-red nails raking the soft flesh of his back and heightening his gratification.

The centipede crawled around the inside of Lenard's jacket, growing ever more agitated by the man's movements and the sharp tang of human sweat.

Lenard was delighted that his gut instincts about the woman had not let him down, if anything, his anticipation had, in fact, underplayed the lady. She was incredibly well-preserved given the age he thought her to be (he hadn't asked, that would have been just plain crass). Her body was firm, trim, and remarkably devoid of the telltale ravages of child-birth (those all too familiar toe-pointing titties, stretch marks, and a loose hole, to name but three). Yep, she was indeed one fit specimen for her age, and up for anything and everything: a rare creature indeed. Lenard figured that he owed it to himself to try out for a return match after he let her and her students out of the Mountainview, and before she went back to San Diego: he'd give anything for another taste of the Bug Lady.

You can certainly ask for nothing, he told himself.

The F250 T-boned Lenard's Lexus hard, sent it skidding sideways across the Desert View Avenue/Miracle Hill Road intersection and into a street light.

It was all no more than a split-second, silver blur in his peripheral vision – Lenard Levandowski didn't know what hit him.

The impact of the Ford truck snapped Lenard's brain stem and killed him before his head smashed open on the side window and slopped its gray, gooey contents out onto his lap.

Death came in an instant to Lenard Levandowski, and someone would say later that it was just like flicking off a light switch.

CHAPTER FIVE

1

"Okay, people," Jane raised her voice to attract her students' attention away from the lure of the steamy, geothermal pool, "it's almost midday and we've not even started yet." Shetried to hide the exasperation in her voice, reminding herself that they were giving up their weekend, and *she* was supposed to be keeping this whole expedition fun. Discretely, Jane shifted her weight to her left leg to ease the ache in her groin that had dulled down to a mild throb: a not entirely unpleasant reminder of her antics the night before.

"I've unpacked everything. By myself," Mel complained. "Thanks for all your help, guys," she added with an extra dash of sarcasm.

Fred smiled that broad, winning smile of his. "That's okay, honey – happy to be of service," he chirped. Fred had spent the past hour resting on one of the poolside recliners and trying to sneak a peek down the top of Martha-Ray's cut-away swimsuit that she wore as a compliment to her micro-mini skirt. The gal might be a little on the plump side, he thought, but she certainly had a rack well worth an ogle.

"Sorry, Mel. I got distracted," Darlene apologized. "I *have* been scouting around though," she sucked up to Jane.

"And?" Jane quizzed, "what have you found?"

"Nothing."

"We've been here for two hours, and you've found nothing?" Jane said with disbelief in her voice. If Darlene got any more hopeless, Jane wouldn't be surprised if one of these days she'd simply forget to breathe.

"Exactly," Darlene said with a wise-owl nod, "absolutely nothing at all. Not a single spider or silverfish, not even a cockroach – and you'd expect a place like this to be crawling with cockroaches."

"Perhaps if you looked a little harder, instead of making goo-goo eyes at Fred, you'd have found *something,*" Jane said, and although she'd made every effort to make her scolding come across as light-hearted, she saw Darlene's face redden. "Now, if you'll all gather 'round, I'll show you what we're looking for today," Jane distracted.

Jane grabbed the equipment bag that she'd instructed Mel to bring along from the faculty. She placed it on a recliner, unzipped it, and addressed her students, all the while doing her very best to ignore the pleasant throb between her legs.

"We have everything we need here to capture living *gigantea* specimens. And I'd like to emphasize the word *living*, is that clear?"

The students nodded.

"We have flashlights, collecting jars – extra-large, nets… " Jane stopped, ground her teeth, to stay calm. "Why *exactly* do we have two bottles of tequila?"

"I thought we could party a little later. Itwould be rude not to," Mel replied. She knew that she could pretty much get away with murder now that she and the esteemed professor were fuck buddies. "After we've caught us some centipedes, of course," She smiled.

"We will see about that, Melanie," Jane said. She put the liquor bottles to one side and continued, "We also have a snake hook and one of these each." She held up a long-handled garbage grabber, the type used by the orange-suited correctional facility people one sees picking up roadside trash. "It is vitally important that you use these to pick up any 'pedes you find. For Christ's sake, *do not* use your hands. They can – and *will* – bite through gloves." Jane threw each of the four students a pair of thick, red industrial gloves. "Even these."

"How are we supposed to use a snake hook and a grabber thingy at the same time?" Fred asked.

"You'll be in pairs: one person can pin the 'pede's head down while the other can grab and maneuver it into a collecting jar," Jane said. "It's just like catching a venomous snake, and I'm sure you've all seen that done on TV." She studied four surly faces, searching for the faintest glimmer of enthusiasm.

None.

"And that brings me to another important point," Jane continued, make sure that you subdue the right end of the 'pede."

"They have the fake head at the butt end," Mel chipped in.

"That's correct, Melanie, and the best way to avoid grabbing the wrong end is to remember that the legs get longer the farther toward the posterior end of the 'pede you get," Jane explained. "Therefore, the end with the shortest legs is the anterior, ergo the *bitey* end," she offered them another grain of humor.

Still no takers.

"It is imperative that you do not take any risks with these animals. They are nervous, aggressive creatures and will give you a nasty bite." Jane pulled an *EpiPen* out of her back pocket. "But, in the – hopefully unlikely – event of a bite, I always carry one of these with me."

"An EpiPen? Are you allergic?" Martha-Ray asked.

"Not that I know of, but I'm sure as hell not going to take any chances," Jane smiled. "There's one for each of you in the first aid kit," she paused, peered into the dark recesses of the canvas bag. "Where's the first aid kit, Mel?"

Mel looked sheepish. "Ah, I couldn't find one in the lab, so I brought what I had in my medicine cabinet at home." Mel fished a small baggie from her shorts pocket and placed it on the wooden recliner.

Jane prodded the baggie. "Two *Scooby-Doo* band aids and a bottle of hydrogen peroxide?" she spat. "What fucking use is that going to be if anyone gets bitten? For Christ's sakes, Melanie!"

"It's okay, Professor, we'll just be *extra* careful, is all," Fred mediated, "everyone with me?"

The others agreed, desperate to avoid an unpleasant scene.

"I am *so* sorry," Mel apologized, "I really did look all over for a kit in the lab. I'm sorry."

Jane sighed and figured it best to let this one go, "okay, I guess we'll just have to stick to Fred's extra careful strategy then." She pulled her thin laptop out of her black backpack, switched it on. Jane's computer was a solid state hard drive – less memory capacity than a regular drive but instantly on and fast as hell.

"If you will all take a look at these clips of *gigantea* in action, you'll have a good idea of the animal we are looking for and the best places to look." Jane clicked open the first of the movie clips on the computer.

It showed a close-up of a Giant Centipede crawling along a mocked-up rain forest floor. It climbed over logs, rocks, and leaves, gliding over the damp terrarium moss with fluid ease, its legs moving in rhythmic waves. It crawled over the camera, and as its legs filled the screen, Jane shuddered.

"As you can see, 'pedes like damp, warm places. They

hide under rocks, logs, piles of debris, anything that will prevent them from drying out," Jane narrated.

The next clip was of an amateur collector smiling at the camera as his pet *gigantea* crawled up his arm. He then placed it into a glass vivarium with a live, white mouse.

"Oh no," Darlene gasped as they watched the mouse sniffing around, oblivious to its impending fate. In a reddish blur, the centipede lunged with lightning speed at the mouse. It sank its wickedly curved forcipules into the rodent's back and wrapped its segmented body around the poor creature; a blink and the movement would have been missed. The mouse's mouth gaped wide open in a terrified, silent scream as the centipede began tearing chunks from its still-living lunch and blood and clods of fur stuck to the arthropod's face. Centipedes, the students learned here, are quite the messy eaters.

"As you can see for yourself, centipedes are quick. Should you find one, for God's sake, don't take your eyes off it – not even for a second," Jane warned them.

The third clip showed a graphic close-up of a male centipede depositing a sperm-sac onto a patch of moss. "And here we have, what you've all been waiting for," Jane laughed, "*Scolopendra* porn."

For once, the students giggled along with her as they listened to the tinny voice-over on the laptop explain that *'centipedes do not mate in the conventional way: in fact, there is no physical contact at all. Following a brief courtship dance, the male spins a silk pad upon which he deposits his spermatophore. The female centipede simply scoops up the male's sperm with her telson, or final segment, and uses it to fertilize her eggs.'*

"And who said romance was dead," Mel joked, and everyone chuckled along.

The voice-over continued as the video showed the female 'pede taking the spermatophore into her body *'– in fact, some species dispense with the male completely and are parthenogenetic.*'

"Babies without sex?" Fred interrupted, "that's like decaf' coffee – I mean, what's the freakin' point?" The girls looked at him with eyebrows raised.

Next up, a video that showed a centipede covered in small centipedes.

"They carry their young – like scorpions?" Martha-Ray enquired. "Well, I didn't know that."

"She's not carrying them. They are *matriphagic,*" Jane corrected. "They're eating their mother," she hit the point home and watched a grimace form on each one of the faces before her. "They will resort to that when there's not enough food around. I guess you could say that it's nature's ultimate sacrifice."

The movie sped up into time-lapse and showed the baby centipedes reduce their mother to nothing in a matter of seconds.

Another clip: this one featured the revered British Naturalist and every zoologist's hero, Sir David Attenborough. He was standing in an immense cave, knee-deep in a mountain of bat-droppings. The entire surface of Batshit Mountain was alive and glinting with thousands upon thousands of tiny, golden cockroaches. Attenborough wore a gas-mask against the deadly stench of ammonia that emanated from the guano and was pointing up at the ceiling. The camera panned upward. Dangling head downward from the roof of the cave were dozens of centipedes, all clinging to the rock with grappling-hook rear legs. They were snatching bats clean out of mid-flight.

"That is *so* awesome," Darlene broke the silence, "how the fuck do they *do* that?"

"They sense the bat's heat and scent," Jane explained. "The 'pedes' eyesight is pretty poor, so they rely on their other senses." She shivered as she watched the centipedes pluck the bats out of the dark cave air with laconic ease. "And as you can see, they're pretty damned good at it."

With more than a large amount of relief, Jane clicked off the laptop. For as many times as she had seen those clips and hundreds of others that featured her lifelong nemesis, *Scolopendra gigantea,* they still turned her damned stomach. "I think we're ready to get started," Jane broke the uneasy silence, "I'd suggest that we start looking anywhere there may be damp and places to hide," Jane directed. "You all need to pair up: Fred, you go with Martha-Ray. Mel, you go with Darlene."

"What about you?" Mel enquired. "You're on your own."

"I know what I'm doing, Melanie. I'll manage, but thank you for your concern," Jane reassured. Actually, she was looking forward to a little alone time. The last thing she wanted was to be stuck with a surly, grumbling student for hours on end or to risk possible injury from a 'pede because she'd put her trust in one of them.

The students grabbed the equipment and drifted toward the exit.

"And don't forget what Mr. Levandowski told you all about the Fifth floor," Jane paused for effect. "Stay the hell off of the Fifth Floor!"

2

The Fifth Floor was a hellish mess. The old caretaker really hadn't been joking when he'd warned them off.

"So, you really like Darlene, then?" Martha-Ray made with the chit-chat as she and Fred poked around. Despite Fred's propensity to play the asshole, Martha-Ray did actually like the guy; she figured he was much smarter than he let on, and he could be funny and charming when he wanted to be. Oh yeah, and had the body of Adonis.

"Yeah, she's one heck of a hot babe," Fred replied, practically drooling as he spoke. "I just can't take my eyes off that sexy bod' of hers."

"I can imagine," Martha-Ray said, already beginning to feel awkward. "I mean, if I were a guy, I'd imagine she was quite easy on the eye."

"Easy on the dick too!" Fred laughed as he forgot himself, "the most fuckable pussy I've ever come across – if you'll pardon the pun!"

"Pun pardoned," Martha-Ray laughed at Fred's embarrassment as her face warmed at her own.

"Oh shit, I'm sorry," Fred stumbled, "I forgot –"

"– that I'm a girl?"

"Yeah," Fred's face glowed bright pink, "No – I don't mean that you're mannish or anything. You're obviously a girl, you've obviously got – "he stalled.

"Tits?" Martha-Ray mocked, "a vagina?"

"Err – I was going to say two X chromosomes," Fred stammered, "but those are good indicators too." He smiled at the girl. "It's just that you're more like one of the guys. Not that I think you're a rug muncher or anything like that," he continued to dig the conversational hole for himself. "Shit, you *are* a lesbian, and I've offended you?"

Martha-Ray smiled. "It's okay, Fred. And no, I'm not. I can assure you that I love cock as much as the next girl," she laughed and found herself relaxing into the sexy banter despite her natural coyness when it came to the subject. "And besides which, I think there are quite enough sapphic shenanigans going on in the faculty as it is, don't you?"

"Eh?"

"Oh, come on, Fred. Don't tell me that you don't know."

"Don't know what?" Fred was puzzled.

"That our beloved Professor of Zoology is dining at the Y with Melanie Hernandez? I thought *everybody* knew!" Martha-Ray declared with a gleeful chuckle.

"Nah," Fred shook his head as if the act of thinking about such matters physically hurt his brain. "She used to be married," he paused, "to a man. And then there was all that stuff about her and the Dean." Now, there was a story Fred *had* heard. Gory details, frat house embellishments, and all.

Martha-Ray laughed a kind laugh at Fred. Beautiful, chiseled Fred with his strong arms, broad chest, and thick, muscular legs: Fred, who would never look twice at a plump, plain girl like her. "I can't believe that you got to the age of twenty-one still so perfectly naive – I think it's *so* sweet," she chastised. "Like, *everyone* knows; Professor Lucas is a raving bisexual – she loves guys *and* girls!"

"Oh yeah. Gotcha," the realization dawned on Fred, gradual as always. "I've seen plenty of that shit on the internet. It's hot as hell watching a girl with a guy and another girl." He smiled at Martha-Ray and chuckled, "And I guess if you're bi, you're never gonna be stuck for a date." At that, they both laughed away the awkward and continued on with their quest.

Martha-Ray found herself sneaking around the forbidden fifth floor behind Fred like an errant school kid who'd broken into the neighborhood Haunted House on a dare: all tippy-toes and speaking in hushed whispers. It was foolish, really, as there was no one about to catch either herself or her partner as they prowled around. And, whilst it was off-task, she knew that Fred was as anxious to explore the mysterious, wrecked building as she was, even if it meant temporarily neglecting their hunt for their multi-legged quarry.

They discovered that, in all, there were four Penthouse suites on the Mountainview's salubrious Fifth Floor, each one more extravagant than the last, save the blasted-out room. The landing area between the rooms was strewn with splinters of wood, lumps of plaster, random items of clothing, jewelry, a single shoe, underwear – it was as if the occupants of that floor had left in one hell of a hurry, scattering their clothes behind them in a bizarre Hansel and Gretel attempt to be able to locate their way back.

Everything was, of course, coated with the ubiquitous Mountainview layer of fine, powdery dust.

"Let's check these two out first," Martha-Ray suggested, indicating to Fred the least damaged of the suites.

"Sure thing, boss," Fred agreed, happy to go along as long as he wasn't expected to make too many decisions: decision-making tended to make his head ache and invariably turned out wrong in the end.

Fred shouldered a door and felt around the wall for a light switch. Found it, flicked it on, and made his way in.

The light that illuminated the room was scant and casted gloomy, nebulous shadows, and Fred had to pause a second or two for his eyes to adjust. He saw the bed was unmade, a tangle of clothes scattered around , and an expensive designer suitcase upended in the middle of the floor as if it had been discarded in the middle of being unpacked.

"Looks like someone left in a hurry," Martha-Ray said over his shoulder. "You check under the beds and whatnot, and I'll go take a look at the connecting suite; give me a shout if you find anything."

Fred nodded and ogled his field-trip partner's voluptuous booty as she made her way to the door that connected the two rooms. If it wasn't for Darlene and her easy, most generous loving (plus the unavoidable fact that she was just a few floors down from where he was standing right now), Fred figured he could have some serious fun with Martha-Ray – didn't they always say that the homely girls were the dirtiest in the sack? Snorting, Fred clicked on his flashlight, dropped to his knees, and started looking in earnest for centipedes.

Martha-Ray opened the unlocked door to the adjacent suite and peered in to the gloom. She clicked on her flashlight, and immediately, a flurry of movement caught her eye. She snapped her head around to follow and caught a fleeting glimpse of rusty red and pointed, yellow legs disappearing beneath a wooden crib in the corner of the room.

"Aha," she rejoiced quietly, "strike one to team Martha-Ray!" Wielding her snake hook like a blind man's cane, Martha-Ray stepped carefully toward the crib, pointing her flashlight beam directly where she guessed the creature would be hiding and noted that the light – and *ergo* her hand – was trembling.

Fred was up on his feet again, his skin crawling. The vivid mental imagery of the giant centipede he'd watched on the Prof's laptop racing across the faux-forest was too strong in his mind to allow him to stay on the floor for any length of time; those things could be absolutely anywhere in the room, just waiting for the chance to crawl over his skin with their innumerable spiked legs. Shivering despite the clammy heat, Fred made his way toward the bathroom, upturning items of clothing, examining beneath each with the harsh beam of his flashlight as he walked. He had it figured out that the bathroom would be a more likely location to find a centipede: damp, dark, plenty of water. And he wouldn't have to crawl around on his belly under any beds and risk finding himself up close and *too* fucking personal to one of those hellish animals.

There was that, *and* he needed to pee.

3

By pure happenstance, inside that particular suite's bathroom, Jackson Booth was standing in the darkness, holding his breath. He put a finger up to his lips to silence the three guys he had holed up in there with him and hoped that they could see his gesture. All four stood motionless and watched the shadowy movements in the thin sliver of light that crept under the bathroom door.

Jackson hoped to hell and back that Lee, Johnny, and Mikey would be able to keep their dumb mouths shut. They were an excitable bunch at the best of times, especially when they were on something – as he suspected Johnny Psycho was right now – and could be worse than a bunch of preschoolers to keep quiet under pressure such as this. As much as he wanted to get his hands on the guy who was tantalizing a door's breadth away, Jackson wanted to do so on his terms, not like this. Not by accident. Nonetheless, in preparation of the possible event, Jackson pulled his gun out from his waistband and held it tight in his sweating palm.

Jackson's breath caught in his throat as the bathroom doorknob began to wiggle loosely as Fred tugged at it from the other side.

4

Martha-Ray popped the flashlight into her mouth and thrust her snake hook toward the centipede that pressed itself against the wall beneath the crib, its head poised back like a rattlesnake ready to strike. Confident that she'd remembered rightly which end of the creature Professor Lucas had explained, was the business end, Martha-Ray lunged forward and pinned the creature's head down with the snake hook. The centipede thrashed and struggled against the hook, its body clanking hard against the cold metal to make a sound like a small, muted bell. Martha-Ray pressed hard against the hook, driving the centipede further into the plush carpet, and she was astounded at just how strong the animal was as more than once it threatened to whip the hook right out of her sweat-slicked hand. The centipede wound the back-end of its long, fat body up along the smooth hook, its legs finding purchase in the miniscule irregularities in the metal; had the creature been any longer, it would soon be digging those legs into the pudgy, vulnerable flesh of Martha-Ray's hand.

She reached for the grabber that protruded from her backpack, biting down hard on the rubber handle of the flashlight as she bore down hard on the snake hook. The last thing she needed was for her – and incredibly pissed – captive to wriggle loose: Christ only knows what these things were capable of. She'd read about a species of Asian hornet that will chase and sting an attacker for miles, long after the perpetrator is no longer a threat to the hive; the conclusion being that the wasps drive themselves into such a frenzy of anger that they simply *can't* stop the attack. Martha-Ray had watched film footage of the things in action – they were a good three inches long and looked like they had flown straight up from the inky pits of Hades – as they chased down and stung to death a wild cat that had strayed too close to their nest. Martha-Ray's own hypothesis was that the wasps were pure evil and did what they did because they enjoyed inflicting pain and killing things.

So, although Martha-Ray could not be definite that these centipedes would exhibit similar behavior as the hornets, she mentally prepared herself to get the hell out of Dodge should her captive specimen escape and come at her for revenge; she certainly thought the thing looked pissed enough to hunt her down, given the opportunity.

Martha-Ray held onto the grabber as if her life depended on it, and she reached for the myriapod's head. "Come to Momma," she whispered as the grabber's orange rubber fingers grasped the segments behind the animal's head that served as its neck. She took the pressure off of the snake hook and pulled the wriggling creature up off of the floor, amazed at just how heavy the thing felt. Letting out the stale breath she'd been unconsciously holding since she'd first spotted the centipede, Martha-Ray stood up and moved away from the crib.

As far as she could tell in the badly lit room, her 'pede was a good catch. Prof' Lucas would be very happy indeed. The animal was an easy two feet long, quite possibly longer, its head broad as a dollar bill. Its matte black eyes glowered at her with what she perceived as pure hatred (always one for the anthropomorphisms, was Martha-Ray, she'd have it talking to her in a Nick Junior cartoon voice next) as it thrashed its dark red body like crazy trying to gain freedom. The centipede twisted its head to snap at the grabber's metal pole with fangs that shone like patent leather, all the while trying to find purchase on smooth aluminum with its finger-length legs.

Martha-Ray felt elated and nauseated all at the same time, fascinated at seeing a centipede alive and up close.. To her, the creature secured at the end of her grabber looked like it belonged on another planet; it was too long, to plastic-looking, had far too many legs to be of the same Earth as pandas, smiley dolphins, and fluffy little kittens. She held the thing at arm's length and took a step backward, making sure to keep her bare legs away from the 'pede's flailing rear limbs and the poison they carried. And as she did so, Martha-Ray bumped into something that hung silently from the doorframe.

5

Jackson tensed, made ready to fight – use the gun, even – should the bathroom door open. In his adrenaline boosted state, he was more than prepared to dish out some swift justice to the guy that dared disrespect the man, the legend, Jackson Booth.

The doorknob twisted and turned. Did the guy on the other side of the door not comprehend that the door was locked?! It wasn't as if this were the only fucking bathroom in the hotel – shit, it wasn't even the only one in this *suite*! What was this guy, some special kind of stupid? Jackson saw movement in the gloom as his best boy Johnny Psycho pulled his trademark, oversized knife from his belt.

The doorknob turned again, followed by a dull thump as Fred shouldered the door. Dust floated down on Jackson and his boys as the door shuddered, and its hinges strained inward.

A scream.

Sharp, shrill, piercing the gloom, Martha-Ray's scream shattered the Fifth Floor's silence. It spiked Jackson's adrenaline level a notch or three higher and made his heart pound heavily in his chest. The doorknob quit moving, and Jackson heard Fred's voice through the door, followed by the sound of the guy running away.

Jackson Booth listened to Fred's footsteps leaving the room beyond the door. And once he was satisfied that his intended victim had gone, he finally allowed himself to breathe.

6

"Martha-Ray!?" Fred shouted as he galloped toward the suite next door. "You okay in there?" The lack of response chilled him even more than the scream.

He entered the suite, played his flashlight about the room.

There was heavy breathing, and it took Fred a second or two to locate its direction. When he did, he saw Martha-Ray, caught in his flashlight's beam like a startled burglar. She sat cross-legged on the hotel suite floor, clutching her empty grabber to her chest like some protective amulet.

"Martha-Ray?" Fred stepped over the discarded debris that littered the floor. He crouched down next to the girl and placed a concerned hand on the hot, bare skin of her shoulder. She felt hot and sticky, and she smelled of sour sweat. "Don't tell me you've been bitten already?" He was hoping not; Fred wasn't all that good in situations that required any sort of injury of first aid – even the sight of his own blood had been known to make him barf on occasion.

Martha-Ray shook her head and looked at him with her wide doe-eyes. She seemed to be unable to speak, and her breath was coming and going in the loud, wheezing gasps of a panic attack. She pointed to the doorway to the en-suite bathroom with a shaking finger, and Fred followed its direction with his flashlight.

"Oh, sweet Jesus," he moaned, and bile lurched up into his throat.

There was a baby doorway bouncer hanging from the door frame between the bedroom and the bathroom. It was dusty and age-faded, but Fred could still make out the blue floral patterns and happy, smiling butterflies that cavorted between the flowers. He could also see quite clearly the body of a baby, still strapped in by the safety harnesses.

Fred danced his flashlight beam over the tiny corpse. Although he was no expert, Fred guessed the baby had been little more than six or seven months old when he'd died. After five years, the body had desiccated, and that gave it the surreal, almost *fake* appearance of an ancient Egyptian mummy; paper-thin, flaking skin stretched taut over protruding bones and hollow, black eye sockets that seemed to reflect the dark. There was a disproportionately large, dried-up puddle of putrefied matter spread out beneath the baby boy's corpse. As he had rotted away, it had formed a solid crust on the carpet, and it still whiffed faintly of putrefaction.

Fred shone his light into the baby's face and immediately retched at the sight of the withered skin, empty eye sockets, and the grinning, toothless mouth.

"They left their baby behind," Martha-Ray's voice was quiet, an almost whisper as she finally summoned the breath to speak. "Who does that?"

"Perhaps he was already dead when they had to leave. It sure does look like they left in a hurry," Fred attempted to console Martha-Ray with the best scenario he could muster; the mental image of the baby's spoiled corpse had already burned into his psyche, and he knew in his heart that it would stay with him forever.

Fred helped Martha-Ray to her feet. "Let's go look somewhere else," he said as he gently guided her from the suite, "we shouldn't really be up here."

As they exited the room, Martha-Ray fought hard to get her breath back and compose herself. Fred was probably right, the baby had died in the gas explosion, and his parents had no choice but to leave him behind as they fled for their own lives. Either that, or they had died in the explosion too, and no one had thought to check their room for a small child. After all, no parent would leave their own flesh and blood behind to die, what must have been an agonizing, lingering death. Yeah, that explanation suited Martha-Ray's optimistic sensibilities, even though her inherent common sense niggled that her hypothesis was total bullshit.

She'd seen for herself the scratch marks on the canvas straps that stretched from the top of the doorframe and down to the baby seat. And the ones on the doorframe. Scratches that could only have been made by the tiny fingernails that lay splintered and broken on the floor beneath the infant's dried out corpse. The baby had obviously tried to claw his way out of the bouncer and had been alive for quite some time after he had been abandoned and sealed up in the hotel.

Martha-Ray wanted to cry, for the baby, for his parents, for herself. No matter what the circumstances, what she had just seen was the saddest thing she'd ever seen – was ever likely to see – in her entire life. Instead, she swallowed it down and allowed her mind to begin creating a few more palatable scenarios – before long, she'd more likely than not have convinced herself that she'd simply imagined the whole thing.

They made their way across the wide landing in silence, veering toward the suite with no door.

"You think the door got blown off when the gas exploded?" Fred said, more to bite through the quiet than to state the obvious.

"Probably," Martha-Ray replied, more than happy for a change of subject, "although most of the door bits are actually *inside* the room. That doesn't make sense."

They stepped over the splintered mess and into the suite, eyes scanning the shattered furniture and litter that covered most of the floor.

The suite's bathroom – an internal room – had completely disintegrated in the blast. There were fragments of the porcelain bath, lavatory bowl, and sink basin mixed in with the obviously expensive ceramic tiles that were scattered everywhere. The wall that had divided the bathroom from the rest of the suite was quite simply no longer where it had been, and that gave the room an expansive, open-plan feel to it.

"What the hell happened in here?" Fred sounded puzzled even more so that usual.

"The caretaker guy said it was a gas explosion," Martha-Ray reminded him.

"Why would there be gas in a hotel bathroom?" Fred asked the obvious question.

Martha-Ray fell silent. Good point. There was nothing in a hotel suite like this one that would require gas. Ergo, if there was no gas, there could be no gas to explode. And if that were the case, Fred's question still stood. Just what the hell *had* happened on the Fifth Floor? There had to be a simple explanation, there always was: perhaps, there'd been a gas leak in the kitchens, and it had accumulated on the top floor of the hotel. All it would take was someone lighting a cigarette or flicking a light switch and – *boom*!

"Oh fuck!" Fred exclaimed and broke her reverie. "Take a look at this!"

Martha-Ray saw Fred pointing at the bed, upon which lay a severed arm, unmistakably human. Its flesh was long-gone, the splintered brown bones cracked and crumbling, the skin dried out, withered and flaking away (*much like the baby's – thanks for the reminder*) on the Egyptian-cotton bed spread. Bizarrely, its index finger appeared to be pointing at the steel-shuttered picture window, as if ordering the two of them out of the room.

"I guess there were some casualties. Inevitable I suppose," she told Fred. "Look."

There were more identifiable fragments of human remains dotted around the room. A skeletonized foot, half a dozen vertebrae, a thighbone, ribs. Martha-Ray spotted another pair of arms, which meant that unless severed arm guy had grown three upper limbs, there'd been at least two people in the room when it exploded. There were no skulls to be found; the victim's heads nowhere to be seen.

Fred picked his way through the debris toward where the bathroom had once been.

"I guess they shut the water off," he said, peering at the pipes that jutted up through the splintered floorboards, "otherwise the place would have flooded."

"That's a shame; it would have made the place even cozier for *gigantea*," Martha-Ray said with a forced smile. "It's still nice and damp though – perfect centipede territory, so we'd best keep our eyes peeled." She poked at a hollow gray thing that poked out from under the bed. It looked like a tooth, six inches long, only hollow and clear.

She picked it up, toyed with it, played her fingers on the thin material that felt like sloughed chitin, the outer casing of choice of the arthropods – a substance that was chemically akin to mammalian hair. She crushed it in her hand, and the ancient paper sensation reminded her of the cicada husks that used to cling to the tree trunks in her father's garden.

"So," Fred asked, pensive, "how come they didn't clear the bits of bodies out? Why would they just leave them up here?"

"Your guess is as good as mine, Fred," Martha-Ray told him as she poked around under the room's spilled detritus with her snake hook. "You'd have thought they would have checked the hotel out at some point for people trapped by the explosion," she shrugged; she was certain that there would probably be a logical – and fluffy, perhaps even pleasant – explanation for that as well.

Martha-Ray made her way with caution across the room, toward the connecting door that stood slightly ajar and hung crazily on its hinges like an entryway to a carnival funhouse.

"Unless they didn't know that there were people up here," Fred offered.

"Or unless there was something up here that stopped them from coming up?" Martha-Ray's mind was whirring now. What if the place had been infested with oversized centipedes, and they'd tried to blow them up? "Something dangerous that meant they *couldn't*."

"Might this have something to do with it?" Fred asked. He picked up a twisted chunk of metal with his grabber. The metal had been warped, twisted out of shape by intense heat, but the stenciled yellow trefoil symbol was still unmistakable. "Isn't that the symbol for radioactive shit?" He pulled a face as if he were thinking just a little *too* hard.

Martha-Ray raised an eyebrow at Fred's discovery: sure that it could mean *anything* – or most likely, nothing at all. She pushed open the connecting door. "Jesus shit," she exclaimed, "you gotta see this, Fred."

Fred stumbled over the shattered room toward Martha-Ray, made his way into the adjoining suite.

"Holy fuck," he mumbled, "what the hell was going on here?"

They both stared with disbelief at the sight before them, neither one quick to comprehend what they were actually looking at. There were stacks of huge, brown boxes and white, plastic bottles of chemicals, a tangled array of multicolored wires, and a small wooden crate which was marked with black sharpie; *'C4'*.

Martha-Ray spoke up first. "There's nitric acid, sulfuric acid, and *glycerol*," she read off the bottles, "they were making nitroglycerine."

"This was a bomb factory?" Fred was astounded; he'd read all about terrorist bomb factories, although they were usually found in less auspicious locales that this. Truth be told, the whole thing fascinated him: it was probably the *only* branch of chemistry that had managed to hold his attention across the hazy years of his education. "In a posh hotel? In the middle of the fucking desert? That's insane."

Martha-Ray opened up the *C4* crate and marveled at the neatly packed rows of high explosives nestled snug within, like eggs in a carton. She was confident enough around the stuff because she'd paid attention in chem. lab and knew that the stuff was incredibly stable in most circumstances unless it was deteriorating. There were no signs of rot or the clear viscous fluid that would show that it was: had Martha-Ray seen either, she'd have high-tailed it out of there before you could say *cyclotrimethylenetrinitramine*.

"I can't think of any other explanation, can you? Especially with this," Martha-Ray said, "let me see that again."

Fred placed the piece of metal he'd found into her hand. She studied it closely. There was something about the alien lettering, the all too familiar symbol for radioactive material that set off an alarm bell or two in her head.

"Nah, they couldn't have been..." Martha-Ray nervously coiled the thin shoulder straps of her swimsuit around her fingers. "Not here."

"Been what?" Fred's voice had a quiver of anxiety.

"I'm guessing this came off of a container of some description. And if it did, then that container would most likely have been holding radioactive material," Martha-Ray told him. "Which means that whoever was up here playing chemistry sets was making themselves a dirty bomb. There's no wonder they sealed the place up." And now she was back to thinking about the baby again – now one-hundred percent assured that the poor thing had been left to die all alone.

"Fuck! Does that mean we're going to die of radioactivity, now?" Fred's face paled with worry and a sheen of slick, nervous sweat crawled across his skin.

"I doubt it very much, Fred," Martha-Ray placated, "they tend to make dirty bombs using only low-grade radioactive stuff. It's more about contaminating things long-term than killing people; you'd be in more danger getting an X-Ray right now." She looked into Fred's eyes and saw the fear that had settled there. "Even so, I think we should take the caretaker's advice and go look for centipedes on a different floor," so saying, Martha-Ray pocketed the metal shard and followed Fred as he hurried out of the room like his firm, shapely ass was on fire.

CHAPTER SIX

1

"I got one! Oh my God! *I got one!*" Melanie Hernandez squealed like a giddy four-year-old as she pinned a centipede as long as her leg and the color of dried blood to the lavish hotel carpet. The 'pede thrashed wildly around and aimed its fake head and venomous rear limbs at Mel's lean, tanned thighs.

"Holy shit, look at you go, girlfriend!" Darlene laughed, her own delight barely contained, "he's a beaut' too!"

"Don't just stand there admiring the fucking thing, get the jar!" Mel ordered with more than a modicum of panic in her voice. She could feel the centipede already beginning to work its head loose of the snake hook, and it was waving its jaws in her direction, flexing them maniacally as if cursing her out. She found the strength of the animal to be quite astounding, even allowing for its size, and she had no doubt at all that it wouldn't take too long for it to wriggle free. That thought scared her. "It's looking at me all funny!" she groaned.

"Yeah, he's probably taking all of this personally;

centipedes are known to be sensitive little souls," Darlene mocked as she took her time in ambling across the hotel room with the grabber and specimen jar.

The two girls had identified a likely looking room on the third floor. It had been unoccupied at the time of the explosion and was as pristine as the day that housekeeping had left it, albeit coated with the thick snow of five year's worth of dust. The queen-sized bed was neatly made, the tea and coffee-making paraphernalia organized just so and untouched with the Customer Survey card placed neatly on the bedside table – all ready for the room's next guests who would never book in. In the spacious bathroom, the paper toilet-seat cover was still in its place, and the roll of toilet paper on the fancy gold holder was folded into a sharp triangle at the end. A thick stack of luxurious, fluffy white towels was neatly arranged on the towel-warming rail next to the shower cubicle, waiting for a freshly showered guest. And, as with every other window in the Mountainview, thick sheet steel served as a curtain, which strangled any daylight that may have had designs on entering.

The door to the room had been left unlocked, and a quick peek into the darkness within with an inquisitive flashlight had revealed a pair of centipedes scuttling around without a care in the world. Darlene and Mel had watched the creatures meandering around, observed how they stayed close to the dust-covered baseboards, and paused every now and then to wave their pinkie-thick antennae in the air to taste it, as if on the hunt for their next meal.

Grimacing with effort and distaste, Darlene clutched at the captured animal with her grabber and gingerly maneuvered it into the specimen jar she had placed with great care on the floor. "Looks like we're gonna need a bigger jar!" she laughed as she pushed the 'pede's head down into the jar; mercifully, with the creature's fat, angry head securely in the container, the remainder of the 'pede's long, writhing body followed with minimal effort. "Geddit?"

she giggled.

Mel nodded and gave a thin smile, although she was not in the right mood for Darlene's dumb movie jokes. Tackling the centipede had left her shaken and drained; it was one thing dissecting animals and observing them through glass, quite another wrestling one half as long as your body with the risk of some serious pain if the damn thing took a bite at you.

"Yeah," she sighed, "I get it, Darlene."

Darlene screwed the lid on the specimen jar with a quick, deliberate action, as relieved as her partner to have the centipede contained. Instinctively, she recoiled and almost dropped the jar as the incarcerated creature tried to bite at her hand through the thick glass.

She caught her breath and poked her tongue out at the creature.

As engrossed in their captured specimen as she was, Darlene didn't notice the other centipede dart out from behind the credenza.

"Shit!" Mel shrieked. She jumped backward out of the creature's way and tripped over her own feet. She landed back-first with a dull thump against the built-in cupboards that were home to the huge, flat screen TV.

Darlene scooted back, stifled a scream as the centipede darted between her and Mel. Thankfully, its focus appeared to be on the floor-level air vent on the opposite side of the room, and it scurried toward its goal with alarming speed and squeezed itself through the thin vents, disappearing into the darkest recesses of the Mountainview. Darlene watched, fascinated as the 'pede raced by just inches from her exposed, French-manicured toes. It was almost hypnotic, the way its legs moved in steady, regular waves, and its hideous, waxy body just went on and on and on.

"That was close," she gasped. "For a while there, I thought it was coming to try save its buddy." She tapped on the specimen jar with a fingernail to make a *chink – chink –*

chink sound that served to further aggravate the captive centipede.

"I really don't think that it works like that, Darlene," Mel laughed. "Besides, if it had been – "she said in her very best Voice-Over Man voice, "– *Super Centipede! Protector of the weak! Bringer of centipede justice!* it would have been wearing a little cape." She laughed, and Darlene joined in the merriment, more through nervous relief than good spirits.

Mel pulled herself up with a grunt; she could already feel the bruises forming on the knobs of her spine. The cupboard door swung open.

"Oh my," Darlene gasped. Her eyes lit up and settled on the inside of the cupboard and its clinking contents. "Would you look at that?"

"Oh wow," Mel gasped her agreement as she followed Darlene's gaze, the discomfort in her back instantly forgotten.

The mini-bar concealed behind the cupboard's dark veneer door was crammed with booze, as if it had been replenished just yesterday. As one would expect from any hotel of the Mountainview's caliber, there were to be found the ubiquitous, miniature bottles of spirits, eight-ounce cans of Budweiser, a diminutive bottle each of red and white wine, along with a dark chocolate *Toblerone* and several packets of salted cashews.

"You do know what this means?" Mel asked the rhetorical – and possibly unnecessary – question. "There are over a hundred mini-bars in this hotel, all full of booze. Even in the rooms that were occupied when the place was closed down. Like, no-one ever buys their drinks from the mini-bar, right?"

"And that means –" Darlene grinned.

"– you got it, sister. We're gonna have one hot-shit of a pool party tonight!" Mel giggled as she proceeded to stuff the mini-bar contents into her backpack.

2

The centipede hid in the darkest shadows that she could find. She felt safe in the blackness and relished the warm dampness that soothed her gargantuan body. She lay still, hunkered down in one of the larger air vents that moved the geothermal heat around the hotel. Although the vent itself was more than a yard across, the creature felt cramped and claustrophobic as her vast body squashed into the confined space. Her senses were on high alert now; she had been awakened by the sounds, scents, and air-borne taste of the fresh humans that had most recently invaded her home.

As unused to company as she was, the 'pede welcomed the presence of the humans because it meant something more important to her than anything else right now.

Food.

Humans were no mystery to the creature: she had happened across them on many occasions out in the desert during her erstwhile frequent hunting forays. She knew well from experience what perfect prey they made with their inadequate senses, vulnerable, soft flesh, and slow speed. She twitched her gigantic antennae in the direction of the new smell, and fresh venom coursed into her fangs to fill them with deadly weight.

Mingled with the overpowering stench of human prey was scent of the smaller ones of her kind. They had emitted their pheromones to broadcast their fear at being hunted and captured to every other centipede in the hotel, and to the monstrous creature, it resembled myriad chemical screams.

And now, as she tasted the air, the 'pede could sense one of the human invaders coming closer. The scent brought with it that sweet promise that drove her to hunt, overriding her fearful instincts to remain hidden in the shadows.

The centipede inched toward the scent that tantalized her from beyond the flimsy mesh at the air vent's entrance.

She flinched and shied away from the piercing light that flashed intermittently across her dull, unblinking eyes ,and she crept slowly onward once it passed.

3

Jane shone her torch once again into the huge air vent, convinced that she had just seen something move in there. Her flashlight picked up nothing, shining only far as the abrupt, right-angled bend in the shiny, aluminum vent and no farther. Whatever it was she thought she'd seen had gone, no doubt spooked by her prying flashlight beam.

She had already captured two *gigantea* specimens in the steam room, an achievement of which she was incredibly proud, especially since she'd had no help at all. Both 'pedes she estimated to be approximately twelve to fifteen inches long, slightly smaller than the one the cop had presented to her. And, whilst she was forced to admit to being a little disappointed to have found nothing larger yet, she was no less exhilarated to have found such fine specimens and captured them alive.

Continuing her search, Jane played the harsh beam of her flashlight into every dark corner and crevice that she could find in the poolroom. She was truly enjoying the thrilling, mixed sensations of excitement and fear of hunting something that genuinely scared her.

Jane had given some thought to Darlene's earlier point about the apparent absence of life in the hotel's pool room. Other than the two 'pedes she'd collected, of course, Jane's expert eye had spotted not one other living thing in or around the basement of the hotel and that she found most peculiar. After five years without human intervention, she would have expected to have found the hotel teeming with innumerable invertebrate life and, more than likely, rats and mice, possibly even a 'possum or two. But no, aside from the specimens she'd pinned down and maneuvered so very carefully into her giant glass jars, there had been nothing else at all.

It brought to Jane's mind a particular Caribbean vacation she'd taken with her ex-husband. The resort in which they had stayed was one of those exclusive golf-resorts, and it was sprayed twice daily with a potent insecticide. This had the effect of rendering the whole place entirely and depressingly sterile: devoid of insects and spiders, along with lizards, frogs, and birds to which they were sustenance. In the entire two weeks Jane and her ex had been there, she'd seen not so much as a butterfly or a mosquito pass by – a definite affront to her inquisitive zoologist's eye. And this was the first time in a long, long time that Jane had given even a passing thought to that vacation – their last before the divorce – and it amused her that the Mountainview had rekindled those less than fond memories.

Weird, she thought.

As she carried on her search for more, bigger – *better* – 'pedes, Jane's mind flittered away to its default setting as it wouldn't in such times of quietude.

It had always been the same – for as long as Jane could recall throughout her adult life – that when her brain was left to its own devices and was allowed to slip into neutral, it always came back to the same old.

Such was the lot of the sex addict, she mused.

Jane didn't think that she'd *always* been this way before they'd stuck her with the label *nymphomania*. In fact, she hadn't even learned how to masturbate until her late teens, although, once she had that particular technique down, boy howdy she'd made up for lost time! It had been her husband, Ronnie – *ex*-husband, she corrected herself – who had thrown the epithet in her face the night he'd walked out. '*Raving nymphomaniac*', had been his actual words, the irony that her whole behavioral thing was mostly his fault had been totally lost to the insensitive jackass.

For sure, Jane liked sex, loved to fuck. It was her favorite thing to do. It occupied her thoughts much of the time, and she craved it like an alcoholic would his next drink. In her younger days, she'd masturbated once, twice, sometimes three times a day to keep her wild impulses under control – but the *awakening* of her addiction had been entirely her husband's doing.

Up to a certain point in their short marriage, Jane had been perfectly content with their once-a-week missionary position – doggie on birthdays and special occasions only – and her Rob Lowe fantasies. And then one day, completely out of the blue, Ronnie had merrily announced that '*I'd like us to try swinging*', and despite his wife's obvious reticence, Ronnie had been most insistent that they give the whole swapping lifestyle '*a go*'. He sold it to Jane in terms of it being their very own, very personal experiment in the thrill of illicit sex with no consequences. And it had been Ronnie who had pushed her into fucking other women, the excitement of multiple partners, orgies, and – most arousing of all – no boundaries.

At first, the thought of sharing her beloved husband with other women, and of her having sex with other men had repulsed Jane. But, in the interests of her own, lifelong, and personal philosophy of '*try anything once*' and her ingrained desire to please her man: Jane had set aside her reluctance and better judgment and had thrown herself whole heartedly into the scene.

They'd eased themselves into it by visiting a local swinger's club, ostensibly to observe. Much to her astonishment and delight, Jane had found the whole thing to be an absolute turn-on, as if a long dormant switch had been thrown in her brain. Suddenly, she simply couldn't get enough of the erotic excitement of the acres of sweating, thrusting flesh unashamedly on show, the atmosphere that fairly oozed sexuality, and the up-front honesty and bluntness of the participants. Once indoctrinated, Jane had found the scene in all its machinations refreshing, boundlessly exciting, and of course, highly addictive.

Before she'd known, Jane had found herself totally immersed in the delights of being buried beneath a heaving, sweaty mound of naked bodies on the orgy bed, giving and receiving pleasure with countless anonymous hedonists, of seducing strangers of both sexes – Jane was none too concerned about with whom she derived her gratification – in more Jacuzzis than she cared to count; of spending sleepless nights with hot couples in some nearby fleapit motel with her husband. Playing. Watching. Enjoying. Fucking.

Jane had fallen into her role of Predatory Bitch with aplomb. She would stride into the swinger's clubs brimming over with sexual confidence, wearing her skimpiest black dress, and fuck-me heels. There, she'd hand-pick the hottest people in the place that *she* wished to enjoy, and let them know just how lucky they were to have caught her attention, and from there, she would extract her delight from their willing bodies, usually in full view of everyone else in the club.

Of course, Husband had loved every sordid minute of it; he got his kicks from watching her with other women, men, and whole groups of guys who would just use Jane and leave her spent and dripping with their secretions. But moreover, he lived for the reliving of each and every sweaty, sticky moment in their marital bed for weeks after each encounter. He'd make Jane describe in vivid detail every pussy, cock, ass, and tit she experienced, and how it felt to be such a wanton slut for him and how did she feel when she watched her own beloved husband driving his dick deep inside some girl she'd just licked out?

They were heady times, indeed for Jane, an awakening of a sexual freedom that she could only ever have dreamt about, all made possible by Ronnie Lucas.

And then, Jane had made the unavoidable mistake of

falling in love.

They'd hooked up with a wonderful couple – Cole and Alesha – who Ronnie had found on an online swinger's dating site. The foursome graduated from casual fucking to becoming regular friends out of the bedroom as well since they all got along so famously.

And therein lay the big mistake...

The symptoms had all been there, plain as the nose on Jane's face, but she had chosen to ignore them. And, before she'd known what was happening to her, Jane had fallen head over heels in love.

With Cole *and* Alesha.

She remembered, at the time, how she'd found it peculiar that whilst her husband was more than delighted to see her physically involved with other people, he was seriously threatened by any emotional involvement. Ronnie simply couldn't handle it. When he found out how Jane felt about their new friends, he'd gone off at the deep end and called a halt to the entire lifestyle thing. Since they had agreed at the onset that either one had the power of veto, Jane was forced to go along with her husband's decision, and she was sure she would be okay with that in the long run.

But what she couldn't deal with was Ronnie's ignoring her as she went through the painful gamut of emotions that invariably follow any relationship breakdown. She'd gone through a horrendous time of emotional withdrawal from Cole and Alesha, and not once had Ronnie shown a grain of understanding, or offered any consolation: he'd simply retreated behind a facade of cold indifference toward his wife.

Ronnie Lucas had created his monster and then completely panicked when his wife grasped at the opportunities he'd offered to her like a child lost in a candy store. Deep down, Jane guessed, her husband hadn't been able to handle her newfound sexual confidence and had been terrified when what he'd sparked in her had raced way beyond his control.

And that had been that – end of marriage.

And now, Ronnie was married to the second Mrs. Lucas, a plain, moderately plump girl from Wisconsin, and they were doing the whole family thing complete with dog and a white picket fence, and the last Jane had heard he was happy.

Jane couldn't help but smile as she recalled the piles of naked, copulating bodies she had often found herself beneath, the debauched nights of wild sex with men and women she knew she had no care to ever see again, the frisson of experimenting with fetishes she never knew existed up until the moment she was introduced to them - of exploring the new and the forbidden. And in her more retrospective, philosophical moments, Jane would often wonder if Ronnie had brought about the metamorphosis, or if he had merely catalyzed something latent within her psyche? In other words, was it *his* fault that she couldn't keep her hands off her students, or *hers*?

Jane sighed and absently shone her flashlight into the air vent one more time.

Nothing.

Perhaps she should just tear off the flimsy mesh covering and crawl into the vent? There was certainly more than enough space in there to accommodate her slim frame. That way, she would get to play Big Game Hunter and poke around to see what may be living inside the dark, dank – and vaguely Freudian – air vent, or what might be lurking around the duct's bend.

"I think not," she scolded herself as the hairs on the back of her neck stood to attention. "That's the other thing I have students for," Jane allowed herself a wry chuckle at this and walked away from the vent.

4

The centipede shied away from the light's inquisitive search as her primitive ocelli registered the sharp, painful contrast between the concealing dark and the danger of being exposed by the light. Her antennae twitched, and she tasted the clammy air.

Finally, the light moved away, and she listened awhile to the noises that her tormentor made, which along with the salty tang of sweating flesh informed the creature that there was definitely prey for the taking. She moved with an instinctive caution, smoothly and silently toward the sounds driven by her hunger.

This egress from the air vent was blocked by a thin covering that the centipede could see – and sense – through. She had been confronted with many others like it in around her domain, so she knew through experience that it would take no effort at all to push through the flimsy barrier. In the cover of the shadows, she tapped at the delicate mesh with her antennae, probed at it with her front legs, and tested it, her target closer now.

The centipede pushed her head against the mesh, and it began to give way.

5

The poolroom door burst open and startled Jane. Jolted from her private thoughts, she dropped her snake hook, which rattled noisily to the tiled floor.

"Hey! Look what we found!" Mel shouted excitedly as she charged into the room like a little kid who's just wiped his own ass for the first time. She was followed closely by Darlene, Fred, and hot on *their* heels, a slightly out of breath Martha-Ray. "He's a doozy!" Mel lifted the specimen jar to show off its contents, struggling with both hands to support the weight of its contents.

"It has to be at least twenty-four inches long, probably

thirty!" Darlene was a little more reserved but had a broad smile beaming across her face. "What did you guys get?" she asked Fred.

"Nothing," Fred replied and looked crestfallen, his ego dented at being beaten at something – *anything* – by a girl. "We saw a couple of centipedes – big ones – and we almost caught one." He shrugged his broad shoulders. "But it's pretty messed up on the fifth – I mean, up there." His face reddened at his *faux pas,* and Martha-Ray shot him a withering glance.

"You went up to the fifth floor?" Jane didn't hide her exasperation all that well, "After *everything* Mr. Levandowski said?"

"Yeah, kind of," Martha-Ray admitted on Fred's behalf – the cat appeared to have got his tongue, and he just stood and stared at the Professor like some poor, dumb animal about to get hit by a truck. "To be honest, we went up there *because* of what Mr. Levandowski said," she added as if that went some way toward justification.

"Give me strength," Jane sighed. "I guess it had to be inevitable, especially with you, Fred. Tell a kid not to do something and all that." She rolled her eyes and decided to leave it be for now. After all, it's precisely what she would have done in their shoes.

Jane gathered her students around to check out the two 'pedes that she had caught all by herself, whilst all the while fighting against her own childish self to prevent the creeping feeling of inadequacy. This wasn't a contest after all, and what *was* important here was that they had actually found – and captured – living examples of the unusually large 'pede.

"These are a little on the small side Professor Lucas," Mel teased with an impish grin as she peered at one of the professor's specimens. The centipede within reared up and scraped at the glass with pointed legs that made a faint *scrit – scrit – scrit* sound like dozens of tiny fingernails on a chalkboard. She thought that the creature had what could easily pass as a *determined* look on its face as it did its level best to claw through the side of the jar.

"You know what they say, Melanie, size isn't everything," Martha-Ray giggled.

Darlene snorted and nudged Fred hard in the ribs with her elbow. Fred retorted with a silent, mouthed '*fuck you,*' and then stepped playfully on Darlene's toe to make her squeal.

6

The centipede shuffled back into the safety of the darkness in the vent, fearful of the sudden burst of noise and the overpowering stench of angry pheromones that came along with it; the smell from the smaller centipedes imprisoned by the humans a warning that what she had considered a helpless meal was capable of causing her harm.

She backed away.

Soon, hunger would prevail and override her fears.

And then she would feed.

CHAPTER SEVEN

1

"We found all kinds of weird shit up there," Fred regaled the girls; as always, he was delighted to be the center of their attention. Mel, Martha-Ray, and Darlene sat around him on the cabana bed, and he looked to be as happy as a pig in shit. The students had all too soon tired of gawking at the centipedes they'd captured and of tapping on the jars to piss them off and make them strike at the glass with their fangs. Mel had declared an impromptu break time, and they'd all decided to put their feet up before the next round of critter chasing. The Prof' was still enthralled by the specimens, of course, and whilst Fred played up to his newfound hero status on the bed, she worked diligently across the room, photographing the 'pedes and making copious notes on her cell phone.

Fred had decided against mentioning the baby's corpse he and Martha-Ray had found during their illicit trip to the Fifth; didn't want to spoil the mood, and he was sure that his bug-hunt partner wouldn't want to be reminded of it.

She'd seemed pretty shaken up by the tiny, rotted corpse, and Fred possessed at least enough empathy in his soul to not rake over those particular old coals. Besides, he'd gotten to know Martha-Ray a little and had gained some respect for her as a woman – that, and she looked damned fine the way her heavy breasts bulged out of her swimsuit.

"There were boxes of explosives, bottles of chemicals, and bits of dead people," Fred continued with his voice lowered. "It looked like a bomb factory to me."

"And you'd know what a bomb factory looks like?" Mel chastised. "There's a lot of those on Daddy's ranch, are there?"

"Well, no. But it looked like what I would *expect* one would look like," Fred stammered. He hated the way Mel continually put him down, had no idea what he'd ever done to make her so hostile toward him, especially since she was always the epitome of sweetness to absolutely *everyone* else. Fred considered throwing out a cutting remark of his own, knowing now what he did about Mel and the professor's mutual pussy licking, but no, he checked himself, better to keep that one stored up for a bigger occasion.

"Show 'em what you found," Martha-Ray cut in. She was more than happy to let Fred take the limelight for their clandestine trip to the forbidden floor. She had never been comfortable in the spotlight and was still upset about stumbling upon the baby's body; she'd made her own decision not to raise the subject, mostly so she could pretend that maybe she'd only imagined its sunken face and gaping, toothless grin.

Fred pulled out the shard of thin metal he'd found and placed it on the bed. "It has the radioactivity symbol on it," he explained.

"Fred thinks someone was making a dirty bomb up there," Martha-Ray said with admiration in her tone.

"Really?" Jane stifled the disbelief in her voice. She'd wandered over to the cabana with thoughts of motivating her students back into action; she was positive there'd be bigger specimens to collect if they looked long – and hard – enough.

"I – I guess so." Fred suddenly felt uncomfortable under the scrutiny of his Professor and peers. He was conscious of the fact that there'd most likely to be questions that he couldn't answer – there always was, once he stepped out of his comfort zone – although he would usually (and with much frustration) come up with the answers sometime later. It wasn't that Fred was dumb, it just took his brain a while longer than most to retrieve the information he'd put into it.

"It would go some way toward explaining the overkill when they boarded the hotel," Fred struggled on. "I mean – steel sheets on every external door and window for a gas explosion? And it would also explain why they haven't demolished the hotel yet. There's no way they'd dare pull the building down and risk the contamination getting outside, they'd want to keep it contained," Fred went on, his eyes seeking Darlene's for support. "And heck, it might even explain the oversized Scolopendras we've been chasing. You said yourself that they don't normally grow bigger than twelve inches."

"I'm saying," Mel burst out. She and Darlene giggled.

"It's *Scolopendridae,*" Jane corrected, "and as for the size of the specimens, there are a whole manner of things that could have caused that other than mutation by radiation; they are hardly *Godzilla,* Fred." Jane gave Fred a warm smile; she had no wish to add to his obvious unease. "And my guess would be that they haven't demolished the hotel because the damage sustained in the explosion wasn't really all that severe, and they plan to reopen it one day. And as for the excessive boarding-up – this place is on the outskirts of a small desert town. Do you know how hard it is to legally remove squatters once they've moved in?"

"No, Ma'am," Fred replied in all honesty. "All I know is that what happened up there was no gas explosion –

there's not even a gas *pipe*! And this piece of metal is clearly part of a box that most likely contained something radioactive," Fred used his dramatic voice, once again relishing the attention, especially from Darlene. "We should check this out. Did you bring a Geiger counter?" he asked.

"Of course, I brought a Geiger counter," Jane told him, "just what kind of Zoologist would I be if I didn't bring a Geiger counter to my bug-hunt?"

"You did? Great!" Fred exclaimed.

Jane smiled her wry smile at him. "I didn't bring a Geiger counter, Fred," she laughed and immediately regretted her maladroit attempt at humor. Fred's face flushed and fell as the others sniggered at his expense.

"Oh," he mumbled.

"Mel couldn't even pack the first aid kit, let alone scientific equipment," Jane redirected the group's attention toward Mel; damned if she didn't want a bruised male ego to nursemaid and Mel was a relaxed foil. "I guess that one will have to wait until we get back. In the meantime, I'd say that this was nothing to worry about."

Jane wandered back over to the three centipedes in the specimen jars: she figured she wasn't going to get much more out of her students since they already seemed to be very much entrenched in *weekend mode*. The two smaller 'pedes that she had caught were now coiled up like rusted barbed wire at the bottom of their respective prisons. The larger 'pede that Mel and Darlene had collected was much more active: it agitated and crawled around the bottom of the jar, and as Jane approached, it reared up to stab at the lid with its fangs. Jane picked up the jar and examined the lively specimen, her eyes drawn to the glinting droplets of clear venom it had deposited on the underside of the lid;all the while, she did her damndest not to give away just how much the creatures were making her skin crawl.

Not much of a secret really.

They all knew.

"Okay," Jane announced as she placed the jar back down, "I guess we're done here." She reached for her cell phone. "I'll call Len – Mr. Levandowski…"

"Aw, do you have to?" Mel whined.

"If you want to get out of here and go home, yes I do." Jane began to search for Levandowski's number under her dialed numbers menu.

"But it's Saturday night. And how often are we going to have the opportunity to stay in a place like this – let alone have it all to ourselves?" Mel reasoned.

"Yeah," Darlene backed her friend up, "we could always stay here and party a little." Pausing for effect, she reached inside her backpack. "And hey, look what we found!" She pulled out a fist full of miniature liquor bottles and scattered them across the bed. "And there are *tons* more where these came from!" she giggled.

All four students looked at Jane with childish expectations on their faces. They reminded her of a group of ten-year-olds pleading to stay up to watch the late-night scary movie.

"I guess we could stay a few hours longer and weather out the worst of the storm," Jane conceded, knowing damned well she was out-voted four-to-one. Say no now, and she'd lose their interest for the rest of the semester. What else could she do? For heaven's sake, even the fat girl, Martha-Ray had turned up in a swimsuit! "A few hours," Jane emphasized, "and *then* I call Mr. Levandowski."

Mel and Darlene squealed with delight and took no time at all in stripping down to their inappropriately miniscule bikinis and jump into the warm pool. Fred peeled off his shirt and followed suit. Martha-Ray remained next to Jane and looked at her professor with mournful cow-eyes, guilt written all over her face. "I'd be happy to help you look for more centipedes, Professor Lucas," she said, her voice barely audible.

"Go on, Martha-Ray, have some fun," Jane reassured.

Martha-Ray's face brightened up immediately. She jumped from the bed, pulled down her skirt, kicked off her flip-flops, and hurled herself with very little grace into the warm, welcoming water.

Jane watched with a fond smile as her students let off steam, wishing now that she had the foresight to wear a bikini too. However, since she had not been a part of her student's conspiracy to turn her field trip into a pool party, she'd had no way of knowing.

She glanced around, although not quite sure who she was expecting to be there to be looking in an abandoned, locked hotel, and pulled her shirt up over her head. Jane stripped down to her bra and black, utilitarian panties and noticed with a tingle that she had solicited a sly glance from Mel, who was floating belly-up in the sulfurus water. To hell with it, Jane told herself, it *was* Saturday night after all, and she was totally off the clock!

And with that self-endorsement, Jane Lucas, Professor of Zoology at the U of C and leading virtuoso in all things *Scolopendra*, cannonballed into the pool like a great big kid.

2

Jackson had waited for an hour and change after Fred and Martha-Ray had gone before he dared switch the lights to the fifth floor suite back on (better safe than sorry). He'd been holed up there with his motley crew since they'd sneaked into the Mountainview. Jackson had told Lee and the others that they had to stay put in the suite; he didn't want them wandering around and into the damaged suites across the hallway – at least one of the wrecked rooms looked especially dangerous. His boys had complied without complaint, but Jackson could tell that they were getting restless since they had come close to the guy they were there to see. So close, in fact, they had smelled his cologne.

With time for contemplation, Jackson had begun to wonder if Mel might be being straight with him, after all, and this was actually some kind of buggy field trip. The Mountainview was hardly the salubrious cesspit of debauchery that he'd had in mind when he'd researched Desert Hot Springs on Wikipedia; he'd envisaged a smaller, motel type place, one of those you find on the outskirts of town and that have their own pools out back – pools that often had murky water and smelled a little on the *green* side but populated by a crowd of naked, cavorting hedonists. But this, a boarded up fuck-up of a place with five people – it hardly qualified for *Eyes Wide Shut*.

Still, the irrationally jealous part of Jackson remained convinced that this was all part of some prearranged sex party, despite the down market location. Hell, a rich bitch like Melanie Hernandez probably got off on slumming it with her snobby friends, all part of the turn-on. After all, she was slumming it with *him*, wasn't she?

So, she was here, and *he* was here. Together. That certainly equaled *something* going on, and Jackson was determined to catch her in the act.

"What's wrong with you, man?" Lee questioned. "We coulda' jumped him from the bathroom, grabbed him then and there."

Jackson eyed Lee and wondered why he'd brought him along in the first place. The guy was as thick as pig shit and looked far too much like the retarded one out of the *Goonies* for Jackson's liking. Still, Lee was handy to have around when things got physical; his thick frame, skinned head, and badly inked tattoos made for a fearsome-looking figure, and he wasn't slow at getting into the middle of a scrap. Jackson had seen the guy fight, and he sometimes thought that Lee didn't actually feel pain at all; he was legendary for having beaten three guys near to death despite having a six inch blade stuck in his chest.

Lee had been hanging around Jackson for a few years now, running odd jobs, dishing out beatings wherever necessary, and intimidating clients and rival gang bangers on the gang's behalf. There were times, though, when Jackson had struggled to contain the guy's violent tendencies, which he figured would become a problem at some point. Jackson was no shrink, but he guessed a lot of the kid's difficulties around people were a result of Lee's deep-rooted detachment issues.

Lee's mom had remarried after his father had moved out when Lee had been just three years old. This was particularly unfortunate for Lee on two counts: One, new stepdad made it clear that he didn't want Lee around once he and Lee's mom started popping out kids of their own and Two, mom had married a guy called Brian Lee. And that had saddled the poor kid with the unenviable name of Lee-Lee. Made him sound like a fucking panda, Jackson thought. Nicely thought out there, Mrs. Lee!

"Like I told you before," Jackson explained once again with strained patience. "We're just biding our time up here, waiting for the right opportunity to make our move." He stretched out on the luxurious red sofa, and the fashionably aged leather creaked out loud. "You guys never heard the expression *revenge is a dish best served cold*?"

Three blank faces.

"No, I guess you haven't."

"Lee's right," Johnny dared to venture. "We had our chance to get the guy who's nailing your girl." He fiddled absently with his lock-knife. "That's just goddamned disrespectful, that is." Johnny snapped the knife open with a resounding, hollow click that echoed around the room. He yawned and extended his gangly frame across the bed, his feet puffing up tiny dust clouds from the comforter.

"I hear ya', man," Jackson placated the boy, "and that motherfucker's gonna get what's coming to him soon enough. Might let ya cut the nigger bitch he was with a little with that knife of yours; teach her not to fraternize with a white boy. If you're a *good boy*, that is." He smiled at the sociopath on the bed and said, "You'd like that, wouldn't you?"

"You betcha!" Johnny exclaimed. "You gonna let Mikey pop his cherry up her too?" He looked across the room at Mikey Tyler, the other black guy in the gang.

Jackson sighed. "No, Johnny, no, I am not," he said and looked over at Mikey's young and, and now incredibly disappointed face. "I'm sorry, Mikey, that's one thing you're gonna have to sort out all by yourself," Jackson told him.

"This place is giving me the fuckin' creeps," Mikey blurted out as he crossed the room toward Lee. He'd not been listening; as usual, he was off merrily having imaginary conversations in his head that he now verbalized half-way through. "It's like Mary Celeste, everything's like the people just vanished."

"It's *the* Marie Celeste," Johnny spat, "you shit-for-brains thick-wad! It's fucking German."

Jackson shook his head at the sad irony and outrageous lack of education that he had inadvertently surrounded himself with. Jesus shit, just how *had* he landed himself with this dumb ass bunch again?

"I don't think it's creepy at all, I think it's amazing that everything is just as it was all those years ago. It's like it's been trapped in time," uncharacteristic rhetoric from Lee.

"For fuck's sakes, man!" Johnny jumped right in his shit – with both feet. "You heard what the old man told the fucking bookworms! It's only been five years, not five-hundred! It's not like we're in the fucking Titanic!"

"Well, that's as maybe," Lee defended, "but at least it's got these!"

With that, Lee flung open the mini-bar door and grinned at the chinking bottles and cans of booze that rattled within. He grabbed a small but perfect *Famous Grouse* bottle and twisted off its cap.

"No, you don't!" Jackson leaped from the couch and knocked the bottle from Lee's hand. "We gotta stay alert, focused." He pulled a fat joint from his pocket, lit it, drew down the first flush of acrid smoke deep into his lungs, and waited for that first glorious buzz to kick in. "We got serious stuff to do, and I'm not having you all fucking drunk," he told Lee as marijuana smoke puffed from his mouth, illustrating his words. He passed the bifta to Lee to cheer him up a little.

"Hey!" Mikey enthused as he peered into themini-bar, "they got salted peanuts too!"

CHAPTER EIGHT

1

The students had arranged five of the wooden recliners into a rough circle at the far end of the pool and nearest cabanas. Each one faced inward as if they were around an imaginary campfire. They had also righted the upended bed to cover up the worst of Virginia Mendoza's bloodstain.

"I have to say – and I think I speak for all of us – that this has turned out not all that bad for a Saturday night," Mel announced, her speech already ponderous and slurred. "I'd like to propose a toast to our Professor Jane!" She raised up a diminutive bottle of gin and then downed it in one.

Jane looked across at the girl and allowed her eyes to soak up the sight of the girl's smooth, lithe body, resplendent and barely contained within its floral bikini. Jane rolled her eyes and hoped that her student/lover's alcohol-fuelled over-familiarity would not give away their secret. Now *there* was trouble that Jane could well do without.

"Yeah, we owe you big time, Prof'," Darlene added. She was sitting on Fred's recliner, which was across from the Professor's. Darlene nestled snugly between Fred's muscular legs and was wearing his T-shirt over her bikini. Furtive movement under the shirt gave away the fact that her sometime boyfriend had one of his huge hands on her breasts and was massaging it like one would an executive stress toy. Darlene didn't appear to mind in the least; she was quite tipsy herself and nursed the remains of one of Mel's Tequila bottles between her knees.

"I guess it's the least I could do," Jane said. "After all, you guys were kind enough to give up your weekend for my bug-hunt."

That phrase again.

Levandowski really had gotten under Jane's skin.

Jane lay back on her recliner, determined to put the old man at the farthest reaches of her mind, and concentrated on enjoying the balmy heat of the room, the subdued light, and the pleasant company. She was beginning to feel a degree of camaraderie with her students, although she was feeling more than a little self-conscious at being the only one who had bothered to dress after swimming. Whilst the others had maintained some state of undress, Jane figured it had been enough that they'd seen her swimming in her bra and sensible panties without her lounging around in said undergarments, away from the concealing water.

Mel's recliner was next to Jane's, and the girl was, to all intents and purposes, naked. Her bikini comprised three inadequately sized triangles of cloth and an array of string that managed – more or less – to hold the triangles in place. Her firm breasts bulged either side of the top, and the thin string of her briefs disappeared between her perfectly round butt cheeks – from the back, she did actually appear to be naked.

When they'd all vacated the pool, having been in there so long that their fingers and toes had wrinkled up like little pink raisins, Darlene had covered herself up with Fred's shirt. She'd knotted it to expose her six-pack midriff and leave her bikini briefs on show, and Fred clad only in his swim shorts. Martha-Ray, the usually awkward one, was quite happy to let everything hang out in her cut-away, and the tops of her Rubenesque breasts were merrily escaping out from the plunging neckline.

Jane imagined the atmosphere of sex in the room to be almost tangible. The scent of sweating bodies and pheromones was all-pervading and filled the humid air with the acrid stink of promise. Of course, it could simply have been her overactive imagination at play and her carnal thoughts were nothing more than further evidence of the insatiable nymphomania that her ex-husband had accused her of, but she still liked to run with such thoughts as they made her feel all kind of warm inside. At times such as this, Jane was pleased that she wasn't a man – as there would have been a formidable erection to hide right now. As it was, she could squeeze her thighs together and ignore the damp heat that emanated from deep between them.

"Can I ask you a personal question, Professor Lucas?" Darlene enquired.

"Sure," Jane cringed inside. Here it comes, *the* awkward question now that alcohol had been imbibed and inhibitions lowered: *is it true that you're fucking Mel?* Jane braced herself, mentally rehearsing a response. Perhaps her trust in Mel to be discrete about their dalliances had been misplaced?

"How come you chose to study centipedes?" Darlene asked, "when it's obvious to – like, *everybody* – that you really hate them?"

Jane took a deep breath and tried not to show her relief. "It's not really something I like to talk about, Darlene." Her lip quivered.

"You didn't think that we knew?" Martha-Ray chipped in.

"Honestly?" Jane said, "No, I didn't. I thought I was hiding it well."

Darlene, Mel, Fred, and Martha-Ray exchanged a glance and a smirk.

"It's probably the worst kept secret in the faculty," Mel said and a sly smile played across her luscious lips.

"Well, seeing as though everyone already knows." Jane looked at each of her students in turn, at the serious expressions on their faces. "And as we're all friends chilling out together, I guess I wouldn't mind sharing." Jane smiled to herself. No questions about how she preferred to enjoy her students between lectures and tutorials – live to fight another day girl! "I wouldn't say I *hate* them," she said. "It's more of a phobia, I guess."

"Question still stands," Mel chimed in. "We've all seen how you are around them; your hands shake and everything. You're even squeamish with pictures of centipedes."

"Yeah, and there's the way you always call 'em *'pedes* instead of centipedes," Martha-Ray added. "It's as if you can't even stand to say the whole word."

"Like I said, it's a phobia," Jane began to explain. "I call it *scolopendraphobia* –"

"– irrational fear of giant centipedes," Martha-Ray translated for everyone's benefit. "Is that a *real* phobia?"

"It is to me," Jane laughed. "It's a word I made up, and since *I'm* the scientific expert, I'm allowed to do that. It's probably the most specific phobia in the world." The official word that Jane knew all too well was *chilopodophobia*, which only that covered *all* of the myriapods, and she really had no beef with millipedes or even the smaller members of the centipede clan for that matter. So *scolopendraphobia* was actually more appropriate for how she felt about *gigantea*, and as she'd said – she was the goddamned expert!

"Only it's not an *irrational* fear, is it?" Mel asked. "Those things can really hurt you."

"No more than a bee or a spider can, and 'there are plenty of people scared shitless by both of those," Jane told her. "Do you realize that more people die each year of bee stings than snake bites?"

"Question's still hanging," Darlene chastised and squirmed a little at Fred's touch.

"Okay, okay." A deep breath. "I chose to study Zoology because of my life-long love of animals," Jane explained whilst doing her damndest not to sound all Pollyanna lame. It was the same line she'd been giving out to justify her chosen career path since college, and she'd always thought it sounded like the intro to a Julie Andrews song in a movie with fucking orphans in it. And, each time Jane told the beginning of this story, she feared that might sound like the ringlet-haired, little girl in the kid's books, the one who loved ponies and went on to become an Olympic show-jumper. And it made her cringe every time.

"Apart from giant centipedes," Fred reminded with a grin.

"Apart from the 'pedes," Jane agreed, "Thank you, Fred." She continued, "I chose to specialize in the *Scolopendridae* family partly as some form of perverse aversion therapy, but mostly because I'm a stubborn bitch and there was absolutely no way I was going to let some dumb myriapod get the better of me."

Everyone laughed with her.

"Have you always been phobic of them?" Darlene asked.

"No, not always," Jane told her, "but that's *really* something I don't like to talk about."

"Aw, go on," Martha-Ray moaned, "You can't leave us hanging." Martha-Ray always did love a good personal angst story.

"It's – it's too painful," Jane said, her voice softening, "even after all of these years."

"Come on, Prof'," Mel coaxed, again with that

flirtatious hint toward dangerous familiarity. "You said it yourself, we're all friends here." Surreptitiously, she stroked Jane's leg with a soft foot, which set off a chain reaction of senses that settled into a hot glow in Jane's lower belly.

"Okay, Okay," Jane conceded and gave out a heavy sigh. "But please, you have to understand just how hard this is for me – I've only ever told this story to my therapist. And for God's sake, you must all promise me that you'll never repeat it – if the Dean found out that his Head of Zoology was scared of her specialist subject…"

"– pinkie promise!" Mel squealed with intoxicated glee. She sat up and held aloft both of her pinkie fingers to illustrate just how *really, really* serious she was. She giggled at this, and her bountiful breasts jiggled about deliciously in her scarce top.

"What the hell," Jane crumbled, "if it helps you cynical lot to understand where I'm coming from a little better, what do I have to lose?"

Jane studied the four intense faces that now hung on her every word, and she began, "my parents were eminent entomologists back in the Eighties, I suppose that's how I ended up in the position I'm in today –"

"– I heard that you ended up in the position you are today because you fucked the Dean." A tipsy Darlene blurted out; she could always be relied upon for the most entertaining and inappropriate alcohol-induced Tourette's.

"Darlene!" Mel snapped.

An awkward pause, then Jane smiled. "Yeah, I heard that too," she said.

"Sorry." Darlene looked nothing of the sort. She jumped and let out a squeak as Fred gave her nipple a firm twist.

"As I was saying," Jane continued, "my parents made the decision early on to take me along with them on all of their expeditions. They figured that there was a better education to be had traveling the world and experiencing everything it had to offer. That's how I got to see the Sahara Desert, the Steppes in the Former Soviet Republic, Antarctica, what's left of the forests in England, the Galapagos Archipelago, the Andes and of course, every naturalist's wet dream, the Amazonian Rain Forest." Jane paused. She felt a little sorry for her wide-eyed students; she knew all too well what they were missing out on in their field of study. In today's age of budget cuts and zero finance for anything that wasn't space, computing, weaponry, or green energy-related, this trip to the Coachella Valley was the farthest afield they were likely to get.

Jane picked up her train of thought; "I was ten years old when they took me to the Amazon basin for the first time –"

- and it was absolutely mind-blowing, even when she allowed for the superlative sights she had already seen in her ten short years on the planet.

The young Jane Lucas – Whitacre as she had been then – stared up at the green canopy that towering way above her head. The breathtaking scale of the magnificent trees stretching up to the heavens had filled her with an all-encompassing, inspiring awe, and it had made her feel very, very small indeed. Little did she appreciate it at the time, but these were her golden years of wonder and exploration – where the future Professor Jane Lucas would be molded.

If only she had known then what she knew now?

There was life of every form absolutely everywhere she cared to look. Every branch, twig, and leaf harbored an inhabitant of some description, be it a snake, spider, beetle, or even some non-identifiable viral disease that infected the trees with abundant bulbous cankers that weighed down the branches. Even beneath Jane's feet, the ground simply teemed and heaved with movement; myriad arthropods burrowed and hunted and lived and died in the leaf litter, snaking rivulets of ants went about their busy labors, and naturally, there were the ubiquitous, uncountable quantities of beetles.

Jane had recalled her favorite quote – attributed to both J.B.S. Haldane and Charles Darwin – that 'the Creator, if he exists, must have an inordinate fondness for beetles!' She smiled, that idea must have been inspired by a place such as this.

It was there, standing in the rainforest deep in the heart of South America and waiting for the rain to ease up so she could further explore this magical place that Jane had met with her very first giant centipede.

She'd already known its name – Scolopendra gigantea – from the books on biodiversity that her parents had given her in preparation for the trip. She knew that the creatures had a nasty bite, a bad temper, and could run much quicker that one would give them credit for. And her ten-year-old mind had teased her, 'well duh, they have a hundred legs – of course, they're going to run fast!'

"It's important that you know what lives in the forest," Mom had told her, peering over the top of her then fashionable thick-rimmed, tortoiseshell spectacles in that stern manner that only Mom could pull off. "There are a lot of dangerous things living in the rain forest: things that look like other things, things that look like nothing, and things that can – and will – kill you." Of course, this had been a matter-of-fact conversation with a little girl who had already seen so much of Mother Nature's death-dealing. Jane, far from being scared, had remained totally unphased – actually excited – by the whole idea of potential death at every turn.

Young Jane had devoured each and every one of her mom's books. She'd memorized facts and figures about each of the critters she was likely to come across, which ones to avoid and which ones she could poke at and investigate.

Which is why the maroon red 'pede with the yellow legs that scurried toward her on the forest's leafy carpet had held little fear.

'A bite just a little worse than a bee-sting,' *she'd read. And although she didn't want to get bitten (she knew first-hand that bee stings could* really *hurt sometimes), Jane had known that the eight-inch myriapod was nothing to be too scared of so had spent a happy quarter-hour toying with the creature by letting it crawl up and down a thin stick she'd snapped from a nearby Mahogany tree. She'd been entranced by the way the animal's spiky legs moved in that wave-like motion typical of the genus; and she'd loved the way the centipede had tapped at both the stick and the air with its antennae whilst its flat, unmoving eyes seemed to watch her with as much fascination as she had in contemplating it.*

And then, as quickly as it had begun, the rain had stopped. It was as if the great rainforest God had decided on enough rain for today and simply switched off the faucet. Jane had replaced the centipede carefully back on the ground under a feathery bush and made her way back to the camp where Mom and Dad were fixing dinner.

Jane's parents were – to her – nothing out of the ordinary. Sure, her friends had parents who were accountants, lawyers, bored housewives (in those days, the latter did prefer the term homemakers, *as if cooking and cleaning were a real job) who were usually half way to drunk on the cooking sherry before Husband came home from a hard day at the office. Her mom and dad were just regular folks, plain old Bob and Sue Whitacre. It just so happened that they traveled the globe and studied bugs for a living. No big deal.*

That night, Jane lay in the humidity of her khaki tent and fell asleep to the hypnotic cacophony of animal calls that split the darkness; the sounds of insects and frogs that were broken up on occasion by a solitary monkey or the chirrup of a hunting bat. Intermittently there would be a blood-curdling scream of something caught and killed by something else; 'Mother Nature red in tooth and claw' (she knew this to be Tennyson, of course).

It was screaming of an altogether different kind that had awoken her.

Shrill, piercing, it startled Jane from her deep, dreamless sleep. In a sleepy blur, she had switched on her lantern, unzipped her canvas door, and dashed across to her parent's tent.

Jane would never, ever be able to drive from her mind the sound of her mother's screams. Agonizing, terrified howls filled with panic and so much pain that drowned out the forest's own screams.

As Jane neared the tent, her mother had staggered through the open flap with her arms flailing. Jane could see in the cold light of her lantern that Mom had ripped off her night-clothes and was utterly naked and trying desperately to pull things off of her body. Dark, long shapes that clung to her and tugged at her flesh with long, spiky legs and sharp, tearing fangs.

Centipedes.

There had been dozens of them, maybe even many more than that, it was hard to tell among the flickering shadows and the chaos – they crawled and jostled on Sue Whitacre's pale flesh, clinging, biting, chewing.

Jane screamed, that high scream that all little girls have inside them. Unfortunately, apart from the dense forest and its vast array of uncaring inhabitants, there was no one to hear her.

"Stay back, Janey!" Mom had called out as she collapsed to her knees as the 'pede venom poisoned her system. "Don't come –"

Jane had ignored her Mother and picked up a stick. Bravely, she stepped forward, brandishing it like a sword.

But where was Dad? Why wasn't he helping?

Jane hit at the creatures on her mom, hit them as hard as she could, and hadn't realized that some of the long, dark snakes on her mother's body was actually blood. Mom grew quickly weak and fell face down into the forest floor. There she'd lain, squirming in agony and clawing at the leaf litter with desperate hands as if trying to burrow down in to the earth to escape her torment.

Jane had sobbed as she beat at the creatures that were eating her Mother – even long after her Mom's body had given up, and she lay quite still.

It was then Jane had glanced inside Mom and Dad's tent.

What was left of Bob Whitacre was still in his sleeping bag on the green, canvas cot. The bag itself was a writhing, pulsing mass filled with centipedes, and their movement gave the perverse appearance that Dad was still breathing. Jane saw that his face was completely gone, now nothing more than slivers of flesh that clung to bloodied bone, chewed away by the creatures that had killed him. Half of one eye bobbled around in its socket as if trying to focus on Jane, its movement created by the giant centipede that was busy chewing on the succulent orb.

Dad's other eye had been – quite simply – not there.

The 'pedes coiled themselves around her father's skull, burrowed into his empty eye socket, and the twin holes where his delightfully beaky Roman nose had once proudly sat. The creatures gnawed on the bloodied nubs of his ears and tunneled inside his head, and Dad's jaw hung slackly in the death's head grin she had seen so many times on pictures of human skulls – only this one was her own Father's – and blood-drenched centipedes feasted on his tongue.

Jane had screamed so loudly, and for so long, that it had made her throat bleed.

Jane allowed the shocked silence to finish the story. Mel, Martha-Ray, and Darlene stared at her in disbelief, and Fred looked like he was about to say farewell to his Tequila.

"Oh my God," Mel spoke first, "That is the worst thing I ever heard." She placed a warm, comforting hand on Jane's knee.

"Yeah, that must have been so terrible for you," Darlene added, "you poor thing."

Martha-Ray was tearful. "How on earth did you ever even begin to deal with something like that?"

"Jeez, Professor Lucas, that really is the worse thing I've ever heard too," Fred told her. "There's no wonder you're scared of centip – sorry, *'pedes*."

"And you are *so* brave working with them after-after *that*," Martha-Ray told her. "There's no way on Earth I could ever –"

Jane looked at each of her students in turn, her face terribly deadpan. Then she said, "You should see your faces." She grinned at them. "I wish I'd taken a picture!" Then Jane broke into a laugh as she saw realization dawn collectively on their blank faces.

"You made all that up?" Martha-Ray gasped.

"Yep," Jane nodded.

"No!" Mel was incredulous.

"Your parents weren't really killed by giant centipedes?" Fred finally spoke up, once again never the quickest to catch on. He pulled Darlene tighter to his body, pressed her against his chest.

"Good heavens, no!" Jane said, "not even a little bit; they're both rotting away peacefully in a retirement community in Tampa! The only thing that's going to eat those two is their bingo addiction and boredom." Jane giggled, highly amused by the looks of astonishment on each of the four faces. "Or, quite possibly the alligators," she mused.

Jane had been telling that tale for more years than she cared to remember. Every batch of students would get *The Story* once the opportunity presented itself. And Jane was always sure to make damned sure that it did. She had long ago figured it out to be by far the best way to approach her very obvious phobia toward 'pedes - attack is the best form of defense and all that. It was her way of avoiding the inevitable pranks of fake 'pedes in her desk drawers and lab coat pockets.

And to date, it had never failed her – got 'em every time. Jane was particularly proud of her performance on this occasion, all she'd needed was a flashlight under her chin to uplight her face, and the moment would have been perfect.

"I can't believe you made all that up," Mel said, and she sounded just a tad hurt, "just to make us feel sorry for you."

"It was more to frighten you in the time-honored tradition of scary campfire stories," Jane told her. "Mom and Dad used to scare me shitless with those all the time on our trips, bless their hearts," She explained. "But a little sympathy is always appreciated, no matter how fleeting."

Then, they all laughed together, the traditional teacher/student barrier lowered still further, friendships established.

Job done.

"So, come on, what's the real reason for your Centipedaphobia?" Darlene enquired. As she spoke she slipped one hand behind her back to toy with Fred's balls.

"It's *Scolopendraphobia*, if you please," Jane corrected her with a faux-mocking tone. "Well, if you must know the truth, it was all Indiana Jones's fault."

"Didn't he hate *snakes*?" Martha-Ray asked.

"Yes, he did," Jane replied. "But in the second movie there's a scene where his leading lady is in a corridor filled with bugs –"

"– Kate Capshaw," Fred blurted out, much to everyone's amazement. "She played Willie Scott in a silk dress. She looked hot through the whole movie."

"Thank you for that, Fred," Jane said and smiled at him as one might smile at a puppy that's managed to not pee on the carpet for a whole afternoon. "Well, in that particular scene, there are a few seconds where they show a giant 'pede crawling into the heroine's hair. You can tell that it's a dummy head – most likely they had to do that for Health and Safety purposes – but that image got into my brain and just stuck with me all the same."

"And that's it?" Mel's tone was flat, almost disappointed. "You have a phobia just because of a movie?"

"Yes," Jane replied, "but before you go judging me, just think about how many people developed a terror of sharks after *Jaws* hit the theaters." She paused to watch as the dim lights of realization ignited once more in her student's eyes. The fact that it made no sense made perfect sense – wasn't the whole point of phobias is that they are, by definition, *irrational*?"

"Like I told you before, I was going to be damned if I was going to let something so stupid control my life. Do you have any idea how many people avoid spiders, snakes, the number thirteen, and ladders simply because they have a phobia? There's even a phobia of feathers – and just how the hell do you get to be *scared* of feathers?"

"Well, I'm proud of you," Darlene's voice had become all breathy on account of Fred's fingers working their magic beneath her shirt, "we all are."

The students nodded and smiled. A little patronizing, Jane thought, but get it where you can, Old Girl.

"Thank you, Darlene, Guys. And thank you *all* for understanding." Jane made eye contact with each in turn to let them know that she'd allowed them a peek into an incredibly vulnerable part of her. Carefully orchestrated, of course. Now, she could be *certain* that although they now knew her weakness, their empathy would guarantee no rubber 'pedes left in her office, dead 'pedes dropping from doorways, or any other pranks that juvenile minds were capable of conjuring up for the tormenting of others. No, she was perfectly safe now.

Fred let out a soft moan as Darlene gripped his dick.

"Oh, for Christ's sake, will you two just get a fucking room?!" Mel shouted across at them. Fred and Darlene both looked sheepish and shot Jane an imploring look.

Could we?

"You're in an empty, one-hundred-twenty room hotel," Jane answered their silent question, eager to build on her new status as *cool grown-up*. "It really shouldn't be that difficult to find a room, given the circumstances."

Taking her cue before their professor could change her mind, Darlene leaped off the recliner and tugged hard at Fred's hand for him to follow. He stood up as quickly as decorum would allow, self-conscious at the more than obvious bulge of the impressive erection that tented his swim shorts.

"Careful Fred, you could poke someone's eye out with that," Mel smirked.

Fred's face reddened.

"Thanks, Prof," Darlene beamed, "you're the best!" She pulled Fred toward the pool room door like her life depended upon it.

Jane called after them, "Just remember to –"

"– stay off the fifth floor!" Mel and Martha-Ray shouted in unison. Jane giggled along and watched fondly as Fred and Darlene practically sprinted from the room. As horny as those two were right now, she'd bet a safe twenty there was no way they'd ever get as far as the fifth floor.

"I guess we're staying the night then," Mel sighed. She made sure to make deliberate eye contact with Jane and to fill her voice with promise.

"Yes, I guess we are," Jane replied and returned a smile.

2

It was dark and far later than anticipated when Lieutenant Newman finally made his way back home. The drive from the Pierson Boulevard police station through the dust-clogged town had been onerous, to say the least: the swirling, wind-blown sand had all but obscured the squat, single-story houses that lined the streets – this was one of the roughest sandstorms he'd seen in recent years. A quick glance at the green LED clock in his Buick told him that it was almost ten.

As was usual, Newman had worked longer than planned for a Saturday night, having made a concerted effort to catch up on the expanding knoll of paperwork on his desk. The storm that had hit town earlier in the day and was set to pound Desert Hot Springs through the night had made for a quiet day. It happened every time a wind storm hit, and Newman guessed that criminals these days were just too damned pussy to brave a little wind-blown sand.

Some of the guys had been talking about a fatal RTA downtown in the early morning, but Newman had deliberately kept his head down; let the uniforms deal with that one, he'd thought, there was more than enough paper that needed pushing around on his desk as it was.

Newman clambered out of the car and fought with the vicious wind for possession of the door. Gaining the upper hand, he slammed the door shut, bowed his head against the hot, driving wind, and battled toward his front door as the pissed off storm threw needle sharp sand grains into his eyes.

Once inside, Newman shrugged off his jacket, slung it over the back of one of the tall breakfast bar stools, and grabbed himself a hard-earned, cold Miller Lite from the fridge.

Janet was asleep on the sofa, snoring softly with her face scrunched up against the cushion. She had her well-thumbed *Fifty Shades* paperback tented across her chest. Why his wife wanted to spend her time reading that crap was way beyond Newman. He figured there was already enough pain and suffering in the world as it was.

He contemplated his sleeping wife with a love that ran

so deep that it sometimes scared him. She looked so peaceful, must have had an intense day with their little girl to have fallen asleep so soon. Addie had been the perfect gift from the gods to the Newmans, but Christ, could she run a soul ragged? She seemed to have that knack inherent in all pre-schoolers to need something the second their adult sits down, that on top of demanding a constant level of attention that can be both physically and mentally exhausting. With all of the up and down, the *'get me this, I want to do that, can we play the other?'*, there was no wonder that Mom – the erstwhile and consummate party gal – was sound asleep before ten on a Saturday night.

Janet – exhausted or not – had upheld the Newman family tradition of never going to bed until the respective spouse returned home safely. The cop liked that: it was a delightful thread of romance in his wildly cynical world.

There were the nights – few and far between since Addie had come along – where he'd been the one asleep on the sofa whilst Janet had been out on the town with her sister or some of her friends. And of course, there were the all-too numerous nights where Janet had not been to bed at all when he was working a case and had pulled an all-nighter. Such was the life of a cop's wife, Newman reflected. No wonder the divorce rate on the force was so goddamned high.

"Daddy!" Addison spotted that he was home. She tore herself away from her *Snow White* DVD and dashed over to greet him.

Newman picked up his three-year-olddaughter and twirled her around. She kissed his nose.

"I missed you, Daddy. Mommy's sleeping." She put her finger to his lips and whispered, "shhhhh."

"Hey, Addie-potamus, you stayed up to see your old Dad, that's awesome!" Newman kissed her nose right back.

"I have on my Disney Princess jimmies. Mommy said I could stay up," the little girl yawned.

"Well, I think it's way past your bedtime, young lady. Want me to tuck you in?"

"Yes, please!" Addie grinned and wriggled from his arms.

Newman glanced at his wife and decided to let her carry on sleeping and followed his daughter as she scampered to her bedroom.

Addison had been a surprise. Understatement – she had been a complete and utter shock. A three-year-old daughter at his age? He'd never had thought it. Nor, it seemed, would anyone else. Then again, that was what you got for still being virile and marrying a hot babe ten years your junior. It certainly put Newman in good company; James Doohan, Anthony Quinn, Charlie Chaplin had all fathered children in their twilight years, even into their eighties. Having said that, a vasectomy had ensured no more for Don Newman - as much as he adored his beautiful little girl, he was smart enough to know when enough was enough.

Janet was Newman's second wife, and they'd met at a time when he was just coming out of the other side of a particularly horrific divorce. He'd vowed never to marry again, and such had been the first experience; he'd even put as much down in writing and made his partner at the time promise to shoot him in the head if he ever so much as mentioned the *M-word* again!

And then Janet had walked into his life. She'd had her car stolen and called into the station one afternoon to file a report. It really had been that straightforward.

Addie had come along when the ink was barely dry on the marriage license. And with her, Newman had found himself once more plunged neck-deep into the world of sleepless nights, diaper-changing, and everything stinking of baby powder and spit-up. He'd thought he'd done his part at repopulating the planet with the three kids he had sired during his first marriage. But clearly, Mother Nature had other plans for this particular, overly fertile cop.

Newman had relished every minute of renewed fatherhood. He'd even learned to find amusement from the people who assumed him to be Addie's grandfather on account of his mature years and graying hair. Newman had lost count of the number of times he'd heard *'are you being a good girl for your Grampa?'* and *'I'll bet your Grandad is so proud of you.'* His favorite was that time at the gas station when some bum had knocked on his window begging for loose change. The bum had taken one look at Addison sitting in the back seat of the Tahoe and said to Newman *'I'm sorry, buddy, I didn't realize you had your grandson with you'.* Still made Newman smile, that one; just where would one even *start* being offended?

Newman knew well to keep his mind distracted from the knowledge that he'd be into his sixties when Addison turned sixteen. That thought terrified him; he'd never wanted to be an *Old Parent*. And he'd just keep right on telling himself that Addie was keeping him young when in reality he figured the little one was hurtling him toward an early grave.

But, standing there now to watch his perfect little princess brushing her teeth, Newman knew that it would be a sad day for him when she no longer walked by his side, clinging to his middle finger 'till it ached.

"Come along, Pumpkin, no more procrastinating," he ordered, "into bed." Addison complied with only the merest hint of protest, indicative that she was ready for sleep.

"Daddy?" Addie asked, her eyelids drooping the second her head hit the pillow.

"What, sweetie?" Newman paused at the door.

"What happened to Snow White?"

"Well," Newman replied in a soft, comforting voice, "she bit the apple that the bad witch lady gave her and she fell asleep."

"Yeah," his daughter paused. "And she's dead too."

Newman grinned. "Goodnight, Sweetpea," he

whispered and gently closed the door.

Janet's rhythmic snoring from the living room sounded like someone trying to start up an old chainsaw, a sure sign that she was in the deepest of sleep. Newman figured he'd leave her a while longer before waking her – ironically – to go to bed. Perhaps if their worn-out leather sofa had been a little more comfortable and less prone to cause backaches that were a sonofabitch to get rid of, he would have left her to sleep.

Newman felt the urge to check his e-mails just one last time. It was an obsessive trait he'd adopted since getting his own laptop – a quick look to see if anything had cropped up in the twenty minutes since he'd left the office. He switched on the dark gray laptop that perched on the kitchen counter. It clicked and whirred as if struggling to come to life, eventually illuminating the kitchen with its cold, white light. Probably time for a new one, Newman promised himself; this one was five years old now, ancient in computer terms. There'd come a time, some day soon by the look of things that this silicone dinosaur just wouldn't wake up.

He supped on his beer, contemplated eating the leftover Chinese takeout that had spent all day out on the countertop, and scanned his emails.

One from his Dad in New Jersey, two from his best friend in Ireland, a page full of spam emails about faux-Viagra drugs and penis enlargements that he dropped straight into his virtual wastebasket. One from Ted Buckner, the Medical Examiner.

'Re: *Report, Virginia Mendoza*' It read. Newman clicked the e-mail open.

'*Here you go Don, just got toxicology info back, thought I'd get it to you ASAP.*'

The attached PDF file was the advance copy of the report Newman had asked for on the remains of the girl they'd found in the Mountainview. He'd wanted to have all the facts at his fingertips should the Johnson boy wake up.

The cop's eyes skipped over the tick-boxes and formal bullshit and down to the hand-written block at the bottom.

'Subject's body contains large quantities of acetylcholine, histamine, and serotonin. There are traces of 5-hydroxytryptamine and hemolytic phospholipase A.

All of these are present in the venom of Scolopendra Gigantea (yellow-legged centipede), although the amount present in the subject's tissues suggests a large number of individual envenomations.

The evidence of the venom components in all tissues in the upper half of the Subject's body suggests that the subject was killed by the bisection of the body at the second lumbar vertebra and not by venom. Had this not occurred, subject would have died, nonetheless, through effects of the venom. At the time of writing, the posterior half of the subject's body has not been presented for autopsy.'

Newman grimaced at the final sentence, his team and the forensics boys had searched every inch of the underground area for the missing half of the Virginia Mendoza. They had come up squat and were about to expand the search to the ground floor when Levandowski had stuck them with a court order to get out and stay out. All they *had* found of Mendoza's lower half was the sticky mess of blood and slop on the expensive tiled floor.

He read on.

'Subject's back shows signs of biting and chewing, with sections of tissue severely macerated and missing in part. Although there is no evidence of human tooth imprints; extensive tissue damage leads to an inconclusive on who – or what – caused said biting and chewing marks.'

Newman growled, damn Ted Buckner and his fence-sitting. If he thought Stevie Johnson had eaten the girl, then why the fuck couldn't he just come right out and say so? And if the M.E. thought the boy had not been responsible for the girl's murder, why in God's good name couldn't he say who he thought *was* responsible?

Unless, of course, Buckner genuinely didn't know.

Newman re-read the report. As he did so, he ran a hand through his thinning hair and absently scratched at the top of his head. What really bothered him here was the *quantity* of venom in the girl's body. He cast his mind back to what the foxy zoology chick in San Diego had told him; that one of those centipedes – *'pedes*, she'd called 'em – had a bite no worse that a bee sting. And, while bee stings were not necessarily something you'd go out of your way to solicit, they sure as eggs were eggs wouldn't kill you. Unless, the professor had been quick to point out, you were one of the unlucky few who had an allergic reaction to bee venom, in which case one sting *could* kill you.

"One hell of an allergic reaction," Newman snorted.

As Newman had it figured, there really was only one way that so much venom could have gotten into the Mendoza girl, and that was if there was a hell of a lot more of those damned-ugly things living in the Mountainview.

And that still didn't begin to explain what the hell happened to the butt-half of the poor girl's body.

Don Newman glanced over at his sleeping wife, listened awhile to the soft, reassuring purr of her snores.

He re-read the e-mail one more time.

CHAPTER NINE

1

Fred Westendick swung his legs over the side of the vast white-sheeted bed, and the bulk of his muscular body made a Fred-shaped shadow in the weak light from the bedside lamp. He yawned and stretched his arms over his head, creating a new, Y-shaped shadow.

They'd had a wild one, he and Darlene. There'd barely been time to throw back the dust-laden comforter on the bed and tear off each others' minimal amount of clothing before the sexual tension had gotten the better of them. They had gone at each other with an unprecedented animalistic frenzy which had been simmered nicely to boiling point by their less than discrete poolside fumbling.

Darlene had launched herself at Fred before even the hotel room door had closed. She'd been a whirling dervish of hot body, probing tongue, and grasping hands, jumping into Fred's arms and wrapping her supple thighs around his waist to grind the heat of her pussy against him. Her momentum had toppled them both onto the bed – Fred remembered feeling relieved that the bed had been there otherwise they would have both had hit the floor. He doubted if Darlene had cared much about safety issues by that point in their coupling – she had fallen upon him like some ravenous wildcat: clawing and scratching and biting until they were both sated and entirely exhausted.

Fred studied Darlene as she slept curled up beside him, his eyes tracing the sensuous curve of her body beneath the starched sheet. She had fallen asleep almost as soon as they had both climaxed – a feat they'd achieved almost simultaneously, as he recalled (a personal first) – pretty much before he'd pulled out of her. Too much booze and rough sex, young lady, he smiled to himself.

Fred stood up and tried his best to gauge in the poor light where the en suite would be.

Darlene turned over. Her eyes shut tight; she let out a gentle whisper of a fart. Fred caught a fragrant whiff of tequila and semen, and smiled once more, this time in self-congratulation.

Having successfully located the bathroom, Fred settled his naked butt onto the cool toilet seat. Once in the bathroom, he had found the lavatory primarily by touch without waiting for his eyes to adjust to the darkness that filled to the small, windowless space.

Something touched his big toe. Fred looked down and froze.

A long shape snaked across the room from the shower cubicle to his foot.

"Oh shit," Fred muttered as the centipede ventured onto his toes.

It took a shit-ton of willpower to force himself to remain still. As Fred watched with morbid fascination, the animal crawled over the top of his foot. He could feel the butterfly kiss of its antennae as they tapped at the sensitive skin, the prickle of the creature's claws as it walked over him, and he felt more vulnerable than he'd ever felt in his life.

Vulnerable? Fred was scared shitless.

Fred held his breath and tried not to tense against the weight of the centipede on his toes. He'd read somewhere that snakes wouldn't attack unless they had you figured for food or a threat. But then again, his mind screamed, this wasn't exactly a snake now, was it?

As focused as Fred was on the myriapod as it examined his foot, Fred didn't notice the other long, dark shapes that lurked against the wall behind him.

A movement.

Fred looked up.

Saw three faces and a raised fist.

And in the blink of an eye, darkness descended upon Fred Westendick.

2

Darlene stirred and shifted in the bed as she drifted back into wakefulness. She stretched out an arm, seeking out the warmth of her lover's body. Instead, her hand found only the cool, damp place where Fred's semen had oozed out of her.

Once again, Fred had 'forgotten' to bring condoms, and Darlene's waking mind reminded her of this fact with a bluntness that made her angry at her own stupidity. When would she ever learn with that jackass? It meant *another* fucking trip to the Well Woman clinic on Monday morning for *yet another* dose of *levonorgestrel* – and Christ himself only knew what havoc that stuff was wreaking on her insides.

Darlene reckoned that she might as well bite the bullet whilst she was at the clinic this time and have the full girlie check-over and full STD screening. Fred was a nice guy and all, but Darlene had never once fooled herself that he and she were exclusive.

She groaned, the tequila in her system was making her

head pound and her stomach churn – she could feel the sour stuff sloshing around inside her. Her nether regions tingled too, and she hoped to dear God that Fred had not given her another dose of crabs. She hated to admit it, but the prickling itch between her legs certainly felt that way.

Darlene looked down the bed at the curvaceous form her body presented beneath the bedsheet. In the muted light of the hotel room, it looked to her as if the bedsheet was breathing. As Darlene watched, the bed pulsed and stirred with an alien, rhythmic movement, which she struggled to figure out. Finally, Darlene's horribly hung-over mind dragged itself with great reluctance into a more alert state. And as it did so, it registered the peculiar pins-and-needles sensation in her legs which felt to Darlene like when she'd lay on an arm for too long, and the circulation would rush back upon liberating the limb. It felt like –

Darlene Buchanan threw the sheet aside and screamed with everything her lungs had to offer.

Her legs swarmed with dark, lucent, crawling crawl things. Things that creeped and scurried, entwined and burrowed, things with undulating bodies that created a mass so dense that it looked like one huge, bulbous organism that covered her lower body. She screamed again and tore at the centipedes that clung to her legs. In return, they snapped with savage bites at her hands as she pulled at their repugnant, hard bodies, and their prickling legs snapped off in her hands.

Darlene kicked her legs in a vain attempt to dislodge the animals that numbered so many that they weighed her down, pinning her to the bed. She succeeded only in getting the 'pedes to tighten their grip on her skin and sink ferocious penetrating fangs deeper into the soft flesh of her thighs. Darlene's head spun wild with terror, her heart drummed hard against her ribs, its pulse deafening her ears like the thrumming of hail on a tin roof. In her heightened state, Darlene could feel the centipedes' poison as it coursed through her veins, its progress accelerated by her pounding heart, and every ounce of her body felt as if it was on fire. Driven by her primitive human urge to survive, Darlene thrashed and fought and screamed at the creatures that were eating her alive.

Working in slow motion, Darlene somehow managed to claw enough of the creatures off of her legs to regain some movement. She kicked her legs and grimaced at the surreal sight of the raw, bloodied mess of her legs and the murky stain they'd created on the bed with her blood that appeared tar-black in the feeble light.

As the 'pede's venom streamed through Darlene's body, she could feel her grasp on consciousness beginning to fade away, an overwhelming tiredness was drawing a hazy veil across her mind, and all she wanted to do was lay back down and sleep, even if that meant succumbing to the tortures that the centipedes had in store for her.

Then – *Fuck no*! Darlene Buchanan was made of far fiercer stuff than that!

Despite the delirium that confused her brain, and drawing on every ounce of strength that she could muster, Darlene swung her ruined, bloodied legs over the side of the bed and struggled to her feet. With each movement, she tore away the centipedes that crawled with relentless determination along her naked body and up toward her face.

There was that tingling sensation again, deep inside her sex. Oh, Dear God, no! They were *inside* of her: burrowing, biting, and chewing. Darlene dropped to her knees. She looked down between her legs and could see the rear end of a fat 'pede protruding from between her swollen labia. The remainder of the creature, she knew all too well, had penetrated her vagina and was busy eating her from the inside. Darlene hauled herself up and took a firm grasp at the writhing body that dangled between her blood smeared thighs. Ignoring the excruciating stabs of the centipede's finger-long legs, she pulled.

The creature held fast, digging into her most delicate, tender flesh with legs and fangs, ripping her apart as she yanked on its body. Darlene shuddered with revulsion at the touch of the centipede's hard body in her hand, slick with her blood. As she tugged, the creature thrashed its rear legs at her grasping fingers, slashing her fingers with razor-thin cuts that shredded to the bone. A paroxysm of panic rolled through Darlene, and in a frenzy, she pulled even harder at the rear quarters of the centipede, despite the *give* sensation in her belly. And still, the 'pede clung on, and the unbelievable agony that flared from Darlene's viscera tore through her body like shards of glass.

A random thought floated through Darlene's delirious brain, almost amusing in its absurdity. She had never really grown to love her vagina, had always hated the way her inner labia protruded too far out beyond their outer lips. Despite reassurances from Fred and her many, many other conquests as to just how desirable she was *down below*, Darlene had always referred to her genitals as *The Last Sandwich in Arby's*.

This made her smile.

Finally, overwhelmed by pain and poison, Darlene sank back on her haunches and cried.

3

Fred came to with a start and found himself tied to a chair by his wrists and ankles with what appeared to be – ironically – gaudy, striped neckties. There was a cloth gag in his mouth, and his concussed brain told him through a thick haze that this was not the sign of anything good. He *was* surprised, however, to discover that he had awoken wearing pants. This was significant to Fred because he knew full well that he hadn't been wearing pants when the lights had gone out, metaphorically speaking. Perhaps of even more significance was the fact that the ill-fitting pants around his lower portions weren't his. Meaning: someone had gone to the trouble of dressing him.

As his blurred vision gradually cleared, Fred could make out that he was still in the hotel, in a room that looked vaguely familiar. He spotted through the gloom that the door to the room was slightly ajar – a potential escape route? He could also make out the vague, fuzzy outlines of the four faces that floated in front of his face, two white, two black.

"Couldn't you have waited for him to finish crapping before you hit him?" one of the black guys was shouting in the face of the thin white guy, and the voice sounded distant to Fred as if he was hearing it down a long tunnel. Thin White Guy was sporting a fresh shit stain down the front of his jeans.

"H – He did it *when* we hit him," Thin White Guy protested, "ya know, like he shat himself!" To Fred's concern, the guy fiddled nervously with a large knife as he spoke; he was clearly scared to death of the man who was yelling at him, and that was never a healthy combination for a person tied to a chair. And, as big as the knife was, Fred figured that if Shouting Black Guy turned nasty on Thin White Guy, it would be useless in the latter's defense; the black guy had the air of someone who was not to be fucked with.

The black guy walked over and pushed his face close into Fred's. He slapped his captive's cheek a few times. "Wakey wakey, motherfucker," he said. The pungent stink of weed on his hot breath assaulted Fred's nose and made his sinuses ache and his eyes water. "So you're the cocksucker who's banging my lady," he sneered.

Fred shook his head. He had no idea who this guy was, who any of them were. Darlene hadn't even mentioned a boyfriend.

Jackson was in no mood for bullshit. He reached into his pocket and pulled out a wooden toothpick. "This is what putting your white dick in my woman gets ya," Jackson snarled. He grabbed Fred's right index finger and pushed the toothpick deep under the nail.

Fred bucked in agony and screamed the best he could around the gag. The wooden chair to which he was tied jumped and scraped on the floor as Fred struggled in vain to get away from the searing pain in his hand.

Jackson Booth smiled a toothy grin at his victim and pushed the toothpick still deeper under Fred's nail.

The pain was excruciating; Fred had felt nothing like this before in his life – he'd cracked his clavicle in his sophomore year of high school football, and *that* had hurt like hell. But this, this was way above and beyond that level of pain spreading through his body like a wildfire as if every nerve ending fired off simultaneously and in sympathy. Fred screamed and cried until streams of thick snot ran from his nose, and sweat and tears poured down his face.

Jackson looked down at the jock who writhed and blubbered like a cocksucking pussy, and thought that perhaps he'd remember what this felt like the next time he was tempted to put his dick where it wasn't wanted. He was also pleased that he'd made the decision to get his boys to put some pants on the guy. Torturing him 'till he wept and bubbled snot out of his nose was one thing, but looking at his naked white dick flapping around whilst he did so was where the line had to be drawn. Lee and the others had not had to look too far for a pair of discarded pants, although the ones they'd selected didn't fit all that well. Still, this wasn't a fashion contest, thought Jackson.

He pulled the gag out of Fred's mouth once the screaming had subsided, and the jock was reduced to sniveling. Jackson always found it remarkable how even the very worst pain ebbed after a while, once the nerves had shot their load, so to speak.

"You like that, white boy?" Jackson jeered.

"Who the fuck are you?!" Fred's voice was pleading and angry and pained all at the same time. "I don't know who the fuck you are!" he sounded desperate.

"That's right, asshole, you don't know me. But it seems like you know my bitch really well." Jackson pushed the toothpick in a little more and delighted in the guttural scream that it solicited.

"Will you stop doing that, you *fucker*?!" Fred screamed at his assailant with strident frustration in his voice.

Jackson punched Fred in the face, bloodying his nose with a sickening *crunch*. "Is that better, you piece of shit?" he spat.

"Look, man," Fred spluttered. He spat out a clod of blood and mucus, which formed strings down to his broad chest. "I'm sorry, okay?! I didn't even know Darlene had a fucking boyfriend; she's never said a fucking word to me!" He ground his teeth against the white-hot pain in his finger and the blast of dull hurt in his head that fanned up from his squashed nose.

"Who the fuck is Darlene?" Lee asked the room.

"Yeah, just who the *fuck* is Darlene?" Jackson demanded. Just how many more guys was this asshole cuckolding? "I'm more interested in *Melanie* – the bitch you just finished ass-fucking before my crew so politely requested your presence." Jackson was enjoying himself, getting into his stride now; he loved all the big talk, the playing with words even more than he loved the power that went hand in hand with the inflicting of pain.

Fred laughed. It was a strained, choking noise that sounded like congealed puke gurgling down a drain. "That wasn't Melanie, you dickwad. It was Darlene I just fucked – we've been fuck buddies since Christmas." He swallowed down a fat gob of coppery snot. "Mel's still down in the pool room with the others," Fred smirked. "I've never laid a fucking finger on her – she hates my fucking guts!" Fred couldn't help the incredulous laugh that escaped his lips. "If there's anybody you should have tied to this fucking chair, it's Professor Lucas."

"He's full of shit, Jackson," Mikey interrupted, "we have seen the Professor, and she's a woman; tits and everything."

"Your clown's got that much right," Fred growled at Jackson. He shot a look in Mikey's direction, daring him to react to the derogatory comment. "Didn't you know that your gal loves pussy, *Jackson*?" Fred spat his tormentor's name like it tasted foul in his mouth, laughed in the man's face. "What went wrong, asshole? You put her off men with your pencil-dick?!"

Somewhat predictably, Jackson hit Fred again. This time, Fred was expecting it and rolled with the punch. Jackson's fist deflected off of Fred's face and registered as little more than a stinging slap.

"You don't believe me?" Fred growled. He could see the seeds of doubt he'd sown already beginning to take root as Jackson mulled over this new information. "Go down and take a look – see for yourself. Take your camera phone – you might get lucky and catch some hot girl-on-girl while you're down there!"

Jackson raised his fist again. He could feel the all-too familiar anger coursing through his body. What if the guy was telling the truth? What if Mel preferred to lick pussy, and she was only hanging with him for the free drugs and the thrill of fucking with his head? And how was it that, between Mikey, Lee, and Johnny, not one of them had actually bothered to take a look at who had been in this wise-guy's bed?

"Gonna hit me again?" Fred taunted as the pain in his face competed with that in his finger. "Not man enough to take me on unless I'm strapped to a fucking chair? No wonder Mel prefers screwing women."

Jackson hesitated, toyed with the notion of pummeling the cracker jock in the face 'till his skull caved in and his smartass college brains slopped out. Instead, he backed off. "Untie him," he growled.

"You sure about that, Jackson? He looks awful pissed to me," Johnny said.

"Just fucking do it," Jackson's voice was a measured calm. "Frat Boy here thinks he's some kinda big man who can take on Jackson Booth. Well, we'll see about that."

Johnny unfolded his knife, and with reluctance, cut through Fred's restraints. He skulked back to his spot by the door, not once taking his eyes off of the guy he'd just liberated. This was the most stupid thing he'd ever seen Jackson do, that was for sure; personally, he much preferred his prey subdued and restrained so they couldn't fight back. This reminded Johnny of the time he'd finally gotten around to releasing a possum he'd kept in a box for two days. He'd spent those two days poking at the foul-smelling thing with sticks through the air-holes he'd punched in the sides, but had balked at carrying out his initial plan to actually kill the thing. In the end, he'd felt quite sorry for the animal, so he'd let it go. Instead of showing even a glimmer of gratitude for its freedom, the damn thing had turned on Johnny and torn his fucking hand to shreds. His good deed had cost him a trip to the ER, twenty-five stitches, and a tetanus shot in the ass. Lessons learned the hard way.

Perhaps Jackson was about to learn one of his own?

Fred remained seated, gritting his teeth so fiercely that everyone in the room could hear them grinding in the pregnant silence. He pulled the toothpick out from under his fingernail. *Shit*, his mind screamed, that hurt almost as bad coming out than it had going in.

"Okay, big shot, let's do this. Man to man," Jackson challenged. "And you boys stay the fuck out of this," he barked at his three compatriots, "no matter what." He pulled the gun out from his waistband and placed it carefully next to the flat-screen and wondered just what the hell he thought he was doing. Jackson was not so much of a street fighter these days, he'd grown far too reliant on his Smith and Wesson. He figured the gun had made him soft over the years, in much the same way as when he'd ditched his bicycle the minute he'd passed his driver's license.

As Fred rose to his feet, a movement in the hallway outside caught his attention. Something immense and dark moved by with a fluidity that pinged his memory. It flowed by the gap that the slightly ajar door afforded, and to Fred, it appeared almost metallic in the glinting light beyond. For some reason, whatever it was reminded him of all the times he'd ever been stuck at railroad crossings waiting for an endless procession of freight train cars to go by. "What the fuck was that?" he said and nodded his head toward the door.

"You think you're gonna get me with that one?" Jackson mocked, "you really must think I'm some special kind of stupid."

Jackson made sure that his move was the first one, determined to make it count. Taking advantage of the split-second lull in Fred's attention, Jackson lunged at the jock, clawed hands reaching for the throat.

The fight was over almost before it got started.

Fred's footballer instincts kicked in, and he deftly sidestepped Jackson's move. He then turned on his heels and brought the bony knob of his elbow down hard on the side of the gang banger's head.

Knocked off of his feet, Jackson went down with little grace. His head bounced off the floor with a sickening *thunk* that left him momentarily dazed. He saw Fred's foot raised and aimed squarely toward his stomach, and Jackson lashed out with his own. His Nike caught Fred hard in the balls, and College Boy went down on his knees like a felled tree.

Fighting like a fucking girl now are we Jackson? The chastising voice of his father rang through Jackson's mind.

Only little girls kick guys in the balls. Jackson shook his head to shoo the voice away. Right now, he didn't really give much of a crap what – or who's – sensibilities he may be offending here, if there was one thing he'd learned in life as a *player* was that in a fight there were no consolation prizes for style. You hit the other guy before he hit you and then you hit him so fucking hard that when he went down, he damn well stayed down.

Jackson kicked out at Fred's face, but Fred caught his foot mid-air and twisted it. Jackson yelped as his knee-joint popped with a noise so loud that it made everyone in the room wince. A sharp pain flared up into his groin that made his dick ache.

Fred scrambled to his feet and lunged at his opponent, bloody murder blazing in his eyes. He dropped his weight hard on Jackson's chest and punched his antagonist hard in the mouth, his knuckles grazing against hard teeth.

Jackson fought for breath. Fred had knocked the wind out of him and was now making it near-on impossible for him to draw another lung full. The full weight of the jock crushed his ribs, squeezing the life from him like some overweight, pissed off *Boa Constrictor*. In a desperate attempt to shift the weight and draw breath, Jackson thrust his arms upward to grab at Fred's eyes and claw at his face. He didn't need his father's voice in his head to make him painfully aware that fighting like this meant losing face in front of his crew, but whilst that was the last thing he could afford to let happen here, Fred was heavier and stronger and faster than he'd anticipated. All too aware of his mistake in releasing Fred, and feeling his vision beginning to gray at the edges, Jackson began to panic.

Fred slapped Jackson's hands away and punched at the man's face over and over. His knuckles reddened with blood from Jackson's splitting lips, and he could feel teeth loosening and face bones crunching. This was no Hollywood fight with your good old alternate-one-punch-each choreography. This was fucking real. This was two guys scrapping, trying in earnest to hurt each other, and Fred knew that he needed to make sure that this guy stayed hurt and down as there would more than likely be the other three wise guys to contend with when this was over.

Another punch, a direct hit to Jackson's larynx.

"Motherfucker!" Jackson wheezed as the last of his breath knocked out of him, and he struggled to inhale. He tried to brace himself as the nauseating thud of Fred's fists beat furiously about his face and head, which created crazy, dancing stars that swam behind his eyes. He did his level best to fight back – but the other guy's weight had him pinned – and a random, fleeting thought spun through his dazed mind, that he sure was glad that his boys had put some pants on Fred – he'd hate to get beaten to fuck by a naked guy.

"You want more?" Fred quit pummeling and screamed in Jackson's face, "Do ya?"

Lee stepped forward unhappy at seeing his boss on the wrong end of such a vicious beating.

"I said stay the fuck back!" Jackson squeaked at him and Lee shuffled away obediently.

Johnny Psycho – nee Jones – had never been one for taking orders from other people where he figured he knew best. His warped sense of loyalty had been screaming at him throughout the fight that it was his duty to protect his leader. He focused his eyes firmly on the spot between Fred's shoulder blades and stepped forward, opening up his knife with a satisfying *click*.

Homing in on that noise, the gargantuan centipede burst through the door and grabbed Johnny with its forelegs. It coiled the first quarter of its body around him and stabbed into Johnny's head with gigantic fangs that smashed down into his skull and split it apart with a nauseating *crunch*. Johnny's mouth flew open in a surprised O and his brains spilled out and down his face like pink Jello pudding, landing with a wet *splat* on the carpet. Johnny Psycho didn't even have the chance to scream. Instead, an odd rasping sound erupted from his spoiled throat as it showered blood around the hotel room like some ghoulish ornamental fountain.

And then the giant centipede and Johnny were gone, the entire attack over and done in a matter of seconds. The creature dragged Johnny's wrecked, lifeless body out into the hallway, leaving behind a puddle of viscous crimson flecked with pink gobs of brain. Johnny's knife lay impotent and slick with blood, amidst the gore, a sickening monument to the thug's most unexpected passing.

"Did you see that!?" Mikey shrieked hysterically. "Did you *fucking* see that?!" As if repeating himself would help.

Jackson pushed a stunned Fred from his chest, hauled himself up with a pained groan, and grabbed Mikey by the shoulders. "Shut the fuck up, Mikey!" he hissed. "Unless you want that fucking thing to come back for *you*." Mikey shook his head slowly, the shock made his eyes bug out of their sockets, and he looked like a retard and Jackson hated that.

Fred stood open-mouthed where just moments before he'd been poised to deliver his *coup de grace* to a well and truly defeated Jackson. "Yeah, I'd keep real quiet if I were you," he whispered. "They have excellent hearing; it compensates for their crappy eyesight. Apparently." He would have gone on to tell Jackson, Mikey, and Lee that some centipede species have no eyes at all, but he was interrupted.

"You know what that – *that thing* – was?" Lee quizzed.

"Yeah, it's a fucking centipede," Fred answered and decided at the last moment to abstain from the sarcastic but much warranted '*duh!*' "Only they're not really supposed to be *that* big." Fred struggled to vocalize what his eyes had shown him, knowing full well that what he found himself explaining to Jackson and his two surviving gang members was a biological impossibility.

The four stared at each other in silence, serenaded by the stomach-turning sounds of crunching and tearing from the hallway outside, and the wet, slopping sound of Johnny Psycho's flesh and innards hitting the blood-sodden floor made each and every one of them feel like hurling.

Jackson maneuvered Mikey to the chair they'd had tied Fred to, made him sit down. It was clear that the guy was in shock, his senses abused to the point of breaking. Compliant, soundless, Mikey allowed himself to be led to the chair. He sat down without protest.

"What the fuck was it? What the fuck was that thing, Jackson?" Mikey finally murmured. "It killed Johnny."

Jackson shook his head, opened his mouth to speak. Nothing came out, and his blood streaked lips just moved in silence. The truth was that he didn't know what he had just seen, nor did he believe Fred's B-movie monster explanation. But then, if neither option was the case, just what the fuck *was* the case? Shit, the more he thought, the more his brain fogged over. "Since you're the motherfucking expert, what the fuck do we do now, frat boy?" Jackson's voice was quivering but still just about under control.

"How the hell am I supposed to know?" Fred said.

"Because you're the one who knows all about centipedes and shit. That's why you're here, right?"

"*I'm* not the expert," Fred defended, "I don't really know all that much about them, only what the Professor briefed us on. And I *honestly* didn't know they made 'em that fucking big!"

"We should make a break for it now, while it's eating Johnny," Lee ventured. "Maybe if it's busy it will leave us alone."

"It's right outside the fucking door," Jackson snarled, contempt dripping from his words. "You saw how quick that thing was, just how far you think you're gonna get?" He saw Mikey stand up. Clearly, the thought of running appealed to the boy. "Sit the fuck down, Mikey," Jackson ordered.

Mikey stood there and stared transfixed with wide, terrified eyes at Fred.

"Mikey, I told you to sit the fuck down." Jackson tried not to raise his voice too high, paranoid that the monster in the hallway would make its encore and chow down on *his* head. "Or do I have to make you?"

"Jesus, shit, man!" Lee squealed as he saw what had caught Mikey's attention.

Another centipede, a size more akin to those that Fred's fellow students had captured earlier, snaked its way out from the shadows behind an oblivious Fred. It circled inches away from his bare foot.

All eyes turned to Lee whose courage amounted to jumping onto an armchair like the inappropriate, ethnic housekeeper in the old *Tom and Jerry* cartoons.

Jackson lunged toward Fred, whose gut instinct was to raise his fists. Jackson pushed him aside and stomped a carefully aimed Nike at what he assumed to be the centipede's head. "Got the cocksucker!" he exclaimed as he relished the crackling sound the centipede's hard carapace made beneath his foot. Then the creature's head jerked around, and in the blink of an eye, the 'pede had its forcipules buried to the hilt in Jackson's leg.

"Fuck!" Jackson screamed, and all thoughts of the monstrous creature in the hallway were instantly forgotten. "Oh, Jesus!" He dropped to the floor and kicked at the animal that had coiled itself around his lower leg and was pumping pure, liquid agony into his calf muscle.

Fred grabbed Johnny's knife out of the congealing mess of blood and slashed at the centipede on Jackson's leg. The knife was honed to a razor's edge and sliced through the hard carapace like it was barely there, severing the centipede neatly in two between the fourth and fifth segments.

Separated from its head, the creature's body uncoiled itself from Jackson. It spiraled and thrashed around on the floor like a thing possessed, legs kicking out as if it had been electrocuted. Its jaws, however, did not let go, and Jackson still had the centipede's head attached to his leg.

"Hold still!" Fred ordered and knelt onto his erstwhile opponent's thigh, pressing his full weight onto it.

Jackson screamed as he felt the searing pain of the centipede's venom shoot up the entire length of his leg and set his balls on fire.

Taking care to avoid them sinking into his fingers, Fred carefully pried the centipede's fangs apart. He gingerly pulled them – one by one – out of Jackson's flesh. The animal's head was still very much alive, its eyes staring at Fred's with intense displeasure as its antennae tip-tapped against his hands as an impatient man might drum his fingers upon a tabletop. Undeterred, Fred worked diligently against the powerful muscles until, finally, the jaws pried open, and he wrested the severed head free.

"Got the bastard!" Fred gasped. He threw the head across the room with a look of absolute disgust on his face like he'd just picked up a fresh dog turd with his bare hands. "We'd better get something on that." He looked at the ragged wound on Jackson's leg and saw that the proteases in the venom had already begun their work of digesting the flesh around the twin holes; the damaged skin around the wound already looked black and slimy.

"Shouldn't you suck the poison out or something?" Jackson grimaced.

"That's snakebites, asshole," Fred grumbled. "The venom's already in your system, and anyways I don't want a mouthful of that shit." Fred considered explaining to Jackson precisely what the venom would do to his insides should he be stupid enough to ingest it but figured the dumb-fuck *gangsta* wouldn't care less. "We'll get a tourniquet on it, try to stop the venom from spreading," he said.

Lee whipped off his belt and threw it over to Fred. Fred strapped it around Jackson's leg just above the knee and pulled it tight. Holding one end in his teeth the way he'd seen done countless times in the movies, Fred pulled the belt as taut as it would go. They would have to loosen the belt every half hour or so or Jackson's leg would die from lack of oxygenated blood, at which point the poisons would be free to circulate around the guy's body. Even with his limited knowledge of 'pede venom, Fred reckoned the guy's leg was pretty much fucked either way.

"You saved me," Jackson whispered, although not entirely sure that to show his gratitude was the right thing to do in front of his boys.

"And you saved me," Fred answered, "let's keep it our little secret, shall we?"

Neither of them saw Mikey making his way to the open door until it was too late.

"Mikey! No!" Jackson called out after the retreating figure.

Mikey Tyler slipped through the hotel room doorway in a heartbeat and then he was gone.

"Shit!" Jackson snapped as he scrambled to his feet, "that dumb-ass kid."

4

Mikey's distressed mind had made the decision not to stay in the hotel room and wait for some overgrown insect to come back and make him part of its very own private all-you-can-eat. Fuck that and fuck Jackson with a big fucking stick, it was every man for himself now.

And so, Mikey ran.

He ran away from the dusty room and away from the

repulsive creature that had snatched Johnny and those revolting chewing, crunching sounds that it was making as it devoured his friend.

Mikey had snuck through the door whilst the monster hadn't been looking and had gained himself what he considered to be a reasonable head start before the giant centipede dropped what little was left of its lunch and set off after him.

As he ran, Mikey chanced a glance behind and immediately wished he hadn't.

It was coming.

The living nightmare with uncountable legs hurtled in his direction along the hallway with almost preternatural speed, and Mikey's scared brain took a moving snapshot of the massive body that snaked side to side like a – well, like a *fucking snake*. The thing's head, smeared glistening scarlet with Johnny's blood, waved this way and that in a rhythmic motion that reminded him of Stevie Wonder singing at the piano. As it picked up his scent, Mikey saw the thing's antennae frantically beating the air as it pinpointed his precise position.

Mikey let out an involuntary whimper and picked up his pace toward the sanctuary of the elevator doors that beckoned him, almost tantalizingly out of reach.

The centipede continued its velocity with a poetic grace, its myriad legs moving in undulating waves as it maneuvered with little effort up the walls and along the ceiling, carrying all thirty-odd feet of its body as if the rules of gravity no longer applied.

Mikey slammed hard into the elevator doors and ended his run with a *thump*. He hammered frantically at the red call button. "Come on, come on!" he screamed at the elevator as if harassing the thing would hurry the carriage along. He saw on the display pad above the button that the safe haven of the elevator was currently on the fourth floor and was heading downward.

At least it was moving in his direction, he reassured himself.

Mikey's breath labored with panic and exertion, his lungs ground in his chest, and his heart pounded like some angry, caged beast in his ribcage. As terrifying as it was, Mikey could do no more now than stare at the capacious head of the bloodied horror that rapidly closed in on him; his eyes transfixed by the huge, black-tipped fangs that spread open in readiness for him. And beneath those he could see the gore drenched mouth parts that twitched and churned like an old man's hands.

"Please no," Mikey cried, and thick tears chased each other down along his cheeks. He was far too young to die, and certainly not like this – he'd always fantasized that he'd go down in a hail of bullets defending his gang's honor or in a ball of flame in a street race with his best bitch by his side; not as dinner for some giant freak of nature. Mikey knew all too well that should the centipede get to him, there would be no pleading, no trying to appeal to its sense of fair play – it was no more than a fucking eating machine. There'd be no more appealing to its better nature than to his Mom's vacuum cleaner, no negotiation, no second chances, so just what the fuck was he supposed to do?

He was done for. The thing was barely ten feet away from him now and he had no place else to run. Mikey fancied that he could smell Johnny's blood in the centipede's mouth; it was a dark, meaty stink that rose above the ammonia that wafted from the creature, that made it stink like some old lady's cat had pissed on it. Mikey closed his eyes and sobbed; he didn't want the gaping machinery of the 'pede's mouth parts to be the last thing he saw.

Ding.

The elevator announced its arrival with a cheerful, melodious chime. The doors opened and nondescript, tinny music drifted out.

The centipede was almost upon Mikey now, its antennae almost brushing his body, and Mikey's imagination told him that he could feel the creature's hot breath on his skin. He threw himself inside the elevator and could have kissed it.

As a kid, he'd been told by his elder brothers that the more you hit an elevator button, the quicker the doors closed. Of course, that was complete bullshit, but Mikey slapped that button as quickly as his hand would go and made his palm turn numb. *Well, ya never know, Mikey, ya never know.*

Mikey screamed as the centipede crawled down from the wall. Its feet dislodged a *Van Gough* print that clattered to the floor, its glass shattering. The creature paused for a fraction of a second at the elevator doors, as if unsure about entering. It tested the metal frame with curious antennae, bit at it with black, shiny fangs that were longer than Mikey's forearms and looked like they were made from Bakelite..

Mikey screamed once again, and the centipede glared at him with each and every one of its eyes and shunted its considerable bulk forward.

Then, the elevator doors closed with a remarkable smoothness that belied five years of disuse.

Mikey winced as he heard – *felt* – the monstrous animal thump against the outer elevator doors. The solid smack against the metal doors forced them to bulge inwards and rattle in their frame, and it seemed to Mikey like the centipede was beating on them with a petulant rage at having lost its Mikey meal.

5

"We have to go. Now," Fred told Jackson as they watched the back-end of the centipede's immense body as it hurtled past the door hot on Mikey's tail. Again, that mental image of railroad crossings and counting the carriages played in his mind.

"We can't leave Mikey," Lee argued, "he's just a kid."

"Mikey's made his own decision," Jackson said. "He ran out on us, he's in his own hands now."

Jackson struggled to stand. The pain in his leg had subsided a little as the tourniquet had cut off the blood circulation and numbed it. He grabbed his gun from the TV stand and thrust it back into his waistband.

"I vote we go left, toward the stairs," Fred suggested. "You think you can do stairs?" there was more compassion in Fred's voice for Jackson than he thought there ought to be considering he was addressing the guy who less than a half-hour ago had forced a toothpick under his fingernail. Still, the appearance of an impossibly giant, ravenous arthropod pretty much trumped everything right now.

"I'll be fine. Quit worrying," Jackson growled through grinding his teeth at the dull throb that had settled in his leg. "You're probably right since it looks like Mikey's gone and commandeered the elevator."

"I don't think it's right, Jackson," Lee argued. "Leaving Mikey like this – you could see he was scared, that's all it was."

"You want to go save his sorry ass? Play the big fucking hero against that disgusting monster?" Jackson snarled. "Go right ahead, Lee, be my fucking guest."

Lee fell silent, beaten before he'd actually had the chance to reply. No, he did *not* want to do that, but at least he'd said the right thing, and wasn't that the most important thing? To be seen making the right gestures? He'd seen with his own eyes what the centipede had done to Johnny: how it had smashed his head like some dipshit kid's Halloween pumpkin and chewed him up like a piece of jerky. And he'd heard all of those disgusting sounds the creature had made as it chewed his friend up, bones an' all. Lee hated himself for it because he genuinely liked the boy, but he'd been glad when the centipede had dropped Johnny and taken after Mikey.

At least then the sounds had stopped.

Subdued and reeling with the onset of shock, Lee followed Fred and Jackson when they left the suite and made for the stairs.

6

Mikey leaned his weight against the corner of the tiny metal box that had just saved his life.

He cried.

Couldn't remember the last time he'd cried: most likely it had been the time his Daddy had upped and left him and his Momma back when he was just four years old. He could still recall how hard he'd sobbed and pleaded with his father not to go, cried so hard he thought he'd never stop. But, eventually, he *had* stopped, and when the tears had dried, his heart had felt harder, heavier. Mikey figured he must have cried his lifetime's worth of tears in that one night because in the fourteen years since then, he'd not shed one more. Not one.

Until now.

He felt his heart thumpity-thumping so crazily in his chest that it was painful. The back of his throat felt raw against the heat of his strained breath that was only just beginning to calm down, now that he was away from the centipede thing. That particular monster was now on the other side of two sets of steel elevator doors and two floors above him, he could relax a little, and decide what the fuck he was going to do next.

The harsh light that shone through the elevator's opaque, plastic ceiling flickered and the elevator gave a slight shudder.

"What the...?" Mikey muttered. The last thing he wanted after his miraculous escape was to get himself stuck in the motherfucking elevator.

Sparks and an acrid smell of ozone, spat from the control panel to his left, and the elevator ground, complaining, to a complete halt. The *muzak* sputtered out.

"Oh, for fuck's sake," Mikey groaned. The dial above the door told him that the carriage was stuck between floors two and one. His eyes flicked to the red telephone above the control panel, and he considered trying it.

"Who the fuck are you gonna call Mikey-boy?" he chuckled at himself, "fucking *Terminix*?" He chuckled again, a maniacal sound in the claustrophobic confines of the elevator.

Mikey reached for the emergency button on the control panel that plumed wisps of white electrical smoke. He hadn't the faintest idea if it would work, or who the button would summon, but he had to at least *do something*.

Before Mikey's fingers could reach the shiny red button, the control panel door flapped open and hung before him on its hinges like a broken jaw. Mikey watched with a terror that knotted his guts up tight as a large, soot-blackened centipede crawled out. It crept with a jerking, erratic movement, its head blackened, and Mikey saw that a considerable amount of its legs were missing and an entire antenna singed off. The creature's carapace smoked with curling threads of smoke that made the thing look like some bizarre blood-red cigarette.

"Oh sweet Mother of God, no," Mikey groaned. He stepped back and whimpered as half of the length of the creature made its hesitant way out from the control panel. It was nowhere near as big as the one that ate Johnny, but from what Mikey could tell, this one was easily as big as the one that had floored Jackson. It lifted its head, its lone antenna gesturing as it tasted the elevator's air, and tasted Mikey.

Mikey kicked at the panel door to slam it shut. The steel door sliced the creature in two and bounced back open. "Yeah! Fuck you!" he yelled in triumph as the bisected halves of centipede plopped to the floor and thrashed around in their respective death throes. Clear, viscous fluid oozed out from each severed end and soaked into the grubby carpet.

"Fuck you, fuck you, *fuck you!*" Mikey's maniacal scream resounded in the cramped space as hysteria possessed him. He stomped on the wriggling centipede parts again and again, splitting them open and mashing the resulting mess into the floor.

With one last and incredibly loud *fuck you*, Mikey stomped his final stomp and stood back to admire the results of his frenzy. He was pleased with what he had achieved – it was as if he had struck a blow for poor old Johnny Psycho.

The centipede was by now barely discernible, reduced to just a jumble of split carapace, gore, and disjointed legs ground into the blood sodden carpet. Mikey allowed himself a deep breath, closed his eyes, and he realized that the music had come back on. He listened to it and tried to make out the barely discernible tune.

The fluorescent light above Mikey forced its way through his eyelids and made his world all pink and warm. He took great comfort in knowing that he was not in *complete* darkness (that, he felt would be far more than his fraying nerves could bear right now), although his closed eyes proved an effective physical barrier to the horrors he had just witnessed.

The light flickered as if the bulb were about to expire.

Panicked, Mikey opened his eyes. The ceiling hatch fell open. The flimsy plastic had buckled under the weight of the swarm of centipedes that had collected on it, and like a red, writhing waterfall, they all cascaded into the elevator.

Mikey screamed.

Centipedes tumbled down from the gaping hole in the elevator ceiling; some dropped directly to the floor with a dull, crispy *flump*, while some chose the more leisurely route and crawled down along the walls. Mikey pressed himself against the corner and stared with utter disbelief at the creatures that pooled around his feet, shuddered as they reared up to explore his legs. And somehow he managed to remain still even as he felt the first tentative legs prickling his shins. Perhaps, his terrified brain told him, if he stayed motionless, the creatures would ignore him.

The centipedes varied in size, Mikey guessed from between twelve to thirty-six inches. There were some that were maybe even longer, but it was getting hard to tell as they crawled over each other, entwining and knotting as they bustled in an ever-deepening centipede pool at his feet.

Throwing caution – and his *keep still* strategy – to the wind, Mikey began to scream and dance around wildly to dislodge the centipedes that made their way up his legs. He shrieked out his hysteria, and kicked out violently at the 'pedes that pressed the weight of their glinting mass against his feet. There was the faint, clacking sound as the multitude of chitinous shells knocked, and rubbed against each other and the sound set his teeth on edge and made him cringe – in much the same way squeaking Styrofoam went through him; it sounded to Mikey like the rattling of thousands of tiny bones and the whispering of tormented souls that bubbled up from the pits of hell.

As much as Mikey kicked at the centipedes, they continued their advance, and their numbers continued to swell with the steady stream of creatures that poured down from the ceiling.

Knee-deep in centipedes now, Mikey struggled to pick up his feet to kick them away. Some of the more adventurous centipedes were crawling up his legs, gaining purchase through his jeans and into the soft flesh beneath with their spiked legs. Mikey screamed and cussed and yelled at the animals, even beat at them with his bare hands despite the revulsion he felt at the touch of their loathsome bodies. But the more he pushed and kicked them away, the more it seemed they clamored to get to him, slithering over their fellows to take their first taste of Mikey Tyler.

The first of the bites didn't feel so bad, the adrenaline that flooded through his veins saw to that. But as the centipede bites increased in frequency, and as their ever-increasing pool reached his waist, Mikey's legs had become one blinding mass of the most unbearable agony.

Wailing in terror, Mikey pulled the centipedes away from his body, and they bit at his hands with those vicious fangs that left cruel, jagged holes in his skin. Angry at being manhandled the 'pedes slashed Mikey's arms to ribbons with their razor-sharp legs and before long, they were slick with blood which turned them slippery in Mikey's fingers. He tried with futility to kick against the prickling, biting swarm that had engulfed his lower body, but their weight was trapping his legs and stifled their movement. It was like being stuck in some wriggling, living tar pit that sucked and slurped to draw him beneath its deadly surface.

What Mikey's venom-clouded brain didn't realize was that it was only the mass of the centipedes that prevented him from collapsing. The creatures had stripped away most of the muscle from his legs, and their powerful jaws were already scraping against his bones with the rasping sound of tiny, gnawing dogs. The agony of uncountable mouthparts masticating his flesh was now indiscernible from the torment of the bites that still forced venom into him and the piercing of his skin with prickling legs. Pain was pain now, and Mikey's entire body was aflame with it.

Mikey Tyler stood chest-deep in the hellish swarm as they fed upon him. Their mass held him perfectly upright in the confined space, jostling him around as they fought amongst themselves for the best morsels and choicest parts. They climbed over one another to lunge at his face, and in doing so ripped gaping flaps in his cheeks, keen to avoid the chomping teeth, yet eager for the moistness of the boy's eyes.

The fight had all but gone out of Mikey as the centipedes scuttled and swarmed around him, biting, chewing, *feasting*. A welcome numbness washed over him as the venom attacked his nervous system, and his body began to close down. Mercifully, he didn't feel the warm flood that cascaded down his ruined legs when the creatures chewed through his femoral artery.

There comes a time in such situations when the brain realizes that there is to be no running away, no escape, and death has become an inevitability. And so, Mikey's brain switched off its pain receptors and prepared itself to close down. And he no longer felt anything but the creeping sensation of thousands upon thousands of prickling feet on his skin and the tugging at his flesh as the centipedes burrowed inside of him. That and the gentle pulling at his insides as his belly split open.

Mikey listened with detachment to the elevator music. He was pleased to have finally identified the track it played as *Purple Rain* as performed on panpipes – no doubt tweaked just enough to avoid copyright infringement lawsuits – which was how come he'd struggled to place it sooner. Mikey recalled something his Daddy had once said about this particular Prince track: was it truly a decade-defining rock anthem that underlined a generation?

Or just self-indulgent crap?

As Mikey's dying brain critiqued the music, the elevator restarted and continued its journey to the ground floor.

Upon reaching said floor of the Mountainview hotel, the elevator doors opened and spilled the writhing mass of hellish creatures and Mikey Taylor's ruined corpse out into the lobby.

CHAPTER TEN

1

Jane Lucas squirmed at the welcome, all too familiar tingle that caressed her spine as Mel's tongue probed the inside of her mouth. Jane reciprocated the kiss with verve and ventured her tongue into the warm mouth of her student, wandering her hands over and along over the girl's heated and deliciously smooth skin.

Jane had been pleasantly surprised when Mel had pounced on her almost the very second Martha-Ray had fallen asleep and left them to their own devices. The eager student had slipped off her bikini top and tugged at Jane's hand like a playful puppy, pulling her from the recliner and tumbling with her onto one of the cabana beds. She'd remained silent, no words necessary to portray her intentions – wanton lust had practically sparked from the girl's eyes.

Jane stole a glance over at the sleeping Martha-Ray. The girl was solidly out, had not moved at all in the past half-hourr. She lay prone on her recliner, head back, mouth open, and occasionally she would let out a choking, piggish grunt as if threatening to begin snoring. Then it was back to the silent, rhythmic breathing of deep sleep.

Jane lost herself in the delicious sensations of Melanie Hernandez's soft lips, silken skin, in the warmth, and scent of her near-naked body. The young girl's face, arms, slender waist, and polished legs were marble smooth and such an exquisite contrast to the abrasive stubble that had assaulted Jane throughout her previous adventures with Lenard and Larry-Wayne; this was exactly why sometimes she preferred to share her affections with the fairer sex.

This in turn reminded Jane of Mel's annoyingly bestubbled pussy, which she anticipated would be in an even pricklier state than it had been earlier on in the week. Did the girl really only shave once a month? Jane hoped not. She sighed to herself and ventured a hand downward. To Jane's sheer and utter delight, her roaming fingers discovered that Mel's mound had been waxed to within an inch of its life, and it was silky smooth and velvet-soft. Mel had most likely waxed – Jane contemplated – so as to accommodate the ludicrously tiny bikini briefs she had been wearing all day. Had Mel been aware, Jane wondered, that she had been giving everybody tantalizing glimpses of her fleshy lips all afternoon and that she had made Jane feel almost uncomfortably damp?

Jane smiled as she knew full well that yes, Mel knew damn well that she had.

Jane ran an exploratory digit along the side of the thin bikini material and pushed it aside to slip into the welcoming slit. She sighed her pleasure as Mel's scorching flesh enveloped her finger.

In response, Mel wiggled her hips and whimpered quietly into Jane's mouth as Jane's finger came away slick.

"Professor Lucas!" Fred shouted as he stormed in through the pool room door. The door banged loudly against the wall and rocked on its hinges.

"What the -?" Jane broke away from Mel and sat up

with a start. Mel promptly sat up beside her, covering her own exposed breasts with a dusty bed sheet.

"You're not gonna believe this!" Fred was breathless.

Jane could see that Fred was supporting a black guy with an arm around the waist and the black guy's arm around his neck. They were followed closely by a bald-headed white guy who looked like he belonged in an asylum. The bald guy slammed the door shut behind him and rested his weight against it.

Martha-Ray grunted herself awake. "Oh, hey Fred!" she called across the pool.

The black guy looked across at Jane and Mel.

"You!" Jackson Booth said to the older woman who'd taught him so much. His very own, personal Mrs. Robinson.

"You!" Jane replied.

"*You're* fucking my girlfriend?" Jackson said to Jane, and he stared over at Mel.

"You're fucking *my* girlfriend?!" Mel shouted at Jackson.

"What the hell are you doing here?" Jane snarled at Jackson.

There followed a brief but incredibly awkward moment of silence whilst Jane and Jackson exchanged awkward glances with Mel, who simply looked mortified at the whole situation.

Jane supposed she should be hurt that Mel was two-timing her, but she really didn't care enough about the girl for that. After all, they'd never really pretended to be exclusive. Jane was genuinely shocked, however, to see no show of surprise from either Martha-Ray or Fred at what had just unfolded. Did they know about her and Mel? And if they did, did *everyone* in the faculty know?

This was not the time for worrying about the latter, Jane told herself, whoever knew would still know come Monday. What *was* important right now was why Jackson Booth was there. Anywhere that guy turned up, there were bound to be problems of some description. Jane had always made sure to keep their relationship firmly behind closed doors since, as much as she enjoyed Jackson's firm, eager-to-please body, she certainly knew trouble when she saw it. Had he followed her here to the Mountainview just to make some dumb macho show of himself?

"Well, ain't this just fuckin' awkward?" Jackson broke the moment. He pulled away from Fred and limped toward Jane's bed, pulling his gun out of his waistband as he approached.

"I don't know if I should bitch-slap you for screwing my girl or ask you for a fucking three-way," he sneered at Jane.

"Don't be so crass, Jackson," Jane reprimanded.

"You know I'm not one of those old-time pussies who don't hit women," Jackson grimaced in her face, "in fact, I'm all *for* equality." Jackson gritted his teeth, still acting the macho man in spite of the excruciating pain that hurtled through his leg like an acid burn.

"You lay one finger on me, Jackson Booth," Jane growled and stood up off the bed, "and I'll break every fucking bone you've got." She squared up to the man who knew every single square inch of her body.

Jackson pointed the gun at Jane, his hand shaking, breathing labored.

"What the fuck is going on here?" Lee butted in. "Johnny's dead, Mikey's shit-knows-where, and you're still bothered about some dumb pussy?!"

"Dead?" Jane was distracted from the gun pointed at her. "Who's dead?"

"I'll ask the fucking questions," Jackson gasped. And in that instant, all of the menace drained from his voice, and his skin took on a sickly gray pallor, made his face look swollen and waxy. "What the fuck −?" Jackson crumpled onto the hard tiled floor in front of Jane with a breathy grunt, his gun tumbling from his hand to clatter away. Jackson clawed at his throat with desperate fingers, mouth wide open, as he made strangled, wheezing sounds.

"What happened to him?" Jane demanded to know.

"He got bit," Fred blurted out. "A centipede bit his leg. A big one! But not as big as…" there was panic in Fred's voice, and the words just refused to form.

Jane grabbed the EpiPen – the *only* EpiPen – from her pocket and knelt by Jackson.

Jackson grabbed her wrist as she raised the pen above his chest. "You're not sticking that fucking thing in me," Jackson managed to say, his breath ever more ragged as his throat continued to constrict.

"You're in anaphylaxis. You're having an allergic reaction, you jackass," Jane's voice was calm.

"I don't care what fancy fucking words you use, bitch. You're not sticking me," Jackson hissed.

"Then lay there and die," Jane told him, again with that calm voice. She made to stand up and felt Jackson's hand relax around her wrist.

Jane plunged the EpiPen into Jackson's straining chest and hit the plunger hard with her thumb. Jackson squealed and pushed her away. He pulled the offending article out of his chest and threw it into the pool, where it landed with a tiny *plop*.

"Motherfucker," he managed to gasp as his breath immediately began its return to normal.

A noise from the door startled them, and all attention refocused.

The door swung open and knocked Lee out of the way like he weighed nothing. He whimpered and rubbed his shoulder.

"Darlene?" Fred gasped.

A ghoulish apparition staggered, screaming and trailing blood into the pool room.

Mel's scream joined Darlene's, and their shrill voices

echoed around the warm, damp air.

Jane found herself rooted to the spot. Instincts screamed that it was her professional obligation to go help the poor girl, yet at the same time, it held her legs immobile.

Shrieking like a banshee and in the most unimaginable agony, Darlene stumbled toward the pool. Her face was a bloodied mask of shredded flesh and pink-white bone, one of her eyes was missing, the other oozed blood and thick, clear fluids. Darlene's once bountiful breasts were now little more than flaps of loose skin; emptied of their meat, shredded, they dripped clots of dark blood over the glistening centipedes that swarmed over and burrowed into them.

"Help me," Darlene implored. She held out her hands, Christ-like to show a writhing centipede in each, gripped by lacerated fingers that showed white bone and frayed tendons.

Fred made to move toward his lover but recoiled in horror as he saw the rear-end of a 'pede dangling between Darlene's legs, two-thirds of its body buried where his penis had been only hours before. Fred gulped down the bile that crept along the back of his throat, and his face turned an ashen gray as if he were going to throw up or faint.

Or both.

Martha-Ray added her scream to the cacophony that reverberated around the stone walls as Darlene lurched forward and into the pool. She made a clumsy belly flop that made a huge, crimson splash, and then she sank amidst the feathery cloud of blood that leaked out of her ruined body.

Jane looked down at Darlene's body in despair and hoped that the poor girl was dead and would thus be spared the further agony of drowning. The 'pedes that she had brought along on – and inside – her body crawled away from their feast, wriggling in a distressed frenzy as slowly they began to drown at the bottom of the pool.

Mel and Martha-Ray sobbed quietly, and an uneasy air of disbelief settled over everyone in the room.

"What the fuck did you do to her?!" Fred growled at Jackson.

"We didn't touch her," Jackson protested, "I swear."

Fred stormed over to Jackson, grabbed the man's shirt, lifting his upper body up off of the ground. "You sick bastard! You did this!"

Lee stepped up and pulled Fred away.

"He's telling the truth, man!" he shouted at Fred. "We left her in bed when we grabbed you. She was just all Jim-dandy fine and sleeping when we left her."

Fred shrugged Lee off, close to crying but determined not to show any sign of weakness in front of Jackson and his thug.

Jane stepped between them. "I think now would be a good time to explain what hell happened up there," she said.

"There was this fucking big alien thing," Lee blurted out, "like one of those." He pointed to the three jars that housed the captured 'pedes. "But bigger," his voice lowered to a hushed, almost reverential tone. "Much fucking bigger."

"A centipede bit Jackson on the leg," Fred filled in.

"That? That was fucking *nothing*!" Lee interrupted and shot an apologetic look at Jackson. "Tell her 'bout the real big motherfucker that ate Johnny!"

"He's right, Professor, we did see a big one," Fred told her, and his voice quavered as if he were already beginning to doubt what he'd seen.

"We've seen a lot of big 'pedes, Fred, it's what we came here for," Jane reminded him.

"But the one we saw was really, really, *really* big," Fred's voice was flat scared.

"Could you be a little more descriptive than just adding

more *'really's?'* Martha-Ray joined in, "was it bigger than the one that Mel caught?"

"Listen up, bitch!" Lee spat. "What we saw upstairs was *fucking* big, alright? Is that a better adjective for ya?" there was anger and panic in his voice. "It picked up Johnny like he was nothing and cracked his head open like it was a fucking egg!"

"You *have* to believe him," Fred protested. "That thing must have been at least twenty-five feet, maybe thirty!"

Jane frowned and said, "I might have guessed it." She shook her head at him. "You disappear for hours, come back with these two characters all stinking of skunk, and expect me to believe this bullshit!"

"We're telling you the truth, lady!" Lee was getting himself all worked up again, and pretty soon, he wouldn't be able to form a coherent sentence at all.

"You're fucking high, is what you are," Jane retorted.

"We might be a little high, but we know damn well what we saw," Jackson joined in. He sat up. "That thing up there was – *is* – the biggest goddamned *insect* you ever saw." Jackson rubbed at his leg in an attempt to ease the throbbing that ached down to the marrow.

"Just in case you have forgotten, Fred, you're talking to the world's leading authority on 'pedes, and I didn't get to *be* the world's leading authority by not knowing my subject," Jane lectured. "There is no physical way for an arthropod to grow anywhere near that size, no way at all." She paused. Let that sink in, she thought. "Even the prehistoric genus –""– *Euphoberia,*" Mel chipped in from the bed.

"Thank you, Melanie," Jane sounded impatient. "Even *Euphoberia* only grew to three feet long."

"Perhaps there were some bigger ones, and one survived?" Lee ventured.

"I doubt very much that you've observed some four hundred, thirty-million-year-old throwback in California.

That shit you've been smoking must be really something!" Jane chided, annoyed at having to deal with society's ignorant. "This is not some lame-ass Sci-fi movie." Jane snorted at the very thought; she'd sat through *Magapython Vs Gatoroid* and *Piranhaconda* back to back not so long ago, and whilst they'd totally offended her zoologist sensibilities, she'd thoroughly enjoyed them both much to her eternal shame.

"It's the oxygen," Martha-Ray interjected in an attempt to dissolve the mounting tension. It was obvious that Lee's aggressive posturing meant that he did not take kindly to being treated as stupid or laughed at. She'd read about his sort and figured if he became too agitated, all verbal reasoning would abandon him, and eventually he'd resort to violence. "In prehistoric times, the atmosphere had more O-two in it; around thirty percent to be precise. That's as opposed to twenty-one percent today."

"And?" Lee questioned.

"And that meant that the arthropods – insects, spiders, and whatnot – could grow to be far bigger than they do today," Martha-Ray explained. "They don't breathe like we do, they don't have lungs that pull air into them, they take their oxygen in by diffusion through spiracles on the sides of their body segments."

"That means it just drifts into their bodies," Jane clarified.

"I know what fucking diffusion is," Lee growled.

"That limits the distance the air can travel inside a body before the oxygen runs out because the oxygen is absorbed by the trachea on the way in," Martha-Ray continued, "so the less oxygen in the air, the less distance it can travel into the animal's body, the smaller the creature has to be."

"So, how come we've already managed to catch centipedes three times bigger than normal?" Fred asked, which all in all was a surprisingly intelligent question for him.

"These 'pedes are *longer* and a little wider than usual," Jane told him. "The air is obviously getting all the way in to their bodies to oxygenate them. It's possibly something to do with this place – perhaps the gasses coming up into the spa are oxygen-rich and have elevated the O-two levels down here." Jane fought down her disappointment at this hypothesis: this could have been a one-off incidence after all. "I really doubt if we would find any specimens larger than these," Jane concluded.

"But what if it's like what they say about bees?" Lee asked, his dulled mind churning.

"Bees?" Jane was puzzled.

"I heard this thing that according to the laws of physics, it's impossible for a bee to fly. Only no one has told the bees that," Lee said in all seriousness. "So what if this is the same idea – no one has told the centipedes they can't get bigger?"

"All that myth tells us," Jane smiled at Lee with much condescension, "is something about the laws of physics."

"And what's that Ma'am?" Lee snarled.

"That sometimes, they can be wrong," as the words tripped from her tongue the smile fell from Jane's face. Sure, the whole myth about bees was just that; somebody had done a few calculations and compared bee flight with that of airplanes and concluded – rather absurdly – that bees can't fly. It so happened that the motion of a bee's wings is more akin to that of a helicopter's rotors that create a downdraft, and so yes, they can (*obviously*) fly. Even so, the idea that the laws of physics can sometimes be disproved held true. Had the moronic, shaven-headed thug just maneuvered Jane into destroying her own argument?

Jane pulled her cell phone from her back pocket, took a gut-churning glance at Darlene, at the bottom of the pool surrounded by drowning 'pedes, and sighed.

"I'll phone Mr. Levandowski to come let us out," she said as she hit the dial button.

2

Lenard Levandowski's cell lit up and buzzed like an annoyed wasp in the gallon-sized zip-locked baggie. It vibrated against the keys and loose change that nestled in the bag along with it and composed a jangling, clattering melody.

Larry-Wayne Williaford snorted with disdain as he eyed the baggie in his hand. His apparently now-dead friend, Lenard always killed the ring tone on his phone, said he found the noise too obtrusive. But Larry had it figured that the old reprobate just got a kick out of having something that vibrated in his pocket.

Larry-Wayne looked down at the phone and considered answering it, more out of idle curiosity than anything else, but then the cell phone quit vibrating mid-ring.

"Thank you for coming all the way out to Palm Springs at this late hour, Mr. Williaford," the Medical Examiner said in a rather brusque manner as he ushered Larry-Wayne toward the mortuary, "and in the storm too."

"Nothin' more than the good Lord's flatulence out there, Doc," Larry-Wayne mumbled. "Least I could do for Lenard."

"Of course, of course," the M.E urged, "now, if you'd be so good as to sign this release for your friend's belongings."

Ted Buckner had been the Palm Springs Medical Examiner for nine years now, had been through more than his fair share of the cadaver identifications. This one from Desert Hot Springs had been quick and easy; all he needed was someone to verify the dead 'guy which his driving license had already given away and to sign off on the bottom of the relevant forms.

The difficult part had been patching the old guy's head back together for the viewing. Levandowski's head had been so badly smashed in that his face was hideously distorted and seemed to Buckner like he was viewing it through one of those warped, carnival sideshow mirrors. The mess had been so hellish that it had taken Buckner and his assistant three hours to make the old boy presentable. That meant that they'd not had the time to strip Lenard of his clothing, something Buckner figured could wait until after the weekend.

"There were only three numbers programmed in his phone, I figured you were the one to call," Buckner explained to Larry-Wayne in his usual droning monotone voice. He was far too genteel to mention that of the other two numbers in Mr. Levandowski's phone: one was a local escort agency that specialized in girls who appeared to be somewhat under-aged, and the other was someone identified in the cell phone's contact directory as *Bug Woman*. The former contact, Buckner had recognized from an investigation two years previous in which one of the agency's girls who looked fifteen but who was actually twenty-three had turned up dead, face down, in a ditch on the North side of town. The latter, judging by the pictures Lenard had of her, was into some pretty weird shit indeed. *Bug Woman?* Buckner shuddered to think what she was all about.

Larry-Wayne nodded his acknowledgement of the M. E.'s comment. Just what the fuck was that supposed to mean? *You were the best one to call*?

"Lenard's got no family and no friends, 'ceptin' for me," Larry-Wayne drawled, "I think he's got a half-sister in Anchorage, but they ain't spoken in near-on twenty-odd years 'n some." He noted with some annoyance that the M.E. had just glanced at his watch for the fifth time in as many minutes. "I'll get going now before your storm gets much worse; don't wanna be spending the night in this place like old Lenard now, do I?" Larry-Wayne let out a wry laugh. "Thanks for lettin' me take his belongings an' all," he said as he lifted up the clear baggie and glanced at the keys, battered wallet, loose change, and cell phone that rattled within.

"That's no problem at all, Mr. Williaford." Buckner smiled as he maneuvered Larry-Wayne to the door with a gentle push in the small of his back. "I don't usually work on Saturdays, but I'm heading out of town tomorrow for a family reunion in Laguna Woods and wanted to wrap things up here before I go," he explained with little recognition of his own insensitivity.

"I'll perform the autopsy when get back on Tuesday, but suffice to say, it should be fairly straightforward under the circumstances."

Larry-Wayne shuffled toward the door, his head bowed, eyes sad.

"Mr. Williaford?" Buckner felt a pang of pity for the old guy who'd just seen what was most likely his only friend in the whole world for the last time. "His brain stem snapped immediately on impact with the other vehicle. It was just like turning out a light, if that's any consolation."

"Does that mean it ups Lenard's chances of him coming back from the dead?" Larry-Wayne asked with a growl.

"Er, no," Buckner mumbled.

"Then no, it's *no* fuckin' consolation," Larry-Wayne growled back, "so you can stick your rote platitudes up your fucking ass." He walked out of the room, leaving Ted Buckner just more than a little nonplussed.

On his way out of the building, Larry-Wayne plucked Lenard's cell phone out of the baggie. There was a message blinking on the screen; *missed call.* Below that was another message, this one in red; *no service,* and he saw that there were no little bars to denote any kind of signal. When he pressed a button to see who the missed call was from, up popped a picture of the slutty university woman with Larry-Wayne's dick in her mouth.

"Sly old fucker," Larry-Wayne chortled, "I *knew* you were takin' pictures." He recalled with fondness the woman's protests when they'd suggested using their cameras, and how both he and Lenard had promised with all sincerity to put them away.

Yet here was her full-lipped mouth and Lenard's cock in union; a fitting testimony to his former friend's magnificent last night on Earth. Larry-Wayne made a mental note to take a good look through *all* of Lenard's pictures on the phone back in the comfort of his own apartment. With that to look forward to, Larry-Wayne cheered up a little. He switched off Lenard's phone and plopped it back into the bag where it chinked against the shrapnel of loose change and the Hotel keys.

Ah yes, the Mountainview. What a sweet job Lenard had landed himself there and no mistaking. All he'd had to do was swing by every couple of days or so to make sure the hotel was secure and that no kids or vagrants had broken in. And that had happened only the once, not long after Lenard had gotten the job. A handful of scruffy itinerants had let themselves in, with the intention of squatting in the opulent surroundings, but Lenard had persuaded them to move on with help from a handful of local hoodlums, who came along carrying baseballs bats and sawn-offs. Heads had been cracked, a kneecap or two peppered with buckshot, and the invaders had been well and truly repelled. Word must have got around among the vagrant grapevine because none came back, ever. And, naturally, Lenard had kept quiet to his employers about that particular episode.

And that was pretty much it. A quick sweep of the outside, of the most over-the-top boarded-up building in the universe a couple of times a week, and Lenard Levandowski got to drive a fucking Lexus! And that was not to mention the bank account full of cash that Lenard had accumulated – Larry-Wayne had sneaked a peek at one of Lenard's bank statements one time and had seen for himself how come his friend got to pay cash for his fancy car. Oh yeah, and buy in takeouts and whores anytime the fancy took him.

Larry-Wayne figured that he might just give Lenard's employers – ex-employers he figured they were now – a call and offer his services, what with Lenard being permanently indisposed and all. It seemed to him to be the most decent thing to do under the circumstances.

Happy with that thought, Larry-Wayne Williaford braced himself against the brutal wind that slapped at his face and stepped out into the night.

3

Ted Buckner pulled the crisp, white sheet away from Lenard Levandowski's body and mentally ticked off his to-do list for the evening: have Lenard's body identified – check; e-mail his findings of the Mendoza girl's remains to Don Newman – check; send tissue samples of aforementioned girl's remains to the School of Tropical Medicine at Baylor College – check; get assistant to pick up dry cleaning before he went home – and check!

All done, dusted and good to go. Buckner cast his expert eye over Levandowski's squat, still body. He noted the hair loss, the dry skin, the brittle, broken fingernails – all classic symptoms that the old boy's thyroid was well on its way to giving up the ghost. Buckner bet himself twenty bucks that there'd be nodules in Lenard's throat too, and a quick feel won him the bet.

He'd seen this kind of sickness once before. It had been rife among the guys who'd been caught up in the Three Mile Island disaster, and it had killed a fair few of them well before their time; which meant, of course, that Lenard Levandowski had the tell-tale signatures of mild radioactivity poisoning. It was not near enough to raise alarm bells in Buckner's mind right now, there'd be no need for lead-lined coffins and departmental quarantines this time; a dose of thyroid cancer was nothing to panic about, no matter how advanced it may be. And that was something Buckner wouldn't know until he sliced Levandowski open on Tuesday – something the M.E. was quite looking forward to, as it happened. Still, he thought to himself, low-level radiation is still radiation, and it'll kill you. Maybe not for a long time, but it'll kill you all the same.

Buckner guessed that Levandowski probably would have had another three years in him, four if he was lucky and could have afforded good treatment – if the Ford hadn't knocked the life out of him, that is – and then his immune system would have died its death and taken the old man with it. Buckner scribbled out a post-it note to remind himself to look up Lenard's records when he got back on Tuesday. He'd put another twenty bucks – double or quits – on the guy hailing from Three-Mile, or possibly even Chernobyl, given his name.

The M.E. also made himself a note to see if he couldn't get a hold of a Geiger counter from somewhere. Again, it could wait until Tuesday because now it was quitting time.

As Ted Buckner slid Lenard's body into the morgue refrigerator, he didn't notice the slight, undulating movement beneath the corpse's bloodstained shirt. Humming a toneless tune to himself, Buckner slammed the door shut on the corpse and went home.

4

At around the same time as Jane Lucas was trying to save Jackson Booth's cheating ass from the centipede bite, Don Newman was re-reading the e-mail he'd received from Ted Buckner when the house phone on the desk rang out. The cop jumped at the sound that shattered the silence, startled from his deliberations.

No one ever called the house phone, apart from those

ever-invasive telesales people and his father. Newman very much doubted that even the former would be calling at ten o'clock at night, which left Dad; he *always* called on the house phone as he flatly refused to own a cell phone. He'd it on good authority from his old colleagues at the FBI that cell phones were specifically designed to give you brain cancer. It was all part of a global conspiracy, according to the *reliable* source, to thin out the human population; the main stay of that argument being that there are more people in India with cell phones than there are with toilets.

Personally speaking, Newman reckoned it was more likely because his father had trouble with small buttons since his eyesight had begun failing and was too goddamned proud to say anything. Praying that all was well with his octogenarian father, Newman picked up the phone.

"Newman," he grunted.

"Hey Don, it's Jon at the Eisenhower Medical Center," a cheerful voice sputtered out of the receiver, "sorry to call you so late on the land-line, but the cell tower's gone down in the storm."

"Again?" Newman said. "You'd have thought they'd have learned their lesson after the fourth time that thing went down." He offered a forced laugh. "How can I help you, Dr. Wong?"

"You asked me to call you when the Mountainview boy woke up," the Doctor said.

Newman could hear yelling and clattering in the background, along with the loud, frantic voices of over-stressed nurses.

"Well, he's woken up, alright," Wong added.

"Okay, I'll be right over," Newman said with a heavy sigh and replaced the receiver.

He closed his laptop's lid and padded across the room to wake his wife. "Hey, Hun, I'm home, but I've got to go back out. Police stuff," he whispered, stroking the hair from her face, "I'll take the Mom-mobile."

"Alright, sweetie," Janet Newman replied, and briefly, her eyes flickered open. Newman doubted if she registered the fact that she wasn't dreaming him. "Careful, windy," she murmured, and her head rolled as she went back to her dreams.

Lieutenant Newman kissed his wife's forehead and nose and let himself back out into the blustery night.

CHAPTER ELEVEN

1

"Your legs are all black," Mel informed her boyfriend.

"Ya, don't fuckin' say!?" Jackson retorted with a groan as he shifted his weight around on the recliner and tried his damndest not to show just how much pain he was in.

"Oh yeah," Mel said and smiled her embarrassment away. "I meant black-*er*. Than usual, I mean."

"Looks like its necrotizing already," Jane crouched down to take a better look at the offending leg. It really didn't look good at all. Although the bite wound had finally stopped bleeding, it now oozed a thick, grayish slime. The flesh around the twin punctures the 'pede had dug into Jackson's calf were swollen, puffy, and a particularly unpleasant shade of black. Jane could also make out the poisoned track where the venom was gradually making its way toward the meat of Jackson's thigh; it was well above his knee now and had no signs of stopping, despite the belt that remained strapped tight around his thigh.

"Necrotizing? What the 'fuck is that?" Lee butted in.

"It means the flesh is dying," Jane explained with that curt, clinical tone in her voice, "probably helped along by the proteases in the 'pede's venom."

"So, what you're saying here is that that thing is remotely digesting my leg?" Jackson tried - failed spectacularly – to mask the fear in his voice.

Jane nodded. "It's probably not helped by the fact that this tourniquet is too tight, you need to let me loosen it," she told him as she reached for the belt. "We don't want gangrene setting in."

"As opposed to the poison that's dissolving my fucking leg?" Jackson snapped and batted her hands away.

"Look, I'm just trying to help," Jane flinched.

"Then get me the fuck out of here!"

"He's right," Martha-Ray chipped in, "he really ought to be in a hospital."

"Don't you think I don't know that?" Jane defended, her voice raised. "I couldn't get a hold of Mr. Levandowski, and now there's no goddamned signal on any of our cell phones!" There was that, and the discovery that every hotel phone they'd tried was dead as the proverbial. She had Martha-Ray and Fred try every phone in every room they could get to safely, just in case the lack of cell phone signal was simply because they were in the basement. "I guess that's one fucking bill they forgot to pay," she said with a weak smile.

"We can't just sit here and hope that somebody happens along," Fred stated the obvious.

"When did the old man say he was coming back?" Martha-Ray asked.

"Tomorrow night," Jane replied.

"We can't stay here another twenty-four hours," Lee raised his voice, "not with his fucking leg rotting and that fucking alien insect thing running around!" The boy was scared way beyond shitless, his macho facade failing him big time.

Jane knew that the tattooed boy was right. It was certainly imperative that they get Jackson some proper medical care and quick, although it was probably too late to save most of his leg – Mel's band-aids and peroxide hadn't quite sufficed.

Her mind wandered back to the conversation she'd had with Levandowski earlier that morning. She'd been pretty pissed when he'd casually announced that he'd have to lock the door behind them and that it was more than his job was worth for him to leave the key behind with her. And then there'd been that look in his eye that reminded Jane of how her father would wink when he shared a secret with her. But – and it was a big but – what if he'd been toying with her and had left the door unlocked after all? He was a wily old bastard who loved his games – *mind* as well as physical – and perhaps he felt that he owed *something* to her after the sexual gymnastics he'd put her through the night before?

"We'll try the front door," Jane announced.

"The old fart said he was locking it," Mel said as she pulled on her beach top over her head.

"Well, just maybe he didn't," Jane answered her curtly. "The least we can do is *try*. Unless you're happy sitting by the pool and watching your boyfriend die, that is?" She blanched as she realized that Jackson could hear her, loud and clear.

"He's not my –"

"He's not gonna die," Lee whined, "you said –"

"I know what I *said*, Lee," Jane lowered her voice, "but you've seen Jackson's leg. Unless he gets treatment the venom's going to keep on spreading. Once it gets up into his body…" Jane didn't bother completing the sentence.

Lee and Jane stared at each other.

"So, let's go check out the front door," Martha-Ray split the standoff.

"We should take weapons or something," Fred

mumbled, "just in case that thing decides to come back."

"Grab the snake hooks and the grabbers – we can use the poles to fight off any monsters," Jane mocked Fred. She hoped to God that his weed-high would disperse sometime very soon; he was of no use to her scatterbrained and stoned and harping on about 'pedes the size of trucks.

"Is that a good idea, Ma'am?" Lee butted in.

"I'd say so, Lee," Jane said, "unless you want to face the things that did that to Darlene with just a hook for protection?" She pointed to the pink-stained pool.

"I didn't mean – what I mean is, I saw this movie once, where they cut these centipedes in half, and then both halves stayed alive and killed everyone."

Jane fought back her smile, fearing that it would be misconstrued. "Yeah, I saw that movie, too," she told him. "That's not really something you need worry about, Lee; you can trust me on that. You cut those bastards in half, they'll die – and stay fucking dead too."

Hearing this from the expert seemed to placate Lee, although Jane was sure that she saw the boy's lower lip tremble as he turned away from her.

2

Jane, Mel, Lee, and Fred made their way up the stairs, leaving the pool room behind them. Jane and Mel made a concerted effort to keep a discernible distance from each other, the awkwardness between the two women most palpable. They hadn't had any time to talk about the whole Jackson situation, and there was quite possibly a lot to be said, considering that they had just learned that they had been inadvertent cock-buddies for almost a year.

Jane didn't care too much, truth be told, *c'est la vie* and all that, but she suspected that Mel was hurting more than she was giving away. Of course, the sixty-four million dollar question was – had she been the most hurt by

Jackson's infidelity or her professor's?

Lee and Fred followed on in silence. They had nothing much to say to each other, and the shock of Darlene and Johnny's death weighed on both their minds. Martha-Ray had elected to stay behind with Jackson since he could barely walk; Jane had agreed that she and the posse would come back for him once they'd established whether the front door was unlocked or not.

At the top of the concrete stairs, they reached the door to the hotel lobby. Jane pushed it open.

"Oh, my…" she uttered and stepped back, knocking into Mel. The door swung closed.

"Jesus shit bricks," Lee cussed and strained on his tiptoes to peer over Jane's shoulder, through the tiny rectangle of glass in the door and out into the lobby.

The lobby floor was literally crawling with centipedes.

Thousands of them.

"Now, what do we do?" Mel eyed the front door that suddenly seemed to be a million miles away.

"We do what we came to do," Jane told her, steadying the shake in her voice. Her every worse nightmare was unfolding by the minute, and her nerves were rapidly starting to unravel. "We go see if the front door is unlocked," Jane continued as she studied the 'pedes that filled the room like a glistening, maroon carpet. They crawled around, over, and under each other, entwining their long, glinting bodies like some nefarious pit of serpents. Jane saw that some of the larger creatures would strike out at their smaller companions, killing and eating them. The faint sounds of crunching made her skin break out in gooseflesh.

"We can pick our way through them," Jane said, "probably best if Lee and I go, since we're the only ones with sensible footwear." She looked down at Mel's bejeweled flip-flops that showed off her long, sensual, and infinitely suckable toes, and at Fred's strappy sandals that made his bare feet a perfectly exposed target for hungry, pissed-off 'pedes.

"You expect me to go in there?" Lee was truly petrified now, "with those fucking things?"

For a hardened street thug, he sure was acting like a frady-cat, Jane mused. If only he could feel the creeping terror that coursed through *her* body right now. Jane fought to ignore it; the ringing in her ears that sounded like a dozen people were blowing whistles inside her head, the resounding *thud – thud – thud – thud* of her heart, the drip of sweat down her back.

"If you want to get out of here, then yes, that's precisely what I expect," Jane held firm. "They're just big bugs, Lee. You can poke them out of the way with your stick."

No one sniggered or picked up on the double entendre.

Lee nodded. Yep, as afraid as he was of the crawling things in the lobby, he was doubly terrified of the *Big One* that ate up Johnny Psycho like he was a corncob. He wanted nothing more than to put as many miles between himself and that fucking abomination as he could, probably wouldn't stop running till he hit San Francisco.

"And for Christ's sake, try not to get bitten," Jane added, "I used our one and only EpiPen on Jackson." She shot a withering look at Mel, who gave her a hard stare back.

Gingerly, Jane opened the lobby door and recoiled at the pungent reek of uric acid that assaulted her nostrils. She'd noticed the smell earlier, when they'd first made their way into the Mountainview and although it had been a lot fainter than it was now, Jane cursed herself for having not made the connection. 'Pedes secrete uric acid as pee, and the pervading stink of it in the hotel should have been a portent to her expert mind that there was most likely a large number of the things dwelling in the place. And if she'd known then what she'd be facing now, Jane doubted very much if she would have continued on with her goddamned *bug hunt*.

Jane pointed her snake hook at the lobby floor and

pushed at a 'pede half the length of her own body. Much to her relief, the thing scuttled away. Encouraged by this, and fighting the urge to flee with every nerve fiber in her damp, sweating body, Professor Jane Lucas took her first step toward the front door of the hotel.

She picked her way with short, tentative steps through the carpet of creatures, her memory taking great pleasure in tormenting her with visions of Kate Capshaw reaching into that dark, narrow hole in the brick wall, and the myriad creeping, crawling things jostling against her skin and that ever-present 'pede crawling through her hair. Jane shook her head to clear the thoughts, and sweat splashed from her hair, into her eyes. Jane blinked away the stinging droplets and glanced back toward Lee who now seemed remarkably calm considering his early reticence. He followed her footsteps, stepping with the greatest of care through the crawling mass, bending slightly at the knees to push the more adventurous 'pedes away with the tip of his snake hook.

"Oh shit," Lee grunted, "that's Mikey."

Jane spun around, and across the lobby, she saw the elevator. Its doors opened and closed in a lazy tempo on the bloodied, skeletal remains of whom Jane assumed was the aforementioned gang member. Mikey's ruined body lay half-in, half-out of the elevator, his denuded leg bones – sticking out through the shredded denim of his jeans – were tripping the elevator's safety mechanism and forcing the doors to open only to try closing again.

The congealing pool of Mikey's spilled, slippery viscera undulated and seethed with a mass of crawling 'pedes that cavorted beneath and within it, and it looked like it had a life all of its own. Mikey's head was little more than a grinning skull festooned with shreds of wrinkled flesh and thick clots of blood. As Jane looked on, his denuded jaw opened and closed as a centipede crawled through it, and it looked like Mikey was calling out to her. Jane fought hard against the gag reflex that threatened to pour sour tequila up out of her rolling stomach.

"He ran away," Lee said by means of justification, although more to himself than to Jane. "He should have stayed with us." And Lee couldn't help but look into the raw, hollowed holes where Mikey's round, crazy eyes should have been. "Sweet Jesus, Mikey," Lee gulped down hot, salty bile and tears and tore his gaze away from the vision of gore and mess that was once the closest thing to a friend he'd ever had in his miserable life.

Lee felt a strong tug and looked down to see that a centipede was crawling up his metal grabber pole. The thing had coiled its body around the pole, and like some bizarre snake made out of Legos, it gripped the smooth aluminum with its claws. There was something just not right in Lee's book about a bug so damned big that you could *feel* its weight, and he felt himself freaking out. Lee inhaled deeply and held that breath. Slowly, firmly, he shook the snake hook to dislodge the creature. The centipede held fast and continued its steady advance toward his hand.

What the fuck do you do? Drop your only weapon or let the thing crawl up onto your hand? Lee lifted the hook and whipped vigorously it over his head. The centipede flew off the end and hit onto the floor to send its brethren scurrying off in all directions.

"Cocksucker!" Lee shouted out loud as he stomped with all his might onto its head. It felt good to feel the thing's *crunch* beneath his foot; one might even say therapeutic.

Jane turned around, startled by the sudden noise. She saw Lee lift up his foot to examine the clear blood and squished entrails that had splattered over his Nikes. He grimaced, and Jane shook her head at him.

"You really shouldn't do that," she chastised. "They can still bite when you think they're dead." Still, it *was* gratifying to see one of the creatures squashed and dead, even if it was only one among so many.

It was at that moment that Jane's peripheral vision picked out something that struck her as strange. All of the 'pedes in the lobby had turned to face them.

All of them.

The creatures had ceased their tireless crawling and were standing perfectly still, their glistening, blank faces pointing at Jane and Lee. It was as if *en masse* they were watching, waiting.

"Oh fuck," Jane muttered. She stood, rooted to the spot, not daring to move one more step. She recalled the iconic scene in *The Birds* in which the titular creatures had flocked to one large tree and had just sat there in silence, their beady little eyes filled with hatred and menace.

"What are they doing?" Lee asked, his voice cracking.

"I don't know, but this can't be good."

"I thought you were some kind of expert on these fucking things."

"I am," Jane defended, "and *I've* never seen this type of behavior before."

"What do we do?" Lee trembled.

"We keep going, I guess, while they're still." Jane took a step forward, another one.

And then another.

The 'pedes just watched.

Only they weren't really *watching*, Jane knew that much. Their eyes could just about discern light from dark, possibly some movement, as well – but obviously, it was enough for them to know precisely where she and Jackson Booth's thug were.

Jane continued on slowly toward the hotel door, keeping her wary eyes on the motionless 'pedes that surrounded her. She had read every article ever written on *Scolopendra gigantea* – fuck, she had *written* most of the definitive ones – and none of them had ever mentioned any kind of swarming behavior.

Not one.

Then again, group behavior had never actually been studied in *gigantea* before, chiefly because of their solitary lifestyle and intrinsic tendency toward aggression and cannibalism.

Was it possible that they could exhibit behaviors similar to those seen in locusts? Locusts were just your ordinary, run of the mill, solitary grasshoppers. But, given a specific set of circumstances, they would band together in their hundreds of millions and deviate from their regular, peaceful behavior to become a voracious swarm capable of untold damage. Add to that the shoaling behavior seen in numerable fish species and the flocking habits of many birds, and perhaps one could deduce that swarming behavior is potentially inbuilt in *all* species? True swarming behavior typically entailed the individual animals behaving as a single organism (*super-organism* was the phrase coined by some and also applied to the social insects – Jane had never much cared for it, she found the phrase misleading) and in some instances made ordinarily harmless creatures very dangerous indeed – just look at how normally law-abiding humans act in a riot situation.

But most intriguing of all was the mystery of how the individuals comprising a swarm managed to communicate with each other to avoid collisions, cannibalism, or fighting over the sudden decrease in space. Take a look at how a humble grackle flock spaces itself out across a street side wire – you could measure the distance between each individual bird to within a fraction of an inch. It was as if they had a set of unwritten bird rules by which they all abided.

Jane was astounded – and terrified – at the possibilities that her hypothesis presented, both professionally and for her chances of surviving this nightmare. A swarm of giant 'pedes acting as one? That *didn't* really bear thinking about right now; it was certainly one for the safety of her laboratory, though, once she was no longer *surrounded* by her subject. As Jane reached the hotel door, she'd already decided that swarming behavior in myriapods should be her next research project.

Jane pulled the door open to face the rust-red steel door that stood between her and the howling, gritty winds outside. She looked across the lobby at Fred and Mel, and forced a *here goes* a smile.

"So, open it already," Lee said.

Jane pushed at the cold steel door with every ounce of strength and resolve she could muster.

It held tight.

Jane sighed and rested her forehead on the chilled door and closed her eyes. Outside, the wind wailed its banshee song. "I should have guessed this was never going to be that easy." She said.

"At least we tried," Lee placated, "there'll be another way out."

"No, Lee, there won't!" Jane raised her voice to the man. "In case you didn't notice, when you sneaked in, this place is sealed up tighter than a duck's ass!" her voice shook. "This was a one-off chance that the caretaker had forgotten to lock the door, and he *hasn't,* so we're fucking stuck in this God-forsaken place!"

Lee said nothing and simply stared at her like a kicked puppy. Jane even thought she heard him whimper.

"We'd best go back," Jane said.

Lee remained quiet, staring wide-eyed at the Professor. His gaze drifted upward, above Jane's head.

Jane followed the youth's crazy stare up along the sweeping wall that ran the full height of the hotel from the lobby to the skylights on the roof. The only noise that came out of her mouth was, "What the…?"

A centipede that defied everything, Jane thought she knew, hurtled down the high wall. It was of immense proportions, and its huge dull, black eyes burned into her.

The monstrous 'pede's bright yellow legs cast a startling contrast against the desert-colored wall and created a pattern of deep indents in the plaster as its spiked feet sought purchase on the wall.

"I told you," Lee muttered as the color drained from his thin face to leave it pallid and glistening with sweat.

Jane wanted to run, to hide, but she simply couldn't tear her eyes away from the monstrosity that appeared to be fixed on *her*. She had doubted Fred, Jackson, and Lee and their stories of a bus-sized creature making a meal of a grown man, but it had turned out that they had been right all along.

This thing was huge.

Impossibly, *fucking* huge.

The centipede raced down along the wall, showering the people below it with puffs of dry plaster. As it ran, its body zigzagged, and it weaved its head from side to side with its antennae twitching as it homed in on its prey.

"We'd better run," Jane whispered as if a lowered voice could somehow render her invisible to the creature.

Taking her own advice, Jane finally found her feet and sprinted from her spot beneath the 'pede, no longer caring about stepping on the centipedes that scuttled away from her pounding feet.

Lee followed hot on Jane's tail as she raced toward the door chased by the monstrous centipede that had now reached the lobby floor and raced after them. As it ran, the creature scattered the smaller centipedes with its pointed claws, and those that didn't move quickly enough were unceremoniously kicked out of the way by the giant's undulating legs or simply crushed underfoot.

As she ran, Jane's imagination tormented her with the ghost of the giant 'pede's warm breath on the back of her neck, although her rational brain told her that was an impossibility. Her mind's eye played out the video clip she'd shown her students, only with herself as the mouse;

held in a tight death grip in the 'pede's unyielding legs and staring deep into the creature's gaping maw as its maxillipeds yawned open wide to feast on her body. Jane fought the urge to scream, the terror trapped in her chest made it tight and ready to burst. Although she dared not glance back at the unfeasible animal, Jane knew that it was maintaining its unrelenting pursuit – a breathless, silent killer, and all the more terrifying for that.

An agonizing age passed before Jane reached the lobby doors. Lee had raced well ahead of her and was already through them when Jane slammed through. She dared a peek over her shoulder and saw that the 'pede was dangerously close, its fangs poised to strike. With the last of her strength, Jane pushed her body through the doors and heard the comforting sound as they slammed shut behind her. She collapsed to the floor next to Lee, her lungs burning through exertion, her breath labored and painful.

Mel and Fred leaned their weight against the double doors and watched through the tiny windows as the centipede hurtled toward them.

There was a loud, dull *thump* as the centipede smacked its hard body against the doors. Fred and Mel were bounced inward with the impact but kept their weight against the doors and prayed to whatever God may be listening, that the thing couldn't figure out door handles. The centipede charged the doors again, this time the doors rattled in their frame, and the hinges bent inward.

"It's coming in!" Fred barked.

"Hold the door! Hold the door!" Mel's panicked voice was shrill, painful to the ears.

Jane added her own weight to Lee's, against the doors, and the creature pushed once more at them with its colossal head. Close up through the small rectangles of glass, Jane thought, the ocelli demonic, and through them, she would be able to see directly into hell. She heard the thing's antennae as they *tappity-tapped* on the doors, as it tasted for its prey, sounding like the eerie clicking of Deathwatch beetles in ancient rafters.

Another push and the four were pushed inward under the 'pede's strength. Thankfully the doors held.

Like a child tiring of a game, the centipede gave up its attempts to force open the lobby doors and instead crawled up them to the wall above. Jane studied the creature as it went by, framed by the twin windows, its vast bulk maneuvered upward in a seemingly endless procession of red segments and clicking legs. The scientist in her could do nothing more than marvel at the sheer size of the creature; it was a perfectly magnified specimen as if she were observing it beneath some gigantic lens. And although the colossal size of the creature defied all logic and everything she knew about *gigantea*, there could be no denying what she saw; the creature's head was easily as broad as the hood of a small family car and the black fangs it had neatly tucked beneath were the size of her forearm and fed by venom glands that were human head-sized balloons of muscle.

As the 'pede ascended, Jane marveled at its shining underbelly; each one of the glistening red segments that looked like plastic and spanned five feet, and then some and were home to the vivid yellow legs that were, in some parts of the animal, much longer than her own.

"Sweet mother of God," was all Jane Lucas, Professor of Zoology and world-renowned *Scolopendra* expert, could bring herself to say, "just how the hell did that happen?"

CHAPTER TWELVE

1

Lieutenant Newman walked with brisk intent into the Intensive Care Unit without so much as a nod or a wave to the surly-looking Sister at the nurses' station. It had taken almost three times longer than normal for him to drive the eleven miles to the Palm Springs hospital because of the motherfucking windstorm, and he was in no mood for the usual niceties. The dumpy nurse must have picked up on the cop's mood and did nothing save stare after him as he approached the doctor who was standing by the door to room three.

"Thanks for calling me, Dr. Wong," Newman said and extended a hand.

"No worries, Don," The doctor said, "He's resting again. We've had to keep him sedated since he came out of the coma; his anxiety attacks have been quite aggressive."

"Yeah, I heard," Newman grunted and hoped that whilst he was there, there wouldn't be a repeat performance of the commotion he'd heard over the 'phone.

The doctor ushered Newman into the room where Stevie Johnson lay. There was a heavy bandage around the boy's head, which covered his entire scalp and left eye. Newman could see an ominous black stain oozing through the bandage over the covered eye, which lent the unfortunate boy the appearance of some badly thought-out Halloween pirate. His limp body was hooked up to an impressive array of medical equipment that blinked, blipped, and whirred around him, all serving to monitor his every life function as well as doing his breathing for him, feeding him, and removing his waste.

"We had to amputate the right hand," Wong informed Newman, "it was badly mauled, and most of the flesh was liquid by the time they brought him in. Do you have any idea if it was a centipede that did this?"

"I've got some creepy-crawly expert in San Diego looking at the one the paramedics picked up; we should know more in a few days," the cop told him.

Wong shook his head. "I saw plenty of snake bites in my time in ER. People would wander too far into the desert and step on a rattler – some of those snakes were big, too. I've seen people lose legs, arms, and even die if they didn't get to the hospital in time." Wong contemplated a moment. "Matter of fact, I hear there's been an upsurge in snake bite cases around here in the last year or two. I'm not sure if that's because of an increase in snakes or an increase in stupid people," he said, "but I've sure as damnation never seen anything like this from an insect."

"They're not insects," Newman corrected. "Apparently."

The doctor ignored Newman. He pried open Stevie's mouth and shone a penlight inside. "His esophagus is blistered and scratched. It looks like something sharp and corrosive was dragged out of his throat."

"One of the witnesses said they saw the centipede crawl out of his mouth," Newman informed him, "although the expert I spoke to said that would have been unlikely to have happened while the boy was still alive."

"Well, *something* crawled up this boy's throat," Wong said. "*And* he's been bitten by more than the one animal. A hell of a lot more." The doctor lifted a corner of the boy's head bandage to peep underneath. "His scalp was badly necrotized due to the enzymes in the venom, and we had to cut most of it away to stop it spreading to his face." Wong sighed. "We now have to wait and see if we got all of it."

"And if you haven't?"

"Then it spreads to his face," Wong told Newman without emotion. "We may still be able to save him, but who'd want to live their life without a face?"

"Couldn't you transplant him a new one?" Lieutenant Newman asked.

At this, Wong laughed a slight, coughing laugh. "Lieutenant, we're in Desert Hot Springs, not Sacramento. We've only just started doing appendectomies through keyhole surgery; I think face transplantation is a little above our pay grade."

Stevie Johnson awoke with a wild scream that shattered the hospital ward's quiet. He sat bolt upright in his bed with his remaining, uncovered eye darting to and fro like he was searching for something. "It got Virginia! It fucking bit her!" he yelled, "it fucking *ate* her!"

Wong looked around nervously at the nurses and orderlies who were already gathering.

"What got her, Son?" Newman asked.

Stevie made to grab the cop without realizing that he no longer had a hand, and the stump of his arm hovered as if his phantom fingers were actually gripping Newman's arm.

"It was a snake! A big, big snake!" Stevie cried. "But it had *legs*! It had fucking *legs*!"

"How big was the snake, son?" Newman stared deep into Stevie's one, crazed eye and tried his best to ignore the stinking, black ooze that seeped from beneath the bandage and trickled down the boy's face.

"It was as big as my car, man!" Stevie screamed, "as big as my fucking car!" With that, Stevie Johnson threw up a thick gob of stinking yellow bile and thrashed around on the bed like some snared animal. The heart monitor next to the bed beeped frantically then flatlined as the sticky sensors tore from his chest.

Two thickset orderlies bustled into the room, followed by the plump no-nonsense nurse who wielded an impressive looking syringe. The orderlies pinned the writhing Stevie Johnson face down to his bed whist No-Nonsense stuck him in the ass with the fat needle. In a heartbeat, the boy was calm.

"He's delirious," Wong explained to Newman. "It's a symptom of the *hydroxytryptamine* and *hemolytic phospholipase A* from the venom. They also cause heart palpitations and nausea. To be quite honest with you, with the amount of toxins in the boy's body – most of which we have no anti-venom – I'm quite astounded that he's still alive."

"Been hitting the Medical Journals, Doc?" Newman gave Wong a half-smile.

"Nah, Wikipedia," the doctor replied and grinned back. "You'd be surprised what we doctors learn from that particular resource."

Newman cracked a perfunctory grin, but his mind had already spun off elsewhere.

What if the cute Professor lady had followed up on her idea to visit the Mountainview? He'd figured she'd pretty much dismissed his storm warning the second it had left his mouth, so what if she *had* come to Desert Hot Springs and was in the hotel right now?

Christ knows how many bugs that can do this to a body?

Newman knew Lenard Levandowski well enough to know that, despite his rote *'nobody's allowed in the hotel'* line, and the fact that he had gotten the Police Department thrown out of a fresh crime scene, he wasn't above taking a bribe or two. Just the right financial incentive and the tight-fisted old coot would let just about anyone in to the Mountainview.

Newman had given Professor Lucas Levandowski's number. If she had gone to the hotel, and the old man had let her in, Newman knew for sure she'd be poking around looking for more centipedes – *'pedes* she'd called them – she'd seemed to Newman to have been particularly excited about finding more of the revolting creatures.

And not forgetting that Dr. Wong had just informed him that the Johnson boy had been bitten by more than one centipede, add that to Ted Buckner's report that had bluntly suggested that something bigger than the one Newman had driven to San Diego in a Wal-Mart bag had killed Johnson's girlfriend; things were starting to add up in the cop's mind. Newman began to feel a sick worry in the pit of his stomach. There was no telling just how many of those ungodly things there were in the hotel or how big the goddamned things had gotten.

As big as my fucking car, man!

"Thank you, Dr. Wong, I'll stay in touch," Newman grumbled, "let me know if he starts making any sense." He nodded at the unconscious Stevie Johnson and made his way out of the room, keen to get out of the hospital. If there was one place that made Newman more uncomfortable than colleges, it was fucking hospitals.

And he had to make sure that Professor Lucas wasn't in the hotel.

2

Jane tapped her finger hard on her cell's touch screen: as if by assaulting it that way, she could make the thing work. Fred, Mel, and Martha-Ray all followed suit with their own phones.

"Fucking nothing," Jane growled, "you guys?"

"Nah," Mel grunted.

"Nope," Fred's voice still had a nervous tremble to it.

"Signal's gone completely," Martha-Ray added.

Jane grunted her frustration and threw her phone on the floor: taking the momentary satisfaction in watching the thing shatter. *Well, it won't work at all now, will it dear?* As her Mom would have said.

They were all back in the pool room. Jane had figured it was as safe a place as any to hide out. The monster 'pede had crawled upward back in the lobby, so the opposite direction made a hell of a lot of sense to her. To Jane's relief, the smaller centipedes (the irony was not lost on Jane that she now considered a three-foot long 'pede to be *smaller*) seemed quite content to remain in the lobby and leave them be.

For now, at least.

She – they all – tried to ignore Darlene's body that lay at the bottom of the pool. The naturally replenishing water was diluting the girl's spilled blood, and now there was only the faintest tinge of pink. Jane supposed that somebody would have to go in and fish her out at some point, if only for decency's sake, but there had been a distinct shortage of volunteers as some of the 'pedes that the poor girl had carried in with her were still wriggling around a little. Just how long did it take those fucking things to drown anyway? Jane mused that there'd probably be a PhD thesis in that one for somebody.

Of course, there was no mad hurry to fish Darlene out of the pool, since there was nothing that could be done for her now; her body had finally quit bleeding and had soiled itself, and Jane figured she'd delegate Fred to pull his dead girlfriend out of the water once they'd got this whole god-awful mess sorted out.

Jane's focus had to remain on the living. She studied the people trapped in this hellish – but breathtaking – place with her. With the exception of Jackson and his tattooed henchman, they were her responsibility. And even then, Jane felt a slight pang of responsibility toward Jackson since were it not for her; he wouldn't have come along to the hotel to crash her field trip in the first place. And the poor guy really wasn't looking all that good, the venom had spread ever higher up his leg, and his fever spiked so much that his face dripped with corpulent droplets of acrid sweat.

It seemed odd, but Martha-Ray seemed to be the one who was holding herself together with some success. She sat quietly on her recliner and studied with deep intent the 'pedes that crawled tirelessly around in endless circles at the bottom of the specimen jars. It looked to Jane as if the girl was trying to psyche the creatures out, an attempt to exert a modicum of authority over them. Mel, on the other hand, appeared to be permanently on the verge of tears, and Fred was so obviously in shock and hadn't said – or done – an awful lot save stare blankly into space since they'd returned from the lobby.

"Okay, guys," Jane announced, doing her level best to sound authoritative. "We need to find *another* way out of here," she stated the obvious. Obvious it may be, but then again, no one else had mentioned it.

"You've seen this place," Martha-Ray answered, "it's sealed up tight. We're going to have to wait for the caretaker to come get us tomorrow."

"And you're confident that we'll last that long?" Mel challenged Martha-Ray, "with fuck knows how many centipedes and that giant thing crawling around out there? And that's assuming there is only the *one* giant one."

A pregnant pause and shocked, pale faces – if anyone had thought that the 'pede Lee and Jane had encountered out in the lobby was *not* the only one in the hotel; no one had dared voice it until now.

"She's right," Jane said, "and Jackson needs medical attention. There has to be another way out, and we have to find it."

"And how we gonna do that when we don't know where anything is, Miss fucking brainiac?" Lee snarled. He was still pissed at Jane for making him walk through the red sea of creepy-crawlies for what he saw as no good reason.

"I thought we could look at the fire escape route maps that the hotel has pinned on the back of every door and in every fucking hallway, *Lee*," Jane replied, and relished the opportunity for sarcasm that for some reason always made her feel better. "They're in every hotel by law, just so morons like you can ignore them." Then she smiled her special patronizing smile at the thug.

Lee stepped toward her. "Just who the fuck do you think you –?"

"Leave her alone and show some respect, Lee," Jackson barked.

Lee did as he was told – grudgingly. Jackson may have been sick, possibly even well on his way to dying, but he still commanded the respect of gang leader. But once he was out of the picture, Lee promised himself a piece of professor ass and more than a little payback.

"According to the map I purloined from the back of the locker room door, since the lobby is obviously a no-go, the next best place we should look is the kitchen," Jane continued. She had pulled the map from the door when they had first looked around, an old force of habit that had finally paid off. It showed that the kitchen was on the ground floor – one floor, two flights of stairs above them – and that the back door led out into the courtyard at the rear of the Mountainview.

"And how do we know that the kitchen's not full of centipedes?" Fred asked, his voice was frightfully quiet, almost a whisper.

"We don't," Jane told him. She saw no use in lying to any of them at this point, no need to flower things up. It is what it is and if there were to be swarms of yard-long arthropods hungry for human blood waiting for them, then there was really not much she could do. "At least we have to try," she verbalized. Jane knew that there was a good chance that the kitchen door would be blocked with sheet steel since every other window and door in the Mountainview had been, but there was always a chance – there just had to be. The girl who had gotten herself killed in here a few days back had obviously found a way in with her boyfriend, and Jane doubted if *they* had sought Mr. Levandowski's permission.

Jane picked up her snake hook, and with decisiveness, she said, "I'm going to take a look, I'm damned if I'm going to sit here, and wait for…"

What? Lenard Levandowski? The unlikely but ever so real swarm of 'pedes? The monster, granddaddy 'pede?

Or – *(d) all of the above*?

"I'll come with," Martha Ray told her, "you too, Fred, you need to get out of here."

"I'll stay with Jackson," Mel announced. She'd had enough of running around for now and figured she owed Jackson enough to stick by him when he was hurt. "You go with them, Lee."

Lee nodded, glad to be given an out. Playing nursemaid just wasn't his thing. He hated seeing Jackson sick and sure as hell didn't want to have to sit and watch the man die; it made his entire universe seem out of kilter somehow. Jackson was the one he'd always looked up to, the strong one, the leader. And now he just looked like a scared, sick man. Lee stood up and reluctantly followed his new leader – the strange, smart woman who chose to collect bugs for a living but who – according to Jackson – could fuck for America.

3

Newman pulled up the Tahoe outside the Mountainview.

He was pleased that he'd decided to take the Mom-mobile since it was bigger, sturdier, and more-sure footed on the roads than his saloon, and he didn't plan on taking any unnecessary chances in the storm. As it was, the buffeting wind peppered the vehicle with blasts of sand and rocked it as if attempting to topple it onto its side.

The cop squinted through the vehicle's window. He could make out the vague shape of two vehicles in the overgrown car park at the front of the hotel: a Jeep that had seen better days and a nice, sensible Hyundai; the latter just the type of car he'd imagined a University professor would drive, but the Jeep? Had to be a student's car.

Which meant that Lucas and at least one of her students were inside the hotel.

"Shit," Newman muttered to himself, not caring that there was no one to hear the expletive. Had Janet been along for the ride, she'd have admonished him for cussing – having been raised a puritan, it was the one thing she didn't like about her husband.

Newman drove up to the front door of the hotel, as close as he could get. Cursing under his breath at the thought of stepping out into the storm, Newman opened his car door. The wind almost tore the Tahoe's door from his hand – and its hinges – when he opened it. Newman got out.

"Hello?!" He shouted against the shrieking wind. "Professor Lucas? Are you in there?"

Nothing.

He tugged at the cold, unyielding steel door, half expecting it to swing open and the day be saved. But no such luck – life was never that easy for Don Newman.

Newman got back in his car and drove slowly around to the rear of the hotel, all the while looking for any signs of life: a chink of light escaping through the sealed windows, the faintest sound, smoke. Smoke? What precisely did he expect they'd be doing in there? Lighting campfires and toasting s'mores?

Unfortunately, the heavy steel sheets on the building's every orifice had made the place light-proof and pretty close to sound proof too. If there had been signs of life to see, any indication as to the whereabouts of the professor, Newman couldn't possibly have detected them from the outside. Instinct told him that there *were* people inside, it was his cop's gut feeling *and* the only way to explain the cars parked in the lot. Newman shuddered upon recalling the multi-legged thing that had plopped out of the Wal-Mart bag onto Lucas's laboratory table and the thought that there were most likely more than enough of the repulsive things inside the Mountainview to go around.

"Shit," Don Newman growled once again.

4

Jane shone her flashlight through the cracked door and into the murky kitchen. The piercing beam created bizarre, dancing silhouettes of the pots and pans that hung like dead things in the gloom. Adjacent to the cookware, suspended above the dusty work tops were neat rows of utensils hanging from hooks like skinny, steel marionettes. Jane wrinkled her nose at the cloying, meaty smell that emanated from the room and prickled her nostrils.

Her flashlight picked out the light switch on the wall a few feet from the door. Checking first along the wall for anything unpleasant that may be crawling there, Jane reached out and flicked on the light.

The murk was replaced by the flickering of the fluorescent lights that thrummed to life above Jane, a stark white contrast that took her a few seconds to adjust to. Once satisfied that there were no 'pedes lying in wait for her, Jane pushed open the door and stepped inside.

"I guess this is the kitchen, then?" Lee asked nervously as he followed close behind the professor.

"I guess it is," Jane answered, in no mood for the

obvious, all too easy sarcasm. "Keep your eyes peeled for 'pedes; they could be anywhere." She pointed her snake hook straight ahead and felt like Harry Potter with his magic fucking wand.

The spacious kitchen was pretty much as Jane had expected: the bland, functional stainless steel of all hotel kitchens, and contained all of the equipment necessary to cater for the Mountainview's once renowned, four-star restaurant with room to spare. It boasted four eight-ring gas ranges, three double-wide refrigerators, and a capacious walk-in freezer, which sported an eye level frosted-up five-inch square window.

Jane walked on, the others following close behind. She plucked a blackened, cast-iron skillet from the dangling array of pots, weighed it in her hand to assess its suitability as a weapon. Happy that it would offer some protection against the 'pedes, she gripped its cool handle like her life depended on it. Martha-Ray, Lee, and Fred followed her lead and armed themselves with a honed chef's knife apiece, and Jane knew that each one of them felt just that little more secure in doing so.

And there, at the other side of the kitchen, was the door to the outside.

Treading with extra care, Jane made her way toward it. She cast her expert eyes this way and that as she moved, alert for any sign of movement or anything untoward that may reveal yet more of the crawling nightmare in which she'd found herself.

Fred lagged behind the others. He crouched down to examine the thick layer of white powdered dust that covered the floor; it was festooned with criss-crossed trails made up of countless perfect circles two to three inches in circumference. They looked like an odd attempt at miniature crop circles. "Oh fuck," Fred groaned. He recognized the patterns – they were exactly the same as those he'd seen during his clandestine visit to the fifth floor.

"It's that fucking thing, ain't it?" Lee asked, not able to hide his fear. He looked around at the trails and saw that they were everywhere.

Jane shushed them. She'd already figured it out for herself that the prints were most likely the footprints of the giant 'pede that had chased her through the hotel lobby, or if not *that one*, another just like it. And that meant that the creature visited the kitchen on a regular basis, given the sheer numbers of footprints. She also noted that there were no human footprints, so the kids who had broken into the hotel had obviously found an alternative way in. At that thought, Jane felt her heart sink a little and she found herself dreading arriving at the door. She knew in her heart that it would be sealed up just the same way as the front door, but she didn't want to voice her thoughts and have the others lose their grains of hope just yet.

"Look." Fred pointed his knife over to his left.

Jane looked over and saw the scattered bones. They were animal bones; cat, small dog or raccoon perhaps, all browny-white and picked clean. A little further back, behind the animal bones she made out an amorphous, bloodied mass of flesh, the obvious source of the fetid meat, coppery stink that pervaded the kitchen; the flesh was green and rotting and seeped its rusty colored fluids into the floor.

"Oh my God," Martha-Ray groaned as she spotted the single, bare foot that protruded from the mess. It had five perfectly manicured toes that pointed skyward, and there was a delicate gold ring around the pinkie toe. Opposite the foot lay the distinctive bony contour of a pelvic girdle from which a handful of vertebrae poked out. Martha-Ray doubled up and dry heaved into a sink that cluttered with a dusty pile of unwashed dishes.

Jane turned away: she'd seen enough to know that they had found the other half of the poor girl who had been butchered in the poolroom.

"What's that?" Fred asked as they neared the outside

door, keen to distract his own attention from the all too human remains. He pointed to a dark mass that crammed beneath a counter top.

Jane clicked on her flashlight and pointed it toward where Fred was looking. And saw there, pressed tightly beneath the counter and adjacent to the door, a batch of enormous eggs.

There was – Jane guesstimated – at least a hundred of the things. They were yellow and glistened as if highly polished, each one the size of a football.

"Jesus shit," Lee exclaimed, "they look like eggs."

"They *are* eggs," Jane told him, once more eschewing the sarcasm. "The big 'pede must be nesting here."

Martha-Ray lifted her head out from the sink and spoke up. Her voice choked with thick phlegm, "And centipedes are maternal, which means that it will come back."

Fred and Lee looked at Jane for reassurances to the contrary. Jane shot a hard glance at Martha-Ray. Thanks a bunch, Missy, for stating the fucking obvious. Not what the two already shell-shocked guys needed to hear right now.

"Not necessarily," Jane's attempt to placate fell on stony ground, "we're not dealing with a typical species here, we can't assume anything." She shone her torch under the surrounding silvered work tops and picked out several other batches of gleaming eggs.

Suppressing the inevitable shudder, Jane reached the door to the outside – to *freedom* – and turned the knob.

Of course, the door opened. It had remained unlocked since the hotel had been evacuated.

But the cold steel door they had welded outside of it was just sealed as the front door.

Jane felt the chill flow of hopelessness rush through her, and she took out her pent-up frustration at the steel door. She pushed at it, kicked it, punched it, and swore at it until her hands ached and her throat was sore. Why couldn't she just catch a fucking break here?

Defeated, Jane slumped down to her butt, her back pressed up against the icy, obdurate sheet of steel, and fought back her tears.

And that's when the lights went out.

CHAPTER THIRTEEN

1

Martha-Ray squealed like a little girl in a ghost train as the blackness slammed down around her. Fred and Lee made jostling, panicked noises of their own as they clattered against the hanging pots and utensils as they stumbled around blindly in the pitch dark.

"Calm down!" Jane called out into the darkness, the quiver in her voice belying her own mounting terror. Jane's mind's eye – ever the playful one – once more treated her to a vision of a whole host of malevolent things that would most likely be creeping, crawling, and slithering toward her feet under cover of the darkness. She groped around in her pocket for her flashlight, retrieved it, switched it on. The welcome thin beam of light split the dark and offered a little comfort to the four individuals trapped in the kitchen. She shone it at each of the others in turn and thought their faces appeared even more terrified and ghostly in the probing light.

"If we're lucky, the emergency generator should still be functional. All hotels have to have them, even if it's just to provide enough light for an escape," Jane did her best to reassure. As a child, her best friend's father had been a hotel inspector and often took his daughter and Jane along on visits that coincided with his one weekend per month parental access.

Jane sat there in the darkness, holding her breath and listening to the sound of her heart beat and imagined once more the creeping terrors that would welcome the cover of the dark to venture out from their hidey-holes.

A noise pierced the darkness, a faint, rhythmic tapping.

"Oh, my God! Something touched me!" Martha-Ray shrieked, her voice filled with panic, and she stomped her feet at her invisible assailant.

"There's something in here!" Fred's voice boomed through the black. He stumbled around, clattering against the hanging pots, some of which clanged to the floor and rolled around with the cymbal crash of metal.

"Watch where you're going!" Lee's voice added to the chaos as Fred barged into him. There was the heavy thump of the two guys hitting the floor, coughing as they inhaled a cloud of dust.

"Will you all just keep still!?" Jane hissed, her own paranoia making her skin crawl at imagined scurrying sounds.

Everyone fell silent, and Jane imagined she could hear the soft rattle of chitinous feet and the clacking noise the 'pedes made as they jostled together; in her mind's eye, they were surrounded by the things in the dark. She began to feel the waves of panic welling up inside her, her mouth dried out in an instant, and her chest tightened as if too terrified to draw breath.

As if on cue, the lights flickered back on, accompanied by the reassuring hum of the generator in some other dark recess of the Mountainview's festering bowels.

"See, what did I tell you?" Jane laughed a nervous laugh.

Martha-Ray smiled at her professor with a tear-stained face, relief etched across her broad features. Fred and Lee looked up from their tangle on the floor, soaking up the flickering light as if they could somehow store it in their eyes.

"Okay, smart-lady," Lee mocked as he glowered at Jane, and then at the steel door that held them captive. He clambered to his feet and left Fred slumped on the floor. "Why don't you figure out just how the fuck we're gonna get out?"

"I don't know," at least Jane was being honest with the guy. "I'd hoped that this door might have been unlocked, or at least not sealed up as tight as the front," she sounded desperate, beginning to feel incredibly *trapped* and claustrophobic. "I guess we have to keep looking for another door that *is* open – the girl who was killed obviously found a way in somehow." Jane took a deep breath. "Or we wait for Mr. Levandowski to come by tomorrow night."

"We could blow it," Martha-Ray said, her voice a timid whisper.

"Excuse me?" Jane retorted.

"The explosives that we found on the fifth floor," Martha-Ray explained, "we could use them to blow the door open."

"Are you fucking kidding me?" Lee coughed.

"Hold on, she may have a point," Fred suddenly sprang to life and startled everyone. "I'd reckon there was easily more than enough C4 up there to bring the whole fucking hotel down. We'd only need a small amount to take the door off."

Jane considered what her students were saying. She'd dismissed Fred and Martha-Ray's reports of a bomb-factory at the top of the hotel as tall-story telling and had not given much brain space as to exactly *why* there would be high-explosives in the hotel in the first place; probably because she didn't really want to know. But, if they were to be believed, it did sound like a feasible, although the implications of it going wrong were just too horrific to even contemplate. Jane's mind reminded her once again of the monstrosity that was prowling the Mountainview and Darlene's bloodied, wrecked body, and she figured she'd feel much happier doing *something* other than wander around hoping to find a way out or to sit and wait for Levandowski to show up.

"Okay, I'll bite. I guess anything's worth a try right now," Jane said with some reluctance. "But who's going to go up there and fetch it?"

"No need to," Lee said, "Jackson's got some."

"You're joking, right?" Fred spluttered. "That asshat's had C4 in his fucking pocket this whole fucking time?"

"Only a little piece," Lee said as if that negated the salient point. "It's probably enough to take a couple of hinges off the steel door though," he explained. "It takes some effort to set the stuff off, but when it does…" Lee made that grating, throaty explosion noise that only boys seem to know how to do properly. "I'll go," he said and darted out of the kitchen like Beelzebub himself were hanging from his balls.

2

Don Newman reached the rear door of the Mountainview at the exact moment the power went out inside. He pulled up his car adjacent to the imposing, rusted door and killed the engine. He thought he heard a scream, although it could just as easily have been a squall of the storm. He dropped his window, ignoring the stinging sand that blasted into his face and coated the interior of his vehicle, and listened.

Silence.

The professor and whomever she had brought along for

the ride could be absolutely anywhere in the hotel, he told himself. That would be five floors plus the basement to go at, so Newman figured the best thing he could do now would be and go find Lenard Levandowski and his magic keys to this forbidden paradise.

Newman gunned the engine and drove off. Behind him, the wind-whipped sand had obscured the hotel from view before he'd left the parking lot.

3

Lee split the matchbox sized chunk of C4 in two and pressed each half against the hinges of the steel door. It felt good to be doing something proactive that didn't involve wading through a sea of fucking bugs to get out of this hellhole, and explosives were something he was more than happy to get his teeth into. He could, however, have done without having to deal with the increasingly sick Jackson to get the explosive and gun from him.

Jackson was in a hell of a bad way upstairs, and it had pained Lee to see him like that. He was no medical expert, but it looked to Lee as if Jackson's days of dealing and playing the gangsta about town were pretty much numbered. Lee hadn't seen anyone so clearly staring death straight in the face since his Uncle Tony had died of Aids a dozen or so years back. Still, the white chick with the big tits had been doing her best to keep Jackson comfortable and calm, although when Lee had gone up to retrieve the C4, he was drifting in and out of consciousness and ranting random bullshit in his more lucid moments. Worse still, the wound on Jackson's leg was stinking the place up, and Lee could see that his thigh muscle had all-but liquefied; it had looked to him more like a half-filled water balloon than any part of a human being.

"*You ain't taking my gun!*" Jackson had screamed in Lee's face, "I need it in case she sics that fucking snake-thing on me!" Lee had seen the terrified look on Mel's face as Jackson had raved on, obviously fearing for her own safety. "It's coming for us all, Lee – can't you see that? It's gonna get all of us just like it got Johnny Psycho! *And then it's gonna munch on our fucking bones!*"

In the end, it had transpired that all Lee needed to do was to exercise a little patience and wait for Jackson to fade out again. Once Jackson had slumped in Mel's arms with his sweat greased head lolling against her ample chest, Lee had been able to take the C4 out of his leader's pocket and the gun from his hand with very little effort. As Lee had stepped quietly away, creeping with exaggerated movements like some skinny cartoon character, Jackson had stirred. He shouted after Lee in a voice shaking with revulsion and terror. "It's in my balls, Lee! The fucking thing's poison is in my fucking balls!" And as much as Lee had tried to close his mind to the echo of Jackson's rant, he found that he couldn't.

"I think that'll do it," Lee told the others. He stood back to admire his handiwork. "I guess you need to get back now." He waved Jackson's gun in the air and hoped that he could get far enough away to hit the C4 and still be safe from the blast when it went off.

"Are you sure you can do this?" Jane quizzed.

"Yes, Ma'am," Lee replied, "always was a good shot." Lee still held on to the fond memory of his father taking him to the shooting range for the first time. It had been not too long before the old man had high-tailed it for good, so the trip had been the last one, too. "I reckon a shot in each piece should bring the hinges off," Lee tried to sound confident although he'd never worked with C4 before and had little idea of exactly how much it would take to blow the door. But, as long as he was well out of the way when it went up, Lee really didn't mind if he blew the entire side of the fucking building off.

Jane, Fred, and Martha-Ray stepped outside the kitchen

door and took shelter behind the wall to the side, all the while keeping a nervous eye out for any tell-tale movements in the shadows that surrounded them.

Lee hunkered down behind one of the imposing, steel refrigerators at what he hoped was a decent shooting distance from the carefully positioned explosives.

"Fire in the hole!" he shouted.

Instinctively, Jane clapped her hands over her ears and ducked her head, braced herself for the blast.

Lee swallowed down a deep breath, took aim, and fired Jackson's gun at the C4.

4

"I could have told you it wouldn't work," Mel told them, her tone matter-of-fact. She stood up from the recliner, her thighs damp and reeking with Jackson's sick-sweat. "C4 is designed to be stable; shooting a bullet into it won't detonate it."

"You studyin' explosive-ology or something, clever bitch?" Lee snapped. His mood had turned rather quickly from scared to disappointed to downright ugly since his failure to ignite the explosives on the kitchen door; his coping mechanism was to lash out at anyone who had the misfortune to be in his vicinity. Besides, what the fuck could some slutty bookworm college girl possibly know about C4?

"Nah, I saw it on Mythbusters," Mel said without a single hint of irony.

"Aww, well, if it's on fuckin' Mythbusters, it's gotta be fucking right!" Lee used his anger as cover for his frustration and panic.

"I think Mel may have a point," Jane added, not helping Lee's mood. She remembered having watched the episode where the beardy guy and the hat guy had shot bullets into a block of C4, dropped an anvil on it – cartoon style – and even set fire to it, and all to no effect. In fact, the only thing that had caused the C4 to explode was a detonator hooked up to an electric charge. "We need a detonator," she told the group.

"Ain't no detonators up there," Jackson spoke up, a rare moment of clarity in his fevered fugue, his voice gravely and strained. He shifted his weight around on the recliner and grimaced as every nerve-ending in his body fired up. It sent his mind off into a delirious ramble; do nerves actually *feel* pain? Sure, they transmit the signals, but can they feel it themselves? He'd read somewhere that the brain itself doesn't experience the sensation; it simply interprets the nerve signals. Perhaps the same could be said for nerves? And if so, would you have to have nerves for your nerves? "I looked." Jackson's fevered mind jolted him rudely back to the now.

Martha-Ray chipped in, "They have acid and glycerol up there. Perhaps whoever was up there before was making their own nitro' detonators?"

"Yeah, there was tons of the stuff," Fred backed her up, "enough to make gallons of nitroglycerine."

Jane's mind raced ahead; far from the question of why there was bomb-making equipment in the Mountainview in the first place was the question of why they were still discussing how to blast their way out. As incredulous as it seemed, desperate times certainly called for desperate measures, and this certainly did appear to qualify as the former category. Were they actually debating a viable option here?

A snaking, scurrying motion in the periphery of her vision answered the question and reminded Jane of precisely why it was imperative they find a way out of the hotel. As if oversized 'pedes three times bigger than they had any business being were not enough to press her personal panic button, the thirty-foot monster that had laid its eggs in the kitchen certainly sealed the deal. There could be no waiting around for Levandowski – Jane doubted very much that they would survive that long.

She – *they* – had to get out, and fast.

"Would that do what we need it to do?" Jane asked Fred.

"I guess so," Fred answered, and his face blushed pink, uncomfortable with the pressure that had suddenly fallen upon his shoulders. He was fairly confident that even a small amount of nitroglycerine would provide enough explosive energy to detonate the C4. After all, what was a detonator but a small explosive device? "But we're going to have to make it ourselves; there are only the raw materials up there," he added.

"And you know how to make it?" Jane asked.

"Yep, it's basic chemistry," Fred told her, "I'm a little rusty, but –"

"– I can do it," Lee butted in. "It's the only thing I actually learned to do in Lab."

"I said, I can do it," Fred bristled at this clear affront to his ego.

"Back off, *Fratboy*," Lee growled. He advanced on Fred with fists clenched. "Let somebody who knows what they're doing do this. A dick-end like you is more likely to blow us all to hell and back."

"Stand down, Lee," Jackson interjected, "this is no time for your macho bullshit." The pain pitched his voice an octave higher than it should have been, but still it remained commanding. "Let College Boy do it; you can give him any help he needs."

Lee glowered at Jackson but backed down nonetheless. He swore to himself there and then that once he was clear of this place, he was going to find another gang to run with, perhaps even start his own. In the meantime, he'd do as Jackson said; he owed the dying man at least that much respect.

Jane stepped up, still reticent but nonetheless painted

into a corner, "Alright, you guys go make your bombs, but just enough to get us through the kitchen door." She'd calculated that the kitchen was still their safest bet since they knew for certain that the lobby was filled with 'pedes so the front door was a definite no-go. It would take time to set up the explosives, time without interruption, and if there were any of the smaller 'pedes in the kitchen, they had been keeping their distance thus far. Jane toyed with the notion that perhaps it was the giant 'pede that was keeping the others out to protect her eggs? Whatever the reason, Jane figured it would buy them the time they needed to get themselves out of the hotel, and preferably before Big Momma 'Pede turned up.

"You can use the back stairs to bring the explosives down; they lead directly to the kitchen," Jane told Fred. "That way we can avoid the main part of the hotel." *We?* She meant *they*, of course. Just one of the perks of being a leader.

Fred nodded and made his way out of the poolroom with Lee close behind and a grudging truce between the two.

"I'm gonna need ice," Fred grunted.

"I ain't fetching your goddamned ice – I'm not your freakin' ice boy," Lee growled back.

With that, they were gone.

Jane peered into the pool, gloomy and filled with rippling shadows under the dim emergency lighting. The 'pedes that had fallen in with Darlene had finally quit squirming around and lay at the bottom, still and quite dead. Jane felt the tears starting up in her eyes and a bitter remorse as she stared at the motionless form of her student that also rested on the bottom of the warm pool, and she supposed that it was about time they fished Darlene Buchanan out of the water.

CHAPTER FOURTEEN

1

Eucalyptus Apartments comprised an imposing building on the smart side of Desert Hot Springs. Of modern construction, built out of pale sandstone and towering eleven stories above the town's municipal parkland and private golf course, the apartments were home to lawyers, bankers, moneyed entrepreneurs, and the like.

And also, it would seem, hotel caretakers. Newman took in the luxe atmosphere of the home of one Lenard Levandowski and whistled through his teeth as he rode the plush elevator up to the third floor. He was in the wrong business being a lowly cop, he chastised himself – it was evidently caretaking empty hotels that earned the big bucks these days.

The elevator hummed to a smooth stop on the required floor, and Newman stepped out. He strode purposefully toward the antiqued beach wood door, which bore the numbers he was looking for: 341.

He knocked.

Silence.

"Hello? Mr. Levandowski?" Newman called through the door, doing his level best to keep his voice low so as not to disturb the other residents. There were influential people in this place, and you could bet your badge that not all of them would be with people they were meant to be with. Such people in such circumstances tended not to take kindly to cops knocking on doors at this time of the night. "It's the police, Mr. Levandowski. I need to talk to you. Open up."

He waited.

The door cracked open.

"What is it?" A rheumy eye peered through the gloom.

"I'm looking for Lenard Levandowski," Newman told the eye, "I was told that this is his apartment."

The door swung open and a tall man with the graying handlebar mustache blocked the entrance. He wore a powder-blue housecoat and black leatherette house slippers and quite possibly very little else.

"Well, he's not here," Larry-Wayne Williaford informed the cop with gruffness in his voice.

"Do you know when he will be back?"

"He's dead."

"Pardon me?" Newman was taken aback. Levandowski had been alive and well this morning, so far as he knew.

"You'd better come in," Larry-Wayne invited the policeman in to Lenard's apartment.

Larry-Wayne explained to Newman the details of poor, poor Lenard's departure from this world. He embellished the story with just how distraught he was that his best friend was dead and gone, and that he had decided to take care of the apartment until Lenard's estate could be sorted out.

"Saw his corpse myself, and his head was all funny. Like a soccer ball a dog got a hold of," Larry-Wayne told Newman. "Still, somebody had to identify him and pick up his keys and shit from that asshole coroner."

Indeed, it had been well worth the drive to Palm Springs for the die-hard opportunist. For more years than he cared to count, Larry-Wayne had ridden on the back of Lenard's grubby predilections and money, encouraging him and reveling in the debauchery and good times that Lenard seemed so easily to be able to afford. And now that the old pervert was gone, his fair-weather friend had taken it upon himself to be the one to look after 341 Eucalyptus Apartments, along with Lenard's generous bank account. The latter would be purely for any out-of-pocket expenses incurred in taking care of said estate, of course, and there was more than enough in the account to see Larry-Wayne through to the end of his days, provided that he spent wisely. It had been a pity about the Lexus getting wrecked though, Larry-Wayne had always coveted Lenard's beloved car.

"I'm sorry to hear about Mr. Levandowski," Newman sympathized. "But I do need access to the Mountainview," Newman cut through Larry-Wayne's reverie. "Did you happen to pick up the hotel keys from the mortuary?"

"I think they might have been in the bag of his stuff they gave me," the tall man replied. He knew damn well the hotel keys were in among the few belongings Lenard had been carrying when he'd been summoned to meet his maker, but he'd be damned if he was going to give them up; to Larry-Wayne, those keys meant that he had a fair shot of picking up Lenard's job.

"I'm sorry to have to insist, Mr. Williaford," Newman kept his voice pleasant but firm. "I appreciate this is a difficult time for you, but this is part of a police investigation," he kind of lied. "I have reason to believe that there are people in the hotel and that their lives may be at risk. If you do have those keys and are not forthcoming, anything that happens to those people is coming straight back to your doorstep." With that, Newman fixed his eyes on the other man's. It was the unnerving stare he'd learned from watching far too many Clint Eastwood movies as a kid.

"They're back at my place," Larry-Wayne conceded with a heavy snort, "ya can drive me over there."

"That would be just perfect, Mr. Williaford," Newman said with a forced smile.

"Gimme a minute to get dressed," Larry-Wayne mumbled. He shuffled toward the bedroom, opened the door.

Newman heard voices.

As Larry-Wayne went in, the biggest black guy Newman had ever set eyes on lurched out of the bedroom pulling a Red Sox T-shirt over his immense head. He was followed by a petite girl who looked to be no more than sixteen. She wore the most indecently tight, gold booty shorts and a matching tank-top that showed off the pale, stretch-marked belly that betrayed her youthful appearance.

"Oh, hello, Mr. Newman," the girl greeted him.

"Hi, Natalie," Newman replied, clearly more embarrassed at the situation than she was. Shit, her son went to the same Montessori school with Addie – they'd even had play dates over at her house.

"Come on, then," Larry-Wayne snapped as with a sad expression he watched his evening's entertainment leave. "Let's go get those damned keys."

2

Lee grumbled under his breath as he trudged along the poorly lit, third floor hallway. As he walked, he kept his eyes glued to the floor, wary of the nasty, creeping things that he knew were out to get him. He clutched the thick, plastic thirteen-gallon bag tight to his chest, which was still cold from the last batch of ice he'd lugged up the two flights of stairs. That's two flights of stairs, five times. That was ten flights of stairs in all and Lee was fucking well exhausted. He'd have much preferred to have used the elevator had it not been crawling with killer fucking centipedes and all messy with Mikey's fucked-up corpse.

Despite his protest to Jackson, Lee *had* been designated Ice Boy, and he vowed that this would definitely be his final trip since the college boy had made a start on mixing the Nitroglycerine; if Fred wanted more ice, he could fetch the motherfucking stuff himself. Lee was still fuming about being usurped as explosives-maker, just what the fuck did some meathead, bug-collecting jock know about making nitro'? Lee had been mixing his own since high school once he'd discovered how easy it was to break into the Chemistry Department's storeroom and gain access to the unlimited supply of raw materials.

Like your first sex, Lee knew, you never forget your first home-made explosion. Nor – like sex – did that thrill ever diminish. He still remembered with fondness the time with three of his best buds, in the far corner of the school playing fields after school, standing around a stripped-down bicycle frame they'd stuffed with ammonium nitrate fertilizer and gasoline. The bang when the makeshift bomb went off had left Lee's ears ringing for days and gouged out a crater fifteen feet across and two feet deep in the field.

It had also hooked young Lee on explosives for life.

From that moment on, Lee had actually begun to pay attention in chemistry class, had even instigated his own research on how to make different types of explosives. His studies had brought him to one of the simplest yet effective explosive materials of all; Nitroglycerine.

So, Mr. Fucking University Guy, Lee grumbled beneath his breath, stick that up your big gay cashmere sweater, and fucking smoke it!

Lee sauntered up to the ice machine, punched the dispense button, and held the bag beneath the plastic chute to catch the cubes that tumbled out. He glanced nervously around, worried that the clattering sound the falling ice was making may attract unwanted multi-legged attention.

As the ice filled the plastic bag, Lee – never one to let shit go – continued to fume quietly to himself. It was unjust that Jackson had ordered him to play subservient to the motherfucker, who was at their mercy only a few short hours ago. For Christ's sakes, Lee had watched Fred crying like a two-year-old brat with it's dick stuck in its zipper, seen him with all snot streaming down his face when Jackson jammed sticks under his nails, and now, now he was supposed to be all *'yes sir, no sir!'* But Lee understood that he owed Jackson some leeway since he'd gotten himself bitten by the centipede, the poor guy was obviously in agony, and if he didn't die from the bite, he was going to wish he had –

It's in my fucking balls!

- and Lee even considered that Jackson might have felt bad about torturing the wrong guy, but *that* had been an honest mistake. Poor, cuckolded Jackson had no idea that he'd been doing the dirty with a rug-muncher *and* her old-lady girlfriend. This Lee found funny, in some respects, although he'd never dare laugh about it in front of Jackson, not if he valued his own balls. Even so, that was no reason for Jackson to go make Lee a fucking lackey.

A centipede fell from the icemaker's chute.

Lee let out a most un-masculine squeal, leapt backward, and slammed into the wall opposite the ice machine. The almost-full bag of ice fell from his grasp and shed its frozen load across the floor in a cascade of glistening cubes.

"Fuck!" Lee barked, embarrassed at his own outburst; although there was no one there to witness him scared to crapping his pants over a semi-frozen centipede.

The creature dangled limp and lifeless from the chute, its body gripped by the inner workings of the ice machine. Lee estimated that there were twenty-four inches or so of the thing protruding from the ice machine with possibly the same again trapped inside. It was a big one, for sure, but at least it looked to be quite dead.

Lee began to laugh, at himself, at the ludicrous situation he'd inadvertently found himself in. It was certainly an adventure to tell the grandkids – although part of him doubted if they'd ever believe him. He picked up the bag, there was still some ice in it, and Lee decided there was enough for this last trip.

A movement in the dark, off to his left, caught Lee's attention. He froze and willed his eyes to see through the gloom. And, as he watched, the tiny emergency lights that glowed on either side of the hallway flickered on and off.

"Cunt," Lee cussed again, this time a whisper as he watched the outline of the gargantuan centipede's head gliding into view.

Heart racing, sweat popped out in tiny translucent beads on his skin, Lee pressed himself into the gap between the wall and the ice machine. He held on tightly to the bag of ice as if it promised protection against the monster that ate Johnny Psycho.

Lee held his breath as the centipede came close, its head nudging against the ice machine then recoiling as stray ice cubes rattled down the chute and onto the floor. The thing's body was so long and trailed so far back down the gloomy hallway that Lee couldn't actually make out where it ended, and he saw that it had some legs that were longer than his own. He *could* see, however, the thing's cold, expressionless face, flat eyes, and hideous, twitching jaws.

The centipede's head rose up, and an inquisitive antenna touched Lee's face, and he caught a scream in his throat. The creature tapped at Lee's skin and stroked his cheek with a delicate touch. The antenna's tip traced down along Lee's neck and to his chest, where it investigated the ice bag, pulling away at the chilled touch of the ice. The 'pede then inched forward on its thick, long legs and opened up its shiny black forcipules directly in front of Lee's face, and he got to see directly into the thing's gaping orifice.

Lee's bladder let loose, and the resulting warmth spread quickly down his legs and made him feel uncomfortable and ashamed of himself. He closed his eyes and prayed to a God – *any* god – that, if this was to be the end, that please let it be quick.

The centipede flicked its antennae once more over the ice bag in Lee's hands. It then tasted it with its gigantic maxillipeds as if confused by the cold. Was this food or a threat? Either way, the gap that it was squeezed into was far too narrow for its fangs to reach. Lowering its head, the centipede examined the lower half of Lee's body.

Lee fought against the stale air in his lungs, desperately wanting to expel and draw in fresh air. He didn't dare though, guessed that it would most likely be the last thing he ever did. The centipede tapped and probed at him, appearing to flinch at the stinking wetness on Lee's pants. After what had seemed like an eon, the animal finally maneuvered its vast bulk away and continued along the hallway on bright yellow legs that flowed in perfect waves and beat a muffled, rhythmic tattoo on the carpet.

3

Although he had no way of knowing, Fred mirrored almost exactly the terrorist Jahanzeb's actions five years earlier as he diligently poured viscous glycerol into the acid mixture in a glass beaker in an ice filled bathtub. He and Lee had set up their impromptu chemistry lab in the suite across the hallway from where the terrorists had met their sudden, inglorious ends, and Fred was busy at work.

His finger still throbbed, but Fred was able to mostly ignore it, thanks to a high pain threshold honed through years of playing football. That didn't make him any less pissed at Jackson though, when they got out of this, he'd very much like to kick the man's ass again,just because.

Fred paused to study the liquid mixture's cloudy

interface for any tell-tale signs that he was going too fast, knowing that to do so would mean a destructive oxidation of the mixture would occur, and that really was the last thing he needed right now.

Behind him, the suite door flew open, and Lee dashed in, clutching the bag of ice, slamming the door closed.

"You'll never guess what just happened," Lee was out of breath, gasping to breathe, let alone speak.

Judging by the piss stain on the young thug's trousers, Fred figured it must have been something pretty life-changing, but he decided not to bite, concentrated instead on pouring the glycerol.

"I saw that big motherfucker," Lee said, undeterred by Fred's silence, "the bastard that killed Johnny. I thought I was fucked for sure!"

Fred thought of a suitably acerbic reply, a real zinger that most likely would have been over Lee's head, but as it formed, he became aware of a stinging sensation in his nose. It felt as if his mucus membranes were on fire, and the back of his mouth itched like something was crawling down his throat.

Then he saw the reddish-brown nitrogen dioxide wafting from the beaker.

"Oh," He said.

The explosion tore away a ragged chunk of Fred's face and ripped away his right hand. He registered no pain, just a blinding light and crushing pressure as he was thrown the full length of the spacious bathroom, and then there came the sickening *crunch* as his head smacked against the tiled wall above the toilet. The blast caught Lee and slammed him against the wall, tearing the ice bag from his hands to shower the suite beyond with smashed ice shards that looked like tiny, lustrous diamonds.

The bathtub shattered beneath the explosion, driven downward by the expanding gasses to blow a hole in the floor. Debris showered into the room below and stirred the swarm of centipedes that had made it their lair.

4

Jane was first into the suite: struggling to catch her breath after her panicked dash up five flights of stairs. Her clothes were sodden; she was still dripping wet from having pulled Darlene's lifeless body from the pool.

Mel and Martha-Ray crowded in behind her.

"Oh my God!" Mel cried out, "Fred!" She ran across to where Fred was laying face-down and motionless in a spreading pool of his own blood.

"Help me," Lee's voice was feeble and loaded with terror.

Jane looked around for the source of the voice, willing her eyes to adjust to the gloom. As they did so, Jane could see half of Lee's body sticking out of the floor. Her first assessment was that the boy had been blown in half, but then she realized that he was actually in one piece and dangling through a gaping hole in the suite floor.

"I think he's stuck," Martha-Ray mumbled and shone her flashlight into the hole that had once been the room's en-suite. She illuminated the shattered joists and the splintered floorboards, along with the fourth-floor room below that was enveloped in ink thick shadows that appeared to be moving. Upon closer inspection, Martha-Ray made out the creeping, snake-like shapes of the centipedes that were making their way up the walls. "We have to get him out of there," her voice was flat and emotionless.

Jane surveyed the situation. The floor around the hole looked far too unstable to risk walking on; the few joists that remained creaked and complained at Lee's every movement. If she, Mel, or Martha-Ray were to put too much weight on the joists, everyone in the room would end up in the room below. She could see that Lee was wedged like a cork in a bottle between two splintered joists that protruded into the center of the hole. One errant move, and he'd plunge straight down into the room below. The fall itself probably wouldn't kill him, but Jane reckoned that the 'pedes waiting beneath him most likely would. Aside from his predicament, Jane thought that Lee looked to be in good shape despite the explosion – the half of him she could see, anyway – a few cuts and bruises, scared out of his wits, but otherwise okay. She glanced across at Fred, who by stark contrast she could see was a lost cause. His body was twisted horribly out of shape and spattered with thick smears of blood; the stump of his right arm was sticking out from his body at an unnatural angle with the splintered ends of the bones poking through the lacerated flesh like obscene fingers. There was also a growing puddle of frothy blood around what remained of his head.

Back to Lee, Jane's first instinct was to leave Jackson's unpleasant friend to his own fate and get the fuck off the fifth floor before the whole place collapsed under them.

"We can't just leave him," Mel said as if she'd read her lover's mind.

Jane sighed. *Of course,* they couldn't leave the poor guy, hoodlum that he was, she still felt some of that guilt-ridden responsibility for him. After all, he had been up here trying to help.

"Go collect some bedsheets," Jane instructed, "we can tie them together and see if we can reach him from here."

"Can you get a fucking move on?" Lee sounded desperate, "I think they're crawling up my fucking legs."

Martha-Ray snatched an armful of sheets from what remained of the bed, sending up gritty clouds of dust in their wake. She coughed and spluttered her way over to Jane, who, with a shell-shocked Mel, helped her to knot the sheets together.

"Here, catch this," Jane called over to Lee. She tossed the makeshift rope over for him to catch.

Lee grabbed for it, missed. The beams holding him shifted, squeezing his body tighter and sending a shower of plaster clumps downward. He let out a strangled mewl and scrabbled at the smooth floor with tattered fingernails.

Jane could feel the broken tiles beneath her feet moving. "Get back!" she barked at Mel and Martha-Ray. What she didn't need right now was their extra weight on the crumbling floor.

The three stepped backward. The floor settled. Jane threw the knotted sheets again.

Lee grabbed and kept hold of the sheets this time. He curled his bony fingers around the soft lifeline and gripped with every ounce of his strength. He was beginning to feel the sharp prickle of feet on his legs as they dug through the material of his pissy trousers, and he fought against his every instinct to kick out. "Oh fuck, they're on me," Lee blubbed in anticipation of the sharp stab of fangs that would soon turn his legs and balls as black and septic as Jackson's.

"Try your best to stay calm, Lee," Jane told him. "If you panic now, you're going to fall." Of course, the man was going to panic; it's what she would be doing right now if she were in his position. "We're going to pull on the sheets now," she said as she took the strain. Martha-Ray adopted her position behind Jane and looped the end of the sheets around her thick wrist. Mel positioned herself between Martha-Ray and Jane and took a firm hold of the sheet rope.

Jane pulled, grimaced as her back strained against Lee's trapped weight; for a skinny runt of a man, he was much heavier than expected. Slowly, inch-by-inch, Lee began to move. The boards cracked and groaned, and debris pattered into the gloom below, but gradually they pulled Lee out of the hole.

After an unbearable age, Lee's torso began to pull clear of the shattered beams, followed by his thighs, followed by his knees. Jane carried on pulling, feeding the sheet-rope through her hands in her bizarre tug-of-war. Lee dragged across the floor flat on his belly, his weight spread as evenly as possible across the broken floor.

As Lee emerged, Jane could see that his legs were alive with a crawling mass of 'pedes, and she winced.

A joist snapped with a loud, vibrant *crack*. The bathroom floor trembled and caved in around Lee, and he was sucked back into the hole.

Jane gave a startled shout and pulled back hard on the rope; she felt the sting of the friction burns on her palms.

Lee forced out a primitive wailing noise that made him sound more like a caged animal than a human being. He vanished into the dark hole between the floors.

With her free hand, Martha-Ray shone her flashlight toward where Lee had been almost within their grasp. She could see that he remained suspended by the sheets that had looped around his arms, his lower half once again dangling impotently through the gaping hole in the floor, his legs a seething blanket of jostling centipedes. Below him, the floor of the room swarmed with the things.

"Oh, God, help me!" Lee found his voice at last and began kicking his legs to dislodge the creatures that clung to them.

"Pull!" Jane cried out, panting with the exertion. She, Martha-Ray, and Mel hauled once again on the sheets to drag Lee up through the hole. As he struggled between the joists, the rough wood scraped his legs raw and served to dislodge some of the centipedes, and the creatures fell silently back onto their brethren below in the fourth floor room.

One final, backbreaking haul, and Lee was free of the hole and flapping around on the floor like a freshly-landed trout.

"Get 'em off me!" he squealed, the terror cracking his voice to a shrill shriek. Jane and the others grabbed their snake hooks to drag off the 'pedes and fling them back down into the hole in the floor.

"Lose the pants!" Jane told Lee.

With no hesitation or attempts toward modesty, Lee unbuckled his jeans, shrugged them off, and flung them down the hole, centipedes and all. He made a quick check to make sure there were none of the loathsome animals on his shirt and then he collapsed on the grimy floor in his underwear, gasping like an asthmatic to catch his breath.

"They're coming up," Jane said as the first of the 'pedes crawled up through the hole in the floor. It was quickly followed by another, and another. "We're going to have to make our bomb someplace else."

"You can't be serious?" Mel was astounded, "after this?" She pointed at Fred.

"I really don't see what other options we have," Jane defended, "other than stay here and pray." She nodded toward the swarm of 'pedes that crawled about in the room below. There were so many of them creeping, snaking, and scuttling down there that the room looked like it was some grotesque, living and breathing thing. "I say we grab what we need and take it to the kitchen, there's an ice maker in one of the refrigerators, and Lee considers himself an explosives expert."

Martha-Ray nodded, too scared to argue. She stood up. "What are we going to do about Fred?" she asked and looked over at the bloodied heap that was Fred. Beautiful, handsome Fred Westendick. Fred, who wouldn't look at a girl like her twice. "We can't just leave him here." She stepped over to Fred's body, knelt, and turned him over.

And immediately wished that she hadn't.

Fred's handsome, smooth-skinned face was completely gone, replaced by raw muscle, glistening bone, and exposed teeth that grinned up at her. His tongue lolled out through the loose flap of flesh where his cheek had once been and his nose – that perfect, sexy Roman nose – was completely gone, reduced to twin blowholes in the bloodied meat of his face. Only one eye remained. Dislodged from its socket, it wobbled precariously on Fred's cheekbone as if balancing to stay put, but it still had Fred's twinkling blue color.

Then, Fred let out a long, gassy exhale and a weird rasping sound from deep inside his burned, shattered throat. It was a scream.

"H-he's still a-alive," Martha-Ray stammered, turned her head to the side and threw up.

5

Lieutenant Don Newman pulled up outside Larry-Wayne's grubby apartment block. This was more like it, Newman thought, a castle fit for a dirty old pervert.

"I'll wait here," the cop told Larry-Wayne, having no desire to either brave the worsening wind storm or the man's crumbling apartment block.

"Give me five," the old man grumbled, "I gotta take a dump."

Newman snorted his derision and glanced at his watch. It was already a quarter after one.

"Really?" Newman shook his head, exasperated, "please try not to be too long."

Larry-Wayne unfolded his tall frame from Newman's car and slammed the door behind himself with a resounding *thump*.

6

They'd laid Fred out on one of the cabana beds and covered him with blankets, which had promptly turned a bright, sodden red from the copious amount of blood that seeped from of the remains of his shattered face. Mercifully, there was little blood from the stump of his wrist to be concerned about; the heat from the blast had cauterized the blood vessels with a somewhat ruthless efficiency.

Jane had stuck a length of PVC pipe from the shattered

bathroom into Fred's mouth as an improvised breathing tube; she hoped that it would prevent her student from choking on his own blood and broken teeth and keep his airway clear. She had also suggested that they put a damp cloth over the remaining eye to try keeping it moist, but that had sent Fred into a wild panic. He'd had moaned and writhed around and attempted to pull the cloth away with a hand that was no longer there, and it was as if the darkness scared him.

Dear, merciful God, the boy could still see.

Jane's mind conjured an image she had seen on some gore website a long, long time ago. There'd been a guy sitting in his car with a shotgun by his side. He'd attempted suicide by shooting himself in the head only to have had the gun move (either that or he'd had last-minute second thoughts) and had only succeeded in blasting his face off. Both eyes had remained in the resulting hamburger meat of the guy's face, and they stared out like floating buoys in a sea of gore.

The understated caption beneath the picture had read, '*this guy is still alive*'.

Jane fought the nausea that grappled with her stomach, her mind immersed in the smog of disbelief at the nightmare she had found herself in. Perhaps, sometime soon, she'd wake up?

She and Martha-Ray had carried bottles of acid, glycerol, and a fresh block of yellow C4 down to the kitchen. Behind them, Lee and Mel had carried Fred to the pool room and made him comfortable.

Comfortable?

An oddly inappropriate choice of word under the circumstances, Jane thought. Fred had been blown almost to bits and had been denied the mercy of death with no painkillers on hand; she was not sure how that could possibly ever be construed as *comfortable*, no matter what they'd laid him on. All Jane could hope for was that shock would keep Fred unconscious until they could get him out of the hotel.

Her other casualty, Jackson, appeared to have perked up and was a little more alert now. Sadly, his leg was a complete disaster. It was nothing more now than bloated, distended skin surrounding liquidized tissue, which sloshed around and oozed out putrid and stinking from his rotting pores. Added to that, Jackson had indeed been correct about the state of his precious balls – the 'pede venom had gotten into *all* of his genitals and was rapidly dissolving them from the inside out.

CHAPTER FIFTEEN

1

In the kitchen, Lee busied himself mixing nitroglycerine. He bent over a sink he'd filled with ice, the clear acid mixture in a Pyrex measuring jug. He was cool, calm, collected. He knew what he was doing, more at home alone with the chemicals than with the people upstairs and the calamity around him. He smiled to himself and whistled a thin tuneless tune as he watched the white layer of explosive forming between the acid mix and glycerol. He pipetted it out with a chilled turkey baster and into a glass ramekin with pictures of pears and cherries glazed around its sides.

Why hadn't he been bitten?

Lee's head swam with all the possibilities. He'd been hanging in mid-air, legs kicking, centipedes clinging so tight to his flesh that he had felt their sharp legs pricking his skin through the thickness of his jeans. And yet, not one single bite. He afforded a glance down at his bare legs – he was still wearing just his boxers and T-shirt – no way was he going to don another dude's pants – and studied the red track-marks on his thighs, his body's allergic reaction to the dribbles of poison from the centipede's prickling legs.

Hanging there, he'd convinced himself that he'd be bitten by the things and have all the fun of watching his legs turn to black smush like Jackson's. Perhaps, he mused, there *was* a God looking out for him after all, or a guardian angel at the very least. Or more probably, it was the fact that he'd peed in his pants during his face-off with the granddaddy centipede, and the repulsive things simply didn't like the stink of human piss.

Lee allowed himself another smile. Whatever the reason, he was feeling pretty damned lucky right now.

Another drip of clear, glutinous glycerol into the acid mix, Lee sniffed the air for even the slightest whiff of that dreaded nitrogen dioxide.

2

Jane sat down heavily on a recliner and lamented. Just how the hell was she supposed to explain all of this? No matter what her relationship had once been with the Dean to have landed her the professorship and tenure, he was going to have to fire her ass for this almighty *clusterfuck*.

The tally didn't look good from where she was sitting: one student dead, one maimed for life – if Fred lived at all, and she wouldn't blame him for not wanting to, looking at what was left of his face. And that was without mentioning the illegal trespassing and lack of insurance for the students in her charge, both of which were probably felonies in their own right. This whole shebang was making Jane's sexual indiscretions over the years seem trivial now, although she could predict that *they* would unquestionably be brought up at the departmental witch-hunt that would inevitably follow all of this.

Of course, Jane wasn't to have known that there was a ridiculously huge freak of nature running around the

Mountainview, nor could she have ever anticipated the appearance of her part-time booty call and his bald, tattooed sidekick; although she was forced to admit that she was glad to have Lee around *now*.

Jane Lucas looked over at the bloodstained, sheet-covered mound that was Darlene Buchanan's body, then at Fred's unconscious frame that seeped blood and fluids from his ruined face, and then to Jackson's pain-wracked face and dissolving body.

Yep, this was going to take some explaining, alright.

She began to cry.

"Hey, Jane," Mel spoke softly as she sat down beside her Professor and put a comforting arm around her shoulders. "Everything's going to be alright."

Jane looked at her student; she saw the kindness in her eyes and a maturity she didn't think she'd ever seen before. Of course, Mel *knew* that everything was not going to be alright, but it was good to hear it all the same. Jane forced a smile.

Mel wiped Jane's tears away, a tender gesture. There was no need to be discrete now that their secret, sapphic cat was well and truly out of the bag. "We all need you to be strong," Mel whispered. Her eyes flicked across to Martha-Ray, who sat on the recliner opposite, hugging her knees, and staring a weird catatonic stare into the pool. "*I* need you to be strong." Mel kissed her professor gently on the lips and tasted the salty tears that had settled there.

Jane stared into Mel's beautiful face, welcomed the comfort that radiated from there, the feel of her warm body next to hers; she wanted to say something, *needed* to say something. *Thank you*? *I love you*? But nothing appropriate formed in Jane's numb mind, absolutely nothing at all.

Her attention moved beyond the student's pretty features to a dark shape that moved behind the thin mesh of the air-duct across the room; a shape that filled the dark hole with tenebrous red and glinted like liquid plastic.

Mel followed her gaze.

"Oh no," the words strangled in Jane's throat, "they're coming in."

As they watched, the mesh that covered the air duct burst open, and a horde of centipedes spilled out across the tiled floor. They scurried across the floor, creating that horribly familiar rustling, *chinking* sound as their hard bodies jostled against each other.

As one, Jane and Mel stood up from the recliner and reached for the weapons they had liberated from the hotel kitchen, although in the face of the onslaught of the crawling multitude of 'pedes the chef's knife and a cast-iron skillet seemed hopelessly inadequate, even when paired with a metal snake hook.

The mass of centipedes snaked its way toward them with a single purpose, and yet more poured of the air duct behind them. There were hundreds of the damned things, Jane grimaced, possibly thousands.

Martha-Ray saw the movement from the corner of her eye and snapped her head around and screamed. Jackson followed her gaze and struggled to climb off of his recliner, his useless leg refusing to cooperate.

The centipedes seemed to be coordinating its movements as one huge animal, which was more sizable and somehow even more terrifying than the single, gargantuan creature. They quickly found their way to the four-poster upon which Fred lay and raced up the legs with lightning speed. The 'pedes were upon Fred's unconscious body within seconds, bustling and crawling all over him in a living blanket of ferocious biting fangs. Fred's body twitched and jerked as the 'pede's feeding frenzy pulled him from his merciful sleep and made short work of his remaining eye as they burrowed into ruined face to seek out the warm, succulent tissues within.

Jane looked away as Fred pummeled at the creeping things that were eating him alive; the stump of his right arm flopped around in an impotent wave as the throng of ravenous 'pedes stripped away his flesh to expose the bones beneath, upon which they gnawed with a gut-churning scraping sound. The 'pedes reminded Jane of piranha; the way they worked together to subdue their prey and strip its flesh. She had witnessed first-hand the notorious piranha fish at work in all of their ruthless efficiency, and they had held her fascination; at least you could avoid those particular predators by staying out of the water.

"What the fuck?!" Jackson shouted. "You gotta get me off this thing!" He continued the struggle to move his dying body off the recliner but what remained of his leg simply didn't work anymore.

The glistening swarm began to fan out from Fred and made its way directly toward the horrified people in the pool room.

Martha-Ray picked up her snake hook and swung it at the creatures that came close to her exposed legs. With deliberate, deft twists of her wrist, she flicked some into the wall one way, others into the pool.

Jane pushed Mel with her shoulder to kick-start the mesmerized girl into motion. "We have to go," she said, "*now*."

They began to run toward the door with Martha-Ray hot on their heels, desperate to get there before the 'pedes cut them off.

"You can't leave me here!" Jackson cried out, his voice sharp with terror.

Jane paused momentarily and turned to look at the man who had followed her here uninvited; the man who had hurt Fred and had threatened her. She decided that yes, she *could* leave the guy here.

Jackson flailed around on his recliner, stabbing at the centipedes that climbed up his legs with the pole-end of the insect net Jane had conceded to let him have. His face was a veil of shock and agony, and the wound in his leg gushed with a rotten, black fluid.

Jane continued on toward the door.

Mel turned on her heels and made her way back toward the recliners.

"What are you doing?!" Jane screamed at her, "you can't –"

"– I can't just leave him." Mel's eyes were tearful and pleading. "They'll eat him."

Martha-Ray left Jane's side and followed Mel, wielding her hook.

Jane's conscience informed her that she really had little choice now, although she was fully prepared to fight it; she had no desire to walk headlong into the seething carpet of 'pedes to save a man who was dying anyway. On the other hand, she couldn't stand by and lose more students to their own pig-headedness; she was in enough trouble as it was. Jane gritted her teeth, she chastised her own warped moral code and turned to follow her students into the affray.

Mel swished the long stainless-steel knife at the centipedes that got in her way. As she battled through the creatures, she wished that she was wearing something more substantial on her feet than designer flip-flops and neon pink nail polish. She shuddered at the touch of the 'pede's prickly legs as they scuttled across her bare toes. Thankfully, the centipedes scattered as the sharp blade sliced through them and left trails of severed body parts and pale, sticky fluid on the tiles in their wake.

Martha-Ray followed close behind her colleague. She pushed at the animals with her own hook, making sure to keep her distance from the vicious fangs that swiped at her. She was positive that they were deliberately targeting her exposed feet, determined to use their potent venom to bring her down. She fought the revulsion that prickled her skin as surely as the centipede's feet – no way was Martha-Ray Penderson ending up as arthropod chow.

Jane brought up the rear-guard. She prodded away the

'pedes that made their way toward her with her hook and squished those that got too close. As she slammed the skillet down on the creatures, it threw up sparks and made each blow a resounding *clang* on the floor.

"Help me!" Jackson was angry, impatient as his frantic fight to keep the advancing creatures at bay grew weaker.

Jane scowled at him with impatience. They were going as quickly as they could, butnone of them could afford to step on a 'pede or get bitten, and the floor was alive with the things. It was like treading through a living minefield, Jane thought, as she smashed a myriapod head with a satisfying *crunch-splat*.

They reached Jackson's recliner just as he collapsed, resigned to his fate. Working with unspoken synergy, Martha-Ray flicked the centipedes off of the recliner whilst Jane used her skillet to knock off the ones that climbed up its legs.

"You guys help him up," Jane panted as she kicked out with a well-aimed boot that scattered the 'pedes, "I'll keep them away."

Mel and Martha-Ray picked up Jackson, an arm over each of their shoulders, and took his weight.

"I thought you were going to leave me," he said to Jane, "thank you, babe."

"Save the bullcrap, Jackson," Jane snapped, "I was on my way out."

Slow, but sure, they all made their way back toward the door, Jackson helping out with his one functional leg the best he could while groaning and grimacing against the pain that wracked his body with each step. Jane kicked out at any 'pede that got in her way, shoved at others with her hook, and took great relish in splattering those that got too close with her heavy pan.

As much as Jane fought, the unrelenting creatures kept on coming; advancing in massed groups that scurried toward her with fluidity that brought to mind brooks of stale blood. She began to panic, experiencing that all-too familiar tightening in her throat, the uncomfortable drip of slick, acrid stress-sweat down her back; just the thought of one of the 'pedes touching her skin made her head spin and knotted her guts.

Jane's eyes darted around, searching frantically for an escape route that would avoid the infernal creatures altogether.

The pool?

What if they all jumped in the pool?

And what if they never got out again? The pool was surrounded by a creeping line of 'pedes that were making their way to join those already feasting on Darlene's body. The sheet Jane had placed with reverence over Darlene's corpse was soaking through with blood that looked molasses-black in the gloomy light, and the shroud itself undulated with uncountable gorging 'pede bodies that made it look like Darlene was breathing.

At least Darlene had been dead before they'd gotten to her, Jane consoled herself; in that respect, at least the girl had been lucky. And then, as if just for the sadistic fun of tormenting herself, Jane's memory recalled in vivid technicolor just how her *ephemeroptera* specialist had died in the first place.

Deciding not to voice the pool option, Jane led the others to the door as the expanding ocean of centipedes maneuvered to block off what was their only realistic exit.

Martha-Ray took sole support of Jackson as Mel and Jane kicked and hacked and stomped at the teeming throng of ravenous creatures that appeared to be working in unison to thwart their egress. The crunch of chitin, splash of body fluids, and *squoosh* of hard carapace filled the pool room and echoed along with Jane and Mel's exertion-grunts and the dull *ding* of Jane's pan.

Finally, exhausted, they burst through the door and into the stairwell, dragging Jackson along behind them.

"Made it," Jane gasped as she slammed the door shut behind her. The door closed on one over-bold centipede that had attempted to follow them out, neatly bisecting it.

"Not quite," Martha-Ray replied. She gawped up at the shadows into which the concrete stairs ascended.

The others followed her gaze.

The walls, the stairs, the ceiling were all dotted with fat, yard-long centipedes, each one highlighted as a sickly, waxen glint in the pinprick glow of the emergency lights.

3

After what seemed to Newman to have been the world's longest dump, Larry-Wayne finally emerged from his crappy abode and made his way – head down against the harsh wind – back to the car. He smiled his wan smile and jangled the Mountainview keys above his head as he snatched the door open and climbed in.

"I thought you'd fallen in," Newman growled. There was no humor in his voice.

"Yeah, I think most of me did," Larry-Wayne replied with a grin, and the pungent stench of expensive marijuana on his breath assaulted the cop's nose.

Newman chose to ignore the man's obvious intoxication, and the fact that, Larry-Wayne had insisted on accompanying him to the Mountainview; the man was reluctant to let the keys out of his sight as a child with a security blanket. No matter, Newman at least had the hotel keys now and the priority was to get back across to the other side of town. No time for reprimands or questions.

Without another word between them, Newman thrust the stick shift into *D* and floored the accelerator.

The Tahoe spun its tires on the loose dusting of sand that covered the road and sped off to be swallowed by the hungry storm.

4

Lee held his breath as he watched the small brown feather of gas grow from his mixture. He froze and waited for the tiny reaction to pass. One drop too many of glycerol at this point, and he, too, would end up looking like a *Walking Dead* extra.

He stole a glance at the fancy ramekin that sat in the ice filled sink; he was confident that he had almost enough nitroglycerine to detonate the C4 that he had already packed on the hinge-side of the steel door, adding it to the smaller amount they'd put there earlier. He'd used the high explosive like Play-Doh, this time molding it the full length of the door. He'd even created an enlarged lump into which he would be placing his makeshift detonator. The plan was to decant the Nitro' into a glass turkey-baster he'd found in one of the kitchen drawers and seal off the narrow end with aluminum foil. The baster would slot into the C4 with enough protruding for him to shoot at.

Then, one bullet into the baster and *boom*, the whole freakin' lot would blow.

A movement caught his attention. Lee flicked his eyes toward the group of yellow eggs closest to him. He had noted earlier, upon closer inspection that the eggs themselves were translucent. Their bile color came from the things that wriggled and fidgeted within their rubbery sanctuaries, doing little to dispel his alien theory. Through the clear egg shells, Lee had seen that the baby things within were exact, miniature replicas of the monster that ate Johnny Psycho. And they all looked pretty anxious to be free of their incarceration.

The brown plume dispersed harmlessly into the air, and Lee continued his drip-drip of the glycerol into the acid mix as quickly as he dared; the sooner he was out of this place and away from the embryo monsters that twitched listlessly and peered out at him, the better.

5

The sweat soaked through Jane's shirt, and she caught whiffs of its sharp, unpleasant odor – strange how fear sweat smelled *different* to the regular stuff. Her back was drenched, and sizeable damp patches had spread out from under her arms and beneath her boobs; it was certainly not the most alluring she'd looked for either one of the lovers that were currently in her company, although she hardly had the time to feel uncomfortable about it. Still, in the oppressive, stale heat of the hotel's stairwell, Jane found herself envying Mel in her cool, loose-fitting shirt and insignificant bikini briefs.

They had made their way – slowly – halfway up the staircase, maneuvering one careful step at a time. Jane and Mel had taken on Jackson's weight, and Martha-Ray had volunteered to take the lead, three stairs ahead, to clear the way of centipedes.

The creatures clung to the walls above and around them, eerily still as if watching, waiting for something. Occasionally one would scurry across a concrete stair in front of Martha-Ray, startled at the human's approach.

It seemed to Jane as though the 'pedes were studying *en mass* their prey. She imagined she sensed the countless flat, beady eyes watching them as they made their way to the top of the stairs.

"I guess they don't care much for people-meat after all," Jackson said with a pained grin across his face.

"Shh, keep it quiet!" Jane whisper-barked. 'Pedes were sensitive to sound, and she'd be damned if she was going to solicit another attack for the sake of a wry quip.

Jackson winked at her through his pain but remained quiet.

Martha-Ray prodded a centipede off of the step above her feet. It turned to face her, its body coiled in an aggressive *S*. She froze, watching as it opened its fangs wide as if in admonishment. It then turned and crawled away up the wall to join the others. Perhaps, she hoped, they weren't interested in eating her now that she reeked so badly of sour sweat.

Almost to the top now, the door to the first floor was within easy reach. If the 'pedes would just stay where they were and retain their apathy, Jane figured that she just might make it to the hallway. From there it was only thirty or so yards to the kitchen and the explosives that she prayed Lee had completed. And then it would be a short step out into the welcome night air.

Buoyed up with renewed vigor, Jane shouldered Jackson's weight, and all-but dragged him and the silent Mel up the last of stairs.

The centipedes began to shift as if aligning themselves to monitor the progress of the four people in who had invaded their domain. Moving as one, the creatures began to creep forward.

"Shit," Jane muttered under her breath as the movement caught her attention. Instinctively, she knew that something was not right.

"Are they coming for us?" Mel broke her silence. She gripped her knife tightly, and her knuckles whitened

"Stay quiet, keep moving," Jane ordered. "You too, Martha-Ray," she verbally nudged the girl.

Only a handful more stairs, yet the kitchen seemed a million miles away. Jane knew that they had to keep moving as the 'pedes were gathering pace, streaming along and down the walls and up the gray steps.

Martha-Ray swung her snake hook at the centipedes nearest her on the wall, dislodging them to tumble back down the stairs. It was a hopeless task as for each one she displaced, there were dozens more to take its position.

Jane growled at Jackson, "If you don't help me out here, I'm just going to leave your sorry ass behind." The man's pained look told Jane that he knew damn well that hers was no idle threat. She'd have few qualms at leaving Jackson on the stairs if it meant that she, Mel, and Martha-Ray weren't slowed down. As altruistic as she was being right now, she saw no point in sacrificing three for the one who was most likely going to die anyway.

Jackson swung his good leg and pushed off on the next step up, casting a nervous glancing at the encroaching centipedes. If it were at all possible, he thought, the vile things somehow looked even worse in the gloom, just something about the way their dark shapes snaked along the walls and made them appear to be floating in mid-air.

Jane felt a crunch as a small 'pede died beneath her foot, and the sticky goo of its guts oozed up the sides of her boot.

The surrounding 'pedes quickened their step, spurred on by the scent of their comrade's death.

"Run," Jane whispered.

"I can't," Jackson whined.

Jane ignored Jackson and sprinted up the stairs, pulling him and Mel along with her with an almost superhuman strength that forced Martha-Ray to take the remaining stairs two at a time or risk getting trampled underfoot. The sinister *click – clack – click* rustle of the centipedes as they gave chase filled the stairwell, echoing around the bare walls like a ghostly whisper.

One final, decidedly unfeminine grunt and Jane reached the top of the stairs. She looked behind her at the living carpet of long, jostling bodies.

Martha-Ray pushed open the double-doors, delighted to be within sight of the carpeted hallway. They all fell through the doors in unison, gasping for air.

"Close them!" Jane panted, "close the goddamned doors!"

She let Jackson slump down, disregarding the agonized cry he let out as he hit the floor. She pushed on one of the doors, Martha-Ray and Mel on the other. The door dampeners did their job well, and the doors closed with an agonizing, unhurried movement that gave the swarming centipedes time to gain ground.

Jane put her back to the door, throwing her entire weight at it.

The doors closed, little by little.

As the first of the centipedes crawled through the six-inch gap that remained between the doors, Martha-Ray hit it with her snake-hook, smashing its head. Another ventured through, and again, Martha-Ray thrashed at it with manic swipes to mangle its head into the lavish carpet.

An inch or two now, and still the centipedes attempted to clamber through the gap, scrambling over each other to gain ground. One more of the creatures thrust its broad head through the gap between the doors, forcipules flexing, antennae waving in frantic arcs.

Jane pushed one final time on the doors, and they closed. The intruding 'pede was crushed in two, and its front half continued toward Jackson, while its severed entrails dragged behind it.

Jane reached out a foot and stomped on its head, and the thing quit moving.

They could hear the 'pedes on the stairwell side of the door, their myriad feet scratching at the wood. She caught glimpses of their red bodies as they crawled up the door, their volume of numbers blocking out the small windows in their relentless attempt to follow.

"We did it," Mel sighed, she was close to tears, "we fucking-well did it!" She half-laughed, half-cried, and cuddled Martha-Ray, "*We did it*!"

Jane remained leaning against the doors, momentarily too frightened to move away. If there were enough 'pedes out there, it was possible they could open the doors through their sheer weight of numbers. She shuddered at that thought.

Jane read the sign on the wall ahead. In one direction

was the kitchen, the other, the trash room; they might just make it after all. "Thank you, Martha-Ray," Jane was genuinely grateful, "you're a trooper."

Martha-Ray smiled and struggled to find the appropriate response, unused as she was to taking a compliment. "Least I could do," she mumbled and looked down at her feet, suddenly she felt self-conscious in her tight cut-away and tiny skirt.

"Yeah, thank you, sweetheart," Jackson chimed in, for once actually managing to sound genuine. The exertion and adrenaline rush had over-ridden the worst of his pain by outward appearances, although his increased heartbeat had accelerated the venom's circulation around his body and shortened his life expectancy even further. "Couldn't have done it without ya," he smiled. He turned to Mel and Jane with the cheeky grin they had both fallen for. "What say we ask Martha-Ray if she'd like to make that three-way a *four*-way?" he chuckled.

The giant centipede's head dropped from above, fangs yawning wide, dripping with venom, its jaws twitching and looking for all the world as if the monster was smiling at them. It hung there a split second – suspended by the colossal body that clung to the ceiling – in the midst of the four horrified people.

Mel screamed first, followed by Martha-Ray and Jackson – who squealed more like a girl than the girls. In their panic, the group split up; Mel took one look into the monster's dull, dead eyes, and turned on her heals to run in one direction, whilst Jane and Martha-Ray grabbed Jackson by a hand each and sprinted in the other, dragging the wounded man along the floor.

"Mel!" Jane called over her shoulder. In her blind panic, Mel had run the wrong way, toward the trash room, "it's this way!" But she knew in her heart that the girl couldn't possibly hear her, or if she could, she'd be unlikely to follow. All Jane could do now was save herself and hope that Mel would find her way back to the kitchen. As Jane ran, she glanced behind and saw the giant 'pede crawl down from the ceiling, along the wall and with deliberate, focused movements, run toward her.

6

Mel lost her flip-flops as she ran. They flew from her manicured feet and bounced away into the gloom, but she barely noticed that they were gone. She thought she heard Jane calling after her, but the sound of her own labored breath and adrenaline-fuelled blood roaring in her ears made it impossible to tell.

She ran on toward the trash room. Away from the humongous creature that she just *knew* was close behind. In her hand, she gripped tight her long knife as if the utensil was more of a talisman than the feeble a weapon; she knew it would be against the heinous monster that hunted her.

The hallway ahead was dark, with only the white emergency LED lights set against each wall to provide any illumination, which Mel thought made the long hallway resemble a miniature airstrip. The dark terrified her, but the mental imagery of the colossal centipede with its malevolent fangs and soulless, staring eyes spurred Mel on and uncaring; she plunged into the darkness.

She felt the first of the things against her face, then a second, and then another, more. Intuitively, Mel raised her hand to protect her eyes from the scratching, clinging things that prickled her scalp and pulled at her hair.

Mel screamed out loud and waved the knife blindly in front of her face, not once slowing her step. She felt the jarring resistance as the blade hit and sliced through hard bodies, the sprinkle of warm juices in her face, and the crinkle of cracked carapace beneath her bare foot.

The centipedes, some longer than her own legs, hung from the ceiling and grasped at Mel's head, stopping her dead in her tracks. Taking hold of her with brutal claws, they snaked their bodies in her hair and bit with ferocity at her face. Mel howled, and her terror reverberated through the shadowed, lonely passageway. Ignoring the savage bites to her hand, Mel tugged at the creatures that entwined in her scalp, dislodging some from the ceiling only to have them scurry deeper into her short, thick hair.

Then, using their collective strength, the 'pedes lifted Mel up.

Mel's bare feet left the floor as the centipedes pulled on her hair and bit deep into her flesh to gain their purchase. She cried out and kicked and flailed in vain at the prickle of sharp feet on her exposed skin as she felt some of the creatures crawl down along her body.

Reaching upward, Mel dropped her knife and grabbed with both hands at the long, hard bodies that held her captive. Fighting hard against the living, writhing chains, Mel braved the sharp stabs of the forcipules that assaulted her hands with searing poisons, desperate to be free of the biting, burrowing torture.

Vicious bites tore through Mel's eyelids and brought waves of burning pain to her eyes that tore deep into her brain and lit up her vision with startling white sparks and pretty, twinkling, ice-blue lights.

An inquisitive head poked into Mel's gaping mouth as she screamed, drawn to the warmth and moisture within. Reflexively, Mel chomped down, and her teeth severed the centipede's head, and she tasted the bitter tang of the thing's blood. She gagged on the bitter, disgusting flavor, and the disembodied head dug its fangs into her tongue to pump out its venom. Blood flowed in a sticky, warm torrent from Mel's scalp, down through the tattered flaps of her eyelids and into her eyes to obscure the last remnants of her vision. It then joined the blood that dripped from her innumerable wounds and splashed down onto the floor below, *pitter-patting* onto the carpet. With each drop of blood she shed, Mel weakened as the centipede venom worked its magic on her body.

Melanie Hernandez cried out in agony and horror one last time; her voice struggled out as little more than a feeble bleat. Then, finally, the insidious wash of venom stopped her heart as the centipedes continued to burrow and feed.

7

"Faster!" Jane shouted, and pulled on Jackson's arm. Martha-Ray was doing her very best but was showing signs of flagging. Jane would be damned if she was going to have to go back to drag her student's fat ass to the kitchen; the girl would either make it or she wouldn't. The 'pede had most of its massive body onto the floor of the narrow hallway and was gathering speed in their direction. Jane's mind raced ahead, self-preservation overruling altruism, totally prepared to drop Jackson and leave Martha-Ray to the mercy of the creature if necessary. She had never been much of one for the whole self-sacrifice bullshit – much more of an advocator of Darwin and his survival of the fittest thing.

And if that meant taking Charlie D' literally, and leaving behind the sick and the overweight in her wake, then so be it.

"Don't let the fucker eat me!" Jackson pleaded, much less of a hard-ass when faced with his own demise. He kicked at the floor with his functioning leg as Jane pulled on him, trying to push himself along.

Jane saw the door up ahead. The *sans-serif* printed sign that read **'KITCHEN'** looked beautiful.

The 'pede was gaining ground. It propelled itself with an unswerving, liquid speed, its spiked legs tapping on the ground, head snaking this way and that, antennae twitching.

Jane threw herself at the kitchen door, dragging Jackson in behind her. Martha-Ray followed and joined Jane with her back to the door. Together, they slammed it shut – no dampener this time – and leaned their combined weight against it to keep the monster 'pede at bay.

The giant creature thumped against the door, jarring Jane and Martha-Ray so hard that their teeth rattled. The door eased open an inch or two, but then slammed back shut; perhaps Martha-Ray's extra few pounds served a Darwinian function after all.

The 'pede pushed again, and Jane could feel its colossal weight behind the door, although it wasn't putting its entire strength behind it; the thing was testing the door with gentle pushes. Jane assumed that sooner or later, it would build up to giving the door a proper shove, and there'd be no way she and Martha-Ray would be able to hold it. They had to find something to block the door.

Jackson crawled across the kitchen floor to the sink where Lee was creating busy explosives, oblivious to the drama behind him.

"Nearly done here," Lee told him. "Hey, you look like crap, Jackson."

CHAPTER SIXTEEN

1

"You think you can hold it by yourself?" Jane asked Martha-Ray. The terrified girl nodded bravely, but her lower lip quivered, and fear crawled across her face. "I think I can drag that butcher's block over to keep the door shut," Jane told her, "but I need you to keep the damn door closed."

"Don't worry, I've got this," Martha-Ray assured her Professor as yet another teeth-clattering *thump* rattled the door.

"Okay, on three," Jane called, "one, two –"

"Three!" Martha-Ray shouted. She pressed her feet hard against the floor and leaned with all of her weight against the door.

Jane scooted across the kitchen to the biggest of the stainless-steel butcher's blocks and dragged it with every ounce of strength her slight frame could muster. Her sweating hands were hot and slick, and she struggled to hold on to thick wooden top, grateful for the layer of fine dust that offered at least some grip. The block's steel feet screeched across the tiled floor in a banshee wail of complaint that made Jane's ears ache.

The giant centipede in the hallway continued its assault on the kitchen door. Becoming bolder with each gentle press against the door, it pressed its bulk against the door to create a gap wide enough to poke an inquisitive antenna through. The sensory appendage waved in mid-air, and its tip stroked Martha-Ray's leg tracing up along her thigh to the soft curve of her buttock and then back downward to tickle at her toes. Martha-Ray bit down hard on her tongue to stifle the scream that she could feel building up in her throat at the 'pede's touch. She gave the kitchen door another shove, and the antenna retracted.

"You need help over there?" Lee called over to Jane as she wrestled with the butcher's block – she had it halfway across the kitchen and was flagging somewhat.

"Just concentrate on what *you're* doing!" Jane yelled back in sharp gasps. She pushed at the block, and her back throbbed with its own complaint against the stress she placed upon it, and her legs wobbled like Jello. Even so, there was no way in hell she was about to give up now. Jane moved around to the opposite side of the block, pulling hard on it until its heavy legs scraped on the floor like fingernails down a chalkboard as she inched it toward the door.

Almost there.

The kitchen door burst open and bashed Martha-Ray hard against the wall. Winded, dazed, she reached for the door to close it, but the centipede slithered its huge body through the doorway and twisted its head around to grab her.

"No!" Jane screamed as she saw the creature snatch up her student in its bulky forelegs.

Martha-Ray thrashed and screeched in terror as the 'pede's sharp claws dug deep into her flesh. She pummeled her fists hard on the centipede's head, thumping hard on its deathly eyes to no effect; the thing was unflinching.

Jane lunged forward and grabbed at the knives that hung on the magnetic strips above the counter-tops. She hurled the heavy, honed knives at the creature only to see them bounce harmlessly from its tough carapace as if they were fake, made of rubber. Martha-Ray let out a long, loud terrified scream as the monster centipede unfurled its shimmering maxillipeds and flexed its gaping jaws in a perverse semblance of a grin as the creature readied itself to strike.

Jane stopped dead in her tracks as the 'pede's fangs sank deep into Martha-Ray's chest, cutting off her scream in mid-flow. Ribs splintered, flesh ripped, blood arced, and thick, scarlet blood bubbled from her mouth and cascaded into the centipede's mouth. Still alive, Martha-Ray kicked her legs and beat against the animal with her hands as it injected its poisons deep into her body. Unrelenting and oblivious to Martha-Ray's inadequate assault on its head, the 'pede held tight onto its prize.

Jane turned away and crouched down behind a workstation and felt like a coward. There was nothing more she could do to help Martha-Ray; that much was obvious but somehow it still didn't assuage her conscience.

Martha-Ray sobbed quietly, resigned to her fate, her fleshy body limp in the 'pede's unyielding grasp. The creatures' forcipules had unfortunately missed her heart and denied the merciful release of a swift death. Its venom was already working hard at closing down her body, and she could feel her heart's erratic beat, her lungs leaden and laboring in her ruined chest, and the dreadful, stinging warmth of the poisons that made her fingers and toes itch as if crawling with insects. The centipede maneuvered Martha-Ray toward its immense mouthparts, and the last thing Martha-Ray saw was the yawning, black maw and mechanical jaws that welcomed her.

Holding her in its forelegs in a lover's embrace, the

'pede began to chew at the ample flesh of the girl's belly.

2

Lee couldn't bear to watch, memories of Johnny's demise flooding his mind. So, as the centipede occupied itself with consuming the nice, curvy black girl, Lee returned his focus back to the removal of the final few drops of nitroglycerine from his concoction and into the ramekin.

He glanced down at his Jackson, who lay slumped on the floor beside him. He'd been drifting in and out of consciousness for some time now, and he reminded Lee of some long-drunk bum in a store doorway.

"Ya need to get that door blown, Lee," Jackson mumbled, "ain't got much time now that fucker's in here with ya."

"I'm on it, man. Give me a fucking break, for Christ's sakes," Lee grumbled. What he really didn't need right now was Jackson getting all in his shit and stating the fucking obvious.

With expert attention, Lee poured the ramekin contents into a second glass baster, which he had sealed up at its narrow end with aluminum foil and silver duct tape. *Just why the fuck was there duct tape in a kitchen in the first place?* That stuff got everywhere.

And there it was, in his sweating, shaking hand.

His detonator.

Lee stepped over Jackson and over toward the steel door. Martha-Ray was now mercifully silent although the crackling munching noises that the giant centipede was making as it made short work of her corpse were somehow worse than her screaming.

He got to the door and contemplated the fat sausages of C4 he'd pressed into the hinges. He also became aware that the 'pede had paused its consumption of Martha-Ray to turn its attention to him, attracted by the sudden movement. An old, familiar chill gripped Lee's guts as he stared across the kitchen at the thing's blank, staring eyes.

"Fuck," He whispered.

A noise to the left startled Lee, and his eyes flicked to the dark, damp space beneath one of the shiny workstations. There, a clutch of the translucent yellow eggs was beginning to hatch.

From her hiding place, and through her tears, Jane's attention turned to the 'pede eggs too. Her stomach churned as she watched the soft, yellow-orange baby 'pedes tear slits in the leathery egg shells and slither out all glistening and wet with the slimy juices that had cocooned them. Each juvenile stretched out at around twenty to twenty-four inches, Jane's expert eye estimated, and each was one a perfect miniature of their monstrous mother. And this was far, far worse than the swarms of centipedes she had encountered thus far, as they were all fully grown, albeit a good deal larger than they should be. But she could see that creatures that were emerging from the eggs were destined to match the colossal size of their mother, and that thought terrified the zoologist.

The baby 'pedes crawled around to explore their newfound freedom whilst staying in close proximity to each other, lifting up their heads to taste the air and search for their first meal. They were wet and vulnerable, their chitinous bodies soft but already beginning to darken as they hardened in the warm air. The babies flexed their formidable jaws as if keen to try them out; the fangs appearing disproportionately large, black, and shiny in contrast to the spongy yellow exoskeleton around them. And each one and every one of the young 'pedes packed the same venom-punch as all of the others Jane and her companions had encountered thus far.

Jane saw that the giant 'pede had dropped Martha-Ray's remains – not that there was an awful lot left of the poor girl, just a bloodied lump of raw meat and shredded scraps of the one-piece Martha-Ray had been wearing. The 'pede had then turned its attention to Lee, although it remained frozen in its spot half in, half out of the kitchen doorway.

"Shit," Jane muttered, Lee was her only chance of escaping this hellhole if the 'pede killed him now; Jane knew that her fate would be sealed. She watched Lee as he crossed over from the sink to the door: his nervous eyes trained on the thin, glass baster and its precious cargo.

"Hey!" Jane leaped up from her hiding place. "Hey, you!" she shouted at the giant 'pede. She pulled a hefty stainless steel cooking pot from the rack above her and banged it with a reverberating *clang* on the counter top.

The centipede turned toward her in a lazy, sweeping motion. It lifted up its head and twisted to face her, fangs flexing and dropping shreds of bloody flesh onto the floor.

"Are you crazy!?" Lee yelled over at her.

"I'm keeping that motherfucker off your ass so be grateful!" Jane shouted back. "Just do what you need to do!"

Jane threw the pot as hard as she could at the 'pede, and it bounced off of the thing's head, and Jane saw with some satisfaction that the creature flinched ever so slightly. Her satisfaction was, however, short-lived as the giant 'pede launched itself toward her.

Jane Lucas ran.

Darting to the next work station, Jane plucked two long carving knives from a nearby rack and hurled one at the approaching 'pede. In an ideal world, the knife would have conveniently sliced through the creature's head and buried itself deep into its brain to kill the hellish thing outright.

But no, the knife bounced off with impotence and clattered to the floor. Jane doubted that the approaching 'pede had even registered that it had been hit.

Considering its size, it was amazing just how nimbly the centipede could maneuver its bulky body along the floor and up over the work tops, its massive legs simultaneously clattering on the tiled floor and rattling against stainless steel as it homed in on Jane.

Jane dashed from the sanctuary of the work station and threw herself across the floor, sliding on her butt as the 'pede's head threw a huge, grotesque shadow over her. The monster shifted its body a touch and snaked toward Jane as she came to a sudden stop adjacent to a cluster of unhatched eggs. Jane struggled to her feet and stood her ground, facing her greatest fear with an almost unnatural calm.

The 'pede paused. It looked to be contemplating the zoology professor and her uncomfortable proximity to its offspring. Its hideous face was raised from the floor, and its flat eyes studied Jane from barely an arm's length away, its body coiled like some hell-spawned snake making ready to strike.

Jane gripped her one remaining knife 'till her fingers hurt and ground her teeth so hard she imagined Lee could hear the noise they made from across the kitchen.

Then the centipede made its move, and Jane reacted with a speed she never thought possible. Jane swung the carving knife at the creature and the cold steel sliced through the creature's right antenna. The 'pede recoiled in pain – or whatever passed for pain within its primitive nervous system – and the severed end of its antenna fell and lay twitching on the ground as if it was feeling out for its other half. A clear fluid dribbled from the raw end of the 'pede's ruined antenna and ran down its face; it looked like the creature was crying.

Taking advantage of the 'pede's distraction, Jane ran from her spot. As she did so, she skidded and lost her footing in the creature's bleeding hemolymph, lurching forward with her arms spiraling and feet skidding in exaggerated slapstick movements. By some miracle Jane managed to regain her balance, and she ran toward the far end of the kitchen. There, she was just a short sprint from the walk-in freezer, but farthest from Lee and the steel door.

Jane squashed herself into the tight gap between two capacious refrigerators, having gauged that the 'pede's head would never fit. She hoped to God that her hurried estimate was correct and readied her knife – just in case.

The 'pede recovered itself from Jane's assault and recommenced the hunt, its one remaining antenna waved in the air while the sump of its companion twitched in lame unison. The creature's legs pounded their tattoo on the floor tiles, the rhythmic waves propelling it relentlessly onward like some unstoppable killing machine.

3

Across the kitchen, Lee inserted the explosive-filled turkey baster into the C4 that he'd stuck on the hinge side of the steel door. He added a little more of the C4 around the receptacle itself to hold it in place.

He'd lost track of Jane but was happy that the monster was chasing her and not him. He kind of hoped that she was okay, she wasn't all bad for an old nerdy gal, and he'd like to save more than just his own life here – but if that wasn't to be, he could most probably live with that. Lee finished packing the C4 around his homemade detonator and took a moment to admire his handiwork. Yep, that ought to do it, he thought, if his explosive combination of nitroglycerine and C4 didn't blow the fucking door off its hinges, then nothing would. And right there was a thought that Lee really didn't want to entertain.

He plucked Jackson's gun from the countertop, next to the door, and double-checked the four bullets in the magazine.

Something grabbed a hold of his leg.

Lee jumped, and acting on instinct, swung the gun downward and fired off a precious shot without thinking.

"Jesus, shit, Jackson! What did you do that for!?" Lee

barked. Jackson had let go of Lee's leg and stared up at him from the floor with incredulity.

"You fucking shot me," Jackson growled. The bullet had gone clear through his envenomed leg, which had burst open to spray chunky, stinking pus and black clots of rotted blood across the floor.

"Oh shit, I – I'm sorry, man," Lee stuttered.

"S'okay, dude," Jackson said and forced a weak smile, "I didn't feel a thing. Now, give me the gun. Let me do this."

"No fucking way, man," Lee said. "With all due respect, man, you're in no fit state to shoot straight."

"You're just saying that 'cos I'm a dead man walking." Jackson managed a strangled laugh and a thick, hacking cough.

"Don't say that," Lee sounded like a petulant child, "we just need to get you out of here and to a hospital; you'll be fixed up in no time." Lee hardly believed the bullshit himself.

"Listen to me, asshole," Jackson snarled. He reached out and dug his fingers once more into Lee's calf, and he saw that he was hurting the guy even though Lee was determined not to show it. "That fucker's poison is in my fucking dick. And you and me both know what that means." Jackson fumbled at his pants. "Look."

Jackson struggled his pants and briefs down, and took no relish in the look of sheer disgust on Lee's face, he even thought for a moment there that Lee was about to hurl. Jackson's entire crotch up as far as his navel had turned the same oozing black color as his envenomed leg. There, suppurating flesh oozed and dribbled over skin so distended that it gave his once-magnificent penis monstrous, disfigured proportions and made it look like some repulsive, deformed root vegetable.

"It got my fucking dick, Lee. I can feel it going bad on the inside," Jackson sounded brave but looked dewy-eyed and tearful as he fought against his own terror, all the while hating himself for appearing weak in front of his subordinate. "I really don't want to live like this, man. I mean, if I can't enjoy the pussy, what's the fucking point?"

Lee started to say something, but checked the words before they came out of his mouth. He knew Jackson well enough to know that the man meant what he was saying, and he guessed that were things the other way around and it was himself crawling around on the floor with a ruined leg and putrefying penis, he'd feel much the same way.

Lee handed Jackson the gun.

"Good boy," Jackson grinned, "you know it makes sense. Now, I suggest that you stand the fuck back."

4

Jane pressed herself tighter still into the gap between the fridges and wished there was someway she could magically push herself through the cold wall that was hurting her spine. As her eyes adjusted to the darkness, Jane could see that there was space enough for her to squeeze behind one of the refrigerators should the need arise; but she hoped to God that she wouldn't have to sit among the stale food bits, dust bunnies, and rat droppings that had collected there across the years.

The 'pede had located her now, and paced back and forth in front of the refrigerators, pausing only to attempt to force its head into the narrow gap, only to be thwarted by its own bulk. The myriapod reached its one remaining antenna into the gap, far enough in for the tip to scratch at Jane's face. It tried to push in its maxillipeds, spreading them wide in an attempt to reach its prey with their venom. But no matter how much the 'pede twisted and turned its head, it failed in its attempts, and as if such a thing were possible, the centipede appeared to be getting increasingly frustrated.

Jane held her breath; she felt cramped and claustrophobic in her refuge and wished the thing away.

She could hear Lee and Jackson talking – no, they were *arguing* – their voices muffled by the bulky fridges by the time they reached her ears. Jane hoped that they weren't going to fuck up their one chance of escape, and she also murmured a quiet prayer that Lee's ambitious plan was going to work.

The 'pede moved its head away, and Jane wondered if the animal was actually capable of feeling frustration or at the very least, some arthropod equivalent of that particular emotion? As she watched, the creature's vast body moved away, one shining segment at a time. She exhaled her relief, closed her eyes, and rested her head on the wall. Jane swallowed hard, the giant 'pede was making its way toward Lee, and all she could do was hope that it wouldn't get to him before he could blast the door open. Sweet Jesus, would this nightmare never end?

In answer to her question, a juvenile centipede snaked down the wall behind the 'fridge, its soft body phosphorescent in the darkness. It made its way toward the warmth that it sensed there, excited by the prospect of its first meal.

Jane first felt the young 'pede tickle her scalp as it moved through her sweat-matted hair. Crawling, itching, prickling, the sensation of the thing's feet reminded Jane of the vibrating, wire head-massager her parents had bought her one Christmas. She reached up a quivering hand to investigate, dreading what she knew in her heart she would find there. Jane cried out as her fingers touched the creeping thing that had burrowed into her hair, and she felt the copious spiked legs and long, soft body that made the thing feel like it was made of latex.

Then she felt hard, sharp fangs sinking into the soft pad of flesh of her thumb.

With a horrified cry, Jane pulled the young 'pede out of

her hair with its forcipules still embedded in her thumb and pumping liquid agony into her hand. She leapt from the confined space to be rid of the creature, to smash it into oblivion on the cold hard floor. Ignoring the hot pain in her hand, Jane swung the juvenile 'pede at the ground to bring its soft body crashing down upon the tiles. On the fourth or fifth swing – in her frenzied panic, Jane really wasn't keeping count – the 'pede finally let go of her hand as its vulnerable body burst open and its innards spilled out.

From halfway across the gloomy kitchen, the giant centipede, alerted by the burst of death pheromones, turned to face its offspring's killer.

Jane returned the thing's gaze; was that *hate* in its dulled, inhuman eyes? She could sense – or imagine she sensed – an angry malevolence emanating from the 'pede's demon-face as the thing coiled its body in readiness to protect its young.

The 'pede burst into motion and started back toward Jane, its fangs wide open, dripping with poison.

Startled by this sudden burst of movement, Jane threw her knife at the creature in a vain attempt to cause at the very least a slight hesitation in its advance. Oblivious to the knife that pinged harmlessly off of its back, the creature advanced.

Jane threw herself back into her refuge, but this time she shuffled *behind* the massive refrigerator, eager to put the heavy bulk of both refrigerators between her and the giant 'pede. She had no sooner forced her body between the silvered rear of the fridge when the 'pede's head appeared at the gap, more determined than ever to get to her, its pushing weight moved one of the appliances away from the wall a little and widened the gap.

A grim determination settled in Jane's gut, and she leaned her back against the wall, placed her feet on the rear of the 'fridge somewhere near its middle, and pushed.

The 'pede thrust its head once more at the gap and

snapped with at the air close to Jane with its forcipules whilst its forelegs scrabbled at the slippery steel, vying for purchase. Jane stared at the fangs that waved so dangerously close to her and trebled her efforts at pushing the fridge.

Suddenly the refrigerator toppled forward with a loud clatter as the glass shelves within shattered. It fell with its full weight onto the 'pede, trapping the creature firmly by six of its legs.

"I got you, you bitch!" Jane yelled at the 'pede. She jumped on top of the felled fridge and looked down at the squirming myriapod she had ensnared. The 'pede writhed and snapped its head back and forth thrashing its huge body with an unremitting violence, but still it remained trapped.

"I got the bastard!" She yelled with triumph at Lee who ran toward her. "I'm not sure how long it's gonna hold though," she added. She glanced at the 'pede and saw that it was already beginning to shift the fridge to free its legs.

"Long enough," Lee growled and grabbed hold of the professor's arm. "We need to find cover before the door blows." Lee pulled Jane down from the fridge, and they both stepped with nervous caution around the flailing 'pede. Contrary to all of her feminist instincts, Jane allowed herself to be dragged away; she saw all too clearly that the growing swarm of newly hatched 'pedes was marching toward her and Lee, and that Momma 'pede had begun to chew at her legs that were trapped beneath the fridge.

They ran toward the walk-in freezer.

"Jackson?" Jane said.

Lee shook his head, and his eyes flicked over to Jackson who lay a little short of six feet from the steel outer door with the gun in his trembling hand, pointing it at the explosives Lee had plastered to the hinges.

Jane remained silent. There was nothing she could think to say, although she did feel a slight pang of regret; she and Jackson had enjoyed some pretty wild times together.

Lee yanked on the freezer's handle and braced himself against the blast of cold air that blew out to meet them. A quick check that the freezer's lock was disarmed, and Lee slammed the door shut behind them.

Jane shivered against the cold and could see her breath as it plumed out in front of her face like smoke. She scraped the frost away from the tiny window on the freezer's door and peered out. She could see that the giant 'pede had gnawed through its trapped legs and had left them bleeding clear juices beneath the fridge, and now the creature was heading toward the walk-in. She also saw that the thin, yellow babies were now swarming toward their mother.

The 'pede's head connected hard with the freezer door, and Jane staggered backward, startled by the ferocity of the 'pede's attack. The door rattled, and one of the hinges snapped away, and then the 'pede hit again. This time, the door buckled inward at its middle, and Jane and Lee cowered at the back of the freezer, behind a half-cow carcass that dangled from a hook in the ceiling like the victim of a particularly cruel mob execution.

Another mighty thud, and the door crashed inward. The giant 'pede pushed its head into the cold, searching for the contrasting, tell-tale warmth that would give away its prey's whereabouts; it hesitated momentarily against the chill.

Jane risked a glance at the 'pede from her hiding place against the cow's frozen interior. She could see that the 'pede's head was battered and dimpled through its battle with the door, which along with its severed antenna made the animal look vulnerable, and for the first time since encountering the giant 'pede, Jane didn't regard the thing as an invincible personal demon. She saw that the creature's back was literally crawling with yellow juveniles, some of which were already taking tentative bites at the exposed soft spots between her body segments to make her their first meal

Beyond the 'pede, at the other end of the

Mountainview's kitchen, Jane saw Jackson steady his gun at the baster that was stuck to the outer door with plastic explosive. He pulled the trigger.

CHAPTER SEVENTEEN

1

"Did you hear that?" Newman asked, and his voice was all but carried away by the rushing wind. He grabbed Larry-Wayne's arm to silence him as he rattled the key in the lock of the Mountainview's front door. Newman blinked his eyes against the assaulting wind-blown sand and cocked his head, listening intently for a repeat of the gunshot he was certain he'd just heard.

"Didn't hear nothin'," Larry-Wayne raised his voice against the wind, "can't hardly hear anything agin' all this damned blowin'."

"I think it came from the back of the hotel," Newman told his reluctant companion. "They must be at the rear entrance."

Larry-Wayne mumbled beneath his breath and gave the key another twist only to meet with more resistance as the lock refused to give.

Impatient with the old man's meanderings, Newman pulled Larry-Wayne away from the door and back to the Tahoe.

2

"Shit, he missed!" Lee groaned, "he fucking missed." He looked over at the giant 'pede that blocked the freezer's entrance and then over at Jackson who was staring with disbelief at the gun in his hand. Jackson had an expression of deep disappointment and confusion etched onto his face, that and an all-consuming, sweating pain.

Jane strained to see around the frozen half-cow and over Lee's shoulder, all of her attention taken by the giant 'pede. The thing loomed in the doorway, reluctant to put more than its head into the chilled air, as if instinctively knowing that the cold would slow its metabolism and make its body lethargic. Even so, driven as it was by the overriding urge to eat, the giant centipede advanced toward Jane and Lee – one grotesque leg at a time.

"Down," Lee barked at Jane.

Before Jane could duck, Jackson had fired off another shot.

"For fuck's sake!" Lee cried out as Jackson's bullet ricocheted from the suspended pots above the six-ring stove-top and dinged harmlessly off of at least three of them.

More worryingly, the gun's recoil had bucked the weapon out of Jackson's hand, and Lee could see that now it lay just beyond his reach. Jackson stared stupidly at it as if hoping he was suddenly going to play *Carrie* and develop telekinesis.

"I knew he couldn't do it," Lee snarled, "he's too fucking weak." He quickly weighed up his options as he saw Jackson embark upon a tortuous shuffle over to where the gun lay, shaking fingers outstretched toward it. There was no doubting now that Jackson was suffering unbearable pain, and from where he crouched, Lee could make out the fresh flow of molasses-black juice leaking from the bullet wound he'd inadvertently made in Jackson's thigh. Lee knew then, that despite his best intentions of altruistic bravado, Jackson simply wasn't going to do the job especially with only one bullet left in the gun.

The giant 'pede inched its body further into the freezer. It appeared to be getting bolder as it acclimatized to the cold, as the cold itself dissipated with the ingress of warmer air from the kitchen which turned the environment within less hostile for the cold-blooded creature.

"I'm gonna have to do this myself," Lee told Jane.

She grabbed his arm. "You can't go out there," Jane said with a nod toward the leviathan centipede which blocked the doorway with its gaping fangs and body that swarmed with the seething mass of young 'pedes which tormented with ever more audacious bites at its flesh. Jane really didn't have to say anything else; the terror in her eyes finished off the thought for her.

Lee pulled away from her with steely determination on his face. "I'll bring the gun back and make the shot from here." A smile. "You're gonna have to distract that motherfucker, though," he instructed and pointed at the centipede, as if he really needed to.

Jane selected a frozen chicken from the shelf beside her and hurled it at the 'pede. The creature recoiled as the rock-solid bird dented an eye.

"Perfect," Lee said and he sprinted toward the door.

Jane aimed another missile – a turkey this time – and hit the 'pede squarely on the stump of its severed antenna. It pulled its head back in reaction to the pain and reared up to snap its forcipules in the direction of the assault.

Taking his chance, Lee darted through the narrow gap between the centipede's body and the buckled door frame. He jumped with a graceful agility over the creature's waving legs and was out into the kitchen.

The 'pede turned its bulk around and followed him.

Jane screamed at the creature and hurled yet more frozen food at its retreating body but her stomach sank as she realized that the 'pede had set its sights – and vicious intentions – on Lee.

"Lee!" She screamed.

Lee turned around and his eyes met with the advancing creature's.

He turned back around and continued to run toward Jackson.

As the centipede crawled after Lee, it shed some of its young, their rubbery legs too weak to cling to the smooth, hard shell of their mother. Undeterred, the ejected juveniles scurried after their mother and toward the two men.

Lee got to the gun at the same moment as Jackson. The wounded man grabbed it and clutched the weapon to his chest.

"Give me the fucking gun!" Lee shouted. "You already fucking missed twice!"

"I got this, Lee," Jackson's voice was slow and deliberate, "trust me."

Lee grabbed for the gun, but Jackson held it tight, despite his weakened state.

"Don't be a stubborn prick, Jackson. Give me the gun," Lee grunted.

"I *said* I got this," Jackson retorted, "now get the fuck away from me." He pushed as hard as he could manage at Lee to shake him loose.

Lee fell backward just as the centipede reached them. The movement distracted the creature momentarily from the enticing scent of Jackson's pre-digested flesh and it lunged forward with lightning speed, its ebony-black fangs stretched open and ready.

Lee screamed as the 'pede's fangs sank deep into his thigh and he felt the black, hardened chitin scrape on his femur. The 'pede pinned Lee to the floor and all he could do was beat on the thing's head with his fists as searing, burning pain enveloped him.

Jackson pointed the gun at the centipede, doing his best

to ignore the yellow swarm that had begun to crawl over his devastated leg.

Lee yelled at Jackson, his voice high, "The fucking door, man!" As he screamed, Lee punched again and again at his attacker's head, aiming for the eyes – he'd seen something on the Discovery Channel once that said you should always aim for the eyes.

Or was it the nose?

Or was that sharks?

The first of the baby centipedes reached Lee, slithering down from its vantage point on the giant's head. It bit into his neck as he pulled at it with his hands, its sharp legs making short work of shredding his fingertips. Another one followed, then another, all chomping into Lee's exposed flesh and they had their heads burrowed under his skin within seconds.

Jackson hesitated, and it was just long enough for one of the juvenile 'pedes to crawl onto his shooting arm and sink its fangs into the delicate flesh on the underside of his wrist. Jackson yelped and flung his arm around, almost throwing away the gun in his frenzy.

"The door!" Lee yelled at Jackson again. "Fucking do it!"

Jackson's eyes met Lee's and in that instant both men united in pain and terror. *Make this nightmare stop,* Lee's eyes implored him.

Jackson switched his aim from the giant centipede to Lee's makeshift nitroglycerine detonator on the door, his hand steady despite the juvenile centipede that was gnawing on his arm.

He squeezed the trigger.

3

The bullet hit the baster full on, and the explosion ended the nightmare for both Jackson and his best boy, Lee. The exploding nitroglycerine detonated the C4 that, in an instant of searing heat, destroyed much of the kitchen and its contents, rocked the Mountainview to its very foundations and blasted the heavy steel door out into the night-blackened desert.

Jane had hit the freezer floor as Jackson fired that final bullet. The shock wave of the explosion thundered through her body, rattling her teeth, and concussed her head, which in turn made her ears ring like a wailing fire truck. She felt the blast of angry, heated air roll over her, bringing with it the hot, sharp debris and a sodden mist of blood that rained down amongst the spiraling plumes of fine dust. In what seemed like a slow-motion eternity, the hotel kitchen transformed into a boiling turmoil of clattering metal, disintegrating plaster and shredded, shattered centipede fragments.

The cacophony of clanking and screeching, tearing and splitting filled Jane's head fit to bursting. She closed her eyes very tight, curled herself fetal, and prayed it would all end very soon.

CHAPTER EIGHTEEN

1

Silence.

Jane sat up, and her body shivered against the dark, dust-laden air that clung to her like a malevolent ghost.

She struggled to her feet; her body was aching and groaning its complaints as she shuffled through the smoke and debris.

In the gloom, Jane could make out twisted metal shapes sculpted from the kitchen's structure by the explosion; the inky, dark stains that had once been Jackson and Lee and the pulverized chunks of what had been the monstrous *gigantea*. She stepped gingerly over the creatures shattered body, wary that it may somehow have cheated death only to grab at her with vicious fangs. Her more rational mind told her that was highly unlikely as the 'pedes head had been vaporized in the blast, and its body was split open like a dinnertime lobster.

Dazed, disoriented, Jane stumbled toward the gaping hole where the steel door had once been and through which the warm, stinging winds of the sand storm outside buffeted. As she homed in on the balmy air and neared the hole, Jane could see that one of the industrial sized refrigerators had become wedged in the doorway. There remained a gap only just big enough to fit her head through.

She pushed at the fridge, eager to be outside, and to hell with the storm that blew its howling, mocking wail at her through the hole.

The refrigerator refused to budge.

Jane kicked at the fridge: swore and beat on it until her hands were sore, and her eyes brimmed with desolate tears.

Spent physically and emotionally exhausted, Jane Lucas slouched to the floor and cried.

All this – she'd been through all of this, just to die trapped in the hotel kitchen. *Jesus-shit*, as the late Lee would eloquently have put it. What a *fucking* mess.

A noise.

It came from beyond the refrigerator. A faint, shuffling, scraping noise like the sound of a myriad tiny legs scratching to be let in.

Jane's body set rigid with fear, and her brain treated her to the less than comforting mental image of another giant 'pede reaching for her in the dark with thick, probing fangs and with revenge on its mind.

The fridge shifted and fell away into the darkness outside.

"Professor Lucas?" a familiar voice penetrated the blackness, accompanied by a harsh light that shone into her eyes, blinding her. "Are you okay?" Lieutenant Newman asked as he stepped over the debris and into the hotel. "What the hell happened here?"

Jane looked at the cop with relief etched on her face, and tear stains scribbled in the grime on her cheeks.

"I think I'm the only one left," she told him, her voice cracking.

Newman surrendered his jacket to Jane; she was

shivering so hard that her teeth clattered together and made a most peculiar sound. He gave a supporting arm around the professor's shoulders and escorted her out of what little remained of the Mountainview's kitchen.

2

There'd be time aplenty for explanations later, Newman thought as he stepped cautiously around the scattered remnants of the kitchen that lay sprawled out over the hotel's back parking lot. There was going to be an inquiry into whatever it was that had happened here – of that much he could be certain – if the professor *had* brought students along with her to the hotel and some (or *all*?) had died in there, the cop knew from bitter experience that she was going to have a hell of a lot to answer for when she got back to San Diego.

As for him, he was facing the unenviable attempt at explaining to his superiors precisely how come he got Larry-Wayne Williaford blown up during what should have been a routine police investigation into nothing more serious than criminal trespass.

Newman glanced over at where Larry-Wayne's legs stuck out from beneath the thick steel door. The old boy had been jiggling that goddamned key of his deceased friend's in the lock when the place had exploded and lit up like the Fourth of July. Somewhat impressively, Larry-Wayne had landed over sixty-odd feet away with the door on top of him, his tragic end now illuminated by the Tahoe's head lights.

But for now, Newman's focus was on getting the hell away from the Mountainview before something else blew up. So, he picked his way carefully through the hotel's spilled flotsam of rubble and shattered metal, carefully guiding Jane as he stepped over this, avoided that. As he walked, Newman's flashlight danced around the wreckage and picked out bloodied lumps of flesh, fat stalactites of iridescent yellow, floppy, wet lumps of things that looked a lot like misshapen, deflated beach balls and glinting, maroon-colored shards of fuck-knows what.

The hot, grit-laden air lashed at Jane's and the cop's faces as they made their way out of the hotel and toward Newman's car. As blustering as they were, already the storm's gusts were growing ever more lackluster as the winds began to die down.

Jane allowed the cop to lead on as her legs felt too weak and unreliable. She turned back around to look at the gaping, ragged hole that Lee's makeshift bomb had ripped in the side of the hotel, and her eyes caught sight of the steel door that had held her hostage for what had seemed an unimaginable age. And there, oozing from beneath the crushing weight of the scorched metal sheet was a syrupy, spreading puddle of dark blood and a protruding pair of legs that lay quite still with their toes pointing heavenward. With a shudder, Jane recognized the legs as belonging to Lenard Levandowski's friend – the striped socks being the dead giveaway – he'd been wearing them the night before when she and the two disgusting, perverted men had gotten intimately acquainted. Jane thought that the stripy socks made Larry-Wayne Williaford look like the unfortunate witch beneath Dorothy's house in Oz.

At that, Jane began to laugh hysterically, and she thought she'd never be able to stop.

EPILOGUE

Ted Buckner whistled through his teeth. Never in all his days as M.E. had he known anything like it. You go away for a few days for the first time in Christ only knows how long, and the entire place goes to hell in a handbasket!

It was Tuesday morning and Buckner's first day back in the saddle after his all too brief vacation. He'd let himself in early to make a start on what already had all the makings of what promised to be an uncharacteristically busy day.

When he'd left on Saturday, his morgue had housed only the Levandowski guy. But now, in the space of just three days, the old man had been joined by small pieces of tattooed, white flesh, the smashed-up remains of some black guy that were decomposing at an alarming rate despite the cool of the refrigerated drawers, a black arm that didn't belong to the said guy on account of it being female – and poor old Larry-Wayne Williaford who was considerably flatter than he had been the last time Buckner had set eyes on him.

The Medical Examiner still struggled to deal with seeing people he'd known in life on his slab, even after more years in the job than he cared to remember. Not that he'd known Larry-Wayne all that well but, jeez, the guy had only been in a few days previous to pick up his friend's belongings.

It had taken the lifting equipment from two fire trucks to pull the sheet steel door from Larry-Wayne's shattered corpse. All of the bones in the man's body had been broken – even the tiny ones in his ears – those most likely from the explosion he'd been caught up in before the door crushed him. In a ghoulishly comical twist, when they'd finally hoisted the door from the body, the rescue crew had discovered that Larry-Wayne still had his hand on the key that was sticking in the door's lock.

Oddly enough, there was to be no inquiry. Buckner had already been given the unofficial word on that by the Chief of Police, no less. It had something to do with the Government and Homeland Security and the goddamned Army; the Mountainview had been sealed up tighter than ever before, and a seven-foot, electrified fence adorned with signs that declared *Federal Warnings!* had appeared – literally – overnight. He'd also heard that there were armed guards there now, which certainly threw in a few sinister undertones so far as Buckner was concerned. Whatever was in the hotel that had caused so much chaos and death over the weekend was clearly supposed to stay in there.

Buckner sighed, the relaxation his break had afforded already little more than a pleasant but fading memory. He figured he'd best make a start with Levandowski's body since the old man had been first in and promised to be more straightforward than playing human jigsaw puzzles. Buckner pulled the white stained sheet away from Lenard's body and oddly malformed head. He plucked the scissors from the steel tray at his side and began to cut away the dead man's clothing.

The centipede darted out from Lenard's jacket, up the scissors, and onto the M. E's hand. With lightning speed, it wrapped its long, maroon body around Buckner's arm and clung on with myriad spiked legs that flashed a vivid yellow. Without hesitation, the creature plunged its fangs into the soft flesh at the crook of Ted Buckner's elbow.

Buckner bellowed as excruciating pain spread like wildfire from the creature's bite, and he staggered away from the autopsy table. He clutched at his chest with his unhindered hand and gasped to find his breath as his entire upper body tightened as if someone incredibly heavy were sitting on it. Buckner's legs buckled beneath him, and as he collapsed he pulled over the tray of pristine dissection instruments, which clattered around him on the white tiled floor.

Reaching the floor with a crumpling thump, Buckner's head cracked on the tiles, and his jarred vision blurred a nebulous gray. As the contents of the tray rattled and bounced around him, Buckner saw the hellish creature from his arm crawling up toward his face, its grotesque body snaking, head weaving, antennae twitching this way and that.

Buckner's body had been almost instantly paralyzed by the centipede's potent venom and the onset of heart failure, and he felt almost serene, somehow strangely *detached* from the horror that befell him; it was as if it were happening to some poor schmo in a B-movie.

Buckner mewled as the 'pede bit into his eye, and sticky vitreous humor spurted out from the punctured orb and down his face. Buckner's vision in his remaining eye flickered in and out as the poisons ravaged his body and his heart fluttered with wobbling, erratic beats. And then Buckner felt the cold, prickling touch of the centipede's legs as it feasted on the delicate flesh of his cheeks.

Mercifully, Ted Buckner had all but departed from this life by the time the 'pede crawled down his throat.

END

ABOUT THE AUTHOR

James H. longmore hails originally from Doncaster, a mining town in the south of Yorkshire, Northern England; he relocated with his family to Houston, Texas in 2010. James boasts an honors degree in Zoology and a former career background in sales, marketing, and business.

He is an accomplished, published author (and publisher), and ghostwriter of popular fiction - he writes across a wide range of genres and subjects: novels, shorts, and screenplays. He has written and directed award-winning short movies, is an affiliate member of the Horror Writer's Association, and has run/hosted the popular podcast/radio show *The New Panic Room* since early 2016, In addition, James is the founder and owner of the indie publisher, *HellBound Books Publishing LLC* (est. 2016), which publishes horror, bizarro, and a whole manner of dark fiction.

http://www.panicroomradio.com

http://www.hellboundbookspublishing.com/authorpage_longmore.html

ALSO BY JAMES H LONGMORE

BUDS

Wildus Guidry, amateur scientist extraordinaire, invents time travel. To his bitter disappointment, he discovers his device only transports him mere fractions of a second into the past. Inhabiting the new, alternate world of that fractional past is a variation of *Homo sapiens* that reproduce asexually by budding and uses sex as a recreational pastime and as a means of feeding. Disappointed by his discovery, Guidry and his entrepreneurial girlfriend decide to bring back some of the Buds and open the world's most bizarre and exclusive brothel - the Buds' unique appearance as grotesquely erotic conjoined twins, triplets, quadruplets (and more!) prove to be incredibly popular amongst the brothel's elite clientele. Of course, all goes terribly wrong as the Buds turn out to be not as benign as first thought, and chaos and the end of the world ensues. *Buds* is a unique, sexy take on the popular time travel trope, and a must for all lovers of conjoined twin tales. An erotic, at times brutal and disturbing, story told with lashings of dark humor.

TENEBRION

"The Devil's in the detail."

Amateur filmmakers inadvertently invoke a demon when they break into an abandoned school to perform and film an authentic Black Mass for their entry into a short movie competition.

Dave Priestley and his crew film in Watsonville elementary school – the site of a horrific tragedy nine years before.

Tenebrion – the malevolent demon of darkness – makes preparations of its own within the dark recesses of Hell. The demon requires a specific set of circumstances and sacrifices to rend a fissure between the worlds and set free its brethren; it has manipulated humans for centuries to put things into place, and the moviemakers are the unfortunate, final pieces of its nefarious puzzle.

Priestley, ever the stickler for authenticity and detail, accidentally sets free the denizen of Hell. And while Priestley and his skeptical friends attempt to return Tenebrion to the pit of Hades, it hunts them all down – one by one – for inclusion in its hellish gateway.

AND THEN YOU DIE:

Following a drunken, hedonistic night out in New Orleans, highly successful businesswoman and sexual deviant, Claire Jepson, accidentally soils herself in her car. The resulting excrement comes to life as a sardonic fecal spirit, and not only dishes out a gruesome death to Claire's unfaithful, gold-digging fiancé, but also thwarts a kidnap/murder plot by her employees. It then introduces Claire to a world of depraved pleasures beyond her imagination.

A year later, the errant spirit has spiraled wildly out of control - its insatiable appetite for perverted sex and human flesh and has destroyed Claire's life. Then, to her horror, Claire discovers the fecal spirit must consume her unborn child to attain immortality; she must return to the seedy underbelly of the Big Easy in a heart-pounding race against time to confront the spirit's creator - a high priest of an ancient, deadly order, who is the only one who can put a stop to the spirit's murderous intentions. A wicked, fast-paced story laced with tongue-in-cheek, dark humor, which is at the same time incredibly erotic and stomach churning. Most definitely not one to be read whilst eating!

PEDE:

An affectionate homage to the creature feature! The once luxurious Mountainview Spa Hotel in the heart of California's Coachella valley lies decaying, abandoned and heavily boarded up - the site of a radioactive, "dirty" bomb explosion five years' previously. Zoology Professor, Jane Lucas, harbors a lifelong phobia of *Scolopendra gigantea,* the Giant Centipede, despite being the world's leading authority on the creature. Following the savage deaths of two teenagers who broke into the hotel to cavort in the natural underground spa and the discovery of centipede remains almost three times natural size, the professor teams up with four of her students to investigate.

Their expedition soon becomes a fight for survival when they're trapped inside the hotel with a gang of violent thugs and a voracious swarm of oversized centipedes that infest the place - and then discover another creature even more terrifying is hunting in the Mountainview's deserted hallways: a centipede of impossibly monstrous proportions… ravenous and desperate to feed.

<u>FLANAGAN</u>

"The Devil's Rejects meets Fifty Shades – heart-pounding, gut-wrenching, sexy as all hell, and with a twist you'll never see coming!"

Meet the Sewells, an all-American couple; happily married for ten years, respected high school teachers, still crazy about one another, and with a mutually-shared dark side.

During their annual Spring Break vacation to recharge batteries and reconnect, the Sewells are waylaid by a perverse gang of misfits in the one-horse, North Texas town of Flanagan.

Taken hostage to be the focus of the gang's twisted games, the Sewells are brutalized into performing vicious physical, sexual, and emotional acts upon one another, until events take an unexpected turn, triggered by an unintentional death.

As their circumstances descend into the worse nightmare imaginable, the Sewells find themselves involved in an altogether different situation...

THE EROTIC ODYSSEY OF COLTON FORSHAY

Colton Forshay dreams himself into a bizarre sexual dystopia - a world in which nothing is as it should be, it alternately rains semen and menstrual blood, sickening sex acts and sexual violence are the norm, and the currency is deviant sexual acts.

In this dream world, Colton inexplicably finds he has gotten his dog pregnant and his wife is brutally murdered as a contestant on a popular TV show.

At first disturbed, then intrigued - and shamefully aroused - by his dreams of the other world, Colton is drawn in deeper and begins to spend more time there with the help of sleeping pills. His real-world wife forces Colton to see a psychiatrist, who encourages him to explore the dream world. And thus, our hero embarks on an odyssey with his dog/son, Eric, to discover the disturbing truth behind his dream world.

There, Colton gets caught up with the resistance, who believe the government - lead by a mysterious, telepathic

ocelot - controls the people by means of dreams of another realm, which sounds uncannily like his actual world.
The storyline alternates between Colton's real and fantasy dream worlds, and the two become inexorably blurred until Colton unearths a disturbing truth not entirely against the perverse tastes he's developed.
This is fantastical tale populated by a whole host of bizarre characters, set in an incredibly peculiar world. Chock-full of startling, sexy imagery and told with incredibly dark humor, Colton Forshay is a bizarro tale both engaging and disturbing.

<u>BLOOD AND KISSES</u>

"Think of what late greats James Herbert and Richard Laymon may have given birth to had they ever collaborated"
- Richard Chizmar
The definitive short story collection from James H Longmore - an eclectic mix of dark horror, bizarro and *Twilight Zone* style tales of the downright disturbing. Welcome to the long-awaited collection from the writer of horror novels *'Pede* and *Tenebrion*; a foreword by Richard Chizmar (co-author of *Gwendy's Button Box* with Stephen King), 18 short stories, 5 flash fiction, and a poem - all skin-crawling, soul-shredding tales of the darkest things that skulk among the night's inky shadows and of the everyday gone horribly awry.

Discover the implication of technology becoming self-aware, enjoy the acquaintance of a charismatic new pastor promising his flock a brand new place to worship his God, spend a little time in the company of a nice young man who is inexorably caught up in his home town's terrible secret.

Then, there's Cupid's revelation he's never experienced love, we discover that very emotion alive and not so well among the ruins of a post-zombie apocalyptic world, and bear witness to childhood innocence forever destroyed in a distant, war-torn city.

Observe, too any unsavory individual's obsession with the ever-elusive snuff movie, and join an elderly bunch of forgetful sleuths out to solve the mystery of brutal deaths that occur with alarming regularity at their memory care facility.

Now, have you ever considered what may happen should you have the misfortune to bump into your family's doppelgangers on a long, tedious road trip? And, can you even begin to imagine being the doting father who finally realizes the apple of his eye's true identity, or the parents who spend what is left of their crumbling lives waiting by a silent telephone for news of their addict son?

There is more, Dear Reader, much, much more; for within the pages we have devils, demons and ghosts, lycanthropes, and demi-gods, all rubbing nefarious shoulders with the most vile of Hell's offspring, who have slithered up from the netherworld to doff their caps and wish us all the sweetest of dreams…

<u>FEEDER</u>

A deliciously bizarro, darkly disturbing peek into the world of gainers and feeders: grotesquely obese individuals and those people who facilitate their growth for the lascivious pleasure of both parties. The heroine of the piece, Novella, Embarks upon a journey into the dreadful netherworld that dwells within the obese, fleshy folds of a woman especially engorged for the perverted delights of her Internet audience. Aided and abetted by a former feeder, she fights to escape before the grim portal closes and she's trapped forever in the ghastly realm of fat, flesh, and death most gruesome.

<u>I AM JOE'S UNWANTED PENIS</u>

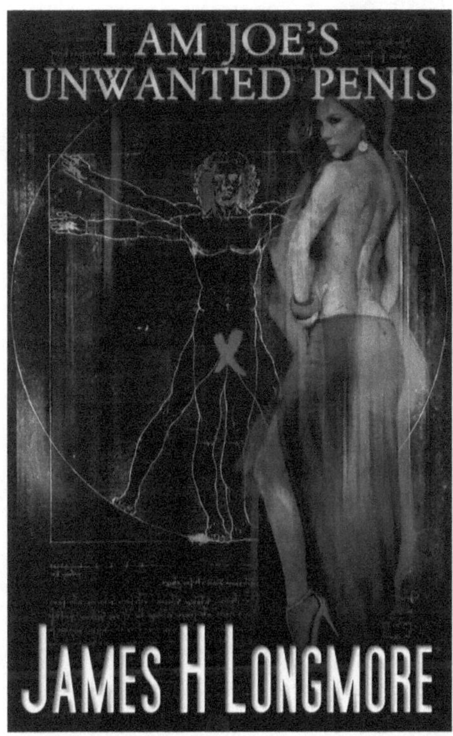

A darkly comedic tribute to the much-loved Reader's Digest series *'I am Joe's…(insert body part here)'* and a bizarre parody of the Bruce Jenner story, *I Am Joe's Unwanted Penis* is told from the point of view of a penis discarded as a man is surgically transformed into a woman.

Upon learning if his high-profile previous owner's regret at having made the transformation, the penis embarks upon a perilous journey for them to be reunited - aided and abetted by a motley, wonderfully personable, and engaging selection of other discarded body parts.

In parts grotesque, laugh-out-loud funny, and undeniably poignant, in others, *I Am Joe's Unwanted Penis* is a buddy-story absolutely like no other!

James H Longmore

**A HellBound Books LLC
Publication 2021**

www.hellboundbookspublishing.com

Printed in the United States of America